STRIP P♣KER

D1042557

STRIP P♣KER

Lisa Lawrence

DELTA TRADE PAPERBACKS

STRIP POKER
A Delta Book

PUBLISHING HISTORY
Brown Skin Books edition published in the UK in January 2006
Delta Trade Paperback edition / February 2007

Published by
Bantam Dell
A Division of Random House, Inc.
New York, New York

This is a work of fiction. Names, characters, places, and incidents
either are the product of the author's imagination or are used fictitiously.
Any resemblance to actual persons, living or dead, events,
or locales is entirely coincidental.

All rights reserved
Copyright © 2006 by Lisa Lawrence
Cover photograph © 2007 by Nicholas Russell/Getty Images
Cover design by Lynn Andreozzi
Book design by Sarah Smith

Library of Congress Cataloging-in-Publication Data
Lawrence, Lisa, 1970–
Strip poker / Lisa Lawrence.—Delta trade paperback ed.
p.   cm.
ISBN-13: 978-0-385-34073-1 (trade pbk.)
I. Title.
PR6112.A989S77 2007
813'.6—dc22   2006021897

Delta is a registered trademark of Random House, Inc.,
and the colophon is a trademark of Random House, Inc.

Printed in the United States of America
Published simultaneously in Canada

www.bantamdell.com

BVG   10 9 8 7 6 5 4 3 2 1

STRIP P♣KER

PROLOGUE: AFRICA

The first time I played strip poker, it wasn't poker at all, it was gin rummy, and it wasn't in London, it was in Africa. I was sitting cross-legged behind one of the acorn-shaped huts with my top off, the slight breeze from the Nuba Mountains making the nipples of my full breasts hard, and Simon was pretty sure I was collecting nines. Didn't matter to me because I wasn't, and I considered myself ahead in the game. After all, he was sitting there in only his tank top, having boldly taken off his shorts first and letting me have a look at his engorged cock, blushing pink at me. As I picked up a card from the deck, he cupped one of my tits and began massaging it, and I told him, "Not fair."

"Hey, I'm losing," he protested.

I flashed a smile at him and arched my eyebrows, saying, "You could have started with your shirt."

"Where would the fun be in that?" he replied, and offered me a wide grin.

He was good looking for a white English man. No weak jaw or poor teeth or sallow skin. No, he had diamond chip blue eyes and soft, almost feminine, curves to his jaw and high cheekbones, a curl of his blond hair falling across his forehead and giving him a boyish look. I hadn't seen the rest of him yet, but the package so far delivered, the girth on him thick, and I had already begun making a circle with my forefinger and thumb to rub him a little, making him harder. I liked Simon. Maybe I wouldn't give him a second glance back home, but we were here, mildly attracted to each other and we were both bored. The good thing was he couldn't play cards for shit.

After my turn, he announced, "Gin! There!"

Of course, he could have been hustling me.

"Get them off, Teresa, come *on*," he laughed, and then an instinctive reflex made him swivel his head around to check if we were being watched.

I doubted anyone would give a damn if they had seen us, although they might have paused in curiosity over his body. Not mine. We were with the Nuba, and while I had come into the Sudan on a British passport with my British name, I was a descendant of these people. They're known for being tall, and I'm about five foot eight, and my complexion is their same dark brown. When I look in a mirror, I recognise one of their flat noses, my face only a little rounder than theirs. While people in the villages of the mountains wore a mixture of Western and native clothing, it wasn't uncommon to see men and women walking around completely nude. So no one would give us more than a second glance. I was the one who stared when I first arrived, watching half-naked Nuba, their heads decorated with white ash, loincloths around their waists, perform the traditional Bokhsa dance—and wearing knockoff Ray-Ban sunglasses.

Simon had made me laugh because he confessed to "feeling bloody physically inadequate next to these guys." Nuba men, after all, can stand over six feet and have impressive physiques. It was really something to watch two of these fellows, naked, covered in white ash and looking like ads for a gym membership, crouch in front of each other and then grapple in traditional wrestling. Simon had a go, and we had a good laugh because he was on his back in seconds.

Now he looked at me, cat smiling after it swallowed the canary, and he waited. I smiled back and rose to my feet, deciding to give him a bonus. I slipped off my panties along with my skirt and stood nude in front of him like an offering. My fingers dug through the pleasantly soft thatch of his blond hair as he got on his knees, as if my body was a temple to him, and then I felt his warm, wet tongue begin these exquisite laps on my pussy. I shuddered involuntarily. His hands were fondling the cheeks of my ass, applying their tender pressure to urge me to open my legs a bit so that his tongue, his beautiful tongue, could probe and explore me further. His lips found my clit and *sucked,* and my knees actually buckled.

"Maybe we'd better get inside," he suggested.

I nodded, forgetting to breathe. At least I had the presence of mind to say, "You'd better have some latex to go with all the aces you threw down."

Yes, yes, he said in a mildly hurt voice, wondering how I could suspect him of being anything but responsible.

It was a hell of a place for a tryst. We had slipped away from the *Sibar*—one of the festivals—but from the open doorway we could look out from the darkness of the hut and still see what was going on. Men and women kept dancing with their arms over their heads, their feet shuffling in circles. The traditional priests, the *kujur,* blessed the cattle. As people laughed and enjoyed themselves, you occasionally heard the *clack, clack, clack* of mock stick fighting.

The on-and-off-and-on-again war felt very far away, at least for now.

I'm home, but I am not home, went the chant in my head again as I rolled onto my back in the dust, and lifted my knees. Simon's well-defined white chest loomed over me, one hand bracing his weight against the earth as the other cupped my breast, and our tongues sloshed together in a wet, luxurious kiss as I felt the tiny red dome of his penis nudge my pussy lips, asking for entry. As I felt his girth fill me, sink into me, and my vaginal muscles spasm with a contraction, my arm hugged his back tightly, and his face was in my shoulder-length hair. I looked at the play of colour of our bodies, our own little Tao symbol, and my mind was distracted momentarily by my choice. Part of me would have liked to have got busy with one of those muscular village men, one of my own kind, but I was practically one step from Martian to them with my British ways, my Western brashness. To be with one of them implied involvement. Simon knew this for what it was. A casual lay over a card game.

"Christ, you are so gorgeous," he whispered, and thrust harder inside me. I matched his rhythm with my hips, and we were a perfect fit, perfectly in tune. I was sucking hard on his chest, leaving purple welts to brand him with my mouth, and he took this as encouragement to pump harder. When I looked down at myself I saw this slick white cock pulling out and ramming back into me with a furious will, disappearing under the tufts of my black pubic hair sprayed with beads of our perspiration. We heard a *clack-clack* of stick fighting again and laughed together, heard the dancing and thought we were being quite mischievous. The two of us off like this while the village went on with its celebration. It was as if we were inside this great pageant, invisible, surrounded by the voices and the low thuds of feet in the dust, and it enveloped us. He didn't have to say a word, we were already moving together, Simon pulling out of me, and me getting on all fours. And as I felt him enter me again, the fullness of him and then his narrow hips against my buttocks, one of his hands cupped my swaying tit as he started a new rhythm. As shadows, we looked out through the keyhole doorway of the hut onto the Nuba people, my people yards away. There were two broad-shouldered naked men making their sticks collide.

"Uhhh ... uhhh ... uhhh ... Give it to me."

Clack, clack. Clack, clack.

I felt Simon pound away, and as one of the combatants up ahead turned, the sun hit him and perfectly outlined all the muscles of his chest, his cock limp but still impressively long, and the young man smiled at his friend with a flash of teeth and great camaraderie. There was such beauty in him, such a noble grace and something more. Something I couldn't define that instinctively hit me in my core, and my legs were trembling and the electric shock of my orgasm began. I heard myself in my little-girl whine, muttering, "Yes, fuck me, come on, fuck me...." And to be honest, part of me had disconnected, feeling myself come but not caring whether it was Simon at all, wishing irrationally the tall young nude out there would drop his stick and come see me. Just look at me with my dangling full breasts and my mouth so wide open in ecstasy I could barely contain my scream. It was the first time I recognised I'd enjoy being watched. But I knew I'd feel a bit choosy over my voyeurs.

Be careful what you wish for.

♦

Khartoum. Dusty. Dirty. Desert. Yecchh. Creeps at the airport who glared at me and then at the photo in my passport. In the land of *sharia*, strict Islamic law, my Destiny's Child CD and my Sony Discman were summarily confiscated.

I am home, but I am not home. That was the mantra that had gone through my head ever since my plane had touched down in the capital. Dad had warned me in a singsong voice, peering at his book in his big overstuffed chair in the old house in Oxford, "You'll be disappointed...." He had done the trip himself years ago. "You won't get bitter, just ambivalent." Whatever the hell that meant.

And so I tried to keep an open mind towards the Acropole Hotel, the looming mosques, the dust storms and ugly government buildings that squatted by the Blue Nile, the grimacing men in their skullcaps, selling melons. In the constant stream of Arabic that washed over you in the streets, you kept hearing the word *abid*. It means slave. It's an insult.

I am home, but I am not home, I thought. The regime in the Arabic Muslim north has been and still is doing its best to systematically exterminate the Nuba and most of the other black peoples in the rich southern half of the country. I can remember sitting on the floor in front of the television at home years ago when the BBC did a documentary on the Old Country and interviewed the governor of Kordofan. "From the Islamic point of view, Nuba culture is very ugly and must be eradicated." Hey, Mom, Dad, did I hear what I think I just heard?

Sometimes back in Soho cafés, earnest young white liberals would suggest to me that Africa was one big, black Balkans, and I would lose my patience. *No.* Sorry. There are no "grey areas" for dissection or dissembling. We're talking removal of magistrates, the slow starvation of supplies and funds from schools, making sure anyone from the wrong ethnic group doesn't get an appointment in the Darfur region. Slavery. Massacres. Oh, and by the way, the big American and European oil companies—Chevron, Total, Orpheocon—used to hire out the government's Arab tribe militias, the Murahaliin, when the Nuba or anyone else interfered with their concession surveys and drilling.

I sure know how to pick a place for a vacation.

I came to meet my grandfather. Since he inconveniently died before I was born, and Dad was never quite sure or forthcoming on how the family wound up in the Land That The Sun Forgot, I would meet my grandfather in his mountains and huts. In the *Sibar,* and okay, yeah, in the shadow of the refugee camps. A British-African girl who normally couldn't live without her fix of the bookshops along Tottenham Court Road and enjoyed trashy American TV on Sky. And here I was in a region the size of Scotland where human misery occasionally kept a lease with an option to buy.

These mountains had divided the Nuba up into dozens of different ethnic groups with their own little idiosyncrasies and languages, with Arabic being the lingua franca whether you liked that or not. I chose to play tourist in a region that the government had left alone for a long while, but if you drove twenty miles to the north and stopped at the ring of thorn fences around the swelling refugee camps, the white folks from CARE and Oxfam and VSO told you that it was only a matter of time. Orpheocon wanted to resume its geological survey in the area. Oil meant trouble.

Simon was one of those white aid workers who liked to drift into the Nuba villages. "Every so often, it's nice to take a break and see *happy* people."

Even if it was temporary. With his boyish long face, he was like a young non-gay T. E. Lawrence. He had the look. Fortunately he didn't have any Lawrence-like romantic illusions about where he was, or if he once had, he'd ditched them.

The other white aid workers I met in Kadugli or elsewhere,

always in fading concert T-shirts and khaki trousers, pissed me off with their condescension. "The SPLA are bastards same as the others. Name me someone who actually wants to help these people *selflessly*. . . ." You passed café tables in Khartoum where you heard the Africans were lazy, that they wouldn't accept sensible advice, that they couldn't be *taught*—

With refreshing candour, Simon granted the point that he was here as much for himself as for any impulse to save his fellow man. More, in fact.

"Sure, we get something out of it," he laughed. "All these bright young things with their Master's in International Development—they'll be milking their war stories for years!"

Yes, he wanted thrills. Yes, he found his middle-class life in Purley crushingly vapid and his premed studies disillusioning. Desperate to confirm a vague intuition that he could heal, he had signed up for shit pay and grim working conditions so that he could inoculate African children against tetanus, meningitis and polio.

His blond hair and his Jude Law looks made his tactless humour and his flippant attitude easier to take. He had a habit of strolling around, singing Bruce Cockburn songs. "Lovers in a Dangerous Time" and his particular favourite, a blistering lefty political tune that had the lyrics, "If I had a rocket launcher, some sonofabitch would die." He giggled over that one as if we were supposed to treat the lyrics as ironic.

I know he worked hard, but you'd swear he came off like a slacker from the way he spoke. Like many of the aid workers, he was full of anachronistic talents that he had abandoned in the First World. For instance, he was a brilliant artist—so skilled as a teenager that Disney's animation studios had actually offered him a contract. He turned them down.

"Are you kidding? Why didn't you take it? You could be out in sunny California! Hollywood!"

"Yeah, I could!" he said, mimicking my enthusiasm. "Drawing Dumbo II and becoming an alcoholic!"

I remember after we made love, we quickly washed and changed, but we were still bored, so he laughed and suggested Strip Chess. I rolled my eyes. How about garden-variety chess for now and Strip Chess later? He had a board in his car. When I came with him to fetch it, I noticed the butt of a rifle sticking out of the back of the Jeep.

"What's that?" I asked nervously.

He responded as if I'd asked him about a species of bird. "Oh. That's a Kalashnikov."

"Uh-huh. And, uh, what are you doing with it?"

"I don't have a big dog," answered Simon. "And I doubt it would help with the militias."

"Simon, I can't believe you keep that thing with you! Surely you'll lose your job if the agency knows you've got it!"

"And wouldn't that be a real catastrophe?" he laughed. "I'd lose my precious token salary of £50 a month and have to go back to Uni! Teresa, please don't tell me 'give peace a chance.' I don't think I can handle it, darling."

"No, but . . ."

I let it drop.

♦

It was a couple of days later when I woke up to find many of the Nuba in the village packing up and heading northwest. In my bad Arabic with its atrocious accent, I was able to talk to one of the shopkeepers and learn that the people feared an imminent attack by Muslim guerrillas. I was packing when Simon found me in a hut and said, "There's not going to be an attack *as such*. More like an encroachment—of oil workers."

"What do you mean?"

"It's the Orpheocon concession survey," he explained. "Come on, a bunch of us are going to go take a look."

"Wait a minute, wait a minute! Are you crazy? What if there *are* guerrillas in the area?"

He shrugged. "Then we drive like hell. Away. It'll be all right, we'll be careful."

To this very day, I have no idea why I took leave of my senses and actually got in the Jeep beside him. Riding shotgun so to speak. There were a couple of young Nuba men in the back, friends of Simon, and they accompanied us half out of curiosity and half out of duty to the elders in the village who wanted some kind of reconnaissance done. More of the Nuba were in a Range Rover driving behind us. If these men had to leave their homes, they wanted to know whether their panic over a rumour was justified.

Driving through the beautiful forested hills, thinking how some countries are better at breaking your heart than men. But I didn't really notice the landscape because I was too busy chanting to myself *what are you doing, what are you doing, what are you doing . . .*

Twenty miles, and the Jeep and the Range Rover drove up to five rifles trained on us, not much of a guerrilla band but I suspected it would be enough. The Murahaliin stood with a single white man. Silver hair, pasty complexion, white shirt and tan trousers and, Jesus, desert boots. He even had one of those geeky mechanical pencil holders in his shirt pocket. He stepped forward and gestured to the Arabs to lower their rifles.

"Whoa, ho, ho! There's no need for that."

He saw a white man driving the vehicle and assumed we posed no threat. Beside his motley group of Murahaliin bodyguards, I noticed one of those surveying thingies on a tripod and plenty of maps weighed down on the ground by a backpack and a thermos. The Humvee in which he and his men drove out here had the yellow Orpheocon logo on its doors. When he spoke to us, I heard a British accent.

"You're trespassing, you know," he warned us with a cheerful smile. "It's a bloody good thing I wasn't staring out at the hills, otherwise these boys would have shot you."

"Isn't it just?" replied Simon sarcastically. "I suppose you wouldn't be interested to know that a whole village has packed up and is on the road because they heard you were dropping by?"

The oil executive looked at him blankly. "What village?" Thinking better of it, he said, "Look, Mr. . . . ? Let me guess. UNICEF? Christian Aid? Well, whoever you are, I'm not interested in politics. If these people you're talking about are on concession land then I can't say I feel terribly sorry for them. Well and good that they go! And if they're not, then I can hardly be expected to express concern over something that is outside our corporate responsibilities."

"This guy was out when they had the public relations course," I whispered.

Simon glanced at me, his face reflecting my own loathing for the man. He stood up in the Jeep, leaned his elbows on the windshield. Doing his best to keep a lid on his simmering indignation.

"Right. We'll try a different tack. Could you at least tell me, since *you're* here, whether we can expect more Murahaliin swooping in for your 'protection'?"

The Orpheocon man thought this was a scream. Chuckling away, he said, "You know it occurs to me that if I say yes, there are more on their way, I'm doing your precious villagers a favour, aren't I? They're packed already, I suppose."

I tugged on Simon's arm. "Let's just get out of here and join the convoy."

"In a minute," said Simon.

He gestured to one of his friends sitting behind me in

the Jeep to hand him the old, rusting Kalashnikov rifle. I watched Simon raise the machine gun with nonchalant grace, and before anyone could do anything, there was a jackhammer rumble that was deafening, and an angry red blotch erupted in the chest of the Orpheocon executive. He didn't die like in the movies—he merely fell in a lifeless heap in the dirt.

I panicked and foolishly grabbed at the rifle, my hand pulling back with my mild yelp from the still-hot muzzle.

"Are you insane?" I yelled. *"What the hell are you doing?"*

Under my voice, I could hear rifles being cocked on *both* sides. I hadn't seen the guns Simon's pals had brought along. I hadn't a clue that the Nuba in the Range Rover had come armed as well.

A Mexican standoff, African style.

The Arabs faced us with better American weapons, but there were more Nuba with more guns, and if things got worse they were going to lose this bout. And all I could think was: Jesus, Simon's killed us. Whoever wins, those Arabs will pick us off first.

"Why did you do that?" I demanded.

But Simon ignored me. He jumped out of the car and brandished the rifle at the Murahaliin, telling them in Arabic, "You go back now and tell your bosses at the company their concession out here has been revoked!"

I followed him out of the Jeep, but I didn't know what to do.

The Murahaliin said nothing. After a moment in which I thought my heart was going to beat its way out of my chest, the Arabs turned with their sour faces, muttering *"abid,"* and jumped into the Humvee. Simon was already returning to the Jeep. I grabbed his arm.

"What was that?"

"That was the answer," he shot back, his voice angry. His blood was up just as much as mine. "That was surgery."

"That was incredibly stupid," I snapped. "Shit, you murdered him!"

"Come on, Teresa. You're the last person I would expect to complain! For Christ's sake, Orpheocon hires the Murahaliin. Chevron used to hire the Murahaliin! You had Total over here for the French doing—"

"I know the facts," I cut in. "And what you just did makes you one more white man thinking he can solve our fucking problems! For God's sake, Simon, can't you see there's going to be a massive reprisal for this? We could have just sent him on his way! We could have driven them off, we—"

"So I went one better."

"What is this?" I demanded. "You want to feel good about yourself with that soldier-of-fortune shit? Did you get your rocks off?"

"I removed one of the bloodsuckers," he replied. "Maybe if we shoot enough of them, the companies will back out of their concessions, and the regime will have to think twice."

"Doubtful," I muttered.

There seemed little point in arguing anymore. I was the only one standing by the side of the car, holding everyone up. I took my old spot on the passenger side, and Simon drove us back to the safe territory.

I could never look at him the same way again. Not because I thought killing the oil executive was necessarily wrong. He was a bastard profiteer who thought he was invulnerable, immune from the ravages the Khartoum regime and his company inflicted here. He was mistaken. But Simon had shot him down without hesitation and so ruthlessly that I saw now he was capable of practically anything.

And I questioned his motives. I had thought he had

"matured" past the usual White Man's Burden nonsense that "well-intentioned" aid workers came over with, having their little relief-work martyrdom, getting their kicks over exotica and then heading home. I thought he was struggling towards finding a role where he could be useful. And now I saw I was mistaken. He was a shopper like all the others, and he'd merely been looking for something different.

I stayed with the Nuba for a couple of months after that episode and gradually made my way back into the north, taking a flight home to London. Mutual friends who visited Sudan told me Simon did a complete amateur mercenary gig with the rebel SPLA for a little while, and then he, too, fled the country, sneaking across the Ethiopian border and having the cheek to walk into a British consulate to ask for help. I suspect his vanity got a mild thrill out of all the rumours and stories circulating about him, but he dropped off my personal radar.

And, come to think of it, I didn't play cards again with anyone for three years.

1

Stretch limos don't normally impress me. Except I wouldn't think you could get a full-size massage table in one. Goes to show you how good my depth perception is. The legs were sawed off like those of a stool, but I was high enough to look through the tinted windows at all the kids smoking pot and the frustrated map readers at the Eros fountain in Piccadilly. I was lying on my back, nude, which was okay by me because Fitz was naked as well, kneeling at the end of the table, cradling my right foot in one hand.

He had spent the last forty minutes reducing me to a pliant mass of soft flesh, practically every muscle in my body relaxed while the whole limo smelled like lavender and a couple of other massage oils. Alicia Keys's new album was playing on the portable stereo. And there was Fitz, nut-brown biceps flexing and swelling as his fingers worked the ball of my foot, that wide chest of his falling and rising with each breath. When he inched his way forward on one knee,

I looked at the vanity mirror he had propped up and got a terrific view of his ass in the reflection.

He smiled down at me, warm brown eyes and flashing white teeth framed by his funky dreads. I had this honey glaze from the oil on my dark skin, and he was getting this polish sheen of sweat from his efforts. My eyes kept straying to his long, thick dick that kept insistently pointing north. Fitz and I don't have much of a relationship. Sure, we sleep together regularly, but he's more like ... I don't know, sexual comfort food.

As the car made its wide turn onto Regent Street like a sea barge, I glanced down and thought: I'm gonna have to do something soon about that gorgeous cock. Only I was a little busy. His right hand kneading my toes, while his left was working the lubed-up dildo in my pussy, and I heard his voice say gently over the music, "Hey, I don't think I ever showed you this trick. Doesn't work on everyone, but ..."

That tiny buzzing sound of the dildo motor as he plunged it in deeper *just* as the pad of his thumb pressed hard on this point (don't ask me where the hell it is!) in the arch of my foot. And then I was spontaneously, violently, coming. "Shit! Oh, shit, Fitz, do that again, baby!"

My head fell back against the cushioned headpiece of the massage table, my back arching, and I was clawing at the white sheet. I told him hoarsely that I thought we better close the sunroof. They'd probably hear me out there in Oxford Circus.

And then my mobile rang.

I was going to ignore it. Fitz was ignoring it. He sent me into another small convulsion and as I floated down from the high, that damn phone kept ringing on and on, and I saw the number on the caller ID. Helena.

Fitz worked for my friend Helena Willoughby these days. He was with me tonight "on loan" as a way to get me to do a favour for her. I wasn't sure what the favour was going to be, but I was certain it would be a bit dodgy. Of course, if I really wanted or needed to see Fitz, I could call him up any time I liked, but it was Helena who tossed in the frills— what she liked to call "OTT TLC." Over-the-top tender loving care. The limo, the champagne on ice with the Belgian chocolates I loved, not to mention the chocolate-coloured man I could just eat up as well. Seeing Fitz as a "client" made things less complicated, and if Helena wanted to pick up the tab, hey, why not? I could always say no.

"Oh, yeah! Oh, yeah!"

Oh, I was pretty far from saying no.

That damn phone.

"Teresa?"

"Helena, your timing absolutely sucks."

Evil giggling at the other end. "Sounds like you're having a good time. Can I count on you?"

"You know it's going to cost you more than a couple of foot rubs."

I expected her to wind me up further with how he was rubbing more than my feet, but she turned serious. In fact, I could hear a trace of fear in her voice. She was doing her best to keep the tone light, but she was deeply troubled.

"Cost is no object, really. When you guys finish up, can you come out to the house?"

"Listen, honey, if it's that bad, I'll swing over now—"

"No, no," she said briskly. Long nervous breath down through the line. "An hour or two will be fine. I appreciate it, I really do. And you'll be handsomely compensated. Teresa . . . ?"

"Yeah?"

"I haven't, um, seen you for a while," she said carefully. "You kept yourself up, haven't you?"

I laughed in disbelief into the phone. *"What?"*

"I mean you still work out, don't you?"

I checked myself out in the mirror for Helena's sake. Damn her for making me self-conscious about my body. Had I kept myself up? Mmmmm, yes. I saw a young woman closing in on thirty but not showing it too much, I hoped. My legs were still long and toned. I always thought my ass was a little too big, but hey, why was she asking me this? The neck. You start to show age in the neck and around the eyes, don't you? Jesus, she was making me paranoid.

"Helena, why don't you ask Fitz for his opinion when we come in?"

"I'm sorry, darling." A quick goodbye, and then she rang off.

"She wants me to come out to the house," I told Fitz, my fingertips reaching for his still-hard penis, "but we have some time. You know any other pressure points like that one?"

◆

Helena lived out in Richmond-upon-Thames, in a five-bedroom house that was twenty minutes' walk from the rail station and ten minutes' drive from the park. She was always destined to be out there or somewhere in *SW* land, bred from oh-so-respectable middle-tier Knightsbridge stock. The surprise was that her mortgage payments came from good-looking hunks taking out London's female rich and elite, women in their late thirties, forties and fifties. The guys took the ladies to dinner, to premieres and to galas and sometimes to bed. Helena probably ran the most successful male escort agency for "straight dates" in London.

I came to know her because I was initially a friend of her sister Susan. It was that "interesting" period of my life, as I call it, when I dropped out of Uni at Oxford and thoroughly pissed off my family. I was looking for ways to make money that didn't involve long stretches of boredom. Susan put me onto Helena, about ten or fifteen years older than us, who needed someone to do a bit of snooping on a competitor. Long story with a couple of ugly details, but let's just say the guy from the Met who wanted his kickback ended up being bounced from the force.

Since Helena and I had hit it off, we socialised now and then. And she asked me if I knew any guys who were reasonably intelligent, could conduct themselves well and would be discreet enough for her business. The pay was good, and a "date" for an evening didn't necessarily imply sex. That was always negotiated beforehand very, very carefully, and Helena expected her cut. At the time, my fling was winding down with Fitz. I knew he had a dream of opening his own massage centre one day that would offer Swedish, Shiatsu, aromatherapy—you get the idea. Banks don't always care for tall black men coming in and asking for business loans. Hell, banks don't like anybody. If he could get his stake together, good luck to him.

So Fitz went off to work for Helena, and I moved on to other jobs. I've been an international courier, spending my nights on red-eye flights back and forth to Chicago. I did a bit of work in Geneva trying to help another friend sell modern art through her gallery (that's the one that paid for brief gracious living in the Nuba Mountains). And when the appraisals got a bit shady I was asked to look into that, too. Little by little over time, I've wound up earning my keep by solving unpleasant little problems for people. Sometimes all of London looks like it's on the fiddle or has a small secret business going on to get around Inland Revenue.

Helena's trouble came along at the right moment. Rent

was due soon on my flat in Earl's Court, and if I didn't have anything else, I would have to temp again at a media clipping service (yecchh) or at a reception desk (double-yecchh) or scrounge from my friend Richard to lead a few classes at his women's self-defence and kickboxing school, but that would only be good for a few trips to Sainsbury's. So naturally I was prepared to accept Helena's chore. Only the first rule of business is: never show your client how eagerly you want them.

Fitz hadn't quite learned that one yet. As the limo left Hammersmith and snaked its way towards Chiswick and onto North Sheen, he filled me in one smooth, delicious stroke. . . .

♦

Helena kept her house on a permanent yellow alert of show home display, the lights always on as the estate agents advised you, not a grain of dirt on the white carpet, the upholstery of the couches always looking shampooed, not simply brushed. Her sister Susan told me she was a regular addict of shows like *House Doctor* and *Ideal Home* on Sky. And yet I know there was no agency sign on the front, and she wouldn't want to put this gem on the market.

She had this thing for "themes" for each room, one done in Japanese style, one with African masks, her kitchen dripping with Art Deco chrome. All I could think was that she went to this trouble because her client base and her social set were indistinguishable—with the few exceptions of unrespectable middle-class types like me.

She must have been pretty anxious. As the limo slid into the driveway, she was waiting at the threshold. Helena's an attractive blonde wearing her hair short these days. With her green eyes and her full curvy figure, she had been approached years ago to become an escort herself, which is how she got the idea for her business. Someone asked her once why she didn't recruit girls since the demand was higher for female escorts. "Yes, that's true, but I want a quiet life," she said airily. "Men will unzip their flies in a minute when they think they're *owed* something. With my business, the boys drop 'em on command. With girls, you have to give them a reason or a high enough price to open their legs, and after a while, they convince themselves they don't need me to book them dates."

Once upon a time, she had apparently raised hell with the RADA types and a bunch of Sloanies. She still liked her fun. For her, the best fun was the kind that made her money.

Fitz opened the car door for me like a true gentleman, and I stepped out in my little black cocktail number that I hadn't worn for more than thirty seconds with him. As his hand chivalrously touched the small of my back, I could still feel the light glaze of the oil on my skin, and I don't know why I felt mildly embarrassed when Helena had set the whole thing up. I whispered to Fitz that he'd missed a couple of buttons on his shirt, and he and Helena traded a look.

"Would you like a drink?" she asked politely.

I said no, still a bit tipsy from the champagne. Fitz went ahead and had a rum and Coke. His work for the evening was done. We made some small talk about Congestion charges and appalling train service and how my gallery friend out in Geneva was doing, then the lull told us we should get down to business.

"Okay, I'm here, honey. What's the problem?"

"It's like this," she said, casting a wary eye at Fitz.

If he knew what was going on, he wasn't in any position

to help. He took a hint and switched on the telly, finding the football channel in seconds flat. Helena focused on me.

"Teresa, how good are you at cards?"

◆

I looked blankly at her. Gin rummy? Solitaire? It was Solitaire when my parents took my brother and me on a trip to France. Helena offered a patient, amused smile. "No, not those games."

We abandoned Fitz to Manchester United while we went into her study. She'd had this room done in Italian motif, dark wood antiques and Grand Tour prints of Venice on the walls. Her computer stuff, though, was state of the art.

We watched the Windows XP logo come on, then Helena tapped an icon, and a box opened with streaming video. I'm a tech-illiterate, but I was fascinated for a couple of seconds by the incredible resolution of the picture. She tapped another key, and the image became full-size, as good as looking at any television. I watched people sitting at a round green table, little chips in the centre. The sound, however, wasn't fantastic—like listening to voices picked up through closed-circuit television, which this sort of was.

"Call."

"Three queens and a pair of fours."

"Very nice, but I believe a straight flush beats a full house—"

"Web cameras in each room," explained Helena. "We recorded this last weekend."

She tapped a couple more keys for a pull-down menu, and now we saw multiple boxes, multiple images. I peered over her shoulder. With a "May I?" gesture, I clicked the mouse to bring up the green table again.

Yes, that's what I thought I saw. The people playing cards

were dressed in very chic and handsome clothes, but a couple of them weren't dressed at all. Laughter rang around the table as the cards were turned over. A brunette in her thirties peeled her jumper off over her head, revealing a set of luscious milky breasts underneath. No bra. She had obviously come to the game with more enthusiasm than clothes.

I had an inkling of what I was looking at, but I still had to ask. "Helena, what is all this?"

"This," she said, leaning back in her ergonomically designed office chair, "is the newest fad in the underground sex market. Strip poker. Very exclusive, very popular now with the bored upper crust and the nouveaus. The celebrities love it. Roving games—every week in a different location. Has to be that way because a stringer for *The Sun* heard about one and nearly spoiled everything."

"I see chips on the table."

"Yeah, it'll take a few minutes to explain the rules unless you know five-card draw. As you can see, there's more to the game than just getting your knickers off. The chips also represent . . . Well, the twenties are for—"

"You're kidding me!" I blurted out, having already guessed. "Sex acts? They're playing for sex acts?"

"The stakes run higher than your average blow job, darling, believe me. This is where the cream mixes with the cream, so these people insist on me and the other organisers 'clearing' them through regular AIDS tests and checks for other STDs. Private clinic, very hush-hush. Nobody wants to let in the swinger who also fancies a bit of rough down in King's Cross."

She tapped the keyboard to enter a different time index, and three screens for different rooms flicked over to writhing and moaning bodies. Cards were still being dealt while off in a dark corner, a man in a tuxedo shirt was bending a

redheaded woman over a billiards table, taking her from behind. I recognised her—a star of one of the new dramas on
BBC2. Jesus. Some of the card players were distracted and
fascinated, some oblivious.

"How high?"

"The stakes?" Helena smiled, lacing her fingers together.
She clicked the mouse on the View menu again and mag-
nified a chip. "That's a threesome, right there. And that
one . . . Not everyone's willing to play with that one. That's
F-O-D."

"F-O-D?"

"Fuck On Demand, darling. You don't pay up at the end
of the game. The winner collects whenever he or she wishes.
A woman can be giving a PowerPoint presentation right in
the boardroom. She gets the call, and she has to beg off to
her colleagues—the dog's died, her five-year-old's at the hospital. He can take her there on the desk if he wants, even if
it means her job. If a winner shows up at the man's house,
doesn't matter if his wife is wondering who's at the door."

"Christ, who would agree to terms like *that*?"

"Spice of life, darling. No one plays expecting to lose.
What's sexy is the anticipation of winning. Having the
power over a lover."

"And if somebody refuses?"

"Word gets around they welsh, and they usually don't
get allowed in other games. As I say, very few play with
those stakes. And the matter's usually settled discreetly.
These people don't like to have their habits broadcast."

"Maybe I shouldn't ask this, but . . ."

"No, go ahead."

"I don't understand how you make money out of this," I
said. "Maybe I'm being a bit dim."

She touched my arm briefly in reassurance. "No, you're
not. The players each put in a hefty entrance fee for the

game and their ante. That goes to me for organising it, finding or renting the location and the rooms, and for throwing in a couple of 'guests.' "

She saw my expression clouding, so she added, "One or two of my boys might play. Remember, the object of the game is still s-e-x, and the more attractive socialites don't necessarily want to go to bed with the fifty-plus Arab banker who bought his way to the table. So if Fitz or Henry or whoever I've got is up for it, those women have something better to compete for."

I shook my head in amused disbelief. I like to think I'm an emancipated girl. I've had a chance to live out one or two healthy fantasies, but this was as if the Borgias got a chance to run the Olympics.

"Amazing."

"It's huge out in Los Angeles," Helena insisted.

"I'll bet! So what's your problem? Tell me you don't need muscle to help enforce an F-O-D marker."

"No. That's not it."

She paused a moment, sighed and pulled open a drawer in her desk. She handed me a folded piece of A4 bond paper. "This was sent to the home address of one of my escorts, Lionel. He took me into his confidence."

I opened the paper and read:

POKING DRIED-UP OLD BITCHES HAS BEEN PROFITABLE, HASN'T IT? LUCKY AT CARDS, UNLUCKY AT LOVE. YOU'RE GOING TO WIND UP DEAD YOU KEEP SEEING HER

That was it. No typed signature, no pen marks on the sheet or stains from any contact with a coffee mug or water glass. The paper was pristine. When I finished, my eyes met Helena's.

"You're going to tell me I should have taken that to the police, aren't you?"

"No, of course, not," I replied. "You'd only bring the kind of attention to yourself you don't need. Besides, there's not much the Met can do with this. It's on standard laser printer paper, probably knocked out with a Canon machine you can find in any office. A good guess the only fingerprints on it are Lionel's, yours and now mine. Did he keep the envelope?"

Helena shook her head.

"Doesn't matter," I said. "Okay, before I get into what's written here, I still don't see your problem."

The doorbell rang. I was surprised. I wouldn't think she'd invite other guests over while talking about something so delicate. But Helena wasn't fazed at all by the intrusion. As we left her office and walked into the hall towards the lounge, she didn't drop the subject at hand.

"What do you mean?" she asked me.

"I mean somebody bears a grudge," I answered. "*With Lionel.* So have him drop out for a while and do something else for extra money. Whoever 'her' is, cut her off and ship Lionel off to Bermuda for two weeks for his nerves. And have him move house and get an ex-directory number while he's at it."

"No, it's bigger than Lionel," she explained, and she dropped her voice to a confidential whisper as she approached the door. "There's been more than one threat made to someone at the games. The bastard's gone after one of my clients. An important one."

"Who?"

"I've asked her to come over," she said.

And she opened the door on Janet Marshall.

I tried to cover my surprise. There she was, a handsome light-skinned black woman of fifty-two with a brush of freckles on both cheeks, her hair up and dressed in an Yves Saint Laurent suit, both hands clenching her handbag by its gold chain. As Helena introduced us, she smiled tightly, her brown eyes reflecting a touch of embarrassed sadness. After all, she could see already that I had more personal information about her than she wanted strangers to know.

Janet Freeman Marshall had been a Parliamentary Under-Secretary of State for Foreign and Commonwealth Affairs when she was an MP. She did a stint running the BBC and, before that, headed the Commission for Racial Equality. And with the occasional newspaper column in *The Guardian* and an appearance on *Have I Got News for You* when the show was still hot, she had cemented her image as a stylish, successful and outspoken role model for black women. The last I heard, she was on the shortlist for the elite post of High Commissioner in South Africa.

And apparently she liked her sex on the wild side.

"Helena tells me you're a kind of investigator," she ventured.

I didn't know how to take that. "Kind of one, I suppose."

She turned on the charm. "You must be very good for her to bring you into this. She's told me a little about your adventures. That whole business in Chelsea. And did you really stay with the Darfur rebels in the Sudan?"

"It's not as dramatic as it sounds," I told her coolly. "I was trying to help a couple of friends and wound up smuggling in medical aid a couple of times."

"You saved lives, I'm sure."

"I wouldn't go that far. I drove a lorry."

"With modesty like that, you'd never do well at politics," said Janet with a smile. "But that's all right, you get things done while the rest of us wring our hands and blow hot air."

"I hope that's not fishing for a compliment," I answered.

She was taken aback. "Is there a problem?"

"None that I'm aware of," I said.

"Miss Knight," she said gently. "Am I to assume you are not one of those who would have voted for me if you lived in my constituency?"

I was honest. "No, you'd probably get my vote."

"But?"

I didn't feel like getting into this. She was pushing hard. "Let's just say I don't particularly understand the rationale of those who want to send you to South Africa. I suppose from their perspective, any one of us will do. But you've made a point in your career of equating black politics with *West Indian* politics."

She looked mildly hurt, her mouth a tight line. After a pause, she said, "Oh. It's *that* one. Let me guess: you don't think of yourself as black."

"I'm not black," I said. "I'm African."

In the background, Helena was positively mortified. At least she had the good sense not to try to play peacemaker.

Janet Marshall adjusted her posture. She was all about dignity. "Helena thought you might be able to . . . help me. All right, you don't want to do it. May I please ask that you at least respect my privacy?"

"I didn't say I wouldn't help."

Her eyes still holding mine, she slowly nodded. "I understand."

A relieved Helena made her a drink and led us back into her office.

"I've been stupid," Janet said as we took our seats around my friend's computer screen. "And careless. Please understand, Miss Knight, I don't apologise to anybody for my sex life. My husband's been dead for six years, and—and it should be nobody's business but my own." She inhaled quickly, and as she let the air out of her lungs, I could hear the tension and frayed nerves in that long breath. "But . . . we're in Britain, and I've been such a clot. You fall into complacency, you see. You tell yourself they go after other targets, that you're simply not that important. But it's not personal to them, is it? They want to squeeze you for money. Or they like to hurt others."

I didn't respond to this, and after a long pause, Helena said, "Janet received a letter in the post. Similar to the one Lionel got."

"May I see it?" I asked politely.

The great lady reached into her handbag, her eyes glistening, but with a sniff, she resumed her composure and handed me an envelope. Nothing on it, and they told me this is how it came to her house in Notting Hill. "It was slipped through my mail slot first thing in the morning on a Saturday," said Janet. Another folded sheet, its message printed on A4 standard bond, just like the first one.

TIME FOR YOU TO RETIRE UNLESS YOU WANT THE WORLD TO KNOW ABOUT YOUR SATURDAY NIGHTS. SAD OLD BAG, AREN'T YOU? HAVE TO PAY TO GET OFF. WHAT A JUICY STORY IT COULD BE

"What do you think?" Janet asked me.

I chewed on a cuticle as I held the note in my hand, gently swivelling my chair. Helena's told me how this makes me look like a bored sixteen-year-old, and I've tried to tell her this is my "mulling" face. I'm mulling it over. Let me mull.

"I think," I said at last, "we could all use another drink."

"She's warming up," Helena reassured Janet.

I clucked my tongue over that one. Warming up? She was dreaming. Tracking down a blackmailer was slightly out of my league. My friend had evidently done quite a sell job on the prospective ambassador. I didn't know what I could tell them from studying two notes. A few notions were percolating in my brain, but now was not the time to speculate freely. Helena returned with our freshened drinks.

"Have you stopped seeing this Lionel?" I asked Janet.

She looked to Helena, mildly confused. "But I don't see Lionel. Okay, yes, I slept with him once because I won him in a game, but ... To be perfectly frank, I simply didn't find him that attractive. Or very good."

Now I was confused.

"Janet has another regular she prefers," supplied Helena. Janet looked down at her hands as our mutual friend put it as delicately as she could.

"And these are the only two threats that you know of so far?" I asked.

As Helena nodded, I couldn't resist thinking out loud anymore. Janet was studying me with rapt attention.

"Doesn't make sense. From Lionel's note and the one sent to you, you'd think whoever this is believes you're an item. You're telling me you're not. And our blackmailer's not jealous over you—they want to end your political career. So why the death threat to him? Helena, I think I'm going to need all the surveillance tapes of these games."

"Certainly," she said. "They're all on the computer. But I should tell you, Teresa, I haven't organised all the games on the scene. I've loaned out Lionel and the other blokes a couple of times, and I'm sure, Janet has, um—"

"I've gone to more than just the games Helena's set up, yes," admitted Mrs. Marshall.

"Well, the ones that you've taped can be a start," I explained.

I got up from my chair and reached for the mouse, clicking on the poker game that Helena had shown me before. There was the redheaded actress, yeah, a distinguished-looking white fellow with silvering hair, Henry, one of the agency's other escorts, a blonde woman of about forty-five saying how she got slaughtered by the Dow Jones last Thursday before flying home ... And yes, Janet was at this one. I hadn't recognised her before because the eyes can refuse to see what's there, or *who* is there. You just wouldn't think a crusading female politician whose public image has always been about dignity and forbearance would be attracted to a scene like this. Hell, she was as human as the rest of us, with her own needs, and I had no right to judge, especially after cavorting with Fitz in the back of a limo.

I was watching the tape to get an idea of suspects. I didn't have to speak aloud the shared thought that our culprit must be someone on the inside, most likely a player. But as we watched, Janet Marshall unfortunately took centre stage at the game.

She was already nude at the table, and there was a boisterous cheer as something happened—I'm not sure whether she won or lost a hand. I realised now maybe I was looking at her through a second lens of youth. In the tiny box of the webcam view, Janet stood up completely naked, her breasts full but still firm, her tummy having a mild roundness but reasonably flat, her hips only a little bit ample with the years. She was grinning and putting her hand on her hip, muttering something we couldn't pick up on the audio, and I thought: I should look that good past fifty.

A black guy—naked to the waist and with his back to the camera—stood up from the table. Then the two of them went hand in hand towards a settee in the background. I still couldn't catch a glimpse of his face. He was obviously tall—maybe six two or six three. Janet and her partner walked out of the shot of View 1 into View 4 of the sofa.

The Janet Marshall sitting beside us had suffered enough humiliation. In a glacial tone, she said, "I know this part. Helena, do you mind if I use your washroom?"

"Of course not, darling. You know where it is."

On the computer screen, Janet lay down, her eyes glassy with lust, biting her bottom lip, lifting her knees urgently, and for the briefest of seconds, I saw an engorged brown penis, its girth impressive and veins standing out. Her man guided it like a wand to her fleshy gates, and then a couple of other heads bobbed into shot, the players now voyeurs. As the anonymous man finished mounting her, thrusting himself all the way in, Janet's head fell back, and we had this vision of powerful sculpted back muscles, the line of a spinal column down to two *café au lait* hemispheres of sweet perfect ass. I couldn't tear my eyes away. On the screen, a couple of the spectators were cheering as Janet began to moan.

I cleared my throat and clicked the mouse to bring the green table back into full view.

"That was Neil," said Helena. "Neil Kenan. Does modelling work, trying to make it as an actor. He's quite a good one actually. He's also one of my best escorts—and Janet's personal favourite. I've had to break them up a couple of times because they conveniently 'lose' to each other."

"Let me guess," I offered. "You're starting to see 'atmosphere' between the two of them."

Helena rolled her eyes. "I love Janet dearly and Neil as well, but together, they can sometimes be a pain in the arse. She thinks because she's paid for sex with him that *all* his dates through the agency will involve sex. You know not everyone calls us up for that. Sometimes they need arm candy for a function. And I don't think Neil likes Janet playing the games circuit. I tell him to lighten up, that the poor woman was married for thirty years, raised a daughter who, thank God, is in America while this is going on, and she's entitled to some fun."

"Just how jealous can he get?" I asked.

"Neil?" Helena shook her head firmly. "No, no, no, Teresa. You can't peg him for this. Neil's the gentlest, most

caring fellow I know, and that's *men* I know, full stop, darling, including those I feed and care for on this little stud farm."

I didn't know Neil. And I wasn't about to rule him out yet. I looked at the screen, frustrated that no clear view of his face was possible.

"Yes," said Helena, folding her arms and smiling.

"Yes what?"

"Yes, the rest of him is just as gorgeous."

"I just wanted to see what he looks like so I can recognise him on the other tapes."

"Of course, darling."

I laughed and playfully slapped her arm. "Don't! I'm mad at you."

"Me? What did I do?"

"Don't be so cute, Helena," I scolded her. "That's why you were asking if I was fit when you called! You know the only way I'm going to solve this for you is if I get into the game. You don't get to watch if you don't play, do you?"

Helena didn't do a very persuasive expression of contrition. "Teresa, you are a looker. You've done a bit of modelling work, and we'll go into London tomorrow to get you a wardrobe to look the part. You'll need a car, too—we'll get a rental. Something a bit flash. We'll say you're a broker or something—"

"Helena, at least give me a convincing cover story. Something where I can lie well!"

She was patting my arm like a nervous seamstress. "Not to worry, we'll figure out the details. Then you'll help?"

I stamped my stiletto heel into her parquet floor, not caring if I left a mark. "You are talking about me perhaps getting passed around like a sex toy."

Helena grinned mischievously. "Then we'll have to turn

you into a poker expert. Janet will help." She turned abruptly sombre. "She's a good person, Teresa. She doesn't deserve grief like this—neither does Lionel. It's as if they're picking off my customers and friends one by one!"

I looked past her at the computer screen. Maybe I had ended up being a "kind of" investigator because I couldn't resist a mystery. I was intrigued by this puzzle. And okay, I have to be completely honest, I was intrigued by the game.

Bets against flesh. To risk yourself like that, to put yourself on display where others disrobed you little by little with a hand of cards, finally taking you or you taking them ... Yes, it was a turn-on. My mind already guiltily played out little fantasies of all the combinations and potential scenarios.

And more, more than all of this, I watched that incredible muscular brown back on the screen, and the way the muscles of his buttocks flexed with each thrust. I saw Janet Marshall's face bathed in perspiration and ecstasy, and there was a higher pleasure there than I had had tonight with Fitz—created not only from lips and skin, but risk, exhibitionism, danger. Heaven help me, I wanted my own taste.

2

"ome on, Teresa, you're not paying attention," Helena scolded me lightly, laughing. "Stay focussed. Now, what have you got in your hand? Garbage. What is that? What is that supposed to be?"

"Well," I said sheepishly, "I was working on a straight—"

Helena and Janet looked at my cards, looked at each other and laughed. They were ruthless with me. Days like this, coming back again and again to the house in Richmond to play cards, so that I went to bed with little rows of red clubs and black diamonds floating in front of my eyes before I drifted off. Our games at the antique coffee table in the living room were with 5p antes and a £1 betting limit, because Helena said I had to understand money stakes and strategy before I could graduate to the mind games and cut and literal thrust of the strip version of the game. And so she drummed into me "The Poker Facts of Life," as she called them, to help me survive.

"You maximise the pots you win, you minimise the amount of money in pots you lose," she said carefully and then smiled, waiting for my reaction, that *well, yes, isn't that obvious*? And being an amateur, my face told her exactly that.

"Darling, it sounds simple, but it isn't," she went on. "When you put money into a pot that you can't win 'just to see what happens,' you're losing more than you need to. If you don't make players fold with a big bet who would have stayed in and called on a smaller bet, then you win less money than you should. At the end of the night, it's not who has the bigger hand—it's who has the most money. And who lost the shirt off their back."

If you're going to call, pay attention to the amount of your bet and what's in the pot. Better to stay in with a 50p bet for a £10 pot than a pot for £2. Adjust your playing style to whoever's at the table. Check your own tells, don't keep a lookout only for tells in opponents. She made my head swim with it all. Fortunately, I got better. Not great, mind you, but better.

"Perhaps we're going about this the wrong way," said Janet one afternoon after her full house beat my flush.

She was disappointed in my performance. The whole afternoon was, in fact, a "secret test" for me, concocted by Janet and Helena like some reality TV show to measure how I was progressing. Could I spot tells? Did I pick up on bluffing patterns? I wasn't distinguishing myself very well, and if I couldn't play my part, I couldn't stay in the game. And catch the baddie.

"I don't know if she can do it, Helena," Janet complained now. "And this isn't fair, sending her in like a lamb to the slaughter. We need to give her an advantage."

Helena's neatly sculpted brows furrowed, but still she smiled, trying to keep the mood light. "What did you have in mind, darling? You can't have one of those clichéd earpieces, for God's sake."

"Maybe if I was her silent partner at the table," suggested Janet.

"A con," sighed Helena, and from her expression, it was clear she loathed the idea.

I knew already she wouldn't do it, and all the reasons were obvious. We could get tripped up before I made any headway on the case, and if that happened, Helena's sideline would be over. It wouldn't take long for her tarnished reputation on the circuit to affect her regular escort business.

As for me, I was irritated as hell with the idea. "Please don't be overprotective on my account," I snapped.

"It's not *over*protective, it's simply protective," replied Janet.

"A con," Helena said again, shaking her head. "No. Oh, no—no, no . . ."

Janet wasn't paying attention, still focused on me. "What is the problem with doing it that way? It's safer."

And I thought, how like a politician to come up with a sleazy stunt like this—and to consider it safe. Might as well speak my mind.

"Look, my primary job—why I was brought in—was to work the case, and I can't do that if I'm too busy playing pantomime games with you. I'll be there to watch the others. Plus I'll have to go to games you probably can't make because of your other commitments, *and* there'll be times I won't want you there."

Helena didn't try to be the hostess with the soothing words this time. She knew that bringing me in always meant I called the shots on how I operate. Having Janet Marshall as my shadow would severely cramp my style, and while maybe she was a great poker player, I doubted she'd be a good enough actress not to give an unconscious sign to others that we knew each other. It would be important, too, to see the dynamics of our other suspects when she wasn't around.

And there was another reason, the one that prompted her contrite, small voice reply of: "Oh."

She looked to Helena once, but she didn't need to ask the question. Neil. Janet knew I would consider him as a suspect for the blackmail. Maybe she couldn't imagine it of her lover, but I had to. It was my job, so I would be treating everyone as a possible suspect.

♦

"Now we play for the fun stakes," Helena told me after a week. And in less than two hours, she and Janet Marshall had me naked as a babe at the table.

And insisted I stay naked at the table while the game was still in play.

"You can't look like a virgin when I bring you," Helena chided me. "This is a game where women can enjoy losing as much as winning. You have to project that you *want* to be there."

"And even when you're exposed like this, it doesn't mean the game's over for you," Janet confided.

"What do you mean?" I asked.

"A lot of girls give up after they lose their knickers or their bra and sit like an ornament at the table," she explained. "They've resigned themselves to *being* the pot instead of 'workin' it' to turn the tables. They sit back and just wait to be won. Me, personally, I find being nude is when I have the best psychological advantage."

She patted my arm gently and said, "I'm not trying to make you feel self-conscious, but you have beautiful breasts. Use them. Lace your fingers together—yeah? Go ahead, lace them together, now elbows on the table and just frame your tits with your arms—yes just like that—now stare at Helena as if she's a man."

I looked across the green felt, but I couldn't keep a straight face, erupting into giggles. "I'm sorry, I'm sorry!" I sat up again and said, "I understand what you're saying. I don't think I'll break up if I'm facing a guy."

"Oh, I *know* you won't!" said Janet. "Then there's the real obvious one. Arch your back like you need to stretch and tilt your chin up, yawning. Yep, boobs out."

"That's so obvious!" I laughed.

"Yes, and it works," said Janet. "You're not drumming your fingers or whistling, so it's fair. Just don't let yourself fall into habits and make it into one of your tells. Pull one knee up and sit with the heel of your foot on your chair. Little girl lost, ingénue thing. I'm too old for that one, but I've seen girls use it and just *unravel* men at the table. They bluff like mad."

"Really?"

Helena nodded in confirmation.

"And there's other stunts you can pull to keep them off guard," said Janet. "Chances are, the men sitting next to you will be doing their utmost to—ahem—get the best view of your southern exposure. Push your chair back a little to help them." Her eyebrows fluttered suggestively.

"Whoa! I should—"

"I'm not saying you open your legs and give them the whole store, but you might want to encourage their eyes. The more they're looking down there, the less they keep their eyes on their game. You can tell just how well some-one plays by how long they stare at their cards. Strip poker, any kind of poker. Once you know what you have, why keep looking at your hand? Watch your opponents."

"And off the record," said Helena. "You're not supposed to touch another player while cards are in play, but if you're daring, you can always reach out and grab his willy and completely throw him off guard."

"Helena!" roared Janet in convulsive laughter. "You're too rude, man. Grab his willy!"

"Like you've never done that, Jan! I know you, my love."

"Ladies," I said, getting up from the table and collecting my panties off the rug, "I know I need to be good, but remember what I'm there for."

Hell, I had to remember what I was there for.

◆

"Time for the vocabulary," said Helena, trading a knowing look with Janet. "Once I take you through this, maybe you'll change your mind completely."

I waited. I had no idea what she meant by vocabulary. Poker is chock full of its own jargon, like outs and Broadway and rabbit hunt. It seemed that strip poker regulars had come up with their own cutesy lingo to add to it. Well, I didn't know anything about topping or bottoms in BDSM either, so it was all new.

"Betting is strip-betting until the final players at the table are more or less nude," explained Helena. "The betting for sex comes in once everyone's out of their clothes *or* by mutual agreement, partially clad, and in some games, there's no 'strip' at all—they cut to the chase. You can open with a French, which is obvious. You can use a lap dance as your opener. That's called a 'bucket seat.' One popular one with the Sloans and Knightsbridge types is the 'Oxford Salute'—simple spanking, but it's not meant as S&M, more comic relief and flirting.

"Then you raise with different bets. 'I'll read you in Braille' is masturbation. 'Finding Nemo' is going down on somebody, make of that what you will. And 69 is still 69. A 'rug burn' is simple vanilla sex, but if you lose to someone, you can choose whether you 'blow out the candles'—meaning they can have you, but not with spectators, or you 'go neon.' Meaning you do it while others get to watch. Now bucket seats, Braille, Nemo and 69 will be Going Neon anyway, so few people get squeamish about rug burns. But it's always the loser's call, and some women—and men—still exercise their right. Usually because they either want to get wild with someone special or they don't like their winning partner *at all*."

"With all that, where can you go?" I said.

"A lot of places, actually," replied Helena. "There's 'Marble Peach'—anal sex. But that turned off a lot of female participants, and it started to affect membership fees, so a lot of clubs dropped it. I never allowed it in the betting with my games. 'Hang the Curtains' is being tied up—usually with silk bonds—while doing it. The general rule, which I have at my club, too, is no bondage bets that blow out the candles. You want to play it, you play with an audience. No club organiser wants to get dragged into court having to swear that they heard a woman—or man, for that matter— give consent at the table, and then things went way too far after they left."

"I can't believe there haven't been incidents already," I commented, shaking my head.

"There have," replied Helena. "You just never hear about them. Teresa, these are games for big kids with money— money enough to buy their way out of trouble. In the early days, everybody relied on just their word, thinking 'Well, we're special people. Nobody's going to misbehave. Everyone knows everyone.' "

She rolled her eyes in weary dismissal. "Well! When the fad caught on, the definition of 'special people' became pretty elastic to liven things up. Get more players, make it more interesting. I know of at least one alleged rape by an entre-preneur from Brazil. That's a case where the police actually were ready to have him arrested. He skipped, of course."

"Jeez," I said quietly.

Helena lit a fresh cigarette. "I always thought if *I'm* doing the organising, the vetting, the retainer on the clinic to check diseases, I'll bloody well be in control. I tried to antici-pate rough customers. I kept my eyes out for who might push things too far and couldn't take no for an answer. I was *so* careful. But blackmail ..."

"We'll get him," I promised her.

♦

My first game wasn't at Helena's. It was at a private home in Primrose Hill.

Helena rented me a BMW to use on the case, and we drove up to the site of future shenanigans—this huge town-house apartment with fifteen-foot ceilings and windows with a generous view of the park beyond. There were pre-game drinks so that everyone's inhibitions could float away on a river of free-flowing Cava and Gordon's gin, and on the stereo was an eclectic mix of Aaliyah, Elvis Costello dur-ing his string quartet phase, and Justin Timberlake. The ab-sent owner had a thing for abstracts with vivid colours, a Ruzicka prominently displayed on the wall.

"So Helena, this is our new blood?" asked a good-looking white guy with silvering hair and a goatee. He was in a tai-lored pinstripe suit that must have cost £1,000, easy.

"George, darling! George Westlake, let me introduce you to Teresa Knight." She quickly explained how George was a self-made man, owning expensive real estate and a string of luxury resorts in spots like the Bahamas, Spain, Greece and South Africa.

Westlake and I shook hands. "Hello," he said warmly. We could have been sitting down for Bridge.

"Be nice to her," Helena told him. "She hasn't played too many games around the circuit."

Helena had warned me she'd set me up as a novice-intermediate, which would cover any gaffes I made and any sign of jitters.

Westlake laughed and said, "I wish I could believe you, my dear. But you do this every time, and then I find I've been taken by a ringer."

Time for me to be charming. I put a couple of fingertips on his chest as I pretended to lean in with a conspirator's whisper. "Honestly," I said, "I'm a terrible card player."

Joking, he mimicked my tone. "Honestly, so am I!"

We laughed together, and he said, "I guess we'll see."

I had got in because I was vouched for by Helena, who saved me the indignity of going for STD tests at the organizer's private clinic. (She did, however, insist that I get myself tested at hers, and since I was allowed in that night, you know how I fared.) As the predators and prey circled each other, she introduced me around as Teresa Knight, a "Senior Adviser" in scientific appraisal with a venture capital fund that bankrolled biotech companies. This was damn bold, I thought. And at one point, I took her by the elbow off to the side to ask: "Shit, what was all that?"

She laughed and answered, "Take it easy, darling. Half these people are only scientifically literate enough to tell you water's wet. If anyone asks what you're working on now, tell 'em it's to do with stem cell research."

"Uh-huh. Where'd you come up with biotech anyway?"

"I was at my dentist's, and I was so bored, I picked up a copy of *New Scientist*." She downed her glass of champagne and added, "You wanted something where you could lie well, didn't you? Mention science to this crowd, and their eyes will glaze over. It's perfect—gorgeous beauty like you, major overachiever but bored by her career who wants excitement and to get her knickers off."

"Next time, give me a hint about my cover story," I scolded her.

"Teresa," she called just before I moved off to mingle.

I drifted back.

"Smile," she whispered close to me. "You have to look like you want to be here, darling. Look horny."

"Thanks, coach."

I was wearing a Joe Casely-Hayford outfit that would probably look as good when I let it slip to the floor as it did on my back. High-waist trousers, very elegant bright red top, not my usual colour, but hey, it worked.

And I mingled. Now and then, Helena stopped by, filling me in on one or two of the regulars. There was Gary Cahill—Helena knew him from Uni.

"What does he do?" I asked.

"Nothing," answered Helena. "Very rich, very spoiled. Waiting for Mummy to die. Big in the fight to stop the fox-hunting ban, 'our way of life' and all that, even though he spends most of his time in London now."

Cahill's face looked a little too much like Rowan Atkinson to me. When I thought I might be seeing this guy naked in a couple of hours behind a card table, I thought *brrrr.*

"There's Vivian Mapling," said Helena, pointing out a bubbly redhead who looked like she was closing in on forty and hiding behind layers of eye shadow. "Loaded as well and a walking, talking example of how money can't buy you manners. Very into the games. Believe it or not, I think this is shopping for her. She's trying to find a husband who can double her wealth as well as her orgasms."

I spotted a good-looking white guy with chestnut hair

and almost delicate features, high cheekbones and a full sensual mouth. To me, he looked about thirty-five, but Helena said he was about ten years older, maybe a little more.

"Wow," I said, impressed. "He's got good genes. What's his story?"

"Daniel Giradeau. The name's French, but he's actually American. A relative newcomer. He's some big architect out of Chicago, over here on a long-term contract to design some building out in Canary Wharf. Moody sometimes, good in bed—"

"Helena?" I laughed.

"Who says I can't play now and then?"

"All right, good for you."

"Thank you for your blessing. The Japanese girl he's talking to is Ayako Tamaguchi—oh, I can't pronounce whatever it is. Born in San Francisco, so she and Daniel compare notes about homesickness for the US of A now and then. Very, very shrewd. Works for one of the Japanese banks down in EC4."

I studied Ayako. Petite, shoulder-length hair and instead of the constant fixed smile and high voice that's a stereotype with young girls from Tokyo, she was quiet, subdued.

"Hardly ever gets her kit off unless she's winning a hand," said Helena. "A bit of a mystery, her. Not one for chit-chat with the girls, although she seems to like Janet. That surprised me a little."

"Why?"

"Well, uh . . ." Helena shrugged, looking a little uncomfortable.

"Because Japanese people aren't known for their warmth towards the brothers and sisters?" I prompted. "It's okay, Helena. We know. Nice to hear she's not like that."

She went on giving me the curriculum vitae of a few

more guests, some unnecessary. It was surprising who had shown up. An art historian who had got his own mini-series on BBC1. A British gold medallist at the Olympics from a few years back. One *Top of the Pops* flavour of the month, the one other black girl here. I happened to think her CD was rubbish.

And Lionel Young. At my request, Helena kept him in the dark as to my real purpose here—along with the other escorts. Fitz knew I'd been hired, but he and I were old friends, and Helena said he didn't care for the strip poker circuit anyway. No threat to my cover.

As for Lionel, I could see why older ladies liked having him on their arm. His long, dark brown face was more cute than handsome, and maybe that was why he shaved his head, to make him look more mature. He was tall, and his build strained at his tailored light pink shirt. Pinstripe trousers hinting at good legs and leaving no doubt about a tight, firm ass.

Now if we could only keep the sound off. Lionel talking ruined the picture. He had actually gravitated over to us and put his arms around my shoulder and Helena's. Pretty transparent.

"Helena, you remembered my birthday!" he joked.

"What's that supposed to mean?" I asked.

"It means I'm going to unwrap you tonight like a present, babe." Big neon smug grin. "It's fate."

"Oh, really?"

"Yes, really," he insisted, dropping his voice to a whisper. "You see yourself getting with one of these chinless crackers? Honest?"

Then just to wind him up, I pointed to the tall, gorgeous guy with chocolate skin and a movie idol face, hair cut short, talking to Gary Cahill and Vivian in a corner. Brooding eyes, but the mouth smiled easily—brilliant white teeth when his smile flashed. Neil. Had to be. I was pretending to have X-ray vision through his black turtleneck, remembering those powerful back muscles on the webcam when he took Janet Marshall.

"What about I get with him?" I suggested.

"Oh, oh," said Helena, close enough to hear.

Lionel was scathing. "You'll be . . . disappointed."

"So I should count myself lucky that you happened to turn up, I guess."

"I'm thanking God already that you're here. You and me, babe. Magic."

And he drifted away to join a circle of conversation, hand clapping George Westlake on the back.

"That guy works for you?" I asked, incredulous.

"Yes, but he doesn't *need* to," said Helena. "Believe it or not, he's actually very smart at what he does. He's an analyst for Buccaneer Cape Mining. Does quite well for himself. One of my first escorts, and I really needed him until you introduced me to a treasure like Fitz and I recruited Neil. Don't pay attention to all that bluster. Sometimes players flirt and brag like that beforehand, helps shake things up before the games start. Speaking of which . . ."

Our host announced we should get down to it. Actually, what the guy said was that a "high stakes" poker game was about to start (and no mention that the stakes were what we had on). The party could continue, but at a neighbour's house down the street, a large Victorian cottage, directions on photocopied handouts from the catering staff. Sure, it made you wonder why they needed to have the party there first at all, but Helena said it was to sniff out new blood, measure interest and attitudes, pique curiosity. Those curious but unacceptable would simply never pass the tests.

There was a buzz of excited conversation, and those who weren't going to play got their coats.

Helena waved to one and all and said, "Have a good night, everybody!" There were air kisses and hugs, and as she fetched her coat, I moved quickly over to her at the door.

"Hey, where you going?" I said with a note of mild panic.

She was puzzled for a moment. "You're in, darling. The rest is up to you."

"But—"

"Teresa, considering what you may feel you have to do here, or maybe what you feel you *want* to do here, I'm not sure as your friend you'd like me to see you that way."

She had a point.

◆

As we played seven-card stud, I watched the personality dynamics. Lionel and Neil hardly said a word to each other, frostily civil at best. Vivian talked. A lot. But much of it wasn't directed at me. She was polite but mostly indifferent to any comment I happened to make. George Westlake was amiable and charming, asking polite questions of the fresh faces, both men and women, and trying to draw them out of their shells. He came across as a kindly older brother feeling responsible for the newbies. Cahill was boisterous, full of opinions but harmless.

I thought for a while that there was a vibe going on between Giradeau and Ayako. He bid for her a couple of times and lost his pants in the bargain, but he took it in his stride. She gave nothing away. Not who she wanted, who she might have had before or how she felt about him, having tasted the goods.

I think there must have been a long-standing consensual arrangement to take it easy on the newbies for the first few games, because I was almost ignored. George Westlake bluffed me out with a pair of kings to get my top off, leaving me in my black bra, and that was as rough as it got for an hour. Then things got earnest. George had the most clothes on at the table, but that didn't necessarily make him the best player. Few of the women bid on him. Vivian had cackled gleefully away and bluffed Neil down to his birthday suit (gorgeous chest, but I couldn't get a peek yet at what was under the table). And Lionel was down to his Marks & Sparks boxers.

The play moved on to getting it on. With a vengeance, Vivian went after one of the newbies, a newspaper columnist for one of the Sunday papers, and within a couple of hands, the man was on his knees and between her legs under the table. I watched Vivian bite her bottom lip with pleasure, not so into it that she didn't give the rest of us a wink, and then our bawdy redheaded lady grabbed a fistful of the guy's hair and began to moan. Loudly.

After she came, she looked back at all of us and said, "Ah, that was nice." While the journo slunk away to the washroom, inexplicably shamed. Bizarre.

Giradeau took a break to go mix fresh drinks for everybody. Cahill got pulled away by a phone call. New game. Lionel's deal, and he grinned at me as he said, "Well, we got so much new blood tonight, we ought to be merciful. Let's go Old School."

"Please don't on my account," I said tartly.

Five-card draw, the game everyone knows. Each player gets five cards facedown. After a round of betting, the players can discard up to five of their cards for new ones from the deck. Then another round of betting. Ayako won a French kiss from Neil, which they performed together like two old friends. We stayed with five-card draw for a while, and then it was clear that Lionel was gunning for me. The others folded, and it was a showdown between us.

"Well, Teresa, if you can read the numbers on your cards then I think you're ready to learn 69," quipped Lionel.

"Let's see what you got," I said coolly.

Lionel grinned and laid down four queens and an ace. Four of a kind that just cleaned out my full house.

Damn it.

The others. Westlake, Vivian. And Cahill returning from his phone call, quickly picking up the thread. Applauding, making quips like horny teenagers.

"Lucky, lucky Lionel!"

"Sorry, Teresa, you're going down—literally!"

"Well played, though, darling!"

Neil offered only a tight smile. Giradeau chuckled but made no comment.

Well, I told myself nervously, this is new. Having 69 with a guy in front of an audience.

"After you," said Lionel with a smirk and waved to the leather settee near the large picture window.

I'd be damned if I'd look embarrassed.

As I pushed back my chair, I rose from the table dramatically, lifting one eyebrow. My tits looked like they were about to spill out of my bra cups, my nipples exposed, and I had no panties on. I knew instinctively that this was somehow more erotic for the men than if I had been fully nude. I turned on my dainty heel and did a fashion model's runway walk to the settee, doing a panther climb onto it, my hands making the leather crunch and sink under my palms. When I glanced back at Lionel, the head of his cock was a ripe cherry ready to burst at the hem of his boxer shorts.

"Oh, no, you don't," he said as he sauntered over to me. "I want to lie down."

"Chivalrous bastard, aren't you?" I muttered.

Titters and laughs from the card table as I got up, let him collapse down on the sofa and then straddled him, facing away. At least his skin was warm. The tension between Lionel and me seemed to enhance the delight of the players seeing us go down on each other. I suspected he might be showing off and goading me for their sake, but I didn't know, and it didn't matter.

My consolation was that I didn't have to look in his smug face but only down at his cock, more impressively thick than long, the veins in it almost angry with the flush of blood but the whole package still appealing enough for my mouth, and I slid my fingers through the black curls of his pubic hair and prompted an involuntary twitch. My tongue gave him a lick of the ice cream cone just before my lips came down, and I was distracted for a moment by the somewhat aggressive parting of my pussy lips and the stroke of a soft, insistent tongue. I didn't care for his technique, but I felt my juices flow in response to the simple stimulation. There was a burst of applause from the card table.

I bobbed my head faster, sucking him in and out, darting my tongue around the tender skin just below the head. Giving him a nice steady rhythm. In contrast, he couldn't seem to decide on what he wanted to do, his tongue lapping me a few strokes then his mouth covering me and then back to anxious tongue strokes. I found myself summoning an image of Fitz, invoking a fantasy to help me get me off, and I was barely halfway up the curve before I felt the hard organ in my mouth stiffen even more and then a rush of warm cum flood into my mouth. I did my best to wait until the salty stream halted, and then I quickly took my lips away and snatched for a tissue from the box on the coffee table.

And this man with his head between my legs *stopped* and lay back. Creep.

I glared at him over my shoulder, and he was as relaxed and self-satisfied as any pampered house cat. It was only when there were whispers from a couple of the other women at the table that he finally woke up. "Oh," he said in a small voice.

"Don't bother," I snapped, and I slid off him and padded back to the table to fetch my glass of wine and get the taste of him out of my mouth. I snatched up my handbag, excused myself from the game about to be dealt and made for the upstairs bathroom. Fortunately, I had brought along a traveller's kit of toothpaste and toothbrush—

Creep, I kept thinking as I finished rinsing my mouth. Then perhaps as a defence mechanism over that ugly little episode, my brain switched over to professional gear, thinking about the case. It was starting to seem that my original contention was correct. The blackmail and intimidating notes weren't about Helena's clients, just one, and if this was how Lionel behaved with women, he was sure to collect grudges.

Creep, I thought again, and I sat down on the toilet, feeling incredibly frustrated. Lionel had done nothing for me, but I had astonished myself by feeling so turned on by being watched. Now I was all worked up, and I needed to get off. I began to play with my pussy, my breath coming out in anxious huffs, my middle finger dancing on the head of my clitoris, and it was at that exact moment that—

I realised I had left the bathroom door open.

Neil was in the doorway, nude, carrying a giant martini glass and staring down at me. His expression conveyed apology and yet admiration, too. There I sat on the toilet with my legs splayed, fingers touching myself, and as he examined me there, I never saw a cock get hard so fast. He appeared oblivious to his own erection.

"They think I'm mixing drinks," he said by way of explanation. "I thought somebody should check up on you. You looked . . ."

"Pissed off?" I suggested.

He shrugged and smiled. "I was going to say upset."

"Lionel's a pig," I declared.

He nodded. "Yes, he is."

I let my eyes linger on his washboard stomach and the graceful planes of skin leading down to a tangle of dark pubic hair and that bar of hard flesh. He had at least three inches on Lionel, but what I really preferred was that he seemed to be a gentleman. Not too much of one, otherwise he would have ducked out. I wanted him to stay. I moved my hand to caress the inside of a thigh, letting him see all of my pussy as I said, "I need to come. Want to help?"

"We could go back to the game and see what happens."

"Or I could get relief right here, right now."

With an athlete's grace, he sank to his knees in front of me, resting the martini glass casually on the basin. "You seem to be fine with what you're doing. I'll play up here."

His hands disappeared behind my back and unclasped my bra, casting it aside to drape over the bathtub sill. Then those large palms cupped my tits like ripe fruit, and with barely a conscious thought, my finger on my clit increased its rhythm. I felt my nipples squeezed between his fingers, gentle firm pressure of cupping me, and I began to nervously lean ever so slightly forward and back. We didn't kiss, but our mouths were so close together I could taste his breath.

He fondled my tits, a snake tongue darting out to tease a nipple, and then his lips sucked one in. I gasped. My left hand caressed the tight curls on his head, and I lifted his chin so that I could kiss him at last. I closed my eyes as our lips met, our mouths opening simultaneously to learn each other through our tongues, and all the while those massive, brown hands danced along the curves under my breasts, traced their way in circles over the areolae, tantalised and pinched me. We broke away for a moment, and I let him see how drenched I was.

"Get inside me," I ordered him in a husky whisper.

He shook his head. "No, you're almost there. You're turning me on so much like this, baby, just play with yourself—"

"But I need—I need—"

He squeezed my tits harder as he nuzzled the back of my ear and kissed me there, and that was all I needed. I keened helplessly and rocked in spasms, suddenly clutching him with my left arm. The heat, the cascading waves of pleasure ... Like an act of mercy, he brought his right hand down to move my own aside and cover my nether lips. But he didn't penetrate me. I thrust myself against the heel of his hand, still coming, beads of perspiration running down my forehead as my fingers shot out to grip his cock. All at once, I felt warm, wet bullets of spunk rain against my belly, and as I came out of myself just enough to look down, there flew another long stream of semen that hit my thigh. I jerked him a little to prompt another mild lava flow just over the head of his penis, and he bit his bottom lip and shut his eyes. I swear it was the sexiest way I had ever seen a man come. Not a wide-eyed gasp, or tortured, open-mouthed grunt. Neil looked like he was lifted by a beautiful piece of music.

Then we both came back to earth and laughed together at nothing.

I looked down at myself and thought we better quickly

shower. We'd both been missing from the game too long, and while it was understood people would have preferences and targets, it was part of the peculiar manners of the circuit that you didn't just abandon the group festivities for one-on-ones until the end.

He ran the shower and gestured for me to get in. We shared it for a minute in silence, washing ourselves clean, Neil saying pass the soap, and then I felt him lightly massaging my back in swirls of foam. Unnecessary, yet lovely. I turned around, and he soaped my breasts and my belly, taking me in his arms and kissing me like a proper lover. It was gentle and sweet and with a low-amp passion that felt so natural, even inevitable. For what felt like ages, we stood there, my hands tracing the formation of each one of his back muscles, his fingers on the cheeks of my ass, tongues saying all we needed to say in the private shared chamber of our kiss.

"You could have fucked me," I told him, smiling.

"I want to win you," he replied.

"The game is everything, huh?"

"Hey, I like to think I'm not as shallow as that," he said with a self-deprecating smile. "But . . . You know people are in such a damn rush. Internet dating, pick-ups in bars. I don't want to come off sounding like a Neanderthal or something, but I've thought long and hard about what I like, and I like the chase. These games, they don't have to be about getting yourself a sure lay or as much as you can. Maybe some others are here for that, but it ain't me. The most provocative, interesting, charismatic women I've ever met, I've met at these games."

I smiled at his charm. The implication, of course, was that I could be one of them. We both stepped out and grabbed a couple of terry-cloth towels.

"And," he went on, "when I meet them, sometimes that has to be enough. Sometimes it is enough. You want to get with them, you *earn* them."

He certainly put a different perspective on the whole thing. I've never easily dismissed Janet Marshall and Helena's other clients as "slack" or "loose" women, not when there are so many double standards we have to put up with about our sexuality, but I was guilty of assuming that each man here wanted to put his thing in as many holes as he could as often as he could. Maybe Neil was that good-as-gold, one-in-ten-thousand man who *enjoyed* pleasing women, who revelled in the stages of the mating dance rather than just the climax.

No one, of course, is that altruistic, I told myself. He was a good number of years younger than Janet, and men *are* different. They crave young flesh. And perhaps being with such a strong-willed, successful sister like Janet, well ... He seemed too confident in himself to feel emasculated by her, but he might need the games as an outlet for an occasionally bruised male ego.

"So you like the chase."

"I love the chase."

"You're competitive like Lionel?" I teased.

He grimaced at the name. "He's a pig, like you said. So immature. The kind of guy who probably keeps notches on his bedpost. No point in talking about him."

"What's the matter?" I asked.

"Let's just say Lionel and I have had our differences in the past."

"At poker?"

"No ..." He said it slowly, trying to think of a discreet explanation. "No, in another scenario."

"Business?"

"Kind of, but not quite," he answered. "I'd rather not talk about him. Wouldn't think you'd want to either."

"Yeah, you're right," I surrendered.

And in just a few casual words, he had given me enough to keep him in mind as a suspect, despite Helena's loyalty to him. It was obvious he and Lionel had come to logger-heads somehow over Helena's escort clientele. Janet perhaps? I couldn't rule it out.

And speaking of Janet, I didn't know what to think now that the pleasure of the moment was over with Neil. Certainly I didn't feel guilty, I have to tell you. Janet needed my help as much as Helena, and she knew what I would be doing here. She knew Neil still went to games, just as she did. But neither Helena, Janet or even myself had speculated that I might end up with "her" man.

I had an out. The other players could probably guess with the time passed what we were up to, but no one could be sure, and our shenanigans were technically outside the game.

"We better get out there," Neil suggested now, and he kissed me on the cheek and fondled my ass, adding, "I'd better go first."

"Do you think it'll make much difference?"

"Hey, probably not, but we keep up appearances, right?"

"Okay," I agreed, and I picked up my bra and looked searchingly around the bathroom, completely at a loss.

Neil laughed at me. "I've done that! You are fairly new, aren't you? Feel like you should have had more clothes when you came in here?"

"Yeah!" I said, and I laughed at myself with him. And then I boldly slung my bra over my shoulder, not even bothering to put it back on.

When we rejoined the others in turn, we each saw we needn't have gone through the pretence.

When I reappeared, Neil was distributing fresh drinks while a commotion went on behind a circle of the guest/ voyeurs. It seemed to be Lionel's night as Vivian straddled him in a chair and pumped her hips, making that shrill giggle that would get on my nerves if I heard it too often, making quips of her own to go with those of her spectators. She had a curvy, lovely body for her age, but there was a little too much of the up-for-it Essex girl about her. I watched Lionel grunt and strain, trying to hold off his climax, but he failed to change my mind about his staying power.

3

Later. Dressed. About to go home.

"Can I drop you?" asked Neil politely.

I was coy. "Maybe that's not such a good idea."

"Why not?"

"We might get to like it too much."

He offered a gentle reminder. "I said I wanted to win you in the game. Don't you trust me?"

I grabbed his ass briefly and said, "I don't trust myself."

I called for a taxi and got a ride to Helena's even though my own flat was closer. I knew I could sleep over at her place, and I had the bizarre paranoid notion that maybe I ought to play it safe by not going home. *This isn't the movies*, I chided myself, feeling a little ridiculous. Nobody's going to say "Follow that car" and find out where you live. Still. We were dealing with a blackmailer here, someone whose anger was prompting him or her to extremes. And the note had warned Lionel he could "wind up dead."

"Richmond," I told the cabby.

As the cab rounded the park, I knew Helena might also

be eager for a debriefing. And if I was honest with myself, I was dying to talk about the whole experience. As she let me in, I saw that she'd still been up, having thrown one of her favourite movies in the DVD player, of all things the Kenneth Branagh, Emma Thompson version of *Much Ado About Nothing*. Nursing a Baileys on ice and wearing her "dress formal" Japanese robe—the one for company—I realised she had half expected me to drop in.

"I'm told you were a hit," she announced before I even had a chance to say anything. "Westlake called. Said you have the body of a Nubian goddess."

"I hope you corrected him."

"You're not a goddess?"

"*Nuba* as opposed to Nubian."

She told me to go ahead and fix myself a drink, and I reached for the Baileys. Then I kicked off my heels, stretched my feet out on her coffee table and proceeded to vent about Lionel. "Helena, where did you get this guy? He's arrogant, conceited, smarmy, and he's giving *our* men a bad name! I can't believe you get repeat business with this jerk."

She gave me an understanding smile and rolled her eyes skyward. "To be truthful," she sighed, "I don't. Well, not for the kind of services a Janet Marshall or one of my other premium customers expects. The young man's so gorgeous, I had high hopes for him in the beginning, but now he only gets calls to be arm candy at some Barbican event or a charity awards function. The package looks great, but no real delivery. It's one of the reasons I've assumed I must be the target of this all and not simply Janet. I mean, why Lionel? Why not send a note to Neil? Or Raymond or Bobby?"

I tapped my nails against the glass of half-drunk Baileys. "Too early to say."

We drank. On the screen, Michael Keaton was doing his Beetlejuice imitation for the part of Constable Dogberry.

Denzel was still gorgeous as Don Pedro, and Keanu Reeves still sucked as Don John—in my humble reviewer's opinion.

"Teresa," she prompted.

"What?"

"I remember that look, I know that look," said Helena. "You're waiting for something. What is it?"

I smiled. She had guessed the truth, so I might as well fill her in. Yes, I had to wait because there weren't many other leads I could follow up at the moment, and maybe if I let her in on my thinking, it would buoy my client's confidence in me.

"Here's the thing," I explained. "Lionel had himself a good night. For someone supposed to be shaken up over blackmail and a death threat, he seemed pretty full of himself this evening. Now maybe that's macho overcompensation, but still, he came out for the game. So yeah, I want to see what happens next. If our bad guy—or girl—is truly plugged in, they'll know what happened tonight. And they may not like being dismissed. They could send him another note or . . ."

"Or?" asked Helena.

"There's another possibility, but you may not like it," I said.

She waited.

"According to the reviews, he's all flash, no fire. He certainly didn't do anything for me, but I don't want to be biased. Now if there really are better guys to go after—whether it's spite against you or to squeeze money out of them— why him? Unless—"

She saw where I was going. "Unless he's cooked this whole thing up himself and lied about *his* note? I can't believe it!"

"He did sleep with Janet," I argued. "And she did tell us he didn't exactly make her toes curl. He strikes me as a number one egomaniac. Maybe his vanity got bruised, and he's decided a little emotional cruelty and cash would do wonders for his self-image. But we'll have to wait and see if another note comes."

And if it did, and if it was genuine, I had other suspects in mind. If George Westlake thought I was so hot that he could rave about me to Helena, maybe he resented how Lionel got the first taste of a new player. Perhaps resenting Lionel was a well-established habit for him.

And then there was Neil—Neil who got the job done when that weasel couldn't break a sweat, Janet's man Neil. Maybe he didn't want to be Janet's man any longer but still bore Lionel a grudge. Two strong suspects if another note came, and there was nothing to say that just because another one was delivered, it would go to either Lionel *or* Janet. Maybe our blackmailer would turn on someone else.

I had deliberately phrased it "bad guy *or* girl" with Helena because, of course, I couldn't rule out the women. If Vivian was behind it all, she put on one hell of a performance tonight, especially when she was happy to fuck Lionel in front of all the players. She seemed to be the only one so far impressed with his prowess. I asked Helena what Vivian Mapling's story was and if there was any friction between her and Janet.

"Yes, actually," said Helena, as if considering it for the first time. "I noticed she and Janet never quite got on, but I never paid much attention. After all, my clients don't usually mix except at the games, and they still have to behave themselves there. Vivian's not exactly English, well, not completely English. She's got family on one side from Zimbabwe—their kind is probably still calling it *Rhodesia*. God! Vivian's one of those strange girls who profess to be liberal but still leave you with a question mark over what goes on in their fluffy heads. Likes black men, likes Lionel and would love to move on to Neil, so you can see where Janet's in her way. You don't think . . . ? Teresa, I told you, she's in the market for a husband. I can't see her taking her diversions with Lionel or anyone else seriously."

"Like I said, Hel, it's early," I reminded her.

Vivian might not consider Lionel husband material, but sexual obsession could have a twisted logic all its own. Maybe Vivian didn't like competition, and she had always resented the ugly little social presumption that Janet, by virtue of simply being black, could swoop in and take the hunkiest black male at the table. That would explain a little of the frost I felt from her tonight, a matter of colour as well as gender. And why couldn't the notes to Lionel and Janet come from a woman? Manipulating them through threats struck me as a very feminine ploy.

But the language didn't fit. Vivian Mapling must be around forty. Would she really call Janet an "old bag" when she was at best only a decade younger than Janet? Or use a term like "old bitches" for Lionel's note when she was one of Lionel's clients herself? Hmm . . .

A greater mystery was Ayako. Watching, always watching and reserved. What was going on with her?

Helena's mind was still on Lionel, resisting the notion that this could be an inside job, defending him almost as passionately as she had spoken up for Neil the first night I was briefed.

"He's by no means my favourite date for the girls, but he's more of a jerk than in the bastard category," she was saying. "And he doesn't need the money, Teresa. I told you—he works for one of the top European mining concerns. Makes far more money than Janet, at least at what she does right now."

I gave that a pensive "Hmmm." Money wasn't everything, and I wasn't about to rule out my theory just yet.

"I hear you met Neil," she ventured. The way she pronounced the word "met" drove right through *entendre* straight into hyperbole. If tongues played at the games, they also wagged.

I laughed through my embarrassment. "Yes, I did."

"Oh, God," she moaned, collapsing back on her sofa melodramatically. "I was afraid of that! I knew he would zero in on you. You're just his type. He doesn't go for loud and brassy or shy, mousy types, he likes quiet, self-confident women who—"

"Helena!" I broke in, still laughing nervously. "We just messed around, we—look, we didn't have sex, okay?"

"This is getting far too complicated," she said, more to herself than to me. "This could well blow up in my face. Maybe we should let Neil in on what you're really there for, and then maybe he won't put the moves on you again."

"Hey," I said. "Number one, I'm a big girl. Number two, there's already enough people who know what I'm up to, and number three, whatever you and Janet think, I'm not prepared to rule anyone out yet."

"But 'messing around' with Neil could be dangerous if he's the one," she argued.

I kissed my teeth and nodded. "You're the one who brought me in and you *knew* I'd have to do a certain amount of messing around full stop."

Helena shook her head at me. "And I'm beginning to think I'm a bloody fool, putting you in danger like this. Look at you, with this 'trouble is my business' thing going on! You're Lara Croft now, are you? Pour us out another drink, darling. I think I need it."

"You're my friend," I told her. "I'm here to help. And by the way, thank you for the nice, fat advance cheque."

"Is there anything else to do besides sit back and wait?"

"Plenty. Tomorrow I get off my ass and start doing background checks on our players."

"If it's financial, I don't think you'll get any surprises," said Helena. "I do regular credit checks on all my customers and escorts, and there's no one living beyond their means. Some blokes who get themselves into trouble think escort work will mean quick money, but I turn them down flat. If they're in debt, they'll harass and phone you all the time for bookings, and I don't need the headache. And the women are more than solvent."

"It's not that stuff I'm really looking for," I replied. "I don't doubt they're rolling in it. I need to get a bead on who might have pissed off whom, who might have burned someone in a business deal. If there's more than your operation hosting these games then a player can always go elsewhere if he doesn't like the faces at the table."

Helena brightened. "Then I might be able to help with that."

"Oh?"

"You can go where I can't follow."

◆

It wasn't exactly true. She might have got into the scene, but she would have stood out, and I'm not sure she would have been terribly comfortable. The name of the game wasn't strip poker but strip dominoes, Jamaican style. And the location wasn't a genteel *SW* house—oh, no, it was a club off Stroud Green Road near Finsbury Park tube station. Jeez, I never knew this place existed, I told myself. And I came out regularly to this neighbourhood to see friends, pick up hair products and check out stuff at the New Beacon Bookshop.

The club was a cavernous, smoky and barely legal joint.

Instead of the careful screening, credit checks and clinic tests, this came down to the natural selection of the bouncers sizing you up. Honeys and babes were given a wave through while the playas and the scrubs got the rigorous scrutiny. There were white chicks here, median age around 19, but they wouldn't have got in without a black date, and I doubt they'd have a clue where to find the place without one. The unofficial national anthem of the game was Nelly's "It's Getting Hot in Here," and as Sean Paul turned to Jamelia, then segued into Jay Z, you didn't need the music to tell you this was a whole different scene.

This was free-for-all spectator sport, no squeamishness here. There must have been five games going on with large crowds gathered at each one, and you heard the crack of the bones flying down like a hail of construction hammers. It was one of the few things that could be heard above the music, the shouts and the laughing. Players didn't sit so much as they stood over a table and shifted nervously or danced to the tunes, their whole attitude of play keenly watched and reviewed as much as their moves and their bodies. *"A little bit of uh, uh"* and as a tall, shirtless guy with nut-brown skin and a broken nose cleaned the others out, he slammed his fist into his palm, yelled *"Yessss!"* And he pointed to a girl across the table, saying, "Give it up!"

She was pretty, a caramel beauty with a clearly Beyoncé-inspired hairstyle and dye job, reduced at the moment to her leather mini and lacy bra, her panties and top already deposited on the table. She gushed and covered her mouth with her hand, then arched her eyebrows at him and smiled as the onlookers shouted their encouragement.

"Here we go!"

"Come on, babes, come on—"

"Oh, look at them luscious titties, man!"

The girlfriends pretending to cover their boys' eyes, the boys fending them off, and there she was, twirling like a model and dancing a couple of steps, her breasts full and exquisite with large areolae and her right nipple pierced with a silver ring. She gave him a challenging *come here* gesture with her fingers waving back to her palm, and the "Ohhhh!" welled up from the crowd as he stalked over to her and gently pulled on the ring with his teeth. His hands slid down and pushed up her skirt so that the audience behind them could see her pert little ass, and she pushed him off and made a show of wagging her finger at him. This was game five, and by game six, they'd be going at it anyway.

I drifted from table to table, turning down two offers of drinks and one rude offer to "mix the blood" out in a car. I could handle it. With all the wildness going on, you had to expect there'd be fools who assumed every girl who came out tonight would be slack.

I could see how the mainstream press could be shut out of the games for the elite, but I was surprised that nothing of this had leaked out and been covered by *The New Nation* or *The Voice*. There were bound to be critics who would come out of the woodwork to say this would give us all a bad name, did nothing to improve the stereotypes of either black men or women, blah, blah, blah. Whatever. From what Helena had told me of the underground white strip rummy and poker games up in Newcastle and Nottingham, this was fairly tame. Another lost opportunity for the media because the hosts were linked with organized crime and had brought in Russian immigrant prostitutes.

Here, I couldn't help but think these people were playing with fire, given the lack of screening processes (I did see one or two guys using condoms, but there were plenty of others who didn't). But I could say one thing for the club, the atmosphere and spirit of the strip dominoes was a hell of a lot more fun and spirited than the "aren't we so clever" smugness of the Primrose Hill crowd. Here was my kind celebrating their sexuality—they didn't think they were fooling anyone by getting away with a dirty little secret.

I slowly made my way to what looked like the table with the most boisterous crowd. And there she was, the lead suggested by Helena. She was named Shondi, a light-skinned mixed-race girl with her hair in cornrows, but no one was paying attention to her hair at the moment. She was completely naked except for ankle socks and trainers, a layer of girlish baby fat around her belly and hips. I made her for no more than perhaps twenty-three. The men looking on were wide-eyed over her generous breasts jiggling as she lay on her back, her teeth gritted as she squeezed her man's ass cheeks, urging him to go faster as he pumped her hard.

He was a muscular guy with bulging biceps, keeping his import Yankees baseball cap on all the while he fucked her, and though the thickness and girth of him made a few of the women gasp and whisper to each other, the couple didn't look very sexually compatible. He pulled himself all the way out, grinning as he showed off for the ladies and then plunged into her again so roughly, it looked like he had hurt her a bit. She was muttering something to him that I couldn't hear, and the expression on her face made me sure it was a complaint. He didn't make any effort to accommodate her. He kept at his steady pace, doing the jackhammer, and now I got a clue.

He's afraid he'll look like he can't last in front of his pals, I thought. He was another Lionel in a way, but then things turned ugly.

He ducked his head down to suck on one of her breasts, and she let out a small yelp and pushed him off. A wet, purple bruise was left behind, and he made another wolfish grin. No more playing. He kissed her smooth light-skinned stomach in apology, and then he bit her again. Now Shondi glared at him. She shoved him hard so that he popped loose and slapped him on the chest, and she moved to swing her legs out and get off the table.

The guy lost it and barked, "Bitch!" as he grabbed her arm to pull her back, and I couldn't believe what I was seeing. An amateur sex show turning into rape before our very eyes. He had her pinned down on the table by one arm, her left hand sinking her nails into his chest and then trying to rake his face, all the while his other hand trying to force her legs back open.

About now, you'd be asking yourself—just as I was—where the *hell* are the bouncers? Not paying attention, that's for sure. And the cheers and shouts over mutually consenting players sounded almost indistinguishable from the sick catcalls of "Fuck her!" and the cries of outrage over this attack.

The big bruiser's mates formed a cordon to keep two of the bouncers back, and I knew they couldn't see what was going on or how bad it was.

Meanwhile, a couple of girls with their dates squared off with his other buddies, trying to reach Shondi to pull her out from under this thug. It was turning into a melee.

Shit like this is how I get myself into trouble. I don't know how I do it, whether it's rebel brigades in Africa or art fraud in Switzerland, but I seem to show up just when the party's getting started.

I stepped politely forward with my glass in hand, saying pardon me, excuse me, as if I only wanted to get by, and you'd be surprised at how often an unassuming posture like that works. I handed my white wine to a girl next to me and asked, "Can you hold this for me for a second, please?" And she dumbly obeyed, and then I moved in right up to the game table.

"Hello," I said to Mr. Thug.

Distracted and confused. Too surreal for him by half.

And then I performed a *haito,* a haymaker-like blow with the knife-edge of my hand, straight into his temple and staggered him.

Shondi looked in mute shock from me to him, came to her senses, and scuttled free. Still nude but at least another witness now, she watched as Mr. Thug fell more than slid off the table at the opposite end and stormed up to me. His mates were doing their job of keeping the bouncers at bay, but they had shoved their way in enough to get an idea of what was going on, while the rest of the crowd instinctively shrank back from this naked bull.

The fact that he was in his birthday suit somehow made him more intimidating. Bizarre, I know, but true, because you saw every defined chunk of his washboard, every cut of his pecs, and now that he was standing up, I saw he was a towering six foot three. Only the tight sheath of the latex condom on his thing making him appear ridiculous. Shit, the boy hadn't even lost his hard-on yet.

Well, I thought, we can fix that.

"You fucking c—"

He didn't get to finish his obscenity. I saw his left arm rise in slow motion to do a boxer-style jab to my face, and my knee was up a millisecond before he even propelled half his arm extension.

Folks probably assumed I'd kick him in the testicles, but I was going for his belly instead. Part of my shoe caught the tip of his penis, and I'll bet that stung plenty. Mind you, not as much as his rib cage collapsing on him.

He folded and crumpled to the hard cement floor,

stained with beer and cigarettes, and as his buddies turned, the security guys broke through and started yanking the fool up under his arms. Now more bouncers rushed over as reinforcements, better late than ever.

"Holy shit!" somebody yelled.

"You see that? Fucking incredible, man."

So now a sweating, naked girl was walking over to me, looking a bit sore and uncomfortable. She hugged me impulsively and said, "Oh, my God, thank you! Some guys just can't take a hint, can they? I'm Shondi."

"Teresa."

"Let me get cleaned up here and dressed, and I am going to buy *you* a big drink! Maybe five of them!"

Saving her wasn't the icebreaker I had planned, I thought, but so much the better. She came back, giggling to cover her wounded nerves, telling me "Nuff respect!" and waving to a couple of stools at the bar.

She was something. Her girlfriends hovered around her, protective and concerned, and if it had been me, I probably would have taken them up on getting a ride home. Out of that place in a flash, taking stock of how I got into that mess. Not her. I suppose to her credit, she didn't milk the incident for sympathy, and I was astonished that she could still bat her eyes flirtatiously at one or two guys floating past, still clinging to the image of her exposed bootylicious form in their heads. I told her so.

"Fuck the rest of 'em here," she declared, taking a long sip of her Zombie. "I'm not going to play victim for any of these fools. If I walk out of here now, it looks like he's got me scared even after what you did. No way! And you just know there are some hypocrites here who are going to say, well, she has it coming if she's going to play that skank game. But those bitches, they sure like to watch. They'll call you a whore, but they don't look away. You want another?"

I shook my head. I was barely halfway through the first drink she'd bought me. "I don't know if I'd have the guts for a crowd this big," I said.

Her eyes sparkled with fresh interest, and she smiled warmly. "Aha! So you've gone neon, but just with the white folks."

When she caught me recognising the lingo, she knew she was onto me. It was my first clue she had a brain as well as a backside. She high-fived me and said yeah, she still played the South Kensington and Knightsbridge poker games once in a while, but more often these days she came out to the clubs here in Finsbury Park, in Brixton or even Wealdstone, where she kept it real.

"Hey, the thing for me is having them see me," she confided. "It is the most *amazing* turn-on. They are cheering me and just waiting for me to show 'em my goodies, and it is so liberating! I come like I'm going to explode. The bigger, the better crowd, baby!"

"I'm just getting into it," I said. "Went up to this house in Primrose Hill, and it could have been great, but I didn't do too well."

She nudged me. "You lost, yeah?" she giggled. "I hope he was cute, at least. What did you have to do?"

"Four of a kind to a full house, and he wants 69, but he comes in my mouth before he even gets me going," I whined.

"Oh, man, I hate that—"

"Yeah, he was a real dud," I said. "Leon or Lionel or something."

"Lionel?"

And I thought, here we go. It was oh, my God, that's amazing, the guy's my ex-boyfriend, and no, really? Yeah, and let me tell you, he was always shit in bed. Selfish, self-centred, couldn't go down on you to save his life. Said he didn't really like it.

"But what can I say?" She shrugged. "I was with him two years, and he introduced me to the games. I think that why I stayed with him as long as I did, because he didn't mind me getting it elsewhere, which meant I didn't pay so much attention to his lousy performance. It wasn't even the sex, really, that made me break up with him."

"Oh?"

She grimaced at the memory of it and said, "Nah. He was a cheap bastard. Didn't know how to be a real man and take care of a girl, you know? I knew what he was making, and the jewellery he bought me—*when* he bought it for me— was trash. Like, what do you think I am? If I'm going to be your woman, let's see you take out your wallet."

I nodded politely and kept my mouth shut. I never understand girls like this, and I don't think I ever will. In a few brief exchanges, I got her life story and knew what she was about. The daughter of a white liberal oncologist who married a black nursing supervisor, an upscale family that had moved into Notting Hill long before the neighbourhood reflected more diversity or even became fashionable because of movie titles. Trust fund kid.

Instead of rebelling against comfort as I did, she had embraced the whole package. This girl would never hold a job for longer than six months in her life, progressing only from real daddy to sugar-daddy, trading up until fading looks forced her to settle. And she took me for a kindred spirit.

"I mean, like, look at you," she went on. "You're *way* too fine for this place—"

"I don't know about that," I laughed.

"Your clothes, the way you move—"

"You're sweet."

"Lionel doesn't deserve either of us. Cheap, selfish, and he's got no morals, man."

"No morals?" She'd lost me.

She had that irritating habit of younger people whose tone makes everything lilt and go up like asking a question.

"Well, duh, baby, he works for a mining company? I went home to visit my folks, yeah, and Daddy had on this pro-gramme about mining in Africa being used to, like, sift stuff out of riverbeds or dig in these abandoned mines? They're killing all these gorillas down there. They chop down the trees for charcoal, right? So then they need huts, so they, like, cut down the bamboo, and the gorillas need the bam-boo to eat. Then they kill the gorillas for meat and their hides. And they mention all these companies, and one of them was Lionel's. So I'm with him again, and I go, 'How can you work for a place that does this shit? It's our people's parks and stuff.' And he gives me this rubbish about how it's no different to some big company needing cattle for beef and cutting down the rainforest, and hey, are you gonna stop eating burgers?"

She took a breath only to order another round. "And I go, 'Come on, when's the last time you saw me eat that shit?' and he goes, 'Well, what do you mean *our people*? Your fa-ther's white.' *That's* when I lost my temper. I mean, do I need that? I just said, 'I—am—outta here.' "

"Too right," I said, and then I had to bring her back on topic. I didn't care about how the less-than-lovebirds broke up, what I wanted to know was—

"I say 'go older, go with the deeper pockets,' " Shondi went on. "My man now? He can't get me off, but he doesn't mind me playing. Or he doesn't know, same diff." She laughed in self-congratulation, and I jumped in.

"It's horrible about this mining stuff you're talking about," I started. "What were they mining anyway?"

I was already thinking conflict diamonds. My mind played hopscotch, trying to connect the dots. Conflict diamonds.

Black market. South Africa? But no, it didn't fit. The South African government was doing its best to stop any illegal traffic in conflict diamonds passing through places like Sierra Leone and Angola. And even if you were cynical about London's stance on embargoes and other UN-sponsored steps to curb the trade, it had made its position clear. Okay, so what about a deal gone bad involving Lionel? Even if true, that explained someone's motivation to threaten him but not Janet.

And gorillas? I never heard of gorillas being threatened with extinction near diamond mines.

"No, it wasn't diamonds," said Shondi. She dismissed the subject with a wave of her swizzle stick. "It was something else, it was ... Oh, shit, I can't remember. Down in Africa, but it really pissed me off at the time, you know? People should care about stuff like that. Like, I have a conscience, and I was willing to break up with him over it."

Like Dr. Freud said, sometimes a cigar is just a cigar. And maybe a case of blackmail over sex is just blackmail over sex.

◆

I checked out Lionel's career anyway. Yes, he was one of the vice-presidents at Buccaneer Cape Mining, and he did economic risk analysis of new acquisition territories. A quick jaunt over to Blackwell's business bookshop and The Economist bookshop, and I soon had a rough idea of what that meant. Flipping open *Risk Management for Mine Planning*, my eyes fell on a paragraph that informed me: "The siting of an underground mine's headworks, for instance, could affect a range of investment factors. Locating mineral processing facilities at the mine, or transporting the ore for processing elsewhere, could change the hazards and risks associated with both these operations. Choosing open cut or underground mining technology illustrates the differences in the potential and range of risk impacts to financial commitment. Issues such as mining sequence and optimal mining duration could also markedly affect environmental risk, which in turn requires careful negotiation with government authorities and public relations initiatives to secure optimum exploitation."

This little tome could sure take the buzz out of a caffeine high.

I went up to St. Pancras to visit the British Library. First I hit the company's archived bios of senior executives, and working with Lionel's start date I cross-referenced this with back issues in *The Financial Times* and other papers. It only took me a little while to find a classified that gave Lionel's original job description in full. It would be unfair to call him a glorified bean counter, but his degree from the London School of Economics had earned him a comfy chair where others went out and did field reports, and he sat back and assessed whether it was worthwhile to go dig or sift or whatever the hell their miners did in pockets of Costa Rica, Australia and central Africa.

For a moment, my interest was caught by the fact that he not only assessed his own company's potential acquisitions, he also kept a watchful eye on what competitors were doing in the same countries. Had they already drained the well? Were they onto something big where his company ought to be looking? Were they able to grease a few palms better than say, Orpheocon, which had mining operations as well as oil?

In a way, Shondi was right in that wherever these gorillas were that were getting evicted and made into Kong burgers, Lionel had some say over whether it was worth the green

light for Buccaneer Cape to move in. Shondi would probably have another fit if she knew the exotic birds of Costa
Rica were probably in just as much danger from what his
company was doing. But all of this didn't help me much. If
Buccaneer Cape Mining was a corporate villain the way
some folks thought of Starbucks or McDonald's, that still
wasn't Lionel.

I made a note that he was required to travel frequently.
Since he was in charge of the analysis reports, he flew down
with the bosses every so often to these countries to deal
with government, any environmental pressure groups or
co-venture partners. If somebody got nervous, the suits
would point to Lionel and say, "Well, our expert will tell
you . . ."

But unless an Australian politician didn't like what the
firm was doing with bauxite and held him personally responsible, I had a dead end. Lionel and Janet had slept
together, but they had nothing to do with each other pro-
fessionally. If Janet won the plum of the High Commission
in Pretoria, that should be fine with Buccaneer, since the
conglomerate had no mining concerns in *South* Africa.

I remembered George Westlake and Lionel off by themselves far more than Lionel drinking with the other guys. I
couldn't see how they would have business together, since
Westlake wasn't in mining but in luxury resorts. Still, they
had looked pretty chummy.

"Let me guess," I said to Helena back at the house in
Richmond. "It was Westlake who introduced him to the
games."

"Actually, it was the other way around."

"Really?"

"Well, as you can probably tell, I didn't want Lionel at
my games like Neil or, say, Raymond. I think he learned of

the circuit through a work acquaintance—he's never there as one of my escorts. And I think he needed Westlake for something or other in business, and instead of the usual nightclub and cigar scene, he thought he'd score points by ushering him into this 'secret world.' Georgie is clever, rich, cultured, but he's come out of a divorce where he's lost his onetime trophy wife, and now for the first time in fifteen years, he has to know how to start conversations with women. Believe it or not, he's never had a mistress, didn't sow any wild oats, and doesn't have a wide frame of reference when it comes to sex—until the games."

Hmmm. Interesting. I carried around one of those spiral notebooks you can pick up at Paperchase, and inside, I had scribbled down the names of the game players I'd met: Lionel, Neil, Gary Cahill, Daniel Giradeau, Vivian, Ayako... Now I pulled it out and jotted a star and another question mark next to Westlake's name.

And still no second note from the blackmailer—not to Lionel, not to Janet.

♦

The next afternoon, I was up a rock. Literally. I had my belay device, my spring-loaded camming tool—one of those hammerlike adjustable thingies to fit into cracks—plus the whole harness and helmet. I must have been quite a sight panting halfway up this artificial peak with its convenient and not-so-convenient holds and nooks. It's a pretty well kitted-out climbing gym, and the only drag is that you have to take yourself all the way out to Sutton to use it—less of a problem recently, mind you, with all my hanging around Helena's place in nearby Richmond.

I do this once in a while. I'm crazy. I'm absolutely scared of heights, and since I hate having fear of any kind, this is my own "tough love" therapy to get over it. I'm sure the gym owners and coaches still put me in the "novice" category because I've only ascended this rock maybe half a dozen times without chickening out, but that's good enough for me. Funny thing is when I'm climbing—and I don't know about other people—I'm not really looking around, I'm just slogging away when I'm into it.

Or when my mind's on something else. Like the case.

When I came out of my near scrapes and adventures in Sudan, one of my friends shook her head and told me, "Girl, you got to get yourself a hobby." With down time in jets, at home in my flat between contracts and catastrophes, with all the empty silent spaces between the notes, I could see she was right. What I could *not* see was me becoming one of those women who starts gardening. Or having a collection of . . . I don't know, something. I know how to cook for up to three people, and that's as far as I'm willing to dare with measuring cups. I can sew if I have to, but you won't find any knitting needles in my place. Please shoot me if I ever get hooked on *EastEnders*.

Teresa, my love, I admitted to myself, you need something to occupy your mind and your time—something you won't mind dropping for the next gig, the next nosing-around job, the next flight. So I've done my best to acquire some extracurricular activities, to round myself out as a person.

Like scrambling up a rock.

"But these things you do," someone observed, "they're just more skills you're *arming* yourself with to prepare for your next gallivanting adventure, your next 'Teresa crusade.' "

Fair comment, I guess. Learning to climb rocks because God knows where I'll be next time and just what I would have to climb. Maybe it's why I'd thrown myself into the strip poker case so willingly, so enthusiastically. I could rationalize to myself all this sleeping around. Climbing, learning to shoot when I was over in America, taking refresher courses in first aid, and okay, Teresa, yes, you have *permission* now to get it on with these guys even though you *know* there are other ways to learn what you're after. You can take a break. You can play.

That comment about arming myself? It was made by the paunchy sixty-seven-year-old gentleman below me at the moment. He was playing belayer, holding the rope and my safety in his hands. "Lowering," he called up. And down I came like a panto fairy on a wire, shoes touching stone and kicking off again, glancing down at him once and thinking: Man, stick to the three-piece pinstripe jobs, Walter, because that grey track suit does nothing for you. Course, it was my fault he was dressed like that, since I'd recruited him into my suburban mountaineering fantasy.

We have this game, Walter and I. He calls ahead to say he'll be in London and knows he should visit me, and we both pretend he's not checking up on me for my father. One of the most esteemed academics out in Oxford and a longtime family friend, I grew up completely buying he was Santa Claus for five Christmases with that salt-and-pepper beard of his.

"Your turn," I said, as I unhooked my gear and wiped my brow with the back of my forearm.

He let out a noise that was between a grunt and a chortle to let me know that'll be the day and then added, "Miracle that you roped me into this . . . just to hold your rope."

"That's very clever."

"Thank you," he answered, looking like a dignified bulldog.

Walter's got one of those deep bass black man voices that could give James Earl Jones a run for his money. When I was sixteen and very obnoxious while we were living in

America for a while, my brother and I used to get him to say, "*This* is CNN." Then we'd collapse in hysterics. Walter didn't have a clue, but my dad knew what was going on and threw his ball of rubber bands at us.

"I did offer cocktails," Walter reminded me now. "In lieu of."

"This is exercise," I said. "Works the muscles, not the liver. Come on, if you're weren't here, how exciting would your day get?"

"I don't expect coming in for the occasional exhibit appraisal for the Ashmolean to be a cliffhanger, darling—sorry for the pun. Speaking of which, no one's trying to kill you these days, are they?"

"You know that only happens when I go abroad," I lied as I reached for my water bottle. "How's Auntie June?"

"The same. She's well."

Funny. I stopped calling him "Uncle Walter" when I was about twelve, but his wife will always be Auntie June for me.

"How's my dad? Did he ever go out with that lady doctor Auntie June tried to fix him up with?"

Walter shook his jowls, ruffled. He had been sent on a mission, and he was supposed to be gathering intelligence, not giving it away. "First," he sputtered, making a big comical show of being offended, "She does not try to 'fix' your father up—"

"Yes, she does, and you help," I said, kissing him on the cheek. I scooped up my towel and mopped my forehead.

"And second," he tried again.

"And second," I interrupted smoothly, "it's okay. Mum's been gone how long now? Walter, would you please tell my dad . . . I don't know, in whatever tactful way you want to do it, that it's okay now. He shouldn't be rattling around that big house all by himself."

"He has his work. Like you."

I shot him a look. I was being oversensitive, but—

"You know I had to go," I said quietly. "I planned it before she even started to . . . Before she got ill."

Walter nodded, and a sad, apologetic smile cut into his neatly trimmed beard. "I am not your judge, little girl. And I do not want the job, thank you very much. I do think all that . . . atmosphere a while back was because you went to Africa so soon *after*. I think he would have preferred you stay close. For a while. Oh, he's past that anyway, Teresa. He worries about you, we all do."

"Isaac doesn't," I said.

"Yes, well," murmured Walter, "your brother's planning a hostile takeover of Brazil next week. I have trouble keeping up with his *ventures*."

I knew Walter cared about Isaac as much as me, but he always used a tone for my big bro's wheelings and dealings that made it sound like Isaac was navigating a legal tightrope. His *ventures*. Jeez. In truth, my brother is a hell of a lot more legit than I've ever been, knowing how to sweet-talk the banks or foundations for his next import start-up, the next flash music video he's directing for a friend, his next restaurant investment.

Growing up and watching our father tread the choppy political waters at the university and how our mum faced pig-ignorance all through the NHS in her nursing supervisor positions, my brother and I both decided early we'd never suffer working nine-to-five for The Man. Isaac was my first hero that way, proving you could go out and do something creative—or at least interesting—to put groceries on the table. And in retrospect, big brother spoiled me. Having seen his example, I could never settle for a boyfriend or partner who was an accountant or systems analyst, who was screamingly dull but "stable."

Course, I don't think Mum would have been able to handle the shock of what I was prepared to do to cash Helena's cheques—not that I'd have advertised it to her if she were still with us.

"Teresa, darling," she told me once; "if you act like a lady, they will still say you're putting on airs and all kinds of things, but act like one anyway—not for them, but for yourself."

We clashed inevitably over her ideas and mine of what a lady was today. My modern definition included being able to kick butt now and then, and it meant planning trips to remote places "unescorted." I admit there were times when I relished shocking her. I could never shock my father—he seemed to wisely concede from the time I was eight years old that I was untameable. Mums never give up. I don't know what it is with mothers and daughters anyway, since my brother Isaac laughed and told me, "If you don't want her lecturing you on these guys and how many there are, and how serious you are about them, *stop* bringing them home and introducing them!" Isaac learned from the time he was in Uni to keep a tight lid on his romantic entanglements. But my mum was my oldest confidante.

God, I miss her.

And now we're all scattered. Isaac always fighting jet lag, me in London, Dad in Oxford, still so reticent that he has to send out an "operative" to see how I'm doing. If I called him, he wouldn't tell me how he is, he'd tell me of his disappointment in the latest crop of students, how his book is coming along, and ironically, gossip about his pal Walter's latest run-in with the Board and his narrow escape—a scandal Walter could tell me right here if he were inclined. Well, I'll make the call anyway, I told myself, right after I wrap up this case—after, so that I don't have to come right out and lie to my own father about what I was working on. I knew I should call Isaac, too, but there was some truth in what Walter was saying about my brother. If I remembered his last email correctly, he really was in Brazil.

When we had changed and found each other again in the lobby, Walter had a spark of mischief in his eye as we walked to his car. "I've often thought, as I watched you grow up, Teresa, that you're just irresponsible enough to make a brilliant tenured professor."

"I never graduated," I reminded him.

"But if you had, if you had gone all the way, I'm saying you'd have been brilliant," he insisted, enjoying his fantasy. "You'd never be in class. You don't care what other people think, so you wouldn't care whether they learn or not. But you can talk certain powers that be into funding all kinds of sabbaticals and expeditions. Sounds like many of the successful infamous profs I happen to know."

"Dad's never been like that," I argued. "Neither have you."

"Well, when we started, we were naïve," joked Walter. "We wanted to teach. Then our virtues simply became bad habits."

I laughed and told him, "I've never had a virtue long enough to make it a habit."

Me as a professor? I'd get my ass fired for seducing the first hunky student who walked into my lecture theatre. And I'd probably do it out of an instinctive urge to rescue myself from that life.

◆

It was two days after my drink with Shondi that I got confirmation that Lionel's ears were burning. It stood to reason that someone might get curious about me and check out my background, and in this great new age of the Internet, all they had to do was go online and see if this company existed with a corporate website. I was counting on that.

A friend of mine's an accomplished website designer, and the night after the first poker game when Helena sprang her fantastic cover story on me as much as everyone else, I got on the phone and quickly enlisted him to create a whole site for "my" venture capital firm, Aslan Biosciences (okay, yes, I loved the Narnia books as a little girl). The site had links for info, corporate history, etc. Much of the stuff my pal cribbed from actual respectable sites, rewriting here and there to make it just different enough, but it all added up to a nice camouflage blind.

There was only one useful bit of information in there, and that was the phone number for general inquiries—it was, in fact, a second ex-directory line Helena kept in the house unknown to her escort customers. An 020 8 number her PA and receptionist, Wendy, would answer with "Aslan Biosciences . . . Oh, Miss Knight isn't in at the moment, can I take a message?"

I was to be phoned immediately in case anyone came snooping around.

And Lionel did.

He wanted to meet me for lunch. I thought I'd better not make it too easy for him, so I had the receptionist phone back to say tomorrow wouldn't do. How about next Tuesday then? Pick a time, he'd told her. He had cleared his schedule for me.

My, my, I thought, the boy's got a lot on his mind. No, he couldn't swing by my office, especially since I didn't really have an office at all (for the cover story's website, I had picked out a random floor of an office block over on Bishopsgate— it was mostly corporate leaseholds, so no one would be the wiser). No, I'd better come to him. He accepted that easily as I thought he would, since even he couldn't be so dim as to think a woman would invite a casual sex partner to her work environment. Tuesday, it was.

No sooner had I finished putting Lionel on ice than Helena's PA rang to tell me that George Westlake was trying to get hold of me. Unlike my last pigeon, I saw no reason to keep the man dangling.

"Hi, George, it's Teresa Knight returning your call. What can I do for you?"

"Teresa, hi!" I heard the pleased excitement in his voice. It was somewhat flattering. "I, um, was hoping we could meet for coffee this weekend. Saturday perhaps?"

"George," I said playfully, "are you asking me out on a *date*?"

In retrospect, this was pretty *duh*. I don't know why I didn't anticipate this from one of them. I'd just assumed the guys who went to the strip poker games wouldn't be interested in seeing the women outside the circuit, not when they could win them sexually at the table. Helena had said that Westlake was rather taken with me.

"Not really a date as such," he answered, sounding a bit lame. Meanwhile I'm thinking: yep, he wants a date. "More like a small favour."

"I hope I keep my clothes on for this favour," I said.

"Oh, yes, certainly!" He said it so quickly that I figured he was sincere.

"Okay, you're on." He had me intrigued.

♦

I was surprised at his choice of venue. I suppose I shouldn't have been since he was in the hospitality business, but I hadn't expected a white guy in his fifties to pick a spot that good. Yeah, yeah, I know—I'm an age snob. Put away the lawsuit, I'm learning.

George Westlake waited for me outside a café I was familiar with near Oxford Street, wearing black Dockers and a dark silk shirt open at the neck with the sleeves rolled up on his forearms. He looked ... Well, he looked damn good. I remembered him at the game in his pinstripe power suit with the glittering cuff links and the diamond tie pin, and while yes, I had seen this man stripped to the waist and his build was holding up, seeing him in casual wear cast him in a different light. It took ten, no, fifteen years off him. I didn't normally go for older guys, especially white older guys, but he actually looked quite attractive to me today.

I was in crisp, almost paint-on new jeans and a blue halter for the warm weather, clunking along in my open-toed shoes from Debenhams. George and I traded appraising looks and smiled at each other.

"Thanks for coming," he said. "Why don't we get a table inside near the window?"

Café Depardieu is one of those over-consciously hip places that are amusing for a while and then have to re-invent themselves after six months like a nightclub. Its current identity sported a framed movie poster of its namesake back when he did his turn as Cyrano, and there were ceramic sculpture goats for decoration and a wall with a pop art collage of photos from the Vichy regime of WW2. Whoever had decorated the place clearly also wanted to direct music videos. On the stereo was vintage Ella.

We ordered our coffee and talked about pointless things for a minute or two. I spun fabulous lies about where I lived (a flat in St. John's Wood, yeah, I wish), what my work was like (stem cells, remember, talk about stem cells) and my family background (an only child—invoking my dream at twelve years old).

I saw that we would discuss almost anything except the spectacle of me naked and going down on Lionel Young, or

Westlake laying down a straight to avoid Vivian getting his trousers off. Strip poker? Oh, no. "First rule about Fight Club is . . ."

He was telling me all about the Turks and Caicos when I reached out and took his hand in mine and said warmly, "What is this favour you wanted to ask?"

He made an embarrassed laugh and said, "It's ridiculous really. I—um—well, you might know that I'm divorced."

I sure hoped he wasn't about to ask me to be his trophy companion on some convention holiday.

"My wife and I split a couple of years ago, very ugly break-up—anyway that's beside the point."

"I'd heard, yeah."

"I have a daughter, Candice. She's turning nineteen next week, and I haven't bought any of her birthday presents yet. And I could use a bit of female help."

So. George Westlake was recruiting me to play personal shopper.

"Don't you have any female friends who could help you with this?" I asked. "Don't get me wrong, George, I don't mind helping but . . ."

"If you ever get divorced, Teresa, and I certainly hope you don't go through it, you discover that one of you gets custody of your friends. And I know it sounds sexist, but as you get older, you discover your remaining friends are over-represented by your own gender."

"Wouldn't it be easier just to ask Candice what she wants?"

"We, um, don't have an easy relationship these days, with all that's happened between her mother and me. And she's at that age where I'd like to show that I don't have to ask, that I know my own daughter." He looked down guiltily at his coffee. "Even if I don't."

"I take it the mother won't give you any help."

"Not at all."

"All right, then. What did you have in mind? Clothes? You know I may be a little old myself to know what's hip for nineteen-year-olds, George. If it's clothes, I need to know sizes, and—"

"I was thinking more music, movies—DVDs she might like."

"But George, I doubt highly that . . ."

I was about to say why would he think I could guess at his kid's taste when the proud father passed along a photo from his wallet of his little girl. And then I understood. I saw George Westlake's high forehead and eyes in a lovely teen-ager's face—a face that was quite noticeably a light *café au lait* shade that was deeper than his own white complexion.

"Your ex-wife's black?"

"Yes."

"You asked me to help you shop because your daughter's mixed race, so you figure I should know?"

"Yes," he said promptly. Then quickly added, "But not just that. Look, I meant this in no way to offend you. Yes. I asked you to help me because you are a *young black woman*—"

I didn't dive in reflexively with my rant that I'm African. I let him get it out.

"My ex never made a big deal out of heritage, and I wish I could say I took a greater interest in hers, but I know my daughter watches MTV and listens to these black fellows, Sean something, and whatever the other guy's name is, Paul whatever—"

"Sean Paul," I laughed. "It's one guy."

"See?" he said, looking exasperated. "Before I moved out of the house, I'd come in and she'd be watching telly shows I'd never heard of. *My Wife and Kids* or . . . ? That's not it. It's *My Wife's First Kid* or—"

"You had it right the first time," I giggled. "Enough! I'll help you."

"I'm sorry," he groaned. "I'm a sad white male."

"No, I think you're a good father," I assured him. "I thought for a moment this was an elaborate ruse to get into my knickers, but it's just too ..."

"Sad?"

I smiled. "I really want to pick a different word. I want to."

"But you can't."

"No."

"Understand," he said, recovering, with a glint in his eye, "I do still want to get into your knickers."

"Okay then, fairly warned," I purred. "I see you have your preferences. Is it only physical then with you? Black women?"

He let out an embarrassed sigh. "I don't want to be that shallow. I mean ... Well, my wife—my ex-wife—is black with Guyanese roots. Yes, of course, I was interested in what made this woman her, so I took an interest in that culture. But all of today's things ... This hip-hop stuff, who the stars are and the clothes—I think a lot of it must be influenced by America, and it's my daughter's generation, and—I don't want to sound *old,* but—"

"I understand," I cut in. "You're not old. It's not your thing, that's all. It's not the thing for millions here. I'm sorry if I was a bit touchy. You're very brave to at least admit your ignorance."

"Thank you," he said, and there was that touch of boyish shyness again.

I could see what Helena meant. He was playing the circuit, yes, but he'd been off the market for a good long time and had to learn the signals and cues all over again. I found myself beginning to like him. It didn't make me want to take him to bed like Neil, but he was sweet in his gentlemanly way. I like flirting, and flirting with him was fun because despite being rusty, he knew that flirting shouldn't advance an agenda.

"But you do like black women, don't you?" I pressed, leaning a bit forward to draw him out.

"I have to say I do," he smiled.

"Interesting. I guess I could see you going after Janet Marshall. She looks great for her age, and she's really successful—"

"Oh, no," he scoffed.

"Too old?"

"Yes. *I am.* Janet prefers her men young. And fit. Someone like Lionel or Neil is more her speed. Janet's a good friend these days."

"You don't look like a fellow who gives up on what he wants," I remarked.

"Not often." He rested a hand on my thigh for a fleeting second. "But sometimes you change your mind about what you want."

We paid for our coffee, and I led him to the big HMV store close by, where I thought we'd make out like bandits for his daughter. Good sale on this week. I grabbed one of their wire baskets, and he grinned in surprise, making a quip about how it was like we were going to Waitrose or something. Ha, if he only knew how I wish I could afford Waitrose.

He held the basket while I tossed in the latest releases from Outkast, Usher, but no point going for the no-brainer options like Alicia Keys or Twista, his daughter probably had those since they were playing everywhere you went. Then I checked the racks for a couple of artists that were only now starting to cross over to the UK from America. They were soon to hit big and if the kid had any taste, George would score major points for finding them first.

"How are we doing with your budget?" I asked over my shoulder. Okay, he's rich, but it's polite to ask.

"We're fine," he said pleasantly. "Better than fine. It's her birthday, I'll splurge."

"No, no," I told him. "We're done here."

I tagged along behind as he settled up at the cashier's, and he absently handed me a boxed set of Peter Gabriel I had been admiring. "Here you go," he said. "A little thank-you for your trouble."

"George! Wow! How did you . . . ?"

"I spotted you looking at the box," he laughed. "You had the look: 'Do I indulge myself?' And even I know Peter Gabriel's too old for my daughter."

"Thank you." I linked my arm through his, and we walked out of the store like that, seemingly a couple. As we strolled Oxford Street for a bit, I looked him up and down and said, "Since you're making use of my buyer talents, can I suggest something?"

"Go ahead."

"You get all your suits tailored, but your wife used to choose your casual wear, didn't she?"

"I wouldn't say she chose for me, but she would suggest," he said sheepishly. "Okay, yeah, she dressed me. What's wrong with this?" He motioned to his shirt.

"Nothing at all," I reassured him. "I like it. But it's safe. And you could use a dash of colour. Now that you're not with your wife, you must be falling into some old habits. I notice you came to the game in your suit, and I'll bet it's because you feel most comfortable in one. You're not closing a business deal, George, you're making a seduction."

"All right then. Tell me some things I should wear."

"Oh, we can do better than that!" I laughed.

I didn't think he could pull off anything from Diesel, but I led him to Burton and John Lewis, believe it or not, has been doing some really interesting stuff with Italian fabrics lately. I picked out shirts and a couple of pairs of trousers for him. I had him looking pretty good after an hour, and I extracted a promise that he would show up in one of his new ensembles the next time he felt like playing cards. It was around five-thirty when we stood on a side road near Bond Street Station, finished for the day, and he said, "Why don't I buy you dinner tonight? As a thank-you."

I lifted the shopping bag that held my present. "You've already thanked me."

"That was for Candice. I haven't paid you back for helping my wardrobe."

"It's all right," I said. "I should get going. But I want you to know I had a lovely time." In this, I was telling the truth.

I stepped in and kissed him, and he was a surprisingly good kisser (the goatee tickled). I leaned into him only very gently yet I felt an insistent hardness below. He blushed faintly and said, "I need you to stand still for a minute."

To hide him until he calmed down.

"I think being close to you is a bit counterproductive," I giggled.

His trousers made a tent for a very long, impressive bulge.

"Christ, this is embarrassing," he said, turning away from passing shoppers. "I'm sorry, Teresa. To be honest, it's been a while."

"But you go to the games," I said, a little surprised.

"I play but I'm not the best player, and it's not like I'm the most in demand," he admitted. "Vivian bets on me sometimes because she's bored, but she only gets me down to my underwear before she turns her attention to Lionel or Neil—Giradeau, even Cahill or whoever the new face is. I won her once ages ago, but I think she let me win. It was very perfunctory—"

"I don't need to know, George," I said quickly.

"Sorry, too much information. I'm sorry."

"You've got to stop apologising, George. I had a really good time."

"So did I," he replied. He wore an expression of such vulnerable open need. I wanted to be compassionate.

"I wish you'd reconsider," he said.

"Dinner tonight? We both know where that's going." I arched my eyebrows at him and offered, "If you're in a hurry, there's always the games."

"That's not what I ..." He sighed. "I want it to be your choice to have my company."

"It was today. And it always will be. You have nothing to worry about on that score." I gave him a swift kiss on the cheek and said, "I'm going now. You've got a PC at home, right? Got broadband?"

He shrugged a yes.

"Start it up when you get home and call my mobile. I'll have something for you." I flashed a smile intended to dazzle and then strolled away. I would bet anything he was watching my back for a good twenty seconds.

I treated myself to a pasta dinner at Amalfi's in Soho, and then jumped on the tube. I knew it would take George longer to get home since he mentioned he'd bought a new house in Walton-on-Thames. By the time I emerged from Earl's Court Station, my mobile bleeped in my handbag.

"Hi."

"Hi," I said. "You online?"

"I can be."

"Good. But first, I want you to take your clothes off and sit down at the computer."

I heard a rustle of clothing being unbuttoned and shed, and I knew he was complying. "You sound about done. Comfy?"

"It's a little cold."

"You'll warm up, George, no worries." And I gave him a very specific URL.

He told me to hang on and then eagerly typed. After a

moment, I heard him gasp in surprise, and I roared with laughter. "Oh, my God!" he whispered. "It's you! When did you have these taken?"

"About five years ago," I said. "And please do not share them."

"No—no, of course not. You look beautiful, Teresa."

He was looking at the website of a photographer friend of mine who had persuaded me to do a series of artsy glamour nude shots for him. Some pics had made it into a coffee table book he released, but it was out of print and never got wide distribution. Still. I could be found on his website, arching my back and looking sensually aroused by the Pacific Ocean, and then there was the one where I was lying in the sun with a sheer netting for a prop. Hey, I made good money and got a vacation out of it.

"Are you hard, George?" I whispered into the phone.

"Y—yes."

No doubt he had clicked on the couple of pop-up shots of me on my knees, looking into the camera with more than a come-hither look, more like a come-and-stick-it-in-me-now look.

"You have a good time then." I laughed a goodbye and clicked off.

The idea of him sitting there nude at that very instant and masturbating to my pictures gave me a chuckle. And the pictures were a useful consolation prize that avoided me having to shut him down right away. He was a nice guy, and as strange as it sounded, I think I could handle fucking him, but dating him held all kinds of traps.

The big trouble was that shopping with George Westlake on a Saturday afternoon didn't get me any closer to the blackmailer. Unless it *was* Westlake, and no, of course, I wasn't about to rule him out just because he had a black ex-wife and a mixed-race kid. Wandering around HMV, I had slowly drawn him out about his own work, how he had built up his modest empire, and I made mental notes to check out each dropped name, every casual reference.

But I had a feeling they would all check out.

I had already poked my nose into Lionel's business affairs on the theory that someone might hold a grudge and was using his personal life as a pretext to intimidate him. But slim pickings there. Yes, those that screw together do deals together, and my digging uncovered the fact that George Westlake had given Lionel a hefty discount on time-shares in Majorca for a corporate junket. One month later, George's stock portfolio included a tidy profit on some new metals trading. And that was recent. That should make them buddies, not foes.

There was another possibility—friends that had a falling-out.

Change the theory of the crime, and you change the suspects and change the motivations. Suppose it *was* personal.

If George had a thing for black women and he was behind all this, the anonymous notes could be interpreted very differently. After all, Lionel's note had warned him to stop seeing "her," presumably Janet, while Janet's note referred to her "having to pay to get off." Instead of Lionel feeling vengeful after a poor performance, what if it was Westlake venting his jealousy?

I rang Helena to get the lowdown. "Oh, yes, darling, he was terribly smitten with Janet for a while. Made a few plays for her, but she always shut him out, and when she and Neil began their conspicuous losing streak to each other, I think he got the message."

Neil. There was still Neil to consider. *Dummy,* I told myself.

You forgot that Westlake probably knows of her involvement with Neil or at the very least got the hint something was there. Confirmed by Helena. A poker regular obsessed with Janet was one of the first scenarios we rejected because of the logic. Jealousy didn't make sense when you factored in a note to Lionel but *not* one sent to Neil.

And Janet's note had referred to her as a "sad old bag." Again, just as with Vivian Mapling, the language didn't fit. Would George use an insult like that? There was only a couple of years' difference between them.

Yet when he talked about young guys who were "Janet's speed" he had mentioned both Neil *and* Lionel.

If he was our blackmailer making death threats, then my passing on links to my nude shots was upping the ante in a very dangerous game.

4

Tuesday. Time to find out what Lionel wanted. The lobby of his employer, Buccaneer Cape Mining, put on an impressive front. Its top brass had turned it into a gallery for up-and-coming painters, many a little too influenced by Bacon for my tastes, but it's not as if I had the bank account to voice an opinion. Big tanks of tropical fish. BBC 24 and CNBC Europe on large television screens overhead, and the standard coffee table fare of this morning's *Wall Street Journal Europe* and *The Financial Times*.

Lionel came out and smiled at me as if we were old colleagues, shaking my hand and greeting me as "Miss Knight," asking if I'd had any trouble finding the office. Past the desk at front reception, he fell silent, ushering me into his professional sanctum and only then finding his voice to ask if I wanted coffee. I declined. He shut the door, and I heard the tiny click as he locked us in. I already saw that the vertical venetian blinds were closed.

He sat down behind his desk and spoke as if he were

upbraiding one of his own staff. "You've been going around asking a lot of questions about me."

I leaned back in the chair opposite him and folded my arms. And smiled. "You wanted to meet me in person for *that*? I could have told you to go to hell over the phone."

"If you want to know something," he said, smoothly ignoring my reply, "why don't you just come to the source? What? What are you looking for?" He saw me make a big show of looking around.

"The luggage. You must keep it around somewhere for all that ego."

"Then why all the questions?"

"It's a small world, Lionel," I said. "Not that it's any of your business, but I merely traded notes with another dissatisfied customer. You really are giving black men a bad name, you know."

"Shondi," he growled, huffing in exasperation. "Thought as much. She's a big-mouthed slut, and anything she tells you—"

"You're doing the games, and *she's* the slut?"

"Whoa, whoa, hold on," he said. "It's not like that. There's a difference between getting it on with people you know or at least you can be sure of, and letting an entire floor of people see your crack and giving it away to one and all! I *never* took her around to that scene. Not ever."

I was scathing. "Let me guess. The deal was you guys fuck other people, but when it's you two, it's *making love,* right?"

"You don't think there's a difference?" he shot back. "Poor you."

"Sounds like it was you who made up the rules all the time," I argued. "Maybe she got tired of it."

He looked down at his desk blotter. "That's not why we broke up."

"Yeah, I heard why. You two had a political argument that got ugly."

He scoffed at that one, looking genuinely surprised. "Is that what she told you? She substituted that shit about my company and how 'what I'm doing is all wrong' for our break-up argument? Oh, man. Okay, whatever."

I didn't press him on this. It wasn't relevant to the case why the two horny lovebirds parted ways. I was looking for other connections. He calmed down a bit and tried to be charming. "Shondi can do what she likes now. And I've matured since her. I've learned to appreciate a finer type of woman."

Yeah, right.

I knew he wanted to flirt, but he also gave me an opening. "Yeah, I hear the rumours."

"Oh, really? And what do you hear?"

I laughed in his face and said, "I'm not some dried-up bitch who needs to pay for it. And I certainly wouldn't pay *you* for it, Lionel."

"You're out of line," he snapped. "If you're referring to who I think you are, she's a lady. What went on between us was at the games, and she certainly doesn't need to pay anybody for it."

This, I didn't expect. And it put a whole new spin on things. He hadn't even bragged about having Janet or made a denial. So much for my pegging him as the one behind it all. Unless this was the king of all bluffs. Okay, I thought, let's probe a little deeper.

"I hear she's got a man."

Lionel found this hilarious. "Right! And you're sharing him, honey!"

I pretended to be surprised. "Oh, yeah? Sounds to me like he's tired of her."

"He'll never leave Janet, not in a hundred years." He sounded quite certain about it. "No fooling, those two are *connected*. I saw that after she and I hooked up, how they're so deep into each other. It doesn't matter about any of their spats or weird vibes, that's them."

"And so you'll gracefully step aside for Neil?" I taunted.

"I'm not that big-hearted," he sneered. "It's just anyone who gets in their way becomes a bit player in their little melodrama, and when the smoke clears, they go back to each other. Makes me wonder why they bother with the circuit, 'cause they're kind of wasting everyone else's time. Sooner or later, they'll wake up. You can go chase after him if you like, and he won't even think he's playing you. He'll believe what he feels for a while then drop you."

"Don't like him much, do you?"

Lionel picked up a pen, toyed with it a second and then tossed it aside. "He's smug, that one."

"I could say the same thing about you."

"Yeah, but I don't pretend to be a saint," he argued. "You do what you like when it comes to him, and good luck with that. I think you ought to give me another chance."

"I am not having you come in my mouth again, Lionel."

"I'm sorry, Teresa, you were just too damn good. I didn't get to do what I do well."

"You want to fuck me here? Right in your office? There are easier ways to get sacked, Lionel. And I don't envisage you getting me off any better than you did last time."

"Tell you what," he said. "We'll use the cards."

I shook my head. "But I don't need to play."

He studied me carefully. "You're up to something. After something—"

"Paranoid, too, I see—"

"Whatever it is, you can come out and ask me, and it'll

stay in this room—if you win. If I win, we do it right here, right now, and I guarantee satisfaction."

The guy kills me, I thought. If I win, I get to ask—meaning he learns what I'm up to. If he wins, he fucks me. I was hard-pressed to see why I should gamble with him at all.

"You're still making offers, and I'm telling you not interested."

"Ah, but I'll sweeten the pot," he laughed. "You don't come—and you got to be honest with me—I never make a play for you again at the tables. I'll forfeit if it comes down to just the two of us, no lie. Keep in mind, when we sit down at a game, we don't get to pick and choose unless we get a winning hand, and frankly, babes, you just ain't that good—at *cards*."

I gave him an appraising look, letting him dangle for a while. I couldn't fault his logic here, really. He could end up having me on my back, winning a rug burn at the very next game where I saw him, and honour would force me to oblige. Of course, if he were crap again here and now, I'd have only his word that his shame would make him keep his end of the bargain. Of course, he had surprised me several times today.

"You're on."

He opened a drawer of his desk, and pulled out a deck, grinning wolfishly again and pointing out, see, it's brand new. Not even out of its plastic wrapping, no tricks. I said I'd shuffle. Silence between us as my hands made the little cards dance as they rearranged themselves, and then I melodramatically put down the deck like a gavel. He cut first.

"Aces low? High card gets to name the fun?"

"Sure."

He lifted his half of the deck to show me the queen of diamonds. He was already laughing as he passed the cards, and when I flipped over a seven of clubs, he confessed, "I do like camisoles."

"Okay, okay . . ."

"Don't tell me you're going to back out?"

"Did I say that?"

I stood up and unzipped my skirt, letting it fall to the floor, and then I slipped out of my panties. Bare legs and my wedge of fur facing him under the hem of my short suit jacket. I shrugged off the blazer and went over to the small round conference table he had in the corner, opening my legs for him in a lewd pose of come 'n' get it. Then I suddenly started.

"Hold it."

"*What?* What's wrong?"

I pointed to the tiny webcam sitting on top of his computer monitor. "You better tell me that thing is off."

I didn't bother to cover up. If it were on, it didn't matter because I'd rip his computer apart in a moment.

"*What?* No! No, of course, it's not on!" He looked at me in disbelief. "Look at the screen. Program's not even running. You see any minimized icons?"

"Humour me," I told him. "Shut down."

He did. I was leaning over his desk, still half naked, my breasts hanging down. He gave me an admiring look and said, "Now. Can I collect?"

I backed up and leaned once more against the conference table.

As he came around from behind his desk, he loosened his tie and undid his top button, unbuckled his belt with his erection pushing out the fabric of his dress pants. It was strange, like there was an angry compatibility between us, a one-upmanship going on as opposed to the perfect chemistry of Neil and me. I was already brushing my hand underneath his shirt and reaching into his boxers as his hands groped my tits through the silk of the camisole, lowering the thin shoulder straps. The way he massaged my breasts ... Well, at least he could do something right.

It was me who put him inside, tugging on his cock a little, brushing the head of it up against my vaginal lips to increase my wetness, and then he slid effortlessly inside me. He wasn't very long, but he made up for this with the thickness of his girth, his dick like a hard muscle that punished me even as it teased. Half sitting on the wooden lip of the table, I lifted my knees to try to hook my ankles around the back of his legs. I felt his hands sliding down to grip my ass cheeks, and then he lifted me off the table, impatient to lower me down.

The cheap broadloom carpet did nothing to save my back from the hardness of the floor, but I didn't mind. For a moment, we fumbled and wrestled, not at cross-purposes, but competitively, trying to drive each other wild. My fingers played with his balls and then guided his cock in, and I cried out as he managed to penetrate me deeper, my knees lifting, teeth sinking into his chest. He whispered with an almost touching degree of respect, "Can I kiss you?" In answer, I gripped his face and sloshed my tongue eagerly into his mouth. All at once his penis seemed to grow twice its size and become an iron bar inside me.

I whimpered in irritable protest, fearing once again, I'd get cheated. But he was holding his own, fucking me almost with a vengeance, his palms pushing against the floor to ground himself. Pumping me hard in slaps of flesh. I didn't realize I was starting to gasp louder, ignoring the soft thud of footsteps from the office hallway beyond. He whispered once, "Teresa," and I buried my face in his shoulder.

As wet as I was, my pussy began to grip him more tightly, holding him in with a shuddering, hungry sucking to keep that hard pole inside me. He reared up with a grunt and pulled out just enough so that his finger could come down to tease my clit, and then I lost it. I felt the cords of my neck straining, beads of fresh sweat on my forehead as my orgasm engulfed all of my being. Uncontrollable shudders. When I fluttered my eyes open, I saw how he shivered, doing all he could to hold back the tide ready to burst.

"I want to . . . I want to come. Can I . . . ?"

Asking permission. Actually asking permission, even though he knew I had had my turn. Maybe he was just an immature asshole in public. I gave his chin a merciful caress and said, "Give it to me. And if you can get me to the top again when you shoot, you can chase me in any poker game."

He was doing slow, aching thrusts to try to keep his control, and then he kissed my breast as a gentleman might kiss a girl's hand. He knew enough not to just start pumping away for his own selfish pleasure but began to play with my tits again, and I think he got the message. As he sucked a nipple and began to thrust harder, I felt another swell of his cock inside me, and I didn't care at all about disguising my own pleasure. I shut my eyes tight, floating above the floor again while his strong hand cradled me under my ass, and he just drilled me. He was enormous when he shot. My left arm felt back muscles rippling like waves as he shook with his own pleasure, and his expression was stripped of all his bravado, a face vulnerable and pleading: *Teresa*.

Damn perverse, the two of us actually holding each other, as if our rutting on the floor could be anything compared to making love with feelings, a rite of affection that deserved afterglow. He didn't say anything stupid, no comment on my orgasm, thank God. Spent, we lay together, strangers again, neither of us knowing what to make of it but glad it had happened. He would never know that as I shuffled the deck, I had slipped in my own marked card to pick it out when it was my turn (hey, I never said I knew how to play poker, but I had a brother heavily into magic tricks when he was ten). He wouldn't have a clue that I had brought along not only a low card, but a king as well, in case I felt differently.

Yes, I did figure he would pull a stunt like this.

But he was far more successful than I had expected.

"You know something," he said softly. "This has been all you. That was incredible because you are incredible—"

"You have tissues, Lionel?" I asked absently.

"Teresa—"

"I'm sorry," I said. "Thank you. For the compliment."

"Teresa," he started again, and I thought: Don't get maudlin on me now. I waited, and he handed me a bunch of tissues from a box on his desk. I cleaned myself as best I could, knowing there must be a ladies' room somewhere, and I quickly dressed.

"Look, a bet's a bet, but no kidding around, if you've got something on your mind, let's have it," he went on. "You want to ask me something?"

"You've answered it," I said. I waved to him as I turned and did a thief's exit out the door.

Let him wonder.

◆

I walked out of there trying to add up what I'd learned besides the fact that Lionel could scratch an itch when he put his back into it.

His responses to everything I threw at him seemed unaffected and genuine. I gave him a chance to knock Janet, and he didn't take it, quite the reverse. Neil might not be his favourite person, but I didn't get the impression that he thought his rival was behind the letter threat. That was interesting to me, especially since Janet was aware that Lionel had been threatened as well.

But so far as anyone knew, *Lionel* didn't know about *Janet's* letter.

In his ignorance, Lionel would assume his enemy was concerned solely with him. If he could objectively rule out Neil, a guy he resented, maybe I had to widen my net. Trouble was, I had plenty of suspects but no leads.

◆

Wednesday evening. 116 Pall Mall, the Institute of Directors. The Nash Room on the second floor. Big gilt-framed portraits and chandeliers, black people in black-tie formal wear. Helena had arranged to get me on the guest list at the British Black Entrepreneur Association Awards, where Janet Marshall was to be a presenter.

I thought it a good idea to check out Janet in her own milieu. It was a long shot that anyone here tonight could betray themselves as a new suspect or give me a fresh insight, since I was dead certain it had to be one of the poker players. But I thought it wouldn't be a bad idea to tag along. The more I learned about Janet, the more I might learn about our blackmailer. Straw clutching? Sure. But what else did I have? And I wasn't about to put the whole membership of the Labour caucus on my suspect list.

It was refreshing tonight to get a break from Teresa Knight, Senior Adviser in Scientific Appraisal at Aslan Biosciences, and be regular Teresa Knight, Miss sometimes activist and full-time troublemaker. I waved to the occasional smiling faces I knew from visits to the Africa Centre in Covent

Garden or to the School of Oriental and African Studies. I could blend into this crowd with no one questioning why I was here. Good champagne, okay canapés. Janet kissed cheeks and shook hands, working this crowd like she was running again for her old Brixton seat. And who knows? Maybe her presentation tonight would help her chances with Pretoria. The British Black Entrepreneur Association was a young group, and sure, the Black Enterprise Awards are better known, but there were powerful people rubbing shoulders here tonight who could always bend a few ears in Whitehall, around Bank tube station or even Downing Street.

Yes, Janet was willing to stop going to the poker games for a while, cut back on a few public appearances as Helena and I advised. But the blackmailer wanted her to retire, and she said she'd be damned if she would completely turn tail and run.

As for me, socially, I was doing all right. I got hit on five times, caught up with a couple of old acquaintances and was learning nothing for the case until Anthony Boulet floated over to my circle.

Janet had introduced me to him earlier. Anthony Boulet was short, shorter than me actually, with a caramel complexion and a stocky build, and though I knew he must be in his forties, he could pass for thirty-five. The thin spectacles on his face put up a barrier of reflections in front of his eyes, so that it was harder to read his expressions. He was warm with Janet, distant with others. The affection and ca-maraderie between those two was clear to see, especially when Janet hung on his arm and fell into patois for their private in-jokes. Anthony scanned the crowd like he was her own Secret Service bodyguard or something.

"Are you going to go talk to Owolabi tonight?" he asked. The question sounded like discreet advice.

"Lord, no," she declared. "The man knows how to hold on to a grudge, and he just won't let it lie."

"Janet, he's got clout. This is the time to mend fences."

"Anthony, it's going to look really bad if I go toadying around. Either they want me for the job, warts and all, or they don't."

I had eavesdropped for another moment and then moved on. What they always said seemed to be true, that Anthony Boulet was Janet's conscience of restraint, slipping in political tips and occasionally helping her get out of traps. Janet was always macro-agenda, passionate about what she wanted changed, and Anthony went and did the homework on the fine print. You'd think a brilliant guy like that would want a political career of his own, but he was happy to sublimate his ambitions for her success.

I think someone asked him about this for one of those short page-12 newspaper features, and he answered, "In the time that I've worked for Janet, my kids went to school and grew up, and no tabloid ever snapped pictures of them outside our front door. No one asked me fool questions about who I was sleeping with or what friends I keep. Hey, everyone else can have the spotlight."

A solicitor, his office wasn't far from the Middle Temple in EC4, but he was really known as Janet Marshall's second shadow and right-hand man. Until recently, that is, since he'd gone back to private practice. He had done wonders helping her shape policy initiatives at the Commission for Racial Equality. And Janet had managed to find him a place close to her at the Beeb, where he cleaned house over administrative practices. Now that Janet's career was taking her full circle back to her roots in international affairs, there wasn't really a place for him. He'd had a good run. And it was my understanding he was doing all right with a whole list of corporate clients.

And now Anthony Boulet hovered nearby, waiting to catch my attention.

"I wonder if we could have a private word," he said in a low voice.

"What's on your mind?"

He steered me gently by the elbow away from a huddle of conversation. "I wanted to know if you'd made any progress."

"Progress?"

"Janet told me about the note," he explained, looking grave. "Whoever sent it is a real slime. She doesn't deserve any of this. Look at the good the woman has accomplished! When I think of what she might be able to do if she gets this position, it turns my stomach to think those tabloid jackals may get their teeth into her. Say the word, and I'll help any way I can."

I was totally bewildered. Granted, I wasn't playing biotech science girl tonight, but neither did I want someone putting a fedora on my head with a card tucked into its band that said PRIVATE DETECTIVE. All I could do was roll with it.

"I appreciate the offer," I said smoothly, "but I'm only here to get the lay of the land, political-wise." As opposed to getting a lay my other nights on the job.

He grimaced, but I still couldn't read his eyes through the shiny specs. "You don't think someone from *this* crowd?"

"I don't know. The person wants Janet to 'retire.' Who stands to gain if she does? Maybe it's not a personal grudge, maybe it's a political motive."

"Hey, let me tell you something . . ." His voice had an edge now, not pissed, but irritable. I must have struck a nerve. "I think I've got a line on most of the political motivations of the folks in here, and sure, Janet has her enemies. That's politics. But this note had to come from a whack job.

Janet's a trusting, caring soul, and she allows too many un-
stable characters on the outside to get in."

"What do you mean by that?" I asked.

"I mean you're better off looking at her friends. If any
good can come out of this, I hope it teaches her to be more
discerning."

I needed him to spell it out clearer than that, so I said, "A
minute ago, I heard you telling Janet she ought to go make
nice with somebody. Seems to me you've cleaned up a lot of
her messes."

"She's my colleague," he said tightly.

"But you don't like her personal life affecting your work
together," I prompted.

The flint in his voice was getting sharper. "I don't especially like people who can't control their passions, no."

"Anybody ever get a little too passionate?"

He laughed mirthlessly at that one and replied, "Last
year, at another function like this one, Janet was the recipi-
ent of an award instead of handing one out. Two hundred
pounds a plate, a major deal. It was the first time there was
a whiff in the air that Boddington wanted to retire in Pretoria,
and Janet might be considered. She was off again, on again
with her actor *boy-toy,* and that week they were off. And
guess who gets himself worked up and insists on seeing her
that night?"

"I take it there was a scene."

"Not irreparable, but you could hear a loud male voice
behind the closed door, and then one of the catering staff
had to go and fetch Janet. Well! She had to walk out during
one of the speeches, which meant everyone saw her leave
and could get an idea of what was going on. It was the first
time I ever chewed her out. I said your personal life is your
own affair, but if you want me to schmooze for you and

help you get this, you can't have this teenage shit going on. It's not professional. It's stupid, really. She started using him on her dates because she couldn't go to functions with me."

"No?" I asked.

"No." He held up his gold wedding band for my inspection. "It wouldn't look good at all. My wife hates political functions so 99 per cent of the time I go stag. You wouldn't think so, but Neil Kenan simplified her life with his presence—in the beginning. Once people hear he's an actor, they assume he's a bit of amusing fluff for her, and all the speculation on her amours goes out the window. No poking around to see if she's having an affair with a married MP."

"I did hear they're rather combustible, her and Neil," I remarked.

"I try not to know. I will say she can do a lot better. She has done better. It's her own fault, really, she expects men to be exclusive with her when she goes off and . . ."

He stopped. Too late.

"I know about all that," I put in. "I'm checking every one of them out."

"*Good,*" he answered. "My money, it's one of them."

"You don't approve, but you're still very loyal to her," I commented.

He looked directly at me, and for once, the reflection in the specs gave me a clear view. His eyes looked very small behind the lenses.

"You know," he said, "you hear all this psychological rubbish about strong black women, this crap about how black women are pushy in the office, or how black men can be Mama's boys, and I get the snickers now and then. You'll find ten per cent of even this crowd think I'm emasculated.

Janet's been my boss, and her good fortune has meant my good fortune. She is a great manager, full stop. She's a great statesperson, full stop. And when you're working with someone with her level of charisma and her vitality, you *want* to work with her. For her. And you allow certain liberties. There's nothing I wouldn't do for Janet."

Interesting, I thought.

Before I could ask him a follow-up, he looked past me and frowned. "I'll have to catch up with you later, Teresa."

As he moved off, I saw the reason for his retreat. Theodore Owolabi glided up to me with a cautious smile carved into his thick salt-and-pepper beard. A dark-skinned Nigerian-born activist, Theodore had been leading the fight on a whole range of causes, from his own people getting smeared with a bad reputation over notorious credit fraud rings to his push years ago for Britain to accept more refugees from Rwanda. He and I knew each other from the Sudan appeals, and he had come over to say hello—to me. Not to Anthony. No love lost there, but Theo had never been a big fan of Janet Marshall.

"You're keeping strange company these days, Teresa," he laughed, and he kissed me on the cheek in greeting.

"My God, you know, I haven't seen you for ages until tonight. Where've you been? I get rumours about you doing a courier run to Chicago, and then you ended up getting chased down to New Orleans by drug dealers . . . ?"

"They were counterfeiters. That was a few months ago, Theo. Your grapevine needs tending."

"I guess so!" he laughed. "At least you're all right. I hope your client didn't pay you in funny money."

"Cute, Theo."

"Tell me what happened with all this!" he implored.

But before I could roll out the tale, there was a stir in

the crowd, and people turned to watch the host of the award ceremonies. We stood and listened to the usual self-congratulatory stuff, a couple of statuettes were handed out, and then Janet Marshall was introduced to give an award for business in the international community or some such thing.

She started talking about Africa, and standing next to me, Theo leaned in to whisper in my ear, "This is rich. When she took her turn as Treasurer of the Africa-Caribbean Unity League last year, we hit her up for its contribution to Darfur. Can't spare it, but there's money for victims of Hurricane Ivan in Jamaica and the Caymans."

"Theo, you can't twist the facts like that," I chided him. "You used to bitch they weren't giving enough. Now you're rewriting history so that they didn't give anything at all."

"They *did* hardly give anything at all."

"The issue's the proportion, Theo. It's shit like this that made me stop coming to the meetings. And if I remember correctly, she played messenger, and she was out of town for the executive committee vote."

He didn't tackle that one, merely rolling his eyes. I let it go and turned my attention back to Janet at the podium. Her speech was hitting all the politically correct notes about the trendy topic of Corporate Social Responsibility and how black entrepreneurs should lead the way. Then she segued into a scathing attack on big multinationals that are still messing around with the natural resource wealth of African nations.

"The conflict diamond business that put Sierra Leone on the front pages has *not* gone away," she told the audience. "The Coltan trade that's behind thousands murdered, raped and turned into slaves in the Congo *has not gone away*. Is it any wonder that we saw genocide in Sudan's Darfur region last year when the world ignored how oil cartels got into bed in the past with the regime in Khartoum? Black power means economic power, and economic power is becoming increasingly vital for our very survival, whether we live in Brixton or Botswana."

"Sellout," muttered Theo.

I looked at him sharply.

"She is," he insisted. "Labour's girl in Pretoria? Please."

"You're out of line," I told him. I wanted to demand why when somebody finally opens a door for one of us and we decide to step through it, it's selling out? I wanted to argue that if Janet accepted the position, it would be one more of us *seen*. But then Theo saw Janet Marshall one way, and I was beginning to see another.

"I think," said Theo, "I ought to go get myself a drink." And off he went.

It was a few minutes later when Janet and I drifted over to each other.

"How are you doing?"

I was direct. "A little concerned. Anthony Boulet swung by to say that he would help any way he can."

"Why is that a problem?" asked Janet. "Anthony was on my staff when I was an MP, and he followed me into the CRE. I've known him for fifteen years, and he's been my rock. I trust him implicitly. In fact, he was there when the blackmail note arrived, so of course, I confided in him."

"But it wasn't necessary to disclose to him what *I'm* doing," I pointed out. "The less people know, the better, so that I can do my job."

"Anthony's very discreet."

"So are you—but you still told him."

She muttered an apology and repeated her line about Anthony's discretion, and then one of the other speakers hailed her across the room, and I let her go. Perhaps I was making too much of it, but then I remembered something Janet had told me from the very beginning—a fact that had unveiled something else, something that Janet had chosen *not* to tell me. And cast her and someone else in a whole different light. My concern grew. And I realized I had come tonight with my expectations far too low. I had found a whole new suspect.

5

Another poker game was coming up, but I was getting more action away from the table. On Thursday, Daniel Giradeau called Helena—my "sponsor" at that first game—to try to get hold of me, and I passed along my mobile number. Giradeau was something of an enigma to me, which I thought pretty rare with Americans, because usually what you see is what you get. He had been charming at the table, but a little reserved, lots of cautious bets, and his target for the night seemed to have been Ayako. Now he was taking an interest in me.

Hmmm ... Lionel was into collecting. Neil said he enjoyed the chase, while George Westlake wanted to court me and make me his rebound girl. It made me wonder if Giradeau would come up with something else.

♦

Men wanted me. Publishers didn't. Another rejection letter from one of the big London houses—I won't tell you which one, but let's just say that when magic wands became fashionable, this publisher jumped onboard the trend with five different imitators. That same Thursday Giradeau was looking for me, I was in my flat, with Stevie Wonder's *Definitive Collection* cranked up full for "Uptight" and ripping open an envelope with a printed return address.

A while back during my wanderings I got what I thought was a nifty idea for a girl detective series for kids. My readers would be—oh, I don't know, eight to eleven or so. Instead of being an orphaned alien or a magician or just one of those Enid Blyton clones, my plucky little heroine would be a Third World girl of an unspecified locale who first lives in a refugee camp and later in a resettled village of her people. She and her helpers would go looking for a friend who had disappeared or maybe foil a couple of black marketeers—adventures like that. I thought I had a winner because I could remember being intensely curious when I was a kid about how people on the other side of the world lived, and I was absolutely sure they were doing more important stuff than me. Certainly their lives were more immediate.

I don't know why I suddenly thought of writing a kids' book. It's not as if I was getting broody or had a child of my own, but the impulse grabbed me. I had an idea, and no one had ever told me I couldn't be a writer so . . . And I read that a good number of these children's authors were eccentric, single and sometimes misanthropic types, so I figured with my lifestyle, hey, I was entitled to join the club. I got a friend of a friend, Roxanne, a talented graphic artist, to do illustrations for it.

The pictures for my little masterpiece were really something. Mostly pen and ink with provocative watercolour washes of sandy brown and ochre. If you met Roxanne, you couldn't imagine the lady coming up with these ethereal images. She's this buxom white woman in her thirties in a tank top and torn jeans who's usually bent over her draft-ing table cluttered with paints, her airbrush gun, a gigantic ashtray with a mountainous heap of chain-smoked butts, and her foot is often twitching in time to blaring Gwen Stefani.

"I love this," I remember saying when I held up one of her finished compositions.

"What?"

"I said I love this," I shouted, pointing to the little girl drawn against golden hills.

"Hey, if the little fuckers don't like it, they have no bloody taste!" she giggled. Earthy girl, Roxanne.

Of course, it wasn't really up to the kids, but adults in offices thinking they understand what kids like. So far, no hits. Usually I got letterhead with the stock response of "your work is not appropriate to our needs." On the letter I opened to Stevie Wonder in the background, someone had scrawled in pencil in the margin in a feminine hand: "This would be terribly dark in tone for children." I thought: what world do *you* live in, sister?

Well, Dr. Seuss got rejection slips. So did that guy who wrote *Where the Wild Things Are,* I'm sure of it. They wrote weird stuff, certainly weirder than a girl who solves small mysteries in a refugee camp.

I crumpled the rejection letter and tossed it in the rub-bish. Time to put away childish things. For the moment.

◆

If George Westlake was Jermyn Street conservative blues and browns, Daniel Giradeau was Versace colour. He moved in a slow, graceful way, the way I'd seen trained dancers walk, almost in a languid manner. Neil, being an actor, had that grace, but Neil spoke with his hands, and he had a model's ease with his posture and his gait. Giradeau didn't seem to put any effort into it, floating up to you like he was on one of those airport moving sidewalks.

He took me to dinner in the ballroom of the Pantheon Hotel, the runner-up choice on Brook Street for those who thought Claridge's was too steep. The folks at the Pantheon had imitated their more famous neighbour's Art Deco style, right down to ripping off artist Dale Chihuly's chandelier design. Good steak. Not sure about the company. I knew I couldn't warm to Daniel Giradeau right away when I asked what made him decide to become an architect, and he told me he'd got excited by the profession when he read *The Fountainhead* at thirteen.

"You don't strike me as the scientific type, Teresa."

"You want thick specs and my hair in a tight bun?"

"Not what I meant," he laughed.

"You're not what I expect of an architect either," I replied.

"What did you expect?"

"Oh, whenever I see architects interviewed on television, they seem to have their heads in the clouds, talking about light and air like physics professors. Or they come across as very meat-and-potatoes practical types, like engineers. You're very shy about your work."

"I could show you the site, but there's nothing but a hole there. For now. I could always show my blueprints."

"Like I would understand them," I smiled.

"Fair's fair," he answered. "I was a whiz at calculus in school, but I couldn't handle chemistry to save my life.... Something tells me you're not a lab jockey. You like the deal-making side of the science, don't you? That is what your company does, right? Venture capital start-ups? Incubators?"

"You mean the investment term, not the actual—"

"No, not actual incubators," he laughed. "That's what turns you on, doesn't it? The deals."

I was guarded. "I suppose, yeah."

He looked at me, smile frozen on his handsome features, perhaps waiting for me to expand on my answer. I popped a last bite of steak in my mouth and chewed away, leaving him with silence.

"That was good," he muttered, and as the waiter took the last of the plates and melted into the back shadows of the restaurant, he reached into an inside pocket and pulled out a joint. He lit up and had a toke then passed it to me. Couldn't believe it. Not because I don't indulge but because of how brazen he was in lighting up here—and in assuming I would be cool with it.

"I'll wait for a bit," I told him. "It was a nice meal."

"I'm glad you enjoyed it."

He reached down where I couldn't see and then rested a long jewellery case on the white tablecloth. He nudged it across for me to open.

"What's this?"

"It's for you."

I opened it. Lying there was an Elsa Paretti snake necklace from Tiffany's, 18-carat gold and worth close to £4,000.

"What's it for?"

He smiled. "Nothing."

"Just like that? You always so generous?"

"If it has to be about something, okay ... Suppose I told you it's yours if you'll just slip off your panties right now and do as I say."

"Suppose I told you that you've made a terrible mistake," I shot back, trying to keep my voice light. "Just because I play strip poker doesn't mean I'm a whore."

"I didn't say you were," he replied coolly. "It's a gift—"

"*Right.* In exchange for—"

"In exchange for nothing," he interrupted. "I did say nothing. You pushed the issue, and I made a bad joke. Have it. Go ahead. I think I know why you come to the games, and it's the reason why I expected you to take your panties off. Not because of some bauble."

"Oh, really? And why is that?"

He took another drag on the joint, and as he finished, I put my hand out to let him know I wanted a hit. It was good stuff, and I quickly got a buzz. It took some of the edge off this verbal jousting.

"To answer that," he said, "let me first tell you what I see. I see an incredibly gorgeous young woman who because of her work was obviously a high achiever during her university years. She's a demon in the gym and knows how to defend herself. Your hands—you have lovely hands, but your knuckles are pronounced, and that comes from hitting things—bags, boards, whatever. You're used to competition. You're used to telling men what you want when you want it. But you never experimented much sexually in the past, and now you want to try new things, take a few risks. You want to be told what to do for a change. It's exciting not being in control."

"Boy, do you have the wrong number," I laughed.

"I don't think so. I'm offering very different services to what you might expect of the others."

Still laughing, I replied, "Services? Huh. Let me tell you what I see, Daniel. I see a guy who knows that bragging he's got 'ten good inches' won't cut it so he figures a come-on that he 'knows me so well' will get him between my legs instead. You're still treating me like a whore."

"No, I'm treating you as a sexual person," he argued. "We all are, I'm just more honest. It's about sex. It's always about sex. That's what it comes down to."

"Uh-huh." I gestured to the necklace still sitting in its box on the table. "And this is what passes for a romantic gesture to you?"

"Not at all. You're an executive. You dress well. You're used to the finer things in life. Most guys think it's just greed when a woman wants things—they don't understand that certain things give them sensual pleasure, just the way men get off when they're behind the wheel of their favourite car. And I want you to have pleasure."

"If you really want me to have pleasure, Daniel, there's a gold brooch over at Bulgari's."

"We'll see," he laughed.

"And for these pleasurable experiences, you want . . ."

"I want to teach you."

I cocked an eyebrow at him, thinking: *Is this guy for real?*

"Now that your lady virtue has been satisfied, why don't you slip off your panties?" he purred. "No one can see you. I can't see you. You've still got your dress on."

"My underwear stays in my handbag," I warned.

"I'm not into that, trust me."

I made a great show of propping up the dessert menu as a screen to hide my arm movements. Then I had to look like I was adjusting my chair, feeling slightly ridiculous. I slipped my hands under the slits that ran up both sides of my dress, and Daniel barely watched me, taking a sudden interest in the page on liqueurs of his own menu. I deposited my little black thong in my handbag.

"Would you like something?" he asked pleasantly. "They have a Tiramisu here that's exquisite."

"I'm pretty full," I said.

"Share it with me? I like the idea of you taking spoonfuls of it while you've got nothing on down there." He called over the waiter hovering in the background and ordered for us.

"This supposed to be more of your lessons in pleasure?"

"You still don't understand," he said, and his bass voice dropped another octave. "I know you'll end up with Neil Kenan."

"And that doesn't bother you?"

"Not in the least."

"Maybe I don't want him," I teased. "There are other guys besides him. And you."

"Well, good ol' Lionel didn't rise to the challenge that night, did he? That was plain for all to see. But then there's . . . Oh, let me guess. George Westlake? Yeah, I'll bet he's fawning over you like a puppy."

I didn't say anything.

"Don't get me wrong," he continued. "George and I are friends—"

"Doesn't sound like it."

"We are, trust me. And sometimes I wonder myself how a guy like that can be so shrewd in terms of commercial property development for tourist spots and then be like the worst, stuttering, pimple-faced gawky teenager when it comes to women. Do you know he's only ever been with five ladies on the circuit? *No one* bets on him."

"Then maybe I will," I said.

"Oh, please. I'm sure his attention is flattering, but you won't want him. Too passive. There's no heat there."

I was withering. "And you think there is with you?"

"No, but there can be. We have to build it. The most underrated sexual organ is the imagination. I think you're just clueing in that with some guidance, you can turn yourself on better than almost any man. Neil's proved that, hasn't he?"

"Neil's proved . . . ?"

Oh, my God. But we were *alone*.

"Don't you know the organisers of these things always have cameras to make sure there's no trouble?" he asked gently.

Yes—yes, I did. First thing I learned from Helena. But I wouldn't expect some creep to have one in—

He knew enough not to get smug over it. "They do it to cover their asses in case things get out of hand. Most games the cameras just roll, and no one's minding the fort. You and Neil were gone quite a while, and I happen to know where the monitors are. I've played games there before."

Oh, *man*. It had never even occurred to me. The washroom. There are limits, the bastards.

"Before you get cross with me," he put in quickly, "think about it. You were already naked. You show up at the games, knowing you would perform sexually in front of others, and you did—you just gave Lionel a blow job. Do you really think it's such an intrusion on my part? You must know it's considered a faux pas for a couple of players to steal away like you two did."

He shrugged and leaned in to whisper, "What's pissing you off *at the moment* is that you thought I was full of shit, right? The American who knows everything?"

I didn't respond. Hell, I couldn't think of any response.

"Teresa, I don't want to take you home tonight. That's not what I'm after."

"What are you after?"

I had to wait for a response because our dessert arrived. Daniel scooped up the Tiffany box and dropped it casually into my handbag, and I let him do it.

He didn't lie about the Tiramisu.

"What are you after?" I repeated.

"Like I said: your pleasure. Neil had the right idea, but he's making it up as he goes along."

Neil squeezing my tits and nuzzling the back of my ear as he told me to play with myself. *Mmph.* If he was making it up as he went along, I liked his improvisational skills.

I glared at Giradeau. "And I suppose you're the professor?"

"Why don't you find out?"

"Why should I?"

His eyes flicked into a dark corner, flicked back to offer me a steady gaze. "The same reason we do all kinds of things. It amuses us. I bet you think I'm an asshole, but I'm also willing to bet you'd enjoy laughing at me while you're being fucked, knowing I can't touch you."

"Being seen is part of the turn-on," I countered. "But it's being seen by everybody, not just you."

"Of course. But the rest are just spectators. An audience. There can be whole other levels of *communication* going on while you're in your most intimate moment. I bet it's already occurred to you. I bet you'll try to send me a message right when Neil's inside you, humping away. And I will think that's great because you're thinking about me, even if it's with scorn."

"All these head games you're playing," I told him, "why don't you go out and find yourself a nice girl who likes BDSM?"

"I'm not into that scene," he sneered. "Dog collars and caning? That's Halloween shit. I'm talking about communication. When you were in the bathroom with Neil, he told you what to do, and you submitted. He's very intuitive—I'll give him that. He knew that you liked touching yourself that way in front of him, that you could do better in that moment than if he touched you. But being submissive that way is at its most powerful when someone knows how far you'll go, how much you'll give. I want to see you get off and have another man's dick inside you and *know* that you're talking to me and only to me. Maybe you'll tell me you wish it were me. Maybe you'll tell me to go to hell. And all of it while it's happening to you, while he's fucking you. I bet you come like a banshee when you do."

"Or there's my third option of just ignoring you completely and having a good lay," I pointed out.

"There's that. But you lose nothing from a little experiment. Go ahead and think I'm a fool if you like. You'll see."

I stole the last bite of the Tiramisu.

Daniel flagged down the waiter to settle the bill. As we waited for his credit card to return, he asked me casually, "Have you ever ejaculated?"

"Excuse me?"

"You must have heard of it," he laughed. "Female ejaculation. I guess you're one of those who don't believe in it, but it is possible."

Yes, I had heard of it. Since it's supposed to happen through your urethra, I'd assumed it was girls peeing helplessly when they came. Ew, how *gross*.

"You're not urinating, believe me," he said. "I could make you come like that, easy."

"Well, you're not going to try!"

"I don't need to give you a rug burn. As a matter of fact, it's far easier with my hand. I thought you had a sense of adventure."

"This is supposed to be in the interests of science, huh?"

"You're the sceptic."

I gave him a healthy contribution for our tip, and then I led him by the hand. We walked out of the restaurant and through the lobby of the hotel as if we were paying guests. Security could be pretty lax with their conference rooms, making them ideal spots for quickies with a spice of danger. We were soon in darkness, and I reached out to turn on one of those green-shaded lamps on the speaker's podium so that we could at least see each other's faces.

He hesitated, standing there looking at me for a long instant, smiling, and when he kept his mouth shut, he could be very handsome. I told him so.

"I see you're getting into the spirit of things," he commented.

"Oh?"

"Insulting me."

"I thought you liked that. You said treating you with scorn showed I was thinking of you."

"I think I meant that for when you're fucking someone else."

I stayed flippant. "But that's so limiting! So. Where do you want to do this, Master?" I could see in the shadows a long table near the podium, and I chose this as my perch.

"That's fine, as long as you're comfortable."

"I am."

"You might want to do something about your dress," he suggested, and I saw that he was serious.

It would have been rather cumbersome to lift the front panel and try to hold it aside. In for a penny, I thought. It wasn't as if he hadn't seen me before. With a stripper's flourish, I gently tugged on my straps and let the silken fabric plummet to the floor. Naked, I slipped out of my high heels and took two steps up to him.

"Let's see what you got with those magic fingers," I laughed.

At first he looked deep in my eyes, and there was stern judgement there—plus an open resentment that I doubted him. He was really pouring on his whole Smooth Operator, Man of Mystery act, and he should have known by dessert I wasn't buying it. I would play along to an extent because he was another suspect to learn about, and in the damn silliest sense, he was right, it was amusing. It actually did turn me on to play the staring game with him. And being naked in this dim light did nothing to make me vulnerable. If he changed his mind about our ground rules and tried to rape me, I'd kick his ass with my tits out as easy as when I put that guy down to save Shondi.

Janet was right. What had she said? *Me, personally, I find being nude is when I have the best psychological advantage.*

I was wet before Daniel's hands even reached me.

We kissed, and he tasted good. For a moment, my hands fumbled blindly to embrace him somehow, but his own caught mine and laced our fingers. My nipples hardened with the stimulation of our mouths exploring, and my legs fidgeted, opening unconsciously, my back arching. I was ready to have more, but he kept his fingers tightly laced with mine, and no body language would rush his timetable. Okay, okay, I thought. My fingers lifted to loosen the grip and surrender, and only then did he let go and reach for my waist. I slipped out of his arms, backed up and sat on the long table, lifting my knees.

Caressing me, very pleasant but nothing special, fondling my tits, and I found myself growing a little impatient. Perhaps he sensed it, because at last he put all of his right hand to cover my pussy, and I welcomed the warmth of his fingers on my outer vaginal lips. I wanted something to happen. I actually didn't want to be disappointed, but as he played with my clit, I settled down and relaxed, deciding it would be enough to come, to have a regular orgasm.

After a moment, he put his middle and ring fingers into my vagina, and I heard my breathing become ragged with the stimulation. The attention of his mouth shifted from my lips to suck on my left nipple, and now I felt his probing fingers in my pussy just behind my clit, expertly locating my G-spot. I keened in shock at the sudden ecstasy, wrapping a tight arm around his neck while he kept applying firm but gentle pleasure. My juices were flowing, and I felt light-headed, dizzy.

"I'm gonna black out," I muttered.

"No, you're not."

There was a distant feeling inside my body, searching for a definition, and I had to settle for the idea that it was like a prick of a pin. His fingers were vigorously shoving in and out of me, and then I felt an ocean roar deep inside. Oh, my God, and I had never felt *that* before, and as the eye of the hurricane struck, I mewled and cried, and the tingling in my spread legs intensified like an electric shock, and I *saw* my pussy squirt over his hand and arm in an obscene display. I couldn't believe this was me. I wasn't peeing—I knew this. My juices. Incredible.

"Oh, fuck," I cried out. Soaked between my legs, my honey running down into my ass, down to the table. He kept his hand in me for a minute, still gently stimulating my pussy as he kissed me in after-play, and I had another mild orgasm. I felt a higher lift of euphoria than usual, Daniel kissing my breasts and my belly almost apologetically. My arms gave out, and I shivered a little as my shoulder blades touched the cold wood.

"You okay?"

"I've never been happier to say I was wrong."

I felt exhausted, gratefully accepting his help in order to sit up again.

"I don't want to abandon you, but maybe I'd better get some towelling or something from the men's room," he suggested. "I'll be right back, I promise."

I nodded weakly and watched his shadow move towards the heavy door. It was a bit disorienting, the descent after orgasm and Daniel Giradeau suddenly behaving like a gentle-man. Then he was gone. Alone and still naked, I jumped off the table to hide better in the darkness, and I actually stag-gered. Better sit down again, Teresa. I rested for a long mo-ment until I was awake enough to feel a bit on edge at every passing footstep and noise beyond the conference room doors.

Daniel returned, whispering, "Hi" and bringing me over wet towels. I wiped myself and hurriedly slipped my dress back on. After a few minutes of fixing myself up in the ladies' room, I met him at the front door of the hotel.

"I'll get the doorman to hail you a cab," he said, his voice still pleasant but more formal. "I had a really good time. I hope you did, too. I'd like to see you again."

"I don't know," I replied honestly. "I don't know what to think."

He shrugged at that. "Well, *I* would like to see *you* again," he repeated.

He smiled and opened the door of the cab for me. No attempt to kiss me goodnight, no gesture of warmth at all except for that smile. Weird. Like he was driving home his point about the sheer ruthlessness of any relationship between us—sexual experimentation and thrills, nothing more. And I got the eerie sensation that he wanted me to feel deflated, emotionally let down after the high of the orgasm.

If I remarked on his coldness and detachment, he'd no doubt offer a reminder that he'd been honest with me. After all, what was different tonight than fooling around at the games? None of us looked for emotional involvement there.

I got into the back of the cab and dismissed all the irra-tional responses that popped into my head, like telling him to go fuck himself or that he could just forget it. I nodded, and the cab pulled out from the curb. Okay, I thought, we'll play for a little while, long enough for me to learn what you're about.

Bluffing is when you pretend to have something you don't. And as I hooked up with these guys one by one, evaluating my suspects, I slowly came to one conclusion. Our blackmailer would turn out to be someone who wasn't what he or she appeared to be.

◆

I don't know what he did to me back there, but later on that evening, I felt helplessly, overwhelmingly horny. I used my trusty little triple-A battery friend I keep in the bottom drawer of my nightstand, but it wasn't enough. I was so sexually charged, I could barely think straight. I dialled Fitz's number three times and hung up each time before the call went through. I liked him, and he was a good friend these days, but what was between us was in a nice, safe compartment, and if I went over to his place tonight out of the blue, I might give him mixed signals and screw it all up. Shit. It would be very nice if I knew how to reach Neil Kenan, assuming he wasn't lying curled up with Janet Marshall at that very minute.

I jumped into Helena's rented Beamer, driving around and trying to tell myself I was just going for a ride. First I ended up outside the dominoes nightclub in Finsbury Park, parked with the engine running until I realized what I had in mind would be totally insane. I pulled my mobile out of my handbag and dialled George Westlake's home number.

He wants me. He'll do for tonight.

No. It would be cruel. It'll mean something to him, if not to you. I hung up.

Shit. *Soooo* horny.

I turned the car around and headed back home.

♦

Big house near Chelsea Harbour. The scene of the latest poker game. Just a short walk down to the Conrad Hotel and various celebrity homes, and here we were in what I was told was a "his and hers" S&M brothel. No one apparently lived here, but there were plenty of bedrooms for short visits. The organiser had discreetly put away all the flails and whips, but when I poked my head into the wine cellar, I saw nothing could be done about the iron-bar cage in the corner—thankfully empty.

Ground floor lounge about as nouveau vanilla as you could get. Gilt frame mirror above mantelpiece. A genuine Aubrey Beardsley on the wall. Big plaster cast of that exhausted horse head with the tongue lolling they've got in the Elgin Marbles in the British Museum. I don't know when they'll declare pastel colours for settees a war crime, but it has to be soon.

I looked around the table. Some new players I didn't know, a couple of poker virgins, and several familiar faces—George, Daniel, Ayako, Cahill, Vivian. No Lionel tonight.

But Neil had shown up.

"Sit next to me, Teresa," said Ayako in her soft Californian accent. "Safety in numbers."

Cahill guffawed. "Don't believe it, my love. Ayako will turn on you when you least expect it and gobble up the best man at the table. I know because it's happened to me before."

"Hey," I said to Neil, tilting my chin at him from across the table.

"Hey," he smiled. "Good hunting."

Out of the corner of my eye, I noticed Giradeau smirking.

♦

We were playing Texas Hold'Em, probably the most popular game in casinos over in America these days, and reasonably easy to learn. Each player gets two hole cards—two cards dealt facedown. You have your round of betting, and next comes the flop—three cards dealt faceup on the table. Communal cards, anyone can use them in combination with their hole cards to make a winning hand. On goes the betting, and then you have the turn—a fourth card flipped onto the table. Finally, we come to the river—the fifth card dealt to the table.

It was a lively game. A Tory MP got to read Vivian in Braille over on the settee. Ayako, obviously in a playful mood, gave an Oxford salute to one of the newbie males, spanking his bare bottom and kissing him between sharp cracks of her palm against his ass. Then Cahill disappeared into a bedroom for a while with a young Indian solicitor, having won a rug burn, but the girl wanted to blow out the candles. The newbie guy was having a good night—first a spanking then a bucket seat lap dance from Vivian.

I held my own for a while, and then Giradeau made it clear he wanted to be inside me tonight. We played a hand where he won my knickers, and that rattled my cage. I could handle sleeping with him—it was how bad I played the hand that bothered me. In poker-speak, I was "on tilt"—letting emotions affect my judgement. Another hand passed, and the focus shifted to Vivian for a bit, and I thought I had settled down. I managed to play well enough again that a couple of the others told me, "Nice hand," getting out of a tight spot with no counter-stakes. So far, so good.

Helena had warned me, "If you want to bluff, the trick is to play the next hand exactly how you played the winning hand." So I thought I had my strategy down. Unfortunately, I forgot another crucial piece of advice. Don't bluff against a dangerous flop. I had a jack and queen of spades as my hole cards, and the flop came up ace, queen, ten of diamonds. Still too many bets at the table, and dummy that I am, I kept chasing for a king and praying no one had a flush. And then it was Neil versus me.

There's a great exchange in an old W. C. Fields movie, *My Little Chickadee*. A guy asks over cards: "Is this a game of chance?"

And Fields shoots back: "Not the way I play it, no."

I was in way over my head. Bluff. Keep bluffing.

I could barely say my raise, it sounded so silly in my ears. The too cute lingo. And such a request in front of a group of people.

"I think I want you to find Nemo for me."

Like the first game, there was an eruption of clapping and whistles like a television audience at a sitcom.

Wicked grin on Neil's face. "Oh, I think we can do better than that. I think you've got nothing but that necklace around your pretty neck, Teresa. I'll see you and raise you a rug burn."

Ayako folded. Time to see the cards.

Flush. He beat me.

I don't know why I didn't fold earlier. I knew he couldn't be bluffing, I knew it. I shouldn't have taken him on. *But you wanted this, didn't you?* Come on, you didn't lose, you made yourself a gift—

"I'll just get my coat," said Neil, reaching for his wallet and car keys.

"What for?" I said. "You're not done here."

Surprised, amused smiles around the table.

"You don't want to blow out the candles?" he asked, offering me the safer way out. I was touched that he was a gentleman about it. I still couldn't be sure Helena hadn't disobeyed my instruction not to fill him in about me, but I wanted to believe this was Neil's personal chivalry, not acting on orders.

A voice, my own but still a stranger's, said boldly, "I'll go neon."

6

Going neon. Doing it there for everyone to see. By now, of course, I had already performed sex acts for an audience, but the audience changed each time. And the electric charge of nerves over doing intimate things on display never lost its intensity. I was on edge with anticipation that this time it would be different, going all the way, abandoning all my inhibitions for the ultimate act.

As Neil came out from behind the table to gather me in his arms, I had the stroke of luck that his body hid my involuntary shiver. I could feel my honey sliding down the inside of my thighs, already so wet for him. It was surreal, me standing there, naked, and this dark-complexioned man striding purposefully around a card table while a group of people watched, their eyes not knowing whether to fix on me or on the incredible throbbing hard-on above Neil's strong, athletic legs.

His hand reached out and felt huge against my mound even before I tasted his breath and felt the invasion of his soft tongue. "Uhhh," I moaned, because three fingers penetrated me all at once and began to play, and shit, I got to tell you I lifted my leg to wrap around his waist and let him slide them further in. I wished I could have melted into his chest, so wide and firm against my crushed tits, his mouth coming down to suck in one of my nipples. But before my hands could grip more chunks of back muscle, he flipped me cruelly around to take me from behind.

I made a cry of half-hearted protest as I heard the creak and scrape of chairs being pushed back, men and women coming around to flank Neil on either side, his huge black dick pointing north, and his hand, oh, Jesus, his hand cupping me again. My pussy lips on display for everyone, wet sopping pussy for everyone to see how open I was getting, and the fear and the thrill competed simultaneously for my mental attention. They could bang me, one after another, couldn't they? And I wouldn't complain. They're gazing at my crack, and just this alone was making me so wet.

"Give it . . . to me," I rasped.

And in answer, a tree trunk was shoved between my legs. The cone of a missile ramming in and yeah, give it to me, give it to me, as I bent over the card table, palms flat on the green felt. Neil's cock slid out of me, and all I could think as I shut my eyes tight is *they see me*. They see my pussy lips gripping him, willing him back in, and it was a pornographic movie in my head, visualising my own vagina and Neil's penis in and out of me, uh, uh, uh. I opened my eyes and stared into the calm black almonds of Ayako, keeping her place at the table. She reached out and took the weight of one of my tits in her small, white hand, fingering the nipple, teasing it hard, and then I lost total control, both my hands shooting back to grip Neil's thighs as I came.

But we weren't done, not by a long shot. His great hands lifted me under my ass and my thighs, urging me to get on the table and lie on my side. His arm hooked under my leg right under the kneecap, and now everyone had a spectacular view of me dripping for him. I could smell my own juices, and it was beyond being stripped, shamed, embarrassed. All the way to a cathartic liberation. The warm head of his cock nudged just once, one exploratory push against my lips below, and I couldn't hide the exquisite torture on my face. I heard him whisper over me, a simple, brutal command. "Play with yourself."

"Stick it in," I whispered back.

"Play with yourself first."

I did, just as I did for him that first night. My middle finger slid down to my clit and worked a rhythm, knowing my mouth was open, my eyes straying to each fascinated expression. Cahill a mirror of my awe, Ayako looking at me as if I were a beautiful oil painting, Vivian, coolly detached, wishing she were the centre of attention. George was in the background. No one seemed to pay attention to the fact that he was jerking off in his chair. Poor George, always forgotten. For a brief instant we made eye contact. I felt a sympathetic urge to give him something, to somehow share this with him, and my mouth enunciated the words, *do it,* just before I shut them tight at another orgasm.

When I opened them again, a creamy torrent of semen had flown from his cock onto the rug, his penis very red in his fist. And still pointing up. Everyone ignored him except me. And Ayako, who gave him a passing glance, seemingly trying to decide something. Then her attention came back to me. Vivian eyed Neil's cock greedily. Helena had told me that she'd paid almost twice the price to have him as her escort a couple of times, and both times he had turned down gratifying her for extra cash at the end of the evening. She had never won a rug burn from him in a game. Never. She would have loved it to be her on that card table.

And Giradeau. Watching me. Waiting for his silent message, the one he predicted I'd give him when Neil fucked me.

"Play with your pussy," Neil chanted in a hoarse whisper.

"Yeah!" I kept chanting back. "Oh, yeah!"

I felt Neil getting harder inside me, and as he thrust, it wasn't a reward for my obedience so much as giving in to his own urges. Hard shockwaves of brown cock slipping in and out of me, bam, bam, bam, his balls jostling up against my ass as I took him all the way to the hilt. My breasts jiggling with his momentum, and Neil saying loud enough for all to hear, "You want them to suck your tits, don't you? You want them to suck your tits?"

"Y—you're going to split me!"

"You want them to suck your tits, don't you?"

"Y—yes."

"Say it."

"I want them to suck my tits!" I said in a little girl voice.

Neil must have given them a look of permission, me lost within myself, because there was a sudden vampire scramble towards me.

Ayako, the closest, reached me first and took my right nipple into her mouth, sucking me like ice cream. Cahill pawed my left breast hungrily, his tongue flicking an orbit around the areola before his lips came down, and damn it, I made eye contact with Giradeau. It was purely accidental, but no doubt the fool would make a big deal out of it.

Not that it mattered really. Because as I lay on the table, being fucked by Neil, the others sucking my breasts, the only thing I had on was that gold necklace from Tiffany's that Daniel had given me.

Neil rammed away, such wondrous thunder as the base of his cock hit my gates, his hand reaching around to play with my clit a couple of times, my fingers covering his and guiding him, and as he thrust on and on, and the others sucked my nipples, I felt like the card table was a raft drifting on an open calm lake, hands slippery on my skin with the film of my own perspiration.

I began to shudder and go into spasms, the hands gripping me, some comforting, some merely wanting to feed off the energy of my orgasm. Cahill's bold hand came around and its knife edge sank into the crack of my buttocks. Different mouths on my tits, me playing with myself, this beautiful man's cock inside me, and I shook and shuddered, coming violently and thinking, *See my pussy, see my beautiful pussy as I take him in, watch me come, watch me—*

Daniel. I couldn't see him. I couldn't see George anymore either.

Neil thickening inside me.

Ayako close to my ear: "Come on her belly, Neil, please." She sounded so distant, so far away.

The mouths were gone from my nipples, and I keened in grief over their sudden absence. Neil's hands moving me again, posing me, on my back now and thrusting harder as I cupped my jiggling tits and felt Neil shoot a powerful burst inside me once and then he pulled himself free, sliding his cock along the wet mat of my fur and shooting again. Shooting a third time. His spunk actually felt more than warm, as if it were cooked in that cannon-size dick he'd been ramming into me. And oh, he was still jetting across my stomach like spirals of confetti.

I was panting hard. I looked into his eyes for what was there, and he wore the strangest expression. It wasn't conquest or self-congratulatory lust. Something else there, close to a genuine lover's admiration. He'd take me home tonight. I knew that for sure. Fucking me—and fucking me here—was all too easy, as if his sexuality expressed in this room were a mask. I saw it in his eyes, how he seemed to say: "You wanted it like this, but I can take you higher—alone."

I was still floating down. I closed my eyes and did a rag doll surrender. Sticky. Sweaty. Hot. Dirty. I felt the tug of his hand. He didn't want to leave me while the rest of the players stared on as if I were a traffic accident. I felt a head rush and almost swooned, and his protective arm came around my waist to hold me balanced. I saw that George had creamed himself again watching us.

"Show's over, guys," Neil said with a modest grin. And he led me to the washroom off the lounge area.

After we washed in turn and got dressed, he never even asked me, and I didn't suggest it either. We merely walked side by side out to his Ford Focus.

◆

His place. One of the corners of Hackney starting to get gentrified. No pastels here. Definitely a guy place, not that there was a jockstrap lying around or a Page Three calendar, but definitely masculine energy. One of those monochrome landscape prints of New York, pre-9/11 with the Twin Towers, framed on the wall. The lounge furniture seemed to have been bought as an ensemble, good-quality dark wood right down to the old-fashioned settee with wooden armrests. A copy of *The Stage* lay discarded on the coffee table next to one of those Daffy Duck mugs you can buy from the Warner Bros. stores (had to be a gift).

"What'll you have?" he asked. "I keep a reasonably well-stocked bar. You want rum? Gin?"

"I'd better stick to white wine," I said. "I'd like to keep my head clear after that scene. I don't know how we top that little performance."

"I'm an actor," he laughed. "We'll improvise. White wine, it is."

I looked around while he opened the bottle. The rowing

STRIP POKER · 145

machine in the corner, the Hugo Boss jacket left folded on
the back of his desk chair.

"So," I said with a mischievous grin, "this is escort
money."

He looked at me with mild surprise then grinned and
shook his head. He tossed up a hand to say okay, you got
me. He recovered well. I suppose it couldn't be the first time
he'd had to fess up to it.

"Somebody told you."

"Sorry. Somebody did. It wasn't Helena, believe me." I
didn't like lying—okay, I don't really mind lying, but I knew
confidentiality was a two-way street. If Helena insisted her
escorts be discreet, it was important she be the very model
of discretion. And if I weren't playing a client, Helena would
have no business telling me.

"I do. That's not Helena's style." He handed me a glass
and said, "You don't look like you have a problem with it."

"I don't. I have a couple of friends who use them, and
they tell me that with male escorts, unlike the girl kind, a
date doesn't have to mean sex."

"That's right, it doesn't."

"But sometimes it does," I said, moving closer to him.

"I'm very much on my own time now," he whispered,
and he set his drink down on a coaster and put his arms
around my waist. We fell effortlessly into dancing to the
music on the stereo.

"Why do you do it?" I asked.

He offered a small self-deprecating chuckle. It was a nice
relaxed sound that with his bass pipes sent a shiver down
my spine. I could listen to that voice of his for ages.

"Why do I do it?" he echoed. "Well, I'm twenty-seven
years old, and I'm beginning to think maybe I'm not God's
gift to theatre after all. I love acting. I love plays. But there's
such cronyism in the theatre world, and it's so hard to

break in. And then when you think you've had your big break, you learn you've got to prove yourself all over again. And they're so bloody negative in this country! They'll piss on the five commercials you've done, that you're not Royal Academy of Dramatic Art. They'll find something. After a while, you don't mind the struggle, you don't even mind the snickers when you say you're actually an actor, but I do insist on living comfortably."

"And the escort dates give you some spending cash."

"Hell, no! They pay for this whole bloody apartment these days. Sad to say but it's the acting gigs that give me spare change. Wish it were the other way around, but that's life."

"Who's your little pet?" I asked.

I pointed to the black ball sitting on a nine-inch stand next to his computer. Jeez. Another webcam. Was I the only one who hadn't bothered to run out and plunk good money down for one of these? We were one step away from science fiction movies where everyone talked back and forth to monitors.

"A gift from a friend," said Neil.

"Let me guess: a woman friend?"

"A good friend," he said, nuzzling my neck. "That's not really important, is it? Forget that. Here, let me show you." He went to boot up his computer.

"Boys with toys," I said. "If I see a subscription to *Stuff* magazine, you know I'm outta here."

"I'm not that sad," he countered.

But I went over to the coffee table, dug under *The Stage* and picked up his copy of *King* magazine with Mya on the cover, arching my eyebrow and giving him a playful, accusing glance.

"Forget that," he said, "come here and look at this. It's amazing, state of the art." I went over, and his arm reclaimed my waist, his free hand clicking away on the mouse. "Check it out, check it out—"

I heard a tiny faint *whrr* and giggled as the black ball panned and tilted. Neil steered us to the left, and the camera followed. Back to the right, and it moved with us. On the screen, a high-resolution square of video reflected our expressions of childlike wonder at the ball's cleverness.

"There's face-tracking software so it moves with you—within limits, of course. It's great for when I'm practising monologues and stuff."

"That's all you've used it for, huh?"

"It's good for home security."

"Mmm-hmm."

I began to strip in front of the camera. On the tiny screen, there were the slightest jump cuts and ghosts as my body moved. And then I got to work on him. He let me undress him, unbuttoning his shirt from behind so that the screen offered an exquisite brown chest that begged for my fingertips. Yes, I'd seen it before but never tired of the view. Unbuckling his belt, undoing his trouser button, slipping my fingers into his underwear to grip his penis, my hand jerking his cock with a millisecond delay.

Now we were alone and could take our time, and being here was about foreplay, stroking and fondling, the weight of his balls in my palm and the smell of his musk. The way his mouth mapped butterfly kisses down my spine, and his hands caressed under my arms, behind my thighs, rounding my hips. Masturbating each other and me ducking my mouth down. But he was too long, so I teased him with my fingers right at his base, and a rewarding tension sprang the red bulb higher between my lips. He tasted good.

I sucked one of his nipples as I played with his balls, and he came on my belly for the second time that evening.

Playing through the night. Riding on top of him, screaming and then sinking down into his arms and to taste his
mouth. And beyond the sofa, the little webcam movie of
him being undressed played on and on in a programmed
loop. When we made it to bed, he took me from behind, and
in the darkness, I summoned the memory of being fucked
on the card table, others' hands all over me, Ayako sucking
my breast and telling Neil to come all over me. . . .

♦

Three in the morning. When I went to the toilet, I opened
his medicine cabinet and looked inside. I don't think you
need a memo that I'm nosy. I picked up a Boots prescrip-
tion bottle with a label that read: fluoxetine.

"It's an anti-depressant," I heard Neil say behind me. I
had left the door ajar.

I started in surprise and whirled around. "I know. It's Pro-
zac, isn't it? I was . . . I was looking for some dental floss."

He smiled and said, "No, you weren't. You were snooping. I don't blame you. You go home with somebody, you
want to know who you're with."

I held up the bottle labelled as haloperidol. "This is an
anti-psychotic."

"Yes, it is," he said, looking me straight in the eye. "I've
had . . . *problems* that started when I was a teenager. I'm . . .
better. I stopped taking some of my medications for a while,
but when things in my acting career slumped, I thought I
ought to get help again."

"Fair enough," I said, and I replaced the pills in the cabinet.

"Teresa," he said. "If you want to ask me something, just
ask."

"No need," I answered, and kissed him quickly, slamming

STRIP POKER · 149

the door in his face. "Out," I ordered, "doing business here."
And then I sat down to wee.

And told myself that his being a psychiatric patient
meant nothing. Truth is, I didn't want to even consider his
mental history.

◆

Back at Helena's the next day, I did a LexisNexis search on
Anthony Boulet. Wasn't sure what it would get me, but go-
ing through old wire stories about him and his work for the
CRE, the Beeb, helped me think about him as a suspect.

Helena happened to notice my work-in-progress but
wisely said nothing, and I didn't volunteer the bit of info
that made me consider Anthony in the first place—a little
unguarded admission from Janet at the awards ceremony
that she'd probably never guess I'd turn over in my mind.

I wouldn't be tossing out that bomb for a long while.

I would use it when I needed it.

A bouquet of flowers bloomed on my mobile's text display. Neil. I resisted the urge to call or text him back—better
to get on with the job. As my mind replayed him taking me
from behind at the poker game, Helena, hovering over the
desk (well, it was her desk, she had the right), yanked me
out of my daydream.

"Clients! My God, I know they're essential, but they sure
are a pain in the arse. This Mrs.—sorry, unprofessional of
me—this silly cow gets complimentary drinks from *my* private stock when Fitz or Raymond picks her up from the house,
and *still* she expects me to spring for the cost of condoms!
Doesn't want the condoms the boys choose! Oh, no, has to
be her brand selection. Honestly, darling, do I need this shit?"

"You like being rich," I said to the computer screen.

"Thank you, darling. Yes, I do."

And got back to her paperwork.

The phone rang. Helena answered it, knowing already it was her PA at the other end of the house. "Yes, Wendy?"

I waited. Helena listened for a moment, and then by the way she reacted, it was as if her PA had begun to speak to her in Portuguese. "*What?* Say that again . . ." Another long pause. "Oh, my God." Helena listened some more and then said, "No! No—do nothing. I'll take care of it."

"What is it?" I asked.

Helena slid the phone back into its receiver. She looked straight at me, but my face might as well have been a window for her. No direct eye contact, her expression distracted, her face going very pale.

"Lionel's dead."

♦

Days might have passed before we learned anything about Lionel, except that Wendy had phoned his extension at Buccaneer Cape only minutes earlier to offer him an escort booking. The receptionist had broken the news in a shaken whisper, confiding that it looked like Lionel had shot himself and had been found in his apartment. *In the nude,* the receptionist had carefully inflected.

Policemen were questioning employees of Buccaneer Cape Mining to try to determine if they knew of anything that might have pushed him over the edge.

In the meantime, the interim conclusion was suicide. It was enough for the police to keep the more lurid details from being released to the red-top tabloids. And there were more lurid details. I would have to learn what they were.

A couple of days had to pass before my best contact with the police could return my phone call—an old friend,

Inspector Carl Norton. He sounded only mildly surprised that I should phone him about Lionel's death since I had popped up in unlikely places before.

I asked if the police thought Lionel had been murdered, and Carl paused all of two seconds before saying, "Off the record, yes." Then I explained that I was doing someone one of my "exploratory favours," and he asked me who, and I said you know I shouldn't tell you that.

"I think you should, Teresa," he laughed with a mild edge in his voice.

"Come on, Carl, you know I didn't have to phone."

"Sure you did, Teresa. You want to know how the investigation's going."

"Yes, I do."

"If your client is somehow connected in any way to the deceased or has information that could shed—"

"They don't," I said bluntly. If I said it firmly enough I could almost believe it myself. "I do need info, Carl, and I do have info to trade, but not about my client."

"What kind of info?"

"I knew him."

"From where?"

"The office."

"You work for Buccaneer Cape Mining?"

"No, I fucked him in his office."

"Never the blushing type," he sighed. "You always give me headaches, Teresa."

"Can we meet?"

"I think that's a very good idea."

◆

Carl Norton is one of those innocuous-looking fellows you'd never take for a homicide detective with the Met. He's white, rounding his forties, and if you want to be cruel about it, he has a passing resemblance to Fred Flintstone. With a certain amount of swarthiness, what with the dark black eyebrows, dark eyes and dark hair, he's been pegged as all sorts of things—Italian, Greek, Spanish—and in truth, he can claim all this and more in his ancestry.

He's the only member of the Old Bill I know who's been working on his Master's in Modern Literature so that he can escape life on the force. You don't meet too many cops who can talk intelligently with you about Joyce and Ezra Pound.

I got to know him way back on my first snooping job for Helena and learned he was a man who could be trusted when I had to blow the whistle on a bribe-taking colleague. He hooked me up with contacts in the Scotland Yard unit that dealt with art fraud and theft, and I had a line for him on the best Ethiopian and Moroccan restaurants in the West End. I introduced him, in fact, to his wife.

Wearing one of his typical short-sleeve dress shirts with a knit tie and carrying his battered briefcase, he marched up to me a few yards away from St. James's Park tube station.

"Friend or no," he announced as he walked up and traded kisses on cheeks, "you better be telling me the truth."

"I always do."

"Uh-huh," he groaned dismissively. "Start from the top."

I did—as much as I could. If I used my language very carefully I could be accused later of being less than forthcoming, but I wouldn't exactly have lied to the police. I told Carl that someone had threatened Lionel over one of his love affairs, and Carl asked me how I could know this. I confessed that I had learned this thirdhand. At the same time, someone had made a threat of blackmail to a Highly Esteemed Personage, and then I had been brought in. I had been chasing down the theory that perhaps, maybe, possibly, Lionel had faked the first threat to cover himself for the second. Until now.

"Teresa, for God's sake, that's motive! You're going to have to tell me who you're protecting."

"I can't!" I said. "Look, they have an alibi. The kind that's airtight." I had checked this with Helena and Janet even before I dreamed of picking up the phone to reach Carl.

"And I'm supposed to take your word for it?" he asked.

"No, but you can believe *The Independent* and *The Telegraph*." I held up copies of the previous day's newspapers. They were running crowd photos from a charity gala at the Tate Modern from the previous night, the very night Lionel was killed. "This event ran well into three in the morning, and there must be a dozen witnesses who can account for them being there. You tell me: what's the window of opportunity for his murder?"

He conceded the point. "Okay, yes, around one-thirty in the morning, so accepting what you're telling me at face value, your person's covered. For now."

"Well, that was too damn easy," I said. "Why aren't you asking me?"

"Asking what?"

"You just suggested my person had motive, and if they're a big deal, they could afford someone else to do it."

He blew air out of his cheeks and said grimly, "True, but I doubt it. This smacks of the personal."

I raised an eyebrow questioningly.

"You ready for this?" he asked. "It's not pretty."

"I'm sure I saw worse in Africa."

He shrugged over that one, muttering he hoped not, and he pulled out the crime photos. It was indeed not pretty.

I've seen dead before, but never someone dead with whom

I had had any kind of intimacy. Having Lionel's cock in my mouth and his mouth lapping me below could be easily dismissed with the knowledge the guy would move on, just a past lover out there somewhere. A name to be forgotten. A face to revert quickly back to status of stranger.

But now I was looking at the same flesh I had tasted, brutalized and lifeless in vivid colours.

Lionel was naked, his ankles bound by thin leather straps to the legs of a plain chair, both his wrists similarly tied to the armrests, yet with enough slack for some movement of one arm. His body leaned forward and away from camera view because of the impact of a fatal gunshot. His left hand dangled by his side, presumably having dropped the revolver, while his right gripped his penis, grotesquely still half-erect from stimulation at the moment of dying, and then post-mortem lividity must have taken over.

You couldn't see it in the photos, but Carl explained that there were large quantities of the victim's semen discovered on the rug and staining his body. Baby oil had been used as the lubricant, but the medical examiner noticed that the skin on Lionel's penis was rubbed somewhat raw from the repeated friction of his masturbation.

A pornographic video had been found cued back to its menu screen on the DVD player. Presumably, it was playing at the time and played on after he died until its finish.

"What kind of video?" I asked.

"It matters?" he asked back.

"Maybe, maybe not."

"Gay porn, if you want to be precise."

"But he wasn't gay," I argued.

Carl gave me a look to say hey, you would know. We agreed that it was more than likely the DVD had been chosen with the intent of increasing Lionel's humiliation beyond death. Whatever had been playing during the torture, if there had been a video playing, wasn't the one cued up and left behind.

Carl went back to a grisly close-up of Lionel's body. "Shot with a revolver at point-blank range. That's the no-brainer part. But the scene was staged to look like suicide."

"How can you be so sure?"

"Two ways. To be fair, one's out of our league, Teresa. It's the blokes in Forensics who came up with it. After he was shot, the killer quickly lifted the victim's body back up and manipulated his hand in the gun to mimic shooting himself. I guess he thought if he moved him around like a puppet that when he let go, he'd get a natural, convincing pose instead of just dropping the gun by his fallen arm. He thought he was being clever, but he was still a bit dim. When he lifted the body back up in a hurry, tiny spots of blood were flicked onto our victim's leg, mixed with microscopic bits of brain tissue. Well, that splatter pattern would be impossible if you're holding the gun barrel right up to your temple. It had to come afterwards."

"Okay," I nodded. "And the second?"

"Let's see how clever you are, my love, because the answer's right here in the photo."

I looked again carefully. After a moment, I said: "The straps."

"What about them?" Carl prompted.

"I'm guessing, and I could be wrong," I explained, "but if it's suicide, and he's going to shoot himself, why tie up his left arm at all? Why not leave it totally free? Let's say he's into kink and he wants the whole effect, it doesn't look like there'd be enough slack in the strap for him to raise the revolver to his head."

"You're absolutely right," he answered solemnly.

And the implication of this sunk in for me. "Shit," I whispered.

His killer had used him in a sick Russian roulette game—
it was the only explanation for the revolver instead of a
more common semi-automatic pistol. *Click* went the gun as
Lionel's tormentor demanded he jerk off and bring himself
to orgasm, again and again. And each time when he shot
off, *click* went the empty chamber … Utter humiliation, so
that you wondered how Lionel could have achieved an
erection at all. And yet faced with the truth that you were
imminently about to die and to die violently, maybe one
would think, all right, I'll taste the last ecstasy of turning
myself on just before the sudden, sharp end.

The other fluid discovered on Lionel's body was the
residue of tears.

"I thought you might have something for me to break
this open," Carl said in disappointed tones. "But we have to
run with what we've got."

"What do you mean?"

"We're questioning a suspect already, and he looks good
for it. Knew Lionel Young, had a grudge with him, and you've
just told me that Young received a threat over a woman."

"I think my words were 'love affair.' I didn't specify gender." I was totally flabbergasted. *They had somebody?* "Who?
Who are you questioning?"

"Neil Kenan."

7

As you can imagine, I didn't endear myself to Carl by telling him that his prime suspect couldn't possibly have murdered Lionel because he was with me that night. First I sleep with his victim, then his suspect, and I had excluded my client for him. He tried hard to keep his face blank and definitively non-judgemental, but he couldn't resist one snide remark: "Is there anybody else in the GLA you want to provide an alibi for? I mean, you're giving 'em out like flyers today."

"Clever. You're the Old Bill's Oscar Wilde."

"I'm doing a paper on Wilde for my Master's, actually," he said. "We're going to hold on to Mr. Kenan for a little while longer." Before I could protest, he added quickly, "Yes, Teresa, you say you were with him, and I believe you, but he's still mixed up in this somehow."

I asked for his rationale. I was intensely curious to know how the police had managed to connect Lionel to Neil at all. Lionel was an executive working in The City for a mining conglomerate. Neil was paying his dues as a catalogue and store display model, getting gigs in plays that were far from the West End.

The only connection between them was the escort service and the strip poker circuit, and if Carl and the other detectives were clued in about that, they would have dragged Helena down with him. And George Westlake, Gary Cahill, Ayako, Daniel Giradeau, and scores of others in games I had yet to play in. And even Janet.

So what did they have on Neil?

♦

Carl wouldn't tell me, but after we finished talking, I hung around outside Scotland Yard long enough to figure out the answer for myself.

It was an hour and a half later when I saw Neil emerge through the glass doors, looking as haggard as anybody does after a grilling by the cops. He shook hands with a well-dressed young Indian man I could only presume was the legal aid solicitor on call that afternoon, and then he glanced around, failing to see me. He was looking for someone else—I realized it was Janet.

Then he frowned, as if logic had caught up with his naivety. He couldn't very well expect that she would show up here to be by his side.

When he started for the tube station, eyes fixed two feet ahead of him on the ground, that's when I called his name, and he looked up. He was surprised and curious to see me waiting for him.

"Hello."

"Do you want a lift home?" I offered.

"Sure. How did you know to come here?"

"The police asked me about your whereabouts the other night," I lied.

I led him around to the BMW, bleeped the car's alarm, and he slipped into the passenger seat.

"I told the police I was with someone," he said. "I didn't give them your name."

"That's chivalrous of you, but under the circumstances, I think it's okay. They found me somehow." I pointed the Beamer into the jungle of West End traffic. "Is it over?"

"Shit, I hope so," he muttered, and let his head fall into his hand.

"Why would they even look at you?" I asked, pretending to be baffled, but I knew already.

Shondi.

It was the only thing that made sense. When the cops picked through the remains of Lionel's life, they turned up Shondi as his ex-girlfriend. Yeah, I know what you're thinking. She would have been quickly ruled out as the most implausible of suspects. What was missing from my brilliant leap of intuitive reasoning is why she would point the finger at Neil.

"The police know Lionel and I didn't like each other," he offered weakly.

"They drag you in for questions over more than just not liking someone," I argued.

"Being black in this city is enough for them to question you."

"Come on, Neil, that won't cut it with me," I replied. "There's a difference between a bored cop pulling you over, and bored lazy cops wasting even their own time with an interrogation."

He eyed me suspiciously. "How would you know about it?"

"Let's just say I have a brother." Well yes, I do have a brother, but he's never been in trouble. I did once have a friend dragged in, only it wasn't a guy, it was a girl. Okay, it wasn't a girlfriend, it was me. But I couldn't tell him that.

"Teresa, can't you just leave it alone, please? You met Lionel so you know, right? I didn't like the guy! Can't we just leave it at that? What do you want to know this for?"

"Because I care," I answered. "I thought we had a connection."

"We do!" he insisted. "It's just ... Life is getting a bit complicated, well, my life anyway. I'm sorry you got mixed up in all this. Getting questioned by the cops, must have been embarrassing—"

"I'll live," I said. I pulled the car into a fresh parking space and cut the engine. I took his hand in mine. "Why don't you just tell me what's going on?"

"Can you be my friend in this?" he pleaded. "Sure, we sleep together, but this has bloody well scared the hell out of me, and I need a friend now."

I nodded.

He took a deep breath and went on. "Look, you know what I do and you seem cool about it, and you and I are getting along. But babe, I can't pretend I haven't got close to anyone before. There's someone I've been involved with. We break it off and get back together, and we break up again, and then we make up, and everyone says we're nuts, and even *we* can't figure it out."

Janet.

He looked through the windshield, searching for words, and then declared, "I'm ... not proud of everything I've ever done in my life, but I try to be a good person. And I can get jealous like any guy—and no, I know I have no right to, but it's not an emotion that makes sense, is it? Anyway, Lionel won this person in a game, and I could have handled it if he hadn't rubbed my nose in it so much. So I did a shitty thing back to him."

Shondi.

I had to nod politely and pretend I knew nothing about

the strip dominoes circuit as he explained it to me. I had actually guessed it would be cards, but the fine details weren't that important. As I suspected, Neil had decided to pay Lionel back in kind. *You take my woman, I'll take yours.*

I could visualize it all. He had worked the network until he found where Lionel and Shondi liked to play. Humiliating the guy in the nightclub would be so much better than a private party. The tunes were blaring, and there was the firecracker roar of the bones flying down. Shondi, hair done in her elaborate cornrows, wearing a fire engine red triangle top and white shorts. "She was dressed for success that night," Neil remarked acidly. For all that Lionel had claimed about not liking the dominoes circuit, he didn't mind showing her off as he squired her around. But he didn't like to lose, either, and Neil had come with that purpose in mind.

"And I made her peel. Right down to her white pumps. Guys were cheering the show, and I made a big deal out of taking off my shirt and unbuckling my pants, and the thing that *really* pissed him off was that I was about to drop trou, and she was up for it. She licked her lips and came scrambling across the table for me. And then I zipped up again, pointed to one of the other losers at the table and said, 'Go on, man, I changed my mind.' The boy lost it, right there. Took three guys to hold him back, and she tried to throw a glass at me, too."

"Why didn't you just have her?" I asked. "Your grudge was with him, not her."

"I made my point without going through with it. I didn't mean to diss her necessarily—"

"Come on, Neil, you did. You didn't have to offer her like a whore to another guy at the table."

He recanted quickly. "Yeah, okay—yeah, I did a little. I'm not proud of myself, like I said. Shondi is ... Look, to be honest, she's beautiful, but she likes the gutter and maybe she belongs there. To be honest with you, I'll do the circuit because everyone's checked out, but they're animals in there, doing it for a crowd."

"You and I did it in front of others."

"There's a big difference between the little group at the private games and that club."

I wanted to tell him that this was the exact same point that Lionel had made to me. There were degrees. Even Helena said there were limits, and I kept wondering what were they? Unless they were ones of class and money. I think if you gave in to certain appetites, even those wouldn't matter to you anymore.

If you fucked in front of four to seven people, what inhibition was left to stop you from opening your legs in front of fifty? Or a hundred? It made me wonder all over again if I was thinking too much and not feeling enough. After all, I had pegged Lionel for the blackmail, attributing a cash-and-wounded-pride motive. But as Carl had said, the killer had made it very personal. If you lost all your sexual inhibitions, I had to wonder if that meant you could strike a blow as easy as you made a caress.

◆

His place again. He insisted on cooking a meal for me, even though I told him he shouldn't go to the trouble. "It's okay, I like cooking. I actually find it relaxing. I run through lines in my head, practice my diction. Why don't you pour yourself a glass of wine and relax? Put on some music if you like."

I did. I hadn't checked out his CD collection the last time I was here, but then I had been busy making a thorough inspection of other physical belongings. Now I let my fingers do their walking through Courtney Pine, Joss Stone and

Craig David. I selected a Toni Braxton album and threw it on. I caught him smiling at my choice, perhaps thinking he had gained a little insight into me through it. I was glad to see the tension of his ordeal with the cops dissipating. Maybe they still considered him a suspect. I didn't anymore.

As he chopped vegetables on the cutting board and fussed over a sauce, I tuned out Toni and picked up the muttering under his breath. "... When I did speak of some distressful stroke that my youth suffer'd. My story being done, she gave me for my pains a world of sighs ..."

I wandered over to the bookshelf and searched. There was a well-worn copy sitting on the top shelf, and by the time I found the scene, he was already at "She loved me for the dangers I had pass'd, and I loved her that she did pity them."

I knew he'd pause after the speech, so I skipped ahead and called out to the kitchen: "That I did love the Moor to live with him, my downright violence and storm of fortunes may trumpet to the world: my heart's subdued even to the very quality of my lord ..."

He took one step out of the kitchen, still holding a chopping knife and a green pepper, with a big delighted smile of white teeth. "Hey! Listen to you."

"Yeah, right," I laughed. "I signed up for a stage class at a community centre once. I went for one night then chickened out on the rest."

"Too bad. You sounded good."

"I don't think the West End will miss me."

I wandered back into the kitchen and slipped an arm around his waist. The gesture of affection felt natural, easy, as I asked him if I could do anything to help. He shook his head.

"You know that's my favourite play," he said.

"Why?"

"It's bloody brilliant. The poetry, the story ... It's a fantastic part. I think he's the noblest of all Shakespeare's heroes, and that's what makes it so achingly sad. It's my dream role. I see every version I can get my hands on. I got the Laurence Fishburne version on DVD, probably the best one there's been in a while."

I was beginning to see what else drew Janet Marshall to him apart from the hot bod. It was doing a great job of pulling me in as well. Character. He had a lot of it. Despite the sincere speeches about the struggling thespian, the boy was together. He kept a clean house. He was mature. He was cultured and charming. I gave him my opinion of that *Othello* remake, how I thought ol' Larry had been great, but Kenneth Branagh had stole the thing with his slightly OTT Iago. No doubt Helena had traded Shakespeare notes with him, too, when she first checked him out. He listened well, not simply waited for the other person to finish before his next comment. And oh, yeah, he cooked. Gotta like that. And let's not forget he was also incredible in bed.

We were into a reasonably engaging conversation over dinner about different spots to check out on vacation in Spain when Neil suddenly sat bolt upright in his chair. "Oh, no."

"What?"

"Oh, *shit*. What time is it?"

"Nine-ish, I think, eight-thirty, maybe. Why?"

He covered his face with his hands and said, "I was supposed to call this director back this afternoon at six-thirty. He's a knob, but a friend put in a good word for me, and I was supposed to do a reading over the phone for him. *Shit*."

"Oh, Neil, I'm sorry ..."

"Not your fault," he said, standing up and walking away from the table. "When did they let me out? Around five? There was enough time. I simply forgot—that's all. Stupid."

"No, just distracted." I tried to be comforting.

And then like a spring coiled too tight, he simply blew. His hand flew up in an arc, and he knocked a low pile of paperbacks off the mantelpiece. I started, more at the suddenness than the crack of the books hitting the floor.

"They come along and fuck with your life, and no 'sorry for the interruption, mate'—oh, no!"

"Neil," I said calmly.

He stared at me as if I had just materialised into the room.

"Kind of scaring me, babe."

He came out of it. "Oh, God, I'm sorry, Teresa! Please, it's just bad nerves. They were talking to me as if I was actually guilty of killing the dude."

"I know, I know," I said. "But it's over now, and you've got to forget about it—"

"They drag you in, ask you all these questions. I know Helena's going to hear about it, and what the hell is she going to think? I need her bookings—"

"I know, babe. Helena won't think anything. She's cool, you'll see."

"You think?"

"I *know*. Why don't you lie down, and I'll give you a massage."

"You don't have to, Teresa. You've been great, really."

"Shut up. I want to."

"All right," he said. "I'm all yours."

"That's what a girl likes to hear. Now take off your clothes, and let me take care of you."

◆

Around ten o' clock the next morning, Helena called on my mobile, asking if I had heard that Neil had been taken in for questioning over Lionel's murder. Yes, I had, I said, not bothering to mention that the gorgeous form next to me between the sheets belonged to her escort. Nothing to worry about, I said.

Helena made a sound that caught in her throat, something between an "Oh?" and a "Ehm," and then she said she did worry about it, since Neil wasn't answering his mobile or his landline.

"Listen, darling, do you fancy a trip to Surrey? I've got Janet coming over, and she's having a meltdown over this. Found out about it from one of her mates in the Black Police Officers' Association, part of their monitoring of every murder investigation of a black victim and all that—"

"But Neil's in the clear," I said, and I was still saying it after I left the man sleeping with a note that apologised for taking off, conference to go to, sorry, babe, and after I had dragged my butt out to the house in Richmond and begged Helena to put on some coffee.

Janet Marshall had indeed come over, acting like a woman scorned, ready to think the worst of her lover. And there I was rolling my eyes at Helena, wondering why I was needed to hold Ms. Marshall's hand.

"My God," said Janet, "why would they pull him in unless—"

"The police released him," Helena replied quietly.

"They never formally held him," I corrected her.

Both statements did nothing to mollify Janet. "The police let people go all the time because they don't have enough to hold them. It doesn't make them innocent."

Helena's voice was firmer now, trying to bring her back to earth. "Jan, you're being irrational. You're just displacing all your anger and jealousy, and whatever problems you and Neil have, you *know* he's not capable of something like this—"

"He's not," I piped up. "He couldn't." Not the man who took me to his bed.

Janet Marshall turned on me, and her eyes were dark coals. "How?" she demanded. "How can you know?"

It was the first time I had seen a glimmer of her formidable temper, and it wasn't nice to be on the receiving end. Combined with her force of personality and presence, it was the righteous fury that had made her such a skilled debater in committee rooms and helped her demolish the avuncular-sounding yet sinister white males who were her political enemies.

But the flash of imperious rage was another reminder of her blind spot. Her sexuality. Her hunger for love. Mature stateswoman or no, she loved with all the careless extreme passion of a fifteen-year-old.

"How can you be so sure?" she fired again.

I stood my ground. "There are details the cops haven't released to the papers or the public. Lionel was . . ." I didn't know how to put it or whether even to go into it at all. The grisly facts weren't supposed to be my point anyway. "I don't think Neil would be capable of the sadism the murderer brought to the killing."

Then I added quickly, "I doubt many people would be."

I thought that might settle her down a bit, but there was still an edge to her voice. "I *should* know Neil better than anyone," she said.

I marked how she put this: I should know Neil. Did she have a clue about him and me?

"But lately," she continued, "I'm beginning to wonder whether I know him at all."

"The police let him go because he had an alibi," I said. "He was at the poker game."

"Lionel was killed some time *after* the game," argued

Janet, and she glanced at Helena for confirmation. "You said the police put the time of death after."

Helena threw up her hands in a silent appeal to me, since I was, in point of fact, her original source of information.

"Come on, Janet," I snapped. I didn't know why I should feel mildly embarrassed, but I did, and it made me irritable and impatient. "Neil went to the game, so it stands to follow a good-looking fellow like him wouldn't be going home alone that night, would he?"

The question was off her lips before I could even draw another breath. "Who with? Who was he with? Helena?"

Our hostess retreated to fetch the wine bottle. "Oh, no, you don't, darling. Not this again—"

"If he is innocent, I have to know."

"You *do* know!" said Helena. "All of us in this room know, Jan. You're not asking for that reason, you know you're not. It's so tiresome when you do this. I tell women 'Don't fall for the escorts—you know what they are and what they do.' And do any of you listen?"

"Please, Helena."

"Same answer as always, Janet. No. You know better."

"Helena—"

"*No.*"

And there I was, stuck with deciding which was the worse anguish for Janet Marshall—suspecting her man was a blackmailer, a murderer and a sadist, or knowing for sure he was getting it on with someone else, i.e., yours truly. I didn't have to tell her. I didn't owe her anything.

And I'm not even sure I can pin down my motivation. Part of me thought it was the decent thing to do, that she was a big girl and could handle it. Part of me was practical, entertaining the possibility that Neil would get around to telling her himself, and then I'd have worse shit to deal with. A small part of me reacted again to her vulnerability. I sympathized with her just as I had that first night I met her and learned of her predicament. Up to a point.

Because another small, nasty part of my brain, the same place that inspires me to block out the teeth in Prince Charles photos in my royalist neighbour's *Telegraph,* was interested in a twisted way in how she'd take me on.

"He was with me," I said. "He won me in the game."

And I waited.

"I see," she said. You could freeze minced beef at the temperature of her voice. "So the price of your help includes taking my man."

"He wasn't your man that evening," I shot back. "And I think you're a little confused about who I'm trying to help. I'm getting *paid* by Helena and doing this job as a favour to *her.* If I save your reputation, that will be a bonus—it's not my main job. If you get out of this mess unscathed, I only hope you're not as big a hypocrite about your politics as you are about sex."

"You little bitch," she started, but she didn't get to finish because Helena cut in.

"Teresa's absolutely right."

"*Helena!* You're supposed to be my friend!"

"I am, and I'm also hers. And being a good friend, Janet, means I sometimes tell you things you don't to want to hear. God knows, I admire all that you've accomplished, but Teresa's right. You're a bloody hypocrite and a pain in the arse about this. For the umpteenth time, if you want to play the field, darling, you can't ask that Neil be exclusive, *which* by the way would be taking one of my best fellows off my roster. And I've never pointed out to you, Jan, how it's bloody insulting to me each and every time you bug me over his trysts or suggest he ought to retire!"

Janet was flabbergasted. "How is that insulting to *you*?"

Helena folded her arms and tried to summon patience.

I knew what she was about to say and didn't interfere. Janet Marshall had it coming.

"It's insulting because yes, I'm your friend, Janet, but I'm also running a business. And my business is a great hunk of beef like Neil and others like him. When you talk about him giving it up, you're talking about the talent I have on call and what puts food on my table and pays for the villa outside Florence where you were a guest. And you're completely oblivious to that. When Neil decides to quit, that's up to him, but I don't need you coaxing that along."

Janet stood there, stunned for a moment. "I . . . I never knew you felt like that."

"I do."

Janet looked from Helena to me, but the resentment aimed my way was replaced by a peculiar shame, the last thing I would have expected. Then I understood.

In slowly getting more and more attached to Neil, she had lost sight of the rules of the game after the cards were packed up. She would never put up with another woman's jealousy if she had won a fellow fair and square or he had won her. In this bizarre little world of adult play, it would be deemed bad taste. Poor manners.

She excused herself and said she ought to get going. She had a function to go to.

"I'm sorry," I told Helena.

Helena folded her arms, her eyes still fixed on the door that had closed behind Janet.

"Don't be," she said. "She's had that coming for a long time."

She marched into her secondary office, and after a second, I followed, trying to think of some last bit of progress I could report to make her feel better. Wendy was at her desk, eating her lunch, and I noticed that she had borrowed one of Helena's DVDs, *Gosford Park*, and was playing it on the large computer monitor they used for surveillance of the poker games. It gave me an idea.

I went over and held up the DVD case. "Helena, what's on this?"

Wendy was staring at me, justifiably puzzled because the movie was running right there on the screen.

Helena shuffled papers, barely paying attention. "It's on the box, darling." She looked up. "Wendy, isn't that it?"

Wendy, mouth full of tuna salad sandwich, nodded agreement.

I had seen *Gosford Park*. What was on screen now was only about forty minutes into the movie. "So knowing what's on the box, and since you know what's on the screen, you don't bother to watch it, do you?"

Helena's voice had that singsong quality of when you're baffled. "No . . . ?"

"Can I borrow your phone?" I asked.

"Of course."

I dialled a direct extension and waited. After a moment, the trademark sleepy voice answered hello.

"Carl? Teresa. That video that was left on Lionel Young's telly—did anyone bother to scan it all the way through?"

As my idea sank in, I heard him curse.

8

Carl said, "Let me look into it," but I knew what that meant, and I got into the Beamer and drove out to Lionel's apartment.

Carl was, of course, there and sighed in resignation when he spotted me waiting outside the yellow caution tape. Well, come on, I thought. It was the next logical step. If the cops weren't interested in the DVD, it stood to reason they might not even bother to remove it from the machine—hence my friend making a sheepish errand run back to the flat. Carl nodded to the PC on guard duty, and I was waved on in.

"One of my men said he reviewed the tape," he explained, "but I think by 'review' he meant he watched five minutes, fast-forwarded the next ten and left it at that."

Understandable. The first fifteen minutes were pretty coarse stuff, at least to my eyes, but then I had never watched a gay porn movie in my life. Carl picked up the remote and hit the fast-forward for 4X speed, mercifully fast but still slow enough to catch anything that might be waiting.

"Ewww," I commented.

"Your idea."

And then a sudden interruption—Lionel became the star of the video. And it wasn't the producer's idea.

Carl was muttering what the hell, but I picked up the DVD case to be sure. Just as I thought, the movie wasn't even straight-release porn but a bootleg copy, and the give-away was the hilariously poor mock-up of the original cover art with bad spelling in the credits. Lionel had used this CD for his own home movie.

It had hit me back in Helena's house. Wendy watching *Gosford Park* on the computer screen normally reserved for the webcams.

Lionel and me in his office, getting naked and spotting the tiny camera on his monitor. If he had one in the office, it stood to reason he kept one at home. Boys with toys. And there it was, sitting on his home PC monitor just like its twin in his office at Buccaneer Cape Mining.

Lionel's performance on screen was far less vulgar than the opening feature. He sat with a young boy straddling him, light-skinned and mixed race, and the boy couldn't have been more than nineteen. He had that kind of androgynous beauty young boys have. Their mouths crushed and slurped in French kisses, the sound quality too poor to make out Lionel's sweet nothings, and Lionel was playing with the boy's pale brown cock, smiling and looking into his eyes with what was obviously deep affection, if not more.

"You told me he wasn't gay," Carl reminded me. But he saw from the shock on my face that this was a headline to me as well. Not gay to get technical, but certainly bi. Jesus.

Shondi had said he was lousy in bed.

Janet said he didn't do anything for her.

I wasn't terribly impressed with him the first time.

And maybe there was a reason for all that.

Was that why he had made such a special effort for me? Because I was snooping around in his life and might have uncovered this? Or was he just conflicted? Or perhaps he simply swung both ways.

Lionel gazed upward at the kid, smiling, and then they traded places in the chair so that he could sink to his knees. I watched as Lionel took the boy's penis into his mouth and sucked him expertly. The boy's lovely shallow chest flexed and tensed, his mouth gasping with pleasure.

Haunting, the idea that these might have been the last images Lionel saw, the ones that inspired his final erection as he sat nude and pitifully sobbing before his sadistic killer blew his brains out. I had wondered how he could even get it up in that terrible moment, even if ordered by his killer to do so, but the boy . . . He had loved the boy.

Carl punched the remote button for stop and eject. He slipped the disc into its box and declared, "That kid might know more than anybody right now."

No argument here, I thought. "Then you better find him."

◆

I left Lionel's apartment and once I was down the block, I made a panicked call to Helena. She was as stunned as I was by the revelation of Lionel's hidden tastes, and she could understand my follow-up request. I spent an extremely nervous hour drinking coffee in a Pret à Manger, and then I was put out of my misery by Helena ringing me back on my mobile.

"You are very, very lucky," she said.

"What?" I demanded impatiently. "What is it?"

"The escorts submit to regular STD checks every month, but that's doubled if they play in the games, and Lionel went to the clinic only Wednesday. He was clean as a whistle, at least as of then, negatives all around. Results came in yesterday afternoon. Wendy put them on my desk, but I hadn't looked at them yet." She dropped her voice to a whisper and added, "And in case you're still worried, I shouldn't tell you this, but you have nothing to worry about as far as any of the others are concerned."

Meaning *him*, too.

"God, that's good to know. You'd tell me, wouldn't you, Helena? You would, right?"

"Teresa!"

"Sorry! Sorry, sorry. Bad nerves."

"It's all right," she replied smoothly. "It's the age we live in. Look, you had a bad scare, but that's all it was." Now her voice was betraying anxiety. "Please tell me you're not going to quit."

"Quit?" I echoed in surprise. "I'm not going to quit on you, Hel, but maybe I'd better cut back on my poker and work the case harder through regular leads."

"Whatever gets the results," she said, and rang off.

I went home to my flat in Earl's Court. I hadn't been back in days, spending nights at Neil's when I wasn't crashing at Helena's house in Richmond. I dumped my accumulation of bills and junk mail on the kitchen table, and made a point of ignoring what could only be the latest rejection letter for my refugee girl detective story for kids. I stripped off and had a long hot shower. Then I raided my DVD collection for something mindless or at least soothing, and I threw on vintage Eddie Murphy in *Boomerang*. Good for a few chuckles, if only to see how skinny and young Chris Rock used to be, how they cast Halle Berry as the "nice" girl runner-up next to supposedly bombshell Robin Givens (who knew then how far Halle Berry would go?). Halfway through the film, I climbed into bed for an afternoon nap, feeling exhausted, but I tossed and turned like a dervish, forgetting I had fuelled myself up with three cappuccinos. My brain raced with cautionary messages and promises to be on good behaviour.

You've had a good scare, that's how Helena put it, and she was so right. What did you think you were doing with the guy in that office? What the *hell* made you think the only way to crack this case was to literally go under covers? What are you trying to do? Screw up your life? You'll watch it from now on. You have to. Squeaky clean. Nuns will blush when they see you coming.

She said the tests were negative. Nothing to worry about. Not over Lionel. Not *him* either.

I dozed but I didn't exactly dream. It was more like a fantasy playing in my head. I was back in the nightclub, visualizing the scene between Lionel and Neil, and in my imagination, Neil unbuckled his belt, let down his trousers, and this time he went through with it. The crowd let out a cheer when they saw his long, thick cock released from his Jockeys, and I saw Shondi lying on the table, once again only in her little ankle socks and trainers like the first time I saw her.

Neil fucking Shondi in front of the crowd, with Lionel looking on and doing nothing. And then Shondi was hugging me like she did after I booted that creep that was assaulting her, nude and hugging me, saying, "Thank you."

I kept feeling her hugging me in a quick embrace again, thanking me. I remembered the sweet odour of her perspiration. She had smelled good when she was close to me.

I lay there in bed, and I was soaking between my legs. Shondi.

You're projecting, that's all. It didn't mean anything. I

178 · LISA LAWRENCE

tried to pull my mind back to images of Neil making love to me, but they wouldn't come. Reception was experiencing technical difficulties.

I reached for the phone to call him.

Don't, I told myself. Don't do it.

No doubt Janet had belatedly rushed to "her" man's side. Jeez, the last thing I needed was to have her pick up his phone when I called.

Daniel Giradeau had left a text on my mobile, suggesting we link up again.

I got out of bed and dialled his number. In response to his nonchalant hello, I simply asked: "Where?"

It took him all of two seconds to recognise my voice, and then he replied, "Green Park."

It sunk in what he had in mind, but I recovered quickly. "Okay."

"ASAP?"

"What else?" I scoffed. And then I went a little insane.

♦

I was the one who offered very precise directions to the exact spot, the exact bench, where I wanted us to meet, to make what was in my head become real. He was about ten minutes late, but I could forgive him for that, and when he saw me, he called my name in astonishment: "Teresa?" He was surprised at how brazen I was, how I could match him for shock value.

I had stripped off my yellow tube top, my orange sarong and my sandals, standing completely naked in front of him with only the protective cover of bushes and trees. I dropped to my knees and unzipped his fly hastily. Before he could make another protest, I had pulled him out and put him in my mouth, making him hard in seconds.

Dogging. The two of us.

Fucking someone in public places, mostly parks, often with someone else watching. It was supposed to be a phenomenon in London and a few other major cities.

Giradeau fucking me hard from behind, making me collapse to my hands and knees, and when the young mixed couple came along—kids in their teens, black boy and white girl—I panted, "Don't stop! Don't stop!"

"Wasn't going to," he panted back.

Eye contact with the boy, watching me naked right there in the park, and he could see everything. I swore I saw the white girl's nipples harden through her cotton blouse. She looked at me, looked at Daniel and tried not to stare at the huge pink dick driving into me. They traded looks of disbelief, checked over their shoulder to see if anyone else had noticed, and it was the girl who actually led the boy closer. They knelt down a few yards away in front of a tree and watched us, the boy with his back against the rough bark, the girl leaning against him.

We must have put on quite a show, because the boy's arms slipped from around her waist to start fondling her breasts, and she didn't stop him. After a while, he deftly unbuttoned her jeans and slipped his hand down her pants, and she still didn't stop him. She was pretty, and she looked very pretty as she came with her eyes closed to tight slits, her small white teeth biting her bottom lip. The boy had managed to shrug her jeans down so that we could see a forest of fine brunette pubic hair.

I moaned, and as my arms gave out, I lay there in the grass, smelling the earth; Daniel fell on top of me and grew even harder. Warm jets of spunk fired inside me, and my pussy contracted with a fresh orgasm. I craned my neck so that Daniel could kiss me, and then he rolled shyly off my back and with a slightly contrite look to the other couple, ducked into the trees to sort himself out. I sat up, still nude, feeling an amazing euphoria as I looked absently around for my handbag. I needed tissues.

As I wiped myself, I saw that the boy by the tree was frantically getting out from under his girlfriend. She looked at him in both wide-eyed surprise and amusement, laughing and seeming to say what are you doing? What he was doing was opening his trousers and pulling down the hem of his Jockey shorts. He managed to pull out his enormous hard-on before he lost all control and a geyser of semen flew forward.

The girlfriend first started in surprise, and then she moved in to try to help him. She grabbed his cock to jerk him a little, kissing him on his neck, his cheek, trying not to get in the way in case he shot this time all over her. She glanced over at me helplessly, the boy's eyes still on me, and I could see his erection was still powerfully hard to the point of painful.

I looked directly at him as I moved into a squat, my legs open, balancing on the small balls of my feet as I moved to cup my breasts.

He fired a long stream of cum again, his girlfriend's hand jerking him quickly to help him, and then she threw caution aside and kissed him deeply. When they finished and looked my way, I stood up and ducked backward into the bushes, smiling and waving goodbye. I would never see them again.

Daniel was ready with my tube top and sarong, dangling my sandals. When we emerged from the bushes, we passed a pair of foot patrol officers and I burst into nervous giggles.

♦

We went to dinner, eating mostly in silence, and then he took me back to his flat, one of those apartment buildings out near Canary Wharf where corporations rent for long-stay foreign executives. I could hear distant foghorns for the shipping traffic.

It was late by then, but Daniel never even bothered to turn the lights on. We groped in the light spilled from the hallway, stumbled in darkness to his bedroom and fucked once more. I could never call what I did with Daniel Giradeau "making love." It was a satiating of appetites, not something animal or mechanical but a transaction of bodies. Foreplay with him was always a competitive sport. And when he came, it was a reminder that no matter how much we reveal ourselves in orgasm, it's something we ultimately feel alone. I could feel him shooting inside me, but he was one of those guys who repressed every grunt of pleasure, every moan of release.

He was gone by the time I woke up the next morning. Well, you don't leave a woman in your flat unless you trust her and have nothing to hide.

Or you simply don't expect she'll find anything.

Me, big snoop that I am, figured there's always something to find. And now in daylight, I could take a good look around.

I showered, dressed, raided the fridge for breakfast, bolted the door and then got to work.

Daniel's flat, Daniel's surroundings. Despite having his hands all over my body, he had quite deliberately kept himself emotionally closed-off and impersonal, I think. And so it was with his home, although he had at least confessed he didn't think of it as such. Yes, the flat was on a long-term lease, he'd said, in his company's name. His kitchen was full of sleek Bosch appliances, the living room all modular

Sanyo consoles for the stereo, the flat-screen telly (baffling tastes in music—retro seventies funk, German techno-pop, Yo-Yo Ma and a collection of soundtrack albums).

The pictures on the wall were neutral, generic prints of touristy London landscapes, the kind that get left behind by the owner and then ignored by a new resident—someone who didn't expect to stick around. On the coffee table was a neat stack of old *Economist* issues and a couple of copies of *The Telegraph*. Jeez, not even an old dog-eared paperback for reading at night.

Of course, some guys don't really care about their environment, but you'd expect to see some artefact of personality, some remnant of home. Though he'd said he'd been in London for about a year, I found a suit bag but not even an unpacked box of clothes.

His computer was empty. Nothing on it but the usual programmes for business execs, and he didn't use Outlook. It took me a moment, but I realised there was something different about his office set-up—computer but no printer. Hey, lots of folks don't need to spring for a printer, but he had one of the state-of-the-art Canon fax machines next to his tower hard drive, and if it could double as a printer, it wasn't hooked up to be one. Instead, there was a stack of confirmation pages like you get with faxes.

Each one with that standard cryptic message you get with the rest of the page blank, a complete waste of paper: "Transmission: OK." No copies of the outgoing documents he'd been faxing, but that was no surprise. Once you send them, why leave them on the machine?

In the rubbish bin by the desk, I saw torn half-sheets of paper—yet more acknowledgements from the Canon that whatever he'd sent had gone out all right.

The phone number where he'd sent them didn't tell me much—from the codes, I could tell it was a Paris line, but that was about it. I hit the little read-out diary display, and he had received dozens of faxes from the same number. Made me wonder why he didn't simply email the person, but some folks can be old-fashioned.

I hadn't bothered to check out the drafting board. My lover of last night was an architect, and sure enough, under the T-square and little Pyrex triangle were several elaborate sketches of modern designs. Maybe that explained the fax machine. As one of the last of the brave few who still knew how to work a mechanical pencil instead of using Photoshop, he could draw a few squiggles on a sheet of A4 and whip it off to his client.

And yep, there were crumpled balls of sketches in the bin by the table. Okay, move on.

Except there was nothing much to move on to. You always find out something about a person in his home, but this morning, I'd learned little except that Daniel Giradeau liked Alpen, kept mint tea next to his Dark Roast, seemed to shop in Chinatown for healthy veggies but had a bit of a sweet tooth with three boxes of Ferrero Rocher in the kitchen cupboard, and he had a thing for Jennifer Connelly—five of her movies in his DVD collection.

The sum of these parts made me start to lose interest in him—not only as a suspect but also as a man. Yeah, he was a good lay, but I didn't think I was getting the real Daniel Giradeau. I think his entire seductive Master in the Art of Love bit was a role he was playing while away from home. It's not like he'd have revealing tan lines around his ring finger, not here in sunless England, but he was just too much on the make.

I admit it. He could turn me on, and he was sexually *amusing* for lack of a better word. But I had to watch out that he didn't become a pointless distraction.

Like I said before, move on.

◆

Carl rang to say "I don't know why I'm doing this" but that perhaps I wanted to tag along when he went to interview a witness over in Soho. Then he corrected himself to say yes, he did know, that maybe ignorance wasn't bliss, and that if I was up on all the facts, I could keep my big politico client out of trouble. Big politicos in trouble made headaches for the Met.

It's not as if he could come out and say Teresa, I owe you one and here's quid pro quo.

He had tracked down the mixed-race boy from Lionel's home movie, a kid of eighteen named Andre. He wore one of those half Ts for men, which always personally baffles me, since you got a guy showing only his midriff like a girl. Neon blue trousers, tassel loafers. Not picking up any style tips lately from *Queer Life,* but then I doubted he had Sky. The kid rented a bed-sit above one of the restaurants, and rather than call him in, Carl preferred to see cagier witnesses in "their environment." We buttonholed him on a street corner, with the swirls of locals, sandwich shop punters, Nikon-noosed tourists, and yes, gay couples floating by.

Carl didn't say what Andre did exactly to support himself and maybe he didn't know, but I doubted that the boy sold himself on the street. He didn't look like he could handle what came with that sort of life, and I suspected that in between odd jobs, he'd relied on Lionel for quick infusions of cash.

I didn't need to ask Carl whether he was a suspect. Even if you suspended disbelief in that anyone could be stupid enough to leave an incriminating DVD in the box, well, the boy was too slight in build. He was the feminine half of the pair, and if it got ugly between the lovers, no way this boy could overpower a tall, fit guy like Lionel and bind him to a chair.

Andre. Pretty. Pouting. Mincing. Chip-on-the-shoulder. Very suspicious of us coming around to hit him up for information. Carl let the kid assume I was a detective as well.

"So now you need the faggot's help, yeah?"

"Your choice of words, not ours," I put in.

"Black man can't be queer in this world, and that's news to you?" snapped the boy. He folded his arms and lifted his chin as he stared down Old Compton Street. "My baby was so far in the fucking closet. He hated himself, end of story."

"Not end of story," I said. "Somebody murdered him."

He had to look at us for that one.

"Do you know anybody who bore him a grudge?" asked Carl. "Who wanted to hurt him?"

"Oh, fuck ... Oh, Jesus fuck." Reeling from it.

"Come on," pushed Carl impatiently. "It doesn't look like he got rough with you, but did he ever go in for something a little more *athletic* with someone else?"

"What do you mean somebody else?" He lost his temper, tears rolling down his cheeks. "There is no 'somebody else'!"

"He did girls," Carl pointed out blandly.

"He didn't shag the cows to get off," said Andre. "That was for cash. And he pretty much stopped that shit anyway. He just took 'em around so they could be seen with him."

Carl and I looked at each other, both of us thinking how love is blind. We already knew Lionel made enough from his mining company job that he didn't need pin money from escort gigs. More conflicted than his boyfriend could guess.

"Right," sighed Carl. "Any straight enemies, then?"

"The whole bloody world's our enemy! Double jeopardy, man. Black and queer. Told my boy why you go play with the suits and deny who you are, hon? Love me and be happy—we'll manage. And don't get me started on the bullshit black straights throw our way!"

"We're not," I said.

"The love that once dared not speak its name now can't shut up," muttered Carl.

"Mike Nichols," I said, recognising the reference.

"Pays to get an education," replied Carl.

Andre wasn't amused. "What is this?" he demanded, too loud and too flaming for even my taste, putting his hands on his hips. "Like I need your breeder smart-ass remarks?"

"Well, then answer the bloody question," prompted Carl. "Could anyone have known about you two? Somebody who hated him?"

The sincere urgency of the question settled Andre down for a moment. Very quietly, sombrely, he answered: "No . . . I mean he was scared, so scared. He kept saying how we had to be careful, 'cause like, his company every so often gets these hired-gun spies to check out their own people. Bunch of homophobes in there. Oh, shit, they killed my man, didn't they?"

"We don't know that," said Carl. He gave me a sideways glance as he added witheringly, "I think multinational conglomerates have bigger fish to fry than if one of their analysts is gay."

I was neutral. Said nothing. It was like the trees were getting thicker in front of the forest. Blackmailer sends Lionel a note to stop seeing Janet, but blackmailer kills Lionel, knowing he was gay. If he wants Lionel out of the picture why not blackmail him with the very secret that terrified our late Mr. Young?

"They did him," Andre insisted to Carl. "You just don't want to believe it or you want to ignore it!"

"You go to those anti-globalisation rallies, too, don't you?"

"Matter of fucking fact, I do, man. That's a crime, too, now, yeah?"

"No," said Carl quietly, "I just think you might want to expand your horizons a little, mate." And reluctantly, he disclosed a couple of the more disturbing details of the murder, which only got Andre started on torture squads in South America, the dangers of a single world currency, how gays were targeted in Zimbabwe and on we go.

"Bet you anything his killer's in frickin' Harare, dude! Not here! My Lionel . . ." He rubbed his eyes again.

Meanwhile, I was circling back to our killer's original intent: try to pass Lionel's murder off as a suicide. Okay, if that was the intent then his sexual orientation, what with the DVD left in the machine, was simply factored in for the convenience of the staged scenario. Successful black mining executive tortured by self-loathing because he was queer. So he kills himself. But Carl wasn't buying it. I wasn't buying it. Hell, even Andre didn't buy it.

And the boy was bitter. "Couldn't even go to the service for him. His family didn't know . . ."

Which tugged at me a little. Yes, the boy was a bit of a cartoon, but no doubt he was more natural and less "on" with Lionel. They had loved each other. It didn't matter anymore whether Lionel was running away from himself and what he was, whether he actually liked getting it on with me or was using women to hide. He did love this young man. Love is love, I told myself.

And none of any of this speculation was relevant to the case.

"Blind alley," said Carl as we left Andre on his corner of pavement.

I nodded. I had the feeling it wasn't so much that we pursued the trail of evidence into this alley as we were led there down a garden path.

Of course, there was one other possibility.

♦

Poker night. A townhouse in South Kensington. The site, interestingly, was the home of one of the players. This was Cahill's place, so we were back in the land of antiques, Persian carpets and Anglo bric-à-brac clutter.

The talk for a short while, among those in the know, was about Lionel Young and how terrible it was, him killing himself like that. Troubled fellow. What a waste. The perfunctory expressions got on my nerves a little, as if Lionel was a matter of old business with the reading of the minutes that had to be quickly dismissed.

To my mild astonishment, the one person who didn't play the hypocrite was the very person I expected to make a big show of public grief: Vivian. She had been with him enough, booked him several times through Helena, never hid how she liked him. But when I managed to be alone with her in a corner and mentioned how awful Lionel's death was, she took a long pull of her martini and snapped, "What can you expect, darling? He was a bloody queer, taking it up the bum all this time. That's right—I have it on the best authority. Made fools of us girls. He had no ... *business* being here when he went around doing that."

I couldn't help but notice how tightly she held her now-empty glass. I worried for a second it might shatter in her hand.

"Gives me the creeps when I think how I had him. He was a good lay and all, but I don't want to be with some faggot! I don't think it was suicide, if you ask me."

"You don't?"

She dropped her voice to a gossipy whisper. "I bet you anything something went wrong. Well, they're all into kink, aren't they?"

Someone called her from across the room, and she was up and gone without another word—leaving me to wonder how she would know enough details to even speculate on any "kink" involved in Lionel's death.

Vivian was my suspect who inspired my "one other possibility" about Lionel's murder. If she were off the rails with sexual obsession, Lionel's taste in boys would surely be enough to prompt a violent—even murderous—reaction. The loathing in her voice a moment ago. The anger that reflected a perceived betrayal. I tried to fathom it. Was it because of her vanity? That Lionel was such a good conquest for her public displays of lust? And now to discover he might well have been putting on a show? Forcing him to masturbate while bound and under a gun would be a kind of sick justice for "lying to her all this time."

Trouble was, I didn't have the piece of the puzzle for just when and how Vivian discovered the truth about Lionel. More importantly, how did she manage to get Lionel naked and bound—one woman against a fit, strong guy? Yes, she would have had the gun, but at some point she surely would have wanted to check his restraints. And while Lionel might have been forced to tie himself up partway, he couldn't finish the job. She would have had to take the risk of coming close to the chair and risking a struggle. Hell, would she even know where Lionel had lived? Did she have an alibi? I had to check it out.

◆

George Westlake came into the kitchen to freshen his drink and Ayako's while I was snapping tongs over cubes of ice for my G & T. He barely looked at me. I assumed this must have been a preoccupation with Lionel. They were an odd pair to be friends—different ages, different professions and backgrounds—but friends nonetheless, and George must have had a shock.

"Poor Lionel, he would have had a long, good life ahead of him if it hadn't been taken away," said George.

Taken as opposed to taking it himself. Carl and his men must have paid George a visit. Lionel probably wouldn't have had any other players' names in his Rolodex, but he would have kept his buddy Westlake's number on file.

I pretended not to pick up on George's phrasing, since I would have to play out a scene of shock over suggestions Lionel was murdered, what did the cops say and blah, blah, blah.

"Did you go?" I asked simply.

"To his funeral? Yes, I did. It was all right." He turned his attention to chopping up a couple of limes. "Nice service. I invited a couple of the others—Helena, Cahill. Vivian didn't want—" He suddenly remembered his tact. "She didn't feel like going."

That could explain how Vivian learned about Lionel. The cops had told George, and George had confided this information to Vivian. Unless, of course, she knew before and was our murderer. Got to check her alibi, I told myself again.

No Neil at tonight's game. Not that I really expected him so soon after his run-in with the Met.

"How are you holding up, George?"

"Not too well, actually," he confided.

"Sorry."

"I heard you're going out with Giradeau."

And he had heard because I had allowed it to circulate back through Helena. I wanted to see what effect the news would have. As likeable as George was, I realized I couldn't rule him out yet as a suspect.

"Are you?" he asked me flat out. "Going out with him?"

I let out a tired breath. "George . . ."

"Teresa, I thought you and I, well—"

"Oh, come on, George," I said. "Look where we are! You watched Neil fucking me right on a table just like that one. And you got off on it."

"Yes."

"Did you think I was going to be exclusive in my dating? Are you expecting that of me?"

"N—No," he said, somewhat timidly. "No, I haven't the right."

"And if you must know, Daniel did ask me out," I whispered. "You and I had our little shopping trip, and you haven't called. What were you waiting for?"

God, what a bitch, I'm acting, I thought. I was technically in the right, sure, but if he wasn't our killer then I was using a nice guy as my personal cat-toy.

All part of the job and the role I was playing. And there are all kinds of ways to dangle your bait. But boy, it sucked.

"I'm sorry," he whispered, which just made me feel worse. "You're right. I shouldn't be asking you things like this."

Woo, boy.

"Let's forget about it," I said, my hands on his shoulders, and I gave him a short kiss on the lips. I nearly told him to call me, but he already thought I had led him on somehow, and my dance card was getting awfully full lately. Better to see what he does.

I went off to mingle, putting my arm briefly around Daniel Giradeau's waist, playing the flirt.

"What are you two discussing?" I asked pleasantly.

"Gossip," replied Cahill. "There's always a buzz over fresh talent, new blood. God knows Helena got us very worked up over you."

"So who is she?"

"Not a she."

"Oh?"

"Vivian provided the bloke's introduction to our organiser," said Cahill. "Don't know how she knows him, and she's doing her tee-hee girlish act whenever I ask. I presume she caught him in her web at some party. So blame her if the chap turns out to be a dud. But he sounds promising. Might actually be someone worth talking to. He's had all kinds of adventures, apparently."

Giradeau was sceptical. "There's some nonsense going around that he was with one of those corporate military outfits in Iraq, the new dogs of war. Well, people make things up, don't they? To make themselves look better."

"But these fellows are real," Cahill insisted, just for the fun of the debate. "I mean Britain used them, the Americans used them. They have to come from somewhere! You ask him tonight, Daniel. You find out for us." He let out one of his boisterous laughs.

No, Giradeau didn't have to ask, not for my sake anyway.

The guy coming in. Diamond chip blue eyes, boyish curl of blond hair across his forehead, pale white skin lightly tanned. Good body on him, and I should know.

It wasn't Iraq. It was Africa.

Simon. Simon Highsmith, and what is *he* doing here? Second question: what the hell can you do about it?

I tried to melt into a corner by the fireplace as he let Cahill take his raincoat and Vivian give him a showy hug and a kiss on both cheeks. George shyly shook his hand, and Ayako hovered, stroking her glass tumbler. And then he saw me.

He saw me. Surprise on his face, of course. Didn't come over. Avoiding me.

No. Scratch that. He doesn't want to know me here. And since I wasn't coming to him, he knew I didn't want to know him here either. Okay, you know about you, so what's his reason?

Then Cahill called us to the game and went around the table, making formal introductions. And Simon kept hiding in plain sight, pretending we were strangers. Just as I did.

◆

Flip go the cards. Flip, flip, flip, each player scooping up his hand, the soft crunch of the deck as it goes back to the green felt of the table.

"What did you say your line of work was, Mr. Highsmith?" asks Giradeau.

"I didn't," says Simon.

And George puts in: "Why is it that when you sit down at a poker table, people start to talk like they do in Westerns?"

A peal of appreciative laughter around the table, Simon included. Daniel waved to Simon, still expecting an answer to his question. And there I was, waiting for a fairy tale like my own.

But none came. Simon leaned back in his seat and said pleasantly, "I do all sorts of things, Mr. Giradeau. I dropped out of medical school and went into aid work for a while, but I discovered I don't have the temperament to be a martyr. So then I did odd jobs in various parts of Africa, and now I do freelance consulting on setting up corporate branch offices in Third World countries. Charter work, smoothing out the banking stuff, negotiating leases, that sort of thing."

"Oh," said Cahill.

Giradeau nudged Cahill and told Simon in a sotto whisper: "You let him down. He was hoping you were a bandit."

"What?" asked Simon with an incredulous laugh.

"Oh, there are rumours going around the circuit that you were a mercenary in Africa," I explained, biting down suggestively on an olive in a toothpick. "Of course, that could be Vivian's overactive imagination."

"I think I said something like I hope he's a tiger in bed," giggled Vivian. "How we get from that to 'mercenary' is somebody else's fault! Tigers in Africa? Bandits in Africa? Like a kiddies' game of telephone."

Simon looked at me as he replied, "I think present company tonight are far too interesting for the stuffy job descriptions I've been hearing. Each and every one of you. Except Westlake here."

George looked hurt. "Oh?"

"I don't mean it like that, mate," said Simon quickly. "I meant you seem to be the opposite of what you are. I'd have thought a tourist resort mogul would be a far more extroverted personality."

Cahill gave George a supportive slap on the back. "Oh, George here is a wild man, trust us. And he's here, isn't he? We've all got to be a little mad to be doing this, don't we?"

"Or horny," argued Vivian.

Ayako, as usual, smiled but didn't comment.

"If you like, Cahill, I can pretend to be a mercenary tonight," said Simon.

"Sounds more Vivian's fantasy," replied Cahill. "Who knows? Maybe you have a bandolier under your shirt."

"He shoots first, asks questions later," quipped Giradeau, putting on a deep movie announcer voice.

My eyes locked with Simon's. I tossed a chip into the pot and said: "Definitely."

♦

An hour later. George, in a mood, had gone home. Cahill was upstairs with Roxanne, a soap actress and a relative newbie. A couple of other pairings of casual regulars had happened— one flown the coop, one in the guest bedroom. And that left several familiar faces around the table. Simon was down to his boxers. Daniel nude. Ayako in a camisole. Vivian with more clothes on than she probably wanted. And me naked.

Ayako, laughing, had pointed to me instead of one of the boys last game, making me lose my knickers. There was nothing in the rules saying a girl couldn't win and make another girl strip, or a boy versus boy—it just wasn't that common a tactic.

"I need you to distract Daniel," she joked.

But Daniel won a young blonde sculptor who had a big gallery show on, and after she gave him a hand job in the corner, they excused themselves for the night.

New game and Ayako's deal. She shuffled the deck, calling out like an Atlantic City pit boss, "Seven-card stud, high/low, kings are wild in the hole." Oh, oh, I thought. This is going to be interesting.

Seven-card stud. Two facedown cards, four faceup, one facedown. Ayako's deal, Ayako's pleasure, so kings were wild in the hole. Meaning if you got one of them dealt facedown (and that only you could see in your hand), they'd be wild. Hey, it would be too discouraging if kings were wild and everyone could see them as faceup cards.

And high/low? Helena told me this was pretty common in regular stud poker. The pot would get split between the player with the best hand and the one with the worst hand. It supposedly added spice in that more players stayed in the game longer.

As if we needed any more spice. An interesting choice of game, I thought, and why split the pot? Unless Ayako was up to something.

Simon had the highest faceup card, a ten of clubs, so he opened the betting. "Here we go, my darlings. What shall I open with? I'll offer a kiss. It's the romantic in me."

"A kiss?" said Ayako. "That's real daring, Simon. But I think we ought to get right down to it. I'll see your kiss—" Clink went the chips. "And I'll raise you a 69. Daniel?"

"Check."

Eyes fell to me, next to bet. "Check," I said promptly.

"Aha," said Vivian. "Well, I'm sure you taste nice, kissing wise, Simon, but I'd rather feel you between my legs. Right here."

I spotted a couple of grimaces from the other players. Vivian may have had money, but there was always something coarse and predatory in her that put off the women and a few of the men. Helena said it was considered a *faux pas* to come out and say who you wanted and how you wanted them at the table. And yet you could be screwing one of these guys and screaming their name in front of the crowd an hour or two from play.

"Raise you a rug burn," said Vivian, flashing her smile. I expected to see fangs.

Around we went. Daniel folded, and then with a poor-sport sneer, Vivian had to pack it in. It was down to Ayako, Simon and me, and now it became quite clear just who the stakes were. I got the distinct impression I was being ganged up on.

Nope, I don't think she was really after Simon, at least not tonight. But she could be helping him.

The way I figured it, Simon had cooked up his little scheme to get me on my back well before the drinks were topped up. I mean, how do you share a high/low pot in strip poker? Even if he won the low hand for the pot, he could claim me, while Ayako would call in her marker on him down the line.

If you wanted to presume innocence over her suggesting a split pot game, yeah, I guess it could be a "we both win, we'll have each other" scenario. But knowing Simon, he would look for a silent partner for his schemes. Winner's choice of who he took to bed.

"I'll hang your curtains," said Ayako gaily, matching his bid for bondage, "and I'll raise one juicy treat."

"Oh, yes?" asked Simon.

"And what's that?" I asked.

"F.O.D.," she smiled.

I wasn't terribly impressed. For Simon, a Fuck On Demand would have been a nice refreshing pick-me-up over lunch in whatever under-the-counter business he was dealing in these days. He had little to lose, certainly no reputation at risk. I still thought he and Ayako were playing out a scene for my benefit.

To fold now . . . He'd get almost as much kick out of rubbing my nose in that as taking me to bed. To hell with him, I thought. I supposedly controlled the bet, but Ayako had taken the stakes as high as they could go.

"You in, Teresa?"

Simon. Not giving me much chance to think.

I smiled sweetly at Ayako and said, "Call."

The odds were in my favour, after all. If I won, I had Simon on my leash, not that I wanted him or expected him to keep the word of the bargain. If Ayako won, she could have him for all I cared. And well, if Simon won, there was still a 50/50 split he'd take Ayako over me. After all, he'd slept with me already. There was nothing new for him with my body, and his attitude tonight told me it was more about figuring out what I was up to and playing mind games.

I could lay down my hand, call it a day, and let them duke it out. All I was coasting on was a straight.

Then all my suspicions went out the window as Ayako said, "Pig."

Pig. There was a contingency in the game where a player could call this out and win both High and Low. They needed two different five-card hands with their seven. Simon laid down a flush, but there was Ayako with her own flush, and that missing king. Wild card.

And me with a straight.

I laughed away like a fool, saying, "Alas, poor Simon! You get to be this lovely lady's wind-up toy for the night of her choice."

And Ayako shot back, "Not him, beautiful. *You.* I want you."

9

Later. She told me she had wanted me since I had walked into that townhouse apartment in Primrose Hill. And then to watch me coming as Neil fucked me senseless, it just made her toss and turn in her bed for nights on end. "You have no idea," she informed me, smiling as if I had missed some important irony in life.

My mind flashed back to that short instant when most of the players had got up to inspect me *there* as Neil had plunged in. Only Ayako had held her place, reaching out to cup my breast. Duh. You didn't pick up on it, girl, and it was right in front of you.

"Your nipple in my mouth," she said. The reverential tone in her voice, it was like she was talking about ambrosia or something.

She crossed the living room and her small, dainty hand caressed the back of my neck almost possessively, circling around to my jawline and up my cheek. "Look," she said smiling. "I want you, and the 'D' does stand for 'demand.'

But it'll help both of us, I think, if you enjoy yourself. Have you ever thought about being with a girl?"

I laughed self-consciously. Yes. Yes, I had. There were a couple of black female celebrities that I had thought: my God, they turn *me* on. But I'd assumed this was just restless, free-floating sexual energy that didn't know where to put itself. I was discovering a lot of things about myself on this job.

For one, it was far easier "going along" with what Ayako wanted and calling it experimentation than facing your own hidden desires and taking the initiative. To be the object of desire? To be seduced? It kind of left me off the hook. Truth is, I was up for it the longer I had to consider it. She was the "other." We had a mutual exotic turn-on thing happening, and I don't think I could have done it if a white chick had pulled that stunt on me back at the game.

I'll always remember her flat in Knightsbridge for incense, candles, Tokyo poster art in hallway alcoves I couldn't begin to fathom. Very clean, very spare. Chic. Feminine.

She slipped off her silk robe embroidered with a dragon, and she was my opposite in every way. I'm tall, and she was maybe, at best, five foot two. My breasts are full, my body having the right curves with a backside that's not too much, but it's there. Her tits had a girlish smallness to them, her ass a tiny, round peach, and though she had lovely, shapely legs, her hips were narrow, almost those of a boy. Her thatch of pubic hair had been elaborately trimmed.

Look at her, I thought. Her delicate body was the cliché wet dream of every white guy with a Far East fetish, and what it inspired in me was an intimate revelation, that I actually desired her. She came over and sat in my lap as a child would, and I hugged her so naturally, feeling an instinctive urge to pet her and dominate her. I held her tight as we kissed, and she was a good kisser, tasting sweet in a surprising way. I expected a girl-taste to repel me. It didn't.

My breasts seemed to fascinate her, all the largeness and generosity of African features, and she played with my tits and fondled me as a boy would. I heard myself moan casually with pleasure, stroking the supple whiteness of that Japanese skin, and then very tentatively, very carefully, I slid my hand up her thigh and rested my fingers on her mound.

Wet. Wet to the touch. I took my middle finger to taste some of her juice, and she flashed a smile of small neat teeth at me, wicked and catlike. In only a second, she slid off me like an oil slick, collapsing onto the floor in almost a fashion photographer's pose, and with a confidence of taking a steering wheel she parted my legs and inserted two of her dainty fingers into my pussy. My gasp spurred her on, and she withdrew her hand and suddenly pounced on me with her mouth, small exquisite lips and the heat of her breath on my labia.

My toes curled, and I hooked my ankles around the back of the chair with the immediacy of the pleasure. Her tongue seemed to lap with an urgent thirst at my pussy, licking me, seeking my clit, and when she found it, I let out a wail. I staggered like a drunk out of the chair, Ayako laughing and holding on to my thighs like a roughhousing child.

"Come here," I said huskily, and at last we made it to the bed.

Kissing her and losing myself in her small mouth, letting her tug on my full bottom lip, and my hands roamed in lazy, curving trails along her belly and up to her breasts. I ducked my head down to suck one of her tiny nipples, with Ayako whispering in my ear, "I love your hair. I love its texture ..." One of her hands ran through my curls, the other now pawing with amazed delight through my pubic hair.

With Ayako on her side, me letting my shoulder blades hit the embrace of silk, we began to masturbate each other, and it turned into an unspoken competition to see who could make the other come. To feel her hand inside me while I simultaneously penetrated her was an incredible, even empowering turn-on. To be inside someone instead of being filled by a guy. To fill someone else.

Short, sharp exhalations of girlish breath as she stared into my eyes and heard my own ragged breathing, and then I could feel it coming, like ripples of water, a gathering of thunderclouds. But I've nearly got you, honey, I almost got you there, the pad of a finger on your clit, fingers back inside you, kneading the most private, secret part of you. Ayako's fingers pushing in and out of me, trying to get me there first, and my sweet box closed on her sopping fingers, tugging, urging her to stay in, and her eyes widened. She *timber*-ed onto the bed as she wailed, her knees opening out as far as they could go. I moved close enough to rest my cheek against hers, beads of her perspiration mixing with my own. I saw out of the corner of my eye, her teeth grit, the black almonds turning to closed slits.

"Oh, fuck! . . . Oh, fuck, baby!" she said.

She caressed my hair, panting after the marathon, giving me sweet little pecks on my lips like saying goodbye. And then she snuggled down and licked me until I screamed for mercy.

Yeah, I discovered a hell of a lot about myself on this case. What I like. What I'm willing to do, and what I won't. Ayako was a turning point for me. We barely said a word to each other when it was over. We walked hand in hand to her front door, and she kissed me goodbye like she expected we

would see each other again. I smiled and actually thanked
her.

◆

My apartment felt very still, very empty when I came home
later. It felt like I hadn't been back in ages, what with crashing at Helena's and all the bed hopping that I was trying to
call detective work. I felt the instinct to come home after
making love with Ayako. Back to the haven of my private
space to mull over what the episode told me about myself.
What it perhaps really meant.

Not that I didn't do a good job of putting it off and finding other things to do. There was Vivian Mapling's alibi
to check out, for one thing, and alas, she had one. Turned
out she did "design consultancy" work on custom jewellery
(whatever the hell that meant) for a few of her rich and
beautiful friends, and she had jetted off for a couple of days
to Paris. Damn. She was far from being my favourite person
at the games, and I would have liked to have pinned this on
her and wrapped up the case quick. But the sadistic *personal*
nature of how Lionel was killed persuaded me that our blackmailer was also our hands-on murderer, no second party
involved.

Until I felt duty-bound to follow up on Ayako's background. Along with taking my pleasure, I had helped myself to something else in her apartment while she was fixing
us afterglow drinks—a few key pages of banking documents,
work stuff she had brought home from the office and no
doubt expected to get around to later. Since they were photocopies and print-outs, I was pinning my hopes on the notion that if she discovered them missing, she might think
she had forgotten them. I had maybe thirty seconds in her
place while she was in the other room to decide what was

and wasn't important, and still I wound up grabbing things on the spur of the moment. Ayako handled major corporate loans—this you could learn already from her business card. What made me shiver at my desk was recognising the name of a corporation I had done my best to ignore for a long time.

Orpheocon.

Shit, shit, *shit*.

Tell yourself that it's coincidence. Come on, she works for one of the largest Japanese banks, and they're a mega-corp with their dirty little fingers into pies all over the world. It should surprise you if her bank *didn't* have a few dealings with them. Coincidence? Not that I was an expert, but Ayako seemed to do pretty hands-off third-party stuff, much of it related to equities and bonds for financial institutions in the Baltic states.

But this is only the stuff you could get your hands on in a quick rush.

One more lover, one more suspect . . .

♦

Trying to banish Ayako from my mind, I tried to return to my so-called "real" personal life. And I got a mild shock as I tore through my neglected post with a letter opener while flicking my right hand back and forth to my computer mouse to zip through my new emails. And I swear this actually happened. The publisher's envelope I had dismissed as another rejection letter? I finally opened it . . . while clicking on a new email from my brother. "Hey, Sis" yada, yada, yada, and it turns out he took the copy of my kids' book I gave him over to a small publisher in Argentina, and they thought it could do enormously well if I was willing for them to translate it into Spanish. On the continent of Isabel Allende and

Márquez, it seemed they liked their kiddie stories with a little bit of social commentary. Wow.

Then I looked down at the cream stationery in my hand from my latest publishing hopeful in London, and they liked it, too. One problem. They did *not* like Roxanne's illustrations. Too sombre, the editor wrote, too damn dark to be perfectly blunt, and while the manuscript, she felt, managed to walk a fine line in tone, from a marketing perspective the submitted pictures would not do. And the publishing house preferred to assign its own illustrators anyway.

So now I had a problem. I could go with Isaac's folks way over there and perhaps get a few hundred copies sold—in Spanish—and with Roxanne's illustrations, since they didn't have a problem with them. Or I could let this big publisher with divisions on both sides of the Atlantic and even in Europe put out my book but perhaps depict my heroine's refugee camp like a happy, sunny street in Balamory. It was my book, sure, but even though Roxanne dashed off her pictures as a "fun little job" and I knew her only slightly, I had sent the manuscript around as a team effort. It would be a shitty thing to do, I thought, to accept the big player's offer and just dump her. If it were done to me, I'd think: bitch.

So I phoned Roxanne up with the good-news-bad-news scenarios, vintage No Doubt coming loud and clear through the phone, "I'll email my brother back and say we'll accept the Argentine guys if you're cool with it."

"What, are you mad?" she snapped.

"You want to take a pass on them and wait for a British publisher?"

"Teresa," said Roxanne, and I heard her exhale a long stream of smoke from her latest cigarette, "don't be daft. *Take the other one.*"

"But they don't want your—"

"I don't give a shit, love. How much you think they pay illustrators for children's books?" She let out one of her high-pitched giggles and added, "I did it as a larf, and it didn't take me very long. And you forget, you threw some dosh my way up front for the effort ages ago."

Yes—yes, I did. Not a lot, mind you, but I did pay her because if the book never found a home, I didn't want all her work to be for nothing and have her resent me. Everybody's got to eat, and if I didn't like being messed around or ducked by the occasional deadbeat client then I should sign a cheque promptly when I hired someone for myself.

"I'm compensated," Roxanne assured me. "No worries. Do you know how much I make off one of my regular jobs?"

"More than they would ever . . . ?" I trailed off and heard another affirmative giggle over the line.

I thanked her profusely, she congratulated me, and all was right with the world for one hour. I opened a nice expensive Cabernet I'd been saving (actually for when I wrapped up Helena's case) and clinked a "Cheers" with an empty second glass on the dining table.

♦

I was cleaning out the fireplace later, muttering "slob" at myself because of the Pyramids of Ash Giza behind the grate when there was a knock at the door. Uh-huh. That meant a) someone had got past the security lock in the foyer, and b) it could be trouble, because if they were a friendly face, they could have buzzed me through the intercom.

"Hello?"

There was a rustle at my feet, and I looked down. Sliding under the door was a pen sketch of Donald Duck. You'd swear it came off a DVD box. Now Roxanne was a good artist, really good, but even she couldn't rip off a Disney character from memory like that. I only knew one person with cartoon drawing talent.

"Hello?" came the voice behind the door.

Simon. At my home. My *real* home. Not tracking me down through Helena. Who knows how he found me, since my phone number's ex-directory.

Okay, he's here. So deal.

Behind the still locked door: "Miss Knight, I have this wonderful proposition for investment involving RNA strands to use for—"

"All right, all right," I said, and I opened the door and waved him in.

"Anything to drink?" And he cast a hopeful glance at the bottle of Cabernet and the still-empty second glass on the dining table.

"Don't push it," I warned.

"Nice catching up with you, too," he answered cheerfully. "How was your date with Ayako?" When I didn't respond, keeping my face carefully blank, he added, "That good, eh?"

"Don't be too smug. There's always the chance you'll have to go neon some night with Vivian."

He made a dramatic show of trembling at the thought. "Ugh. You're just being cruel."

"What are you up to, Simon?"

"I might ask you the same thing, darling," he replied. "Aslan Biosciences? I particularly like the market slogan: 'From cell to sell.' Nice touch."

I tried a lame bluff. "Who's to say I'm not working for them? That's pretty insulting of you, Si."

He was roaring now. "Oh, please! Maybe others will buy 'smokescreen-dot-co-dot-uk,' but I'm not. It took one quick trip to Companies House to check your business registration. The rest of 'em must be pretty dim! And if I remember correctly, you don't even have a humble Bachelor of Sciences or an MBA, let alone what you'd need to evaluate biotech start-ups!"

I sighed. Give it up, Teresa. "Okay, you know. So what do you want, Simon?"

"I want to know what you're after."

I scoffed at that. "I can't tell you that! You could be the bastard responsible."

He seemed to look above my head as a revelation hit him, muttering, "*Shit.* Why didn't I see it before? And it's so fucking obvious."

"Go ahead and share." And if you're wrong, I thought, I'm not about to dissuade you.

"You're working for Janet Marshall," he said, pacing my living room. "She's up for the High Commission job in South Africa, and someone's putting the squeeze on her. They're going to waltz over to *The Sun* or *News of the World* with nice juicy pictures of her fucking those society types, but first they want to drain her bank account. You do realize they'll take her money and expose her anyway, don't you? You're a fool, Teresa, if you think you can keep a lid on this thing."

"Someone's got to try," I answered. It hardly mattered that he'd guessed wrong about my employer, he was already close enough to the truth. And then he floored me.

"After all that self-righteous arguing of yours back in Sudan, and now you're willing to protect a murderer?" he asked. "Or did you do it yourself? Granted, Lionel Young isn't my model of a businessman, but he had to be the stooge for someone else and to off him for the sake of a political career! Have you actually become one of those . . . ?

How much could she possibly pay you to get you to do a dirty job like—"

Oh, my God, I thought because I had to wonder if he was for real.

Here I was suspecting he might be Lionel's killer. And there he was, thinking the same of me, that I would clean up a politician's messes like some hired gun. He had got it into his head that because he could shoot a man down, anyone could.

And that I had.

Unless he was a very good actor.

"It wasn't you," he said softly, almost to himself. "But if it wasn't you then . . . ?"

Before I could say anything, he added, "Teresa, darling, if you're very smart, you'll tell your Ms. Marshall to book herself a holiday in Martinique or Biarritz or wherever she wants to play and get the hell out of London for a while. And you ought to go with her. This is going to get uglier than I thought."

"Still thinking you know what's best for us, eh, Simon?"

"Teresa, you don't know everything that's going on! Back in the Nuba Mountains, you could say I was playing soldier, but we're *here*. It's a different country this time, a different—"

He cut himself off. I hadn't said a word, simply staring at him. He knew his temper might make him blurt out something important.

"Oh, no," he said, once more cheerful. "I can see this conversation is only going to help one of us."

"You're working for somebody, too, Simon. Tell me who it is."

"Cards on the table, so to speak? Uh-uh. By the way, I like your place."

And with that, he casually walked back to the door and let himself out.

◆

I got two calls at home later in the week, both surprises. The first was that wonderful low voice saying "hello" with such intimate affection that I immediately melted.

"Been a while," I said.

"Yes, I'm sorry about that," said Neil. "You, um, know how I said there was someone I've been close with, and we're on and off again, and . . . ?"

Thud. As in pick up your ego, Teresa.

"And you're on again," I finished for him, trying not to sound pissed off. Well. You predicted a reconciliation, didn't you?

"No, no," he said quickly. And then with a note of bitterness, he added, "They, um, came around a little too late for my taste, and . . ."

"I think you can say *she,* babe," I told him. "It's not making it any more delicate, taking the gender out of it."

He laughed self-consciously and answered, "You don't let a guy get away with anything, do you? Okay. *She* came by and we talked, just talked. And I've had a chance to review our relationship and how this person isn't exactly there for me. Hey, it was you who turned up at the station, not her—"

"Maybe she didn't know," I suggested.

Oh, the lameness.

"She heard about it soon enough," he growled. "Anyway, I think it's time she and I called it a day since we both seem to want different things, and—well, I didn't really call to talk about her. I was hoping you and I could go out Friday night. Maybe do something normal couples do and keep our

clothes on for a little while. Not a long time, mind you—"
Infectious laugh again. "But a little. Drinks, dancing, movie?"

"Does it have to be Friday?"

"Oh, hey, you have plans. Sorry, if you got something on
then—"

"Any other night would be wonderful."

"There's a game on Friday night, isn't there?" he asked,
suddenly remembering. And becoming suspicious.

"I think there is, yeah."

"Is that what you've got going?"

Oh, oh.

I took a deep breath. "Look, Neil. I like you. A lot. But
something tells me you've had these same issues with that
'other person.' And I don't feel like filling her shoes, so let's
get this stuff out of the way right now. I won't ask you to
give up anything—for the time being—if you do the same.
Then if it's good, we can see where it leads. You go and
think about what you really want. Then call if you still
want to be in the dark with me. At a movie or anything
else."

I heard him say my name, but he got tongue-tied. No
counter-argument ready. I took advantage of the pause to
say, "Talk to you later, babe."

He wouldn't know how much I really, *really* wanted him
to call me back.

♦

Second phone call. Even less pleasant and even more out of
the blue. From, of all people, Anthony Boulet, Janet's political right-hand man.

"Teresa, do you have an operative in your employ? You
got a contract fellow who does research or something?"

"I wish!" I said, blown away by the question.

"I'd like to believe you," said Anthony in that peevish way he had, which instantly got my hackles up. "But entertaining the notion for the moment that you don't want to be candid with me, I'll ask you to please call off your dogs."

"I don't know what you're talking about."

"I thought I made it very clear at the awards how loyal I am to Janet. And frankly, I'm insulted you or your ... your Richmond-upon-Thames Madam friend could think I'd have anything to do with this! Let alone murder that loose faggot who—"

"Whoa, whoa!" I said. "What the hell are you talking about?"

"I am talking about your white shill going around digging into my old cases. I do have friends in court archives—the CPS, the Met, the Beeb, all over—and I'm onto you. I know you're doing your job, but I am telling you now: back off. You are barking up the wrong tree, and if you keep it up, it just might fall on you."

Click.

Simon. Couldn't be sure, but my best guess. Digging around and thinking Anthony was a suspect as well? Or was he our culprit, and he was out to create more chaos?

I wouldn't know how to rein him in even if I knew what he was up to.

◆

The Lotus Eaters is one of those private *SW* clubs in London with a very exclusive members' list. There's the attached hotel, an impressive gym, plus a chef who could perhaps spin off on his own and do a Jamie Oliver books/TV/endorsement thing but knows how good he's got it. Saudis are welcome, but no football icons, material girls, or disgraced author MPs who, having served their sentence, now want to be welcomed back to the fold. They hold a lot of posh events there. Sometimes people get naked at them.

Naturally, the poker crowd I'd been seeing lately were all members, except for Giradeau (who maybe wasn't going to be around long enough, or perhaps they didn't want an American) and, surprisingly, Vivian. I would have thought these would be choice hunting grounds for her—not for lovers, necessarily, but for her next financial merger, i.e., a good marriage.

I was wearing another long skirt with a deep slit up the side and an elegant black halter top with a tie neck and sequins around the trim, and I found relatively low heels worked better for the sweep and movement of the skirt. One thing for sure, if I had a bad run tonight, I'd be naked as a jaybird in only three hands. And maybe that was my point. I looked forward to losing, to showing off. I scared myself in liking this so much.

I held out a perverse hope that Neil might actually show up for the game. I had this bizarre fantasy that he would turn up as he had for Janet Marshall in the past, and we would go through the motions of a game merely to be in each other's arms. Put on a show like we did the first time.

Another part of me, however, tingled with anticipation about the unknown, about who I might win or lose to.

Neil didn't show. Mercifully, neither did Simon.

But Ayako did. And so did George. And Daniel. And Gary Cahill. And Vivian.

And Janet Marshall.

♦

Obviously, she had had her fill of playing it safe. Black-mailer or no, she wanted to have fun. No Neil holding her back anymore. She'd show *him*.

"We've missed you, darling," said Cahill. "What's the oc-casion for the return of our prodigal daughter?"

"Independence Day," laughed Janet. She gave me a wink, and it was clear she was tipsy.

"As far as I'm concerned," said Janet boisterously, "this is my night! We only live once, right, Teresa?"

I gave Janet a neutral smile and said, "You want to pack all your living into one go, huh?"

"How is it you Americans put it?" giggled Janet, nudging Giradeau. And then she mimicked a Brooklyn accent as best she could, declaring, "Goddamn straight!"

We played Texas Hold'Em. Nobody expected Janet would play very well when she was so obviously pickled. She was caught out in what seemed to be a couple of silly bluffs and a few lacklustre hands, and it wasn't long before I saw that lovely body I admired for her age live and in person at the table. I even spotted a couple of the stunts she taught me to distract the men. She was witty, she was giggly, she was drinking two drinks to my one, and then she blew us all away by betting the men at the table a rug burn. Not one fellow. All of them.

"You mean F.O.D.?" I asked.

So that she could call in her markers and spread them over a week or something.

"Oh, no!" laughed Janet. "I want an assembly line right here!" Sounding a little too much like Vivian tonight.

Of course, none of them folded. They were guaranteed sex whether they won or lost, the hand a flimsy charade. Not that the cards mattered anymore, but Janet took them all with a straight.

She clapped her hands together like a little girl, throwing back her head and declaring, "*Yes!* Come on, boys!"

She was going neon with all the trimmings, three guys of her choice. And I looked on as the woman who could be our ambassador to South Africa giggled and threw herself down on the rug, opening her legs so that everyone had a generous view of her shaven pussy. Her glistening labia and her hangman's clit. George cast one guilty look my way, his mouth freezing into a tight line of resentment, and I said nothing. I understood. If I didn't want him then he was a grown boy, free to pursue Janet if he wished. And he had wanted her for a while.

As he pawed her full tits, Janet was already breathing hard, and then Cahill thrust in his thin needle of a cock. I watched George kiss Janet greedily, and Cahill came in an anti-climactic rush. Janet half yelped, half laughed, saying, "Wait a minute" before she rolled onto her knees. Giradeau and Cahill traded places, Giradeau fucking her from behind, and now Janet moaned loudly. I was embarrassed yet spellbound. It was one thing to see Vivian, Ayako or one of the other girls in the throes, but Janet—

George still kissed her, but she showed little passionate interest in him—too distracted by the pounding fullness in her vagina. George's hand in her hair, tracing two fingers along her open lips, wiping the perspiration from her forehead. She gritted her teeth as she came, and Giradeau kept hammering away, his hands squeezing the cheeks of her wide backside. At last he seemed to swoon as he pumped her full of his cum, draping himself over her back for a moment, wanting to feel her tits before he fell away.

Then it was finally George's turn, pausing only a moment to insist she roll onto her back, and he opened her legs anxiously before he took his penis in his right hand and guided himself in. He was a construction worker on the job, wanting to drill her violently, and perhaps from other games he knew what would get her off. I watched her second orgasm build in her eyes, brimming with cathartic tears. I watched George come with a long groan, the way his middle-aged buttocks tensed with surprisingly youthful vigour. I was past my embarrassment. It made me wet, watching her taken like that by multiple partners. I was barely conscious of how I had begun anxiously touching myself through a fold of my skirt.

Me with my breasts out and my nipples hard, my halter top long gone, with only a skirt on and no panties. And then Ayako. Completely, exquisitely nude. Her hand down there under my skirt. Fondling me, making me gasp and lean against her. I didn't mind at all. Her little body could be so warm, and tonight she tasted like cherries. Her clever little hands, one of them down below, one of them cupping my tit, squeezing and circling, squeezing and circling in a rhythm she knew drove me wild. Her small white teeth nibbled my earlobe.

I had the uncomfortable mild fear that the men would tire of Janet and turn to Ayako or me and expect us to join in. There was something vaguely unpleasant in the idea of becoming contestant number two for this gang of stud bulls tonight. It was too raw, all because of Janet's open need. And yet I was turned on by the spectacle, couldn't tear myself away. They all knew Ayako had won her F.O.D. with me, so let them think I'm a bi case. And I didn't really know how much was an act for the others' benefit anymore.

George, quietly lying back after his ride with Janet, turned to watch us. He was getting a fresh new hard-on from Ayako's pale fingers on my dark pussy.

He went over to the panting Janet and gave it to her all over again.

She came twice from Giradeau's second turn. She played with her clit to get off while Cahill had another go. He never lasted very long.

By that time, I had turned away, kissing Ayako while all her fingers were inside me, and with my back to the group, only she knew I was stifling a whimper over my own climax.

I leaned against the poker table exhausted, and then I excused myself, glancing over my shoulder to see what was starting to happen in my absence. George Westlake wanted to fuck Ayako. He seemed to always be trying to make it with exotic beauties.

She laughed in his face and said something like "Earn it, George!"

Perhaps meaning the game. And then she turned to Cahill and let him suck on her middle finger, knowing that it had been inside me.

Then it all got too much, as if the group lust in the room manufactured a phoney dry-ice fog that merely blocked you from glimpsing the smallness of all our humanity. All the rampant fucking was simultaneously glorious and vulgar. I stopped enjoying myself. I couldn't enjoy myself any more here. It's not that I had found my modesty again, sure as hell not any prudery—I wanted one-on-one back. Whatever this spectacle was, you couldn't call anything about it intimate. I ducked into a side room of the suite, plopped myself down on a love seat and was surprised to see violet and purple flashes and spots before my eyes. Dizzy. I shook it off, blinked once and twice, and there was Ayako standing in front of me.

"Do you want to come home with me tonight?" she asked.

"I *want* to," I answered. "But . . ."

I thought of the documents I had swiped from her apartment, how they could be a clue to something sinister or could mean nothing at all. Not that I had found anything more incriminating.

Hypocrite. You were more suspicious of Lionel, even of Neil, and yet you still slept with them. And then there's Giradeau, a suspect as much as Ayako, and you keep getting it on with him—

Ayako looked hurt. After watching her in the games and being intimate with her in her apartment, I had wondered if anything could puncture that veil of cool reserve, could make her feel vulnerable.

"When you're ready," she said, keeping a positive thought, some kind of faith in me, and she leaned over—she didn't have to lean much—and kissed me full on the lips, nudging her tongue inside my mouth. I let her. I returned the kiss and caressed her cheek and offered a silent promise, not knowing yet if I would make it a lie.

◆

I showered—I always showered after one of these games. And then, since we were at The Lotus Eaters, I quickly dressed and headed into the main health club of the complex. Sometimes Helena had brought me in as her guest and I knew it had a big dance studio. Perfect for practising karate forms.

I changed into the *keikogi* I'd brought along in a gym bag, knowing I'd be here tonight. I felt like going back to my roots and doing sensible meat-and-potatoes karate instead of sloppy, undisciplined kickboxing. I worked my way through the practice forms from Heian Shodan all the way up to Nijushiho-dai.

I had worked up a good sweat and was doing punching and kicking drills up and down the hardwood floor when Janet came in, wearing a bright pink leotard. Something told me the outfit was an excuse to talk to me.

"Do you mind if I watch?" she asked politely.

Panting a little from the workout, I shook my head.

"There are windows at the dojo where I train. People watch us all the time."

I went back to the drills. When I had punched and kicked my way to the end of the floor, punctuating my last strike with a loud *kiai,* I stood up formally, staying in the moment long enough for a display of proper awareness. Then I relaxed.

Janet studied me intently. She probably didn't understand all of what I was doing, but she knew intuitively I was good at it.

"What's on your mind?" I asked.

"Oh, nothing . . . everything."

I tried to put her at ease. Politicians, like actors, must have a constant appetite for both attention and reassurance. "We both saw a little too much of each other tonight, I guess."

She smiled faintly. "Maybe. I don't know. Look, I, um, I don't know why I'm going to admit to this, but . . . I haven't cared about the respect of anyone under thirty in quite a while. I haven't needed to cultivate it."

Jeez, this wasn't necessary. "Janet, look . . ."

"And then along came Neil, and sure, I paid for him the first few times because I was lonely, but . . . He is under thirty, and he can get armies of girls half my age, but he's interested in *me.* I always figured I would have to give him up sooner or later, and I tried to prepare myself for it, but it's still going to hurt. And then he chases after you—"

"Well, about that—"

"No, please, let me finish. This is hard enough as it is. I'm not going to say what I think you expect me to."

She looked down. She looked away. Everywhere but in my eyes. "I see how strong you are. Up here." She tapped her forehead for reference. "You're no man's fool, are you? Not ever."

"I hope not."

"My husband," she said distantly, eyes shining. "I loved that man for decades. When we made love, it was good but no angels wept over our heads or anything. I had my daughter, we raised her, and I got on with my career and never even looked twice at another man. And after he died, I didn't know what to do with myself. I found myself getting horny and feeling ridiculous, hardly experienced at all. And maybe my body looks one way, but inside, I don't *feel* older. I certainly don't feel any wiser! I feel the way I did at your age. And okay, maybe I'm fighting gravity and putting a lot of hope in face creams, but I still don't want to go out with sad divorced men with bellies and hard luck tales. I want a firm ass and youth and a nice smile."

"I don't blame you," I smiled.

"You wake up one day, and you ask yourself, who are all your inhibitions for? And so I got into the games, and I find out yeah, there are men who *do* want to fuck me. Still. At my age. The games . . . There's bluffing and there are mind games, but in the end, we know what everyone's there for. If they want you, it's immediate. Sometimes it's even better than with Neil because I'm not wondering for how long? Is he with me for the society? Where are we going? Do we have a future? It's raw. You're just taken. You're . . . Well, you know now. You know what it can be. And tonight . . ."

Tonight? Yes, I understood. Tonight was about being stripped naked beyond clothes. She had wanted to forget Neil, practically obliterate him with a new memory of a parade of cocks filling her one after another, of her own mini-orgy that had her as the star. Tonight wasn't about firm ass and youth. She would make do with George Westlake and Cahill and Giradeau.

We had both abandoned our identities in that room in a haze of alcohol and pot smoke, and my little email lie to my consciousness later would be that I'd been on the job.

She was the second woman in the world after that Japanese girl to see me at my most intimate level, and who knows? Maybe she thought I'd been "faking it."

Here she was, fearing that I considered her a tramp.

Janet Marshall. She just kept on lobbying me. And it always made me withdraw. I wished she hadn't come down there.

◆

I was lying in bed, enjoying a pretty good dream. I was back on a holiday in Paris that had turned into a case, only this time there were no au pairs from Somalia and no cops, just me walking down to the big Galerie Layfayette. I was laughing and holding hands with Ayako.

I heard her voice in that faraway muffled dream sound you get when you're asleep. She told me: *We should do it at the cosmetics counter.* And then suddenly we were upstairs in the bathroom fixture department, all shiny chrome shower-heads and pale blue tiles. And I was in a full bathtub under a blanket of bubble foam (it's a dream, don't ask where the water came from). Ayako had a flannel and was soaping my breasts while customers walked by, and then her dainty white hand dipped into the water and fingered me—

When the hand shook my shoulder, I was flustered and disoriented.

222 · LISA LAWRENCE

Helena's very real and audible voice informed me: "Our girl is in a *shitload* of trouble!"

I rubbed my eyes and said, "What? What are you talking about?"

I threw back the covers and, nude, searched for my robe. Oh, man, I barely remembered coming over to stay in Richmond.

A tall side of pale beef, brunette with a nice six-pack and great biceps, padded naked into the doorway with a coffee pot and said absently, "Hel, I couldn't find the stuff you wanted so I whipped up a batch with the Kenyan—that all right, luv?"

I heard what sounded vaguely like Aussie accent. He and I inspected each other for a shocked two seconds, and the long thick member between his legs twitched with fresh life. He blushed and darted behind the wall, saying, "Oh, Christ, I'm sorry! Didn't know—morning!"

"Down, children," Helena told both of us.

"He came from a land down under?" I asked. Couldn't resist.

"Get dressed," she told me, helping me into the robe. "And keep your hands off my fruit."

"Fruit?"

"Kiwi."

"Nice," I said.

She pulled me by the hand into her bedroom, where her large-screen Sony was switched on to the BBC Breakfast show. I saw camera footage of yellow caution tape in front of a smart-looking door. Then a photo inset with the caption MURDER, and cut to a huddle of cops, Carl Norton looking his deeply focussed, rumpled self.

The reporter was ticking off the facts in an appropriately sombre voice: "Anthony Boulet's body was found early this

morning at his Islington house. The high-profile black solicitor was apparently surprised in his home by a burglar.
Cause of death has been confirmed as strangulation by a
rope or cord. No word yet on what was taken from the home
of the man considered to be one of the most prominent
voices in the black community for more than ..."

10

M r. Boulet's wife has been on holiday, visiting family in Jamaica with their daughter, and he was in the house alone," the reporter droned on. "Their 22-year-old son lives and studies in Florida. Police had no comment on a tabloid report this morning claiming that Mr. Boulet had booked a minicab for around one AM to go to the home of Janet Marshall, his longtime friend and collaborator on many high-profile government and equal opportunity initiatives . . ."

"Oh, *shit*!" I said.

"Where did the bastards get that?" thundered Helena.

"Easy," I said in a monotone voice. "They don't say who discovered his body. If his wife and kids are out of town, who's left? Either a neighbour heard a commotion and went to investigate, or he was in plain view to the cab driver through his front window. And one of those little PC shits on the case leaked it. Or maybe the dispatcher phoned up the newspaper for a quick pound."

"Oh, God, this is awful," said Helena. "It's all innuendo.

Who's to know why Anthony would want to come see her in the middle of the night? But the way it looks—"

"Where is she now?" I asked. "Have you tried to reach her?"

"I got you up first."

"Assume her home phone will be ringing off the hook," I told her. "You must have her mobile. Try that."

She did. Janet's mobile was switched off, which meant all we could do was wait. It stood to reason that by now she was either being questioned by the cops or had gone to ground after they'd tracked her down.

I was having guilt pangs myself because I had probably dug the hole a little deeper for her. In letting Carl know that I was dealing with a blackmail case over a Highly Esteemed Personage, it was a no-brainer to connect the dots from Anthony Boulet to Janet Marshall. And if something as ridiculous as the minicab booking could leak out then the whole deck of cards could be spilled into the open.

We went downstairs to have breakfast with the Kiwi, still looking very hunky in a sleeveless T-shirt and faded plaid pyjama bottoms. He was pretty dumb, didn't have a clue about the most basic London tourist sites (Helena had picked him up in a club), but he was still adorable, and I have to say he was a class act. He whipped us up Spanish omelettes.

At four in the afternoon, Helena's doorbell rang, and I opened it to see Janet on the front step, looking very worn out but still in one piece.

"Shit!" I said. "You okay? Get in here."

"I'm all right," she muttered.

Helena rushed forward, and in one smooth motion she had three Scotch glasses out and a bottle. I swore I never saw her break stride at her bar.

◆

Pizza. The police knew Janet was innocent, not even involved and didn't have a clue that Anthony wanted to see
her—because of pizza.

After her OTT behaviour at the poker game, she felt a
wave of remorse and went over to Neil's, insisting she loved
him, please take her back, and that she didn't understand
how their relationship got so complicated. They both liked
their fun, had always thought they were both sophisticated
and had strong enough self-esteem to indulge other appetites, get variety, blah, blah, blah. But jealousy was Human
Nature 101. Irrational. Inevitable. Makes grown adults do
stupid things. Now the two of them had to figure out what
they wanted.

Terrific. That's the advice I gave Neil on the phone. I kind
of expected he'd be doing the figuring out over *me*.

"We talked for hours, just holding each other and hash-
ing it all out."

She avoided my eyes as she said this, and I recognised
that she took no cruel pleasure in defeating me for Neil's affection. No wish to pay me back for my brief dalliance with
him.

"I hadn't eaten anything, and he said he was hungry,
too, so we ordered out," she explained. "I'm the one who
made the call, and I answered the door."

"You're damn lucky the delivery guy remembered you,"
said Helena.

"At the door, I realized I didn't have enough pound coins
to make up the bill for the pizza, so the fellow had to wait
while Neil fished around for some extra money."

The police checked and had established that Anthony
never placed any calls from his mobile or his home phone
to Janet. Not to her mobile, not to her house and not to
Neil's, assuming he even had the number. He merely booked
the minicab to shoot over to her house in Notting Hill.

Janet looked out the window. "God. So right when I'm with Neil, poor Anthony . . . And he was trying to get hold of me." Her eyes brimmed with tears.

I sat down directly in front of her, trying to get her to focus. We were far from out of the woods. "What did the police ask you about the blackmail?"

"Th—they didn't," she answered, mildly surprised at the question. "How could they know? They don't know, do they?" She looked from me to Janet.

"Not yet," I said.

I'd been worrying earlier about Carl making the natural connection from Anthony to Janet, and from Janet back to me, already connected to Lionel. But since there was nothing so far to tie Anthony's murder to Lionel's, he probably thought at the moment he was dealing with two unrelated homicides. After all, he knew I worked for a Highly Esteemed Personage, but he didn't know which one—not yet. If so, good. It bought us time.

"I think you better tell us about Anthony now," I suggested.

Janet still wore her expression of baffled innocence. "What do you mean?"

"You were seeing him," I said. "Come on. If we're going to help you, we have to know everything."

Helena was baffled, too, only her surprise was genuine. "Janet?"

Our stateswoman sat on the couch, the edges of her mouth flickering in a sad smile as she asked me, "How did you figure it out?"

"The clincher is that he didn't phone before booking the cab to come over," I explained. "He must have presumed you were home. Who makes presumptions like that? Lovers do. Even friends call to see if you're there before they swing by. But a lover could drop in, and he would have a key. He could wait. You also gave yourself away that night at the awards. You told me Anthony was there when the blackmail note arrived. Well, weeks ago, you said the note was slipped through your mail slot first thing on a Saturday morning. And if he was there, my bet is he slept over. Right?"

"Yes," she said quietly. "Yes, he did."

"The night of the awards, I actually began to consider Anthony as a suspect. After all, it would have been so easy for him to slip the blackmail note into your mail slot from the inside when you weren't paying attention. This is a man who told me he 'didn't like people who couldn't control their passions.' Mix in a little guilt and self-loathing over cheating on his wife along with an obsessed devotion to you, and it added up to motive. But I gave that idea up."

"Why?" asked Helena.

"Because Lionel still doesn't compute in a jealousy scenario. Why kill him and not Neil? Anthony told me himself how Neil once showed up and caused a scene at an awards banquet. That's the guy he'd be pissed at, not Lionel. And if he was trying to frame Neil, remember, the police only questioned him for Lionel's murder because of a really weak connection with one of Lionel's old girlfriends, a girl named Shondi. I've met her. She doesn't have a clue about you or your life or any of this. And I would be utterly *amazed* if Anthony had ever heard of this girl. All of this speculation doesn't matter anymore now that Anthony is . . ." I sighed. "How was your relationship with him recently?"

"A little strained sometimes, but nothing serious," answered Janet. "I think we both knew it couldn't last. It had pretty much run its course—especially when I got word that Neil was pulled in for questioning. Anthony knew I'd rush to support him."

Yeah, sure. Except that I was the one waiting for him outside the police station. Let it go, Teresa.

"Did Anthony ever come to the poker games?"

"Oh, no," said Janet. "He was appalled that I went! I started going before we got involved, and at first he reacted with this stern disapproval mixed with concern. I told him it was my life, and then after a while, it became a kind of strange in-joke between us. We'd been friends for a long time, and I teased him sometimes with these anecdotes about what went on there. It didn't make him want to go, but maybe . . ."

"Maybe it inspired him to start thinking of you romantically," I suggested.

She nodded. "His kids were grown. His wife is a wonderful person, but they had grown apart. The usual. He insisted the poker games were sordid, but I'm sure he liked some of the spicy details."

"But he never tried it himself?" I asked again. "Not even once?"

She shook her head again. So did Helena.

"What are you thinking, darling?" Helena asked me.

"About motive," I said. "Yes, it stands to reason our killer would assume you'd confide in Anthony about the blackmail. But this is a guy who never came to the games, was outside the circle. In fact, he made almost as good a target as you. High-profile solicitor, well paid, loving wife—perfect for blackmail."

"Yes," said Janet softly. "And now he's dead."

"I'm convinced this is definitely not about sex, and Anthony's murder will prove it." I pointed to Janet. "Is there any chance Anthony would have given you keys to his office for any reason?"

"No," she answered. "No, he had no reason to these days."

"Too bad," I said. "I guess it's back to breaking and entering."

◆

They call it "scrubbing." Basically, you use the lock pick to "scrub" back and forth over the pins while you adjust the amount of torque on the plug, the cylinder that rotates when you insert the proper key. I could get into the whole thing about *wards* and *sheer line* and all that jazz, but no, I'm not supposed to have these kinds of tools, and you should go blame Steve, a tall, bearded shoe-repair and key-cutting guy who looks like a Wookiee and who taught me this stuff at his shop in Stanmore. It's useful to make different kinds of friends.

God bless these traditionalists who had yet to put in alarms.

I was using my picks on a door not far from that quiet island of Barrister Central that sits between the Victoria Embankment and Fleet Street. You turn off the Strand and duck into these mazes and courtyards, and you're passing buildings that go back to the 16th century. You need a map, not because it's big, just confusing, and when I passed the spacious lawn and Temple Church, I knew I had to be crazy. There were regular foot patrol constables that wandered through here and the surrounding streets, and the stunt I had in mind was really dangerous.

But since Anthony Boulet had been a solicitor, not a barrister, his office wasn't at one of the Inns of Court—he'd rented it a short distance away on one of the main streets. Slightly less conspicuous. Helena insisted on tagging along to play getaway driver, but we made Janet wait back at the house in Richmond.

I was in Anthony Boulet's office in ninety seconds. Steve would have been ashamed of me. What can I say? Out of practice.

232 · LISA LAWRENCE

There's a wonderful company in Hounslow that sells beds. They'll deliver them and actually set them up for you, and when they come into your house they put on these slippers that must be made out of the same material as cheap shower caps. Nice considerate touch, respectful of your clean floor and all that. So I'm inspired to wear these over my shoes every time I go out on one of my little trespassing whims, which, yeah, are more frequent than I'd like to admit. I promise I'll get therapy. Right after Helena writes me a big fat cheque. Or maybe after the next one.

Anthony Boulet's office had a décor like most solicitors. If you can afford the rent, you probably have enough to decorate to impress, and this looked like a showroom for The Bombay Company. Books. Antiques. Stuffy. Pompous. Old World globe in the corner. Brass astrolabe as a curio on his desk in between stand-up framed photos of his wife and kids. I couldn't see any evidence that the cops had been here yet, but I assumed they had and would probably come back.

They'd be trying to figure out if anything in Anthony's work could be connected to his murder. But since he wasn't with Crown Prosecution, had never defended your average thug in court and had dealt with corporate and quango clients I bet they'd think there were slim pickings.

I sat down at his desk. And when I booted up his computer, I saw something interesting. Up came the annoying blue screen with that message or a similar one that most of us know:

Because this program was not properly shut down, one or more of your disk drives may have errors on it. Scanpal is now checking drive C for errors.

If he hadn't shut down properly, was it because he'd been in a hurry? Or perhaps he was interrupted.

A bit frustrating, trying to type in gloves. Helena was

outside, sitting with a digital camera around her neck, trying to play tourist. She also had a whistle, which she would blow if it looked like a presence of the Met was about to set foot near the door. Since it was Sunday, I was hoping they would wait.

I clicked on "Recent Documents" and got a long list of files. The older ones had surnames, and when I called them up, they were password protected. Frankly, it was the newer ones that caught my eye, files with incomprehensible names like "capac.doc" and "tan." (As in the colour "tan"? For what, though? Maybe a company name?)

But when I tried to bring them up, all I got for each one was the little flashlight icon that told me the computer was searching. All deleted.

When I checked in his Internet Properties folder, someone had wiped his links and cleared the history.

Shit. Whatever had happened to Lionel, Anthony had definitely been murdered over something bigger than the strip poker games. The answer was on this computer despite what the killer thought. Just because you delete files doesn't mean they're not still sitting on your hard drive, where brilliant geeks can do their voodoo to call them back to life.

I knew a few such geeks, guys as handy with computer viruses and "worms" as my buddy was with a lock pick, but to involve them in this would be a major risk and pain in the ass, since I would have to bring them here (ha, ha, yeah, right, Teresa) or remove evidence from a crime scene, which would be a major no-no.

Maybe I didn't have to.

I crouched down to use my smaller picks on Anthony's desk drawers, and that's when I saw it. I don't think I would have noticed had I not bent on my knees and got the lower perspective to work the drawers.

Lying on the rug, a little under the desk at the opposite

234 · LISA LAWRENCE

end and barely perceptible, was a tiny pile of white powder. What the heck was it and what was it doing there? Then it came to me, because this is what you get when you drop a pill and you accidentally step on it. Paracetamol pancake or whatever it was.

And the desk had been moved. There were two deep indentations for one of its legs, as if it had been pushed, and then someone had realized it had better be pushed back. And since this was a small room, there was no logical reason why it should be moved at all except that one or perhaps two people had hit it with enough force.

A struggle. Anthony had met his killer here in his office first.

I got up and went around to the front of the desk. It was difficult to see, given the darkness of the stain on the dark oak, but it was there, and Carl's forensic colleagues would pick it up. Tiny spatters of blood. My guess? They came from Anthony's defensive wounds in a struggle. Cut knuckles, a scrape, something small.

Anthony Boulet was strangled—a rope, a cord, something that would have left marks on his neck, identified by the authorities. The choice of murder weapon dictated how much attention the killer paid to covering his tracks. Had Anthony been knifed with a large blade, there would have been more blood—enough that the killer would make an attempt at cleaning up. After all, he moved the body so the police would think the murder didn't happen here.

Clever bastard. He must have overheard Anthony phone the minicab company, or he was sitting right across from him when he placed the call. He dumped the body back at his victim's house, and the minicab showing up would bolster the idea that Anthony must have been murdered there.

It was a tight window, but he had made it. The cab was to show up at 1:00 AM, and Anthony was discovered at 1:12 AM.

My mobile rang. I nearly jumped out of my skin. Helena.

"Are you going to be much longer? This is starting to wear on my nerves, darling."

"Come to the door and bring that camera of yours."

"Oh, God! We're going to get caught. Teresa, I cannot handle small spaces with bars. I don't want to be some horrible guard's sex slave!"

"I'll visit you every day in the exercise yard. Now get over here."

I watched her approach from the window, and when she was outside the door, she stretched out her arm to hand me the camera like it was a bomb. Poor Helena. A fantastic Madam. Great at Scotch and sympathy, brilliant hostess. Lousy at special ops.

I clicked off a dozen or more pictures of the room with fine close-ups of the powder, the blood spray and what sat on Anthony's desk. I had no idea if they would be useful or not, but I thought I'd better have them for reference.

Then I rifled through the desk drawers and discovered something else important. There were limits to our killer's imagination. And he definitely wasn't a lawyer. I knew this, because if he were, he wouldn't even have to remember that lawyers *write things down on legal pads*. Nice long yellow foolscap sheets with blue lines. But in our wonderful age of technology, you get a bit of tunnel vision about other people's habits.

Sure enough, there was a pad with Anthony's chicken scratches, leaving me only a little better off than I was moments earlier. I knew I was on the right track because I could make out the date he had scribbled out, which happened to be for the very night he died. The pages underneath were dated going back two weeks, some pages marked with only a couple of lines, some filled to bursting with tinier scribbles into his self-made margins.

"Tan" on his machine became "tant" on the yellow paper. *Tant*. Tant? Whatever it meant to him, he must have simply abbreviated it further when he named the file. I got lucky in that "capac.doc" finally made sense in his handwriting as "electronic capacitors."

There were references to manufacturing plants, components named and where they came from, statistics on quantities. One of the companies named in a list was Lionel's. Buccaneer Cape Mining. Warmer, getting warmer—

But what did Anthony Boulet care about mining? And what did he care about the manufacture of electronic capacitors and where the raw materials came from?

I went to the photocopier, turned it on and let it warm up. Then I dashed off legal-size copies of all the pages. That would certainly show up on the machine's count, but there was nothing I could do about that. Hopefully, the police would overlook that minor detail. Done, I replaced the legal pad exactly as I'd found it, locked up the drawers of the desk and beat the hell out of there.

Helena was standing on the curb, tugging on her ring finger and bouncing a little on her heels like she had to wee. The perfect accomplice.

When we got in her car, I rang Carl at his home.

"What's up?"

"I'm psychic," I announced. "Let me test it out on you. Your lab people have found thanks to the post-mortem lividity that Anthony Boulet's body was moved."

I heard Carl groan at the other end. "Teresa. I'm getting another one of my headaches. Sandra is pushing Mark's stroller even now to Tesco's, and I had this nice afternoon all to myself with Dostoyevsky. Why are you pissing down on my sunshine, mate?"

"Dostoyevsky's overrated. Listen. If you go to Boulet's

office, you'll see a struggle happened there. Tiny blood splat-ter residue and what looks like a crushed pill on the floor. Could be nothing, but I'd really like to know what it is. Will you tell me?"

"Teresa . . ."

"And the killer deleted files from his hard drive."

"I am not hearing any of this—"

"Good news is," I rolled along, "he overlooked Anthony Boulet's notes in his desk. Carl? About that pill left on the floor?"

"Teresa, if this is about his work, does she know anything?"

She. Well, he's not an Inspector for nothing. Might as well be honest with him.

"I don't think so," I sighed. "Whatever it is, it won't leap out at you from the page."

"I'll have to bring her in for more questions."

"When do you want to talk to me?"

Another groan. "Is there anything else you can tell me?"

"Not much."

"If I dragged you into an interrogation room, would it make any difference?"

"To be honest . . ."

I glanced at Helena sitting next to me driving, looking more relaxed and back to her old self. She could get a shark of a solicitor in half an hour if I needed one.

"Thought so," sighed Carl, and he rang off.

◆

Damn it, what was this guy after?

Earl's Court. Hot bath. Herbal tea. Telly on mute. Playing a *Girlfriends* rerun in the middle of the afternoon. On the stereo, Skunk Anansie singing "Just Because You Feel Good."

I was thinking about our bad guy. Mulling. He had killed Lionel and had enjoyed himself doing it. He had murdered Anthony Boulet, but it looked like that was a rushed job, one prompted by necessity. Boulet had to have been close to tripping over something incriminating.

So what the hell was it? What tied a mining company executive to a solicitor investigating the sale of electronics parts to a black female politician and made them all so important that—

The fog lifted. Suddenly it was all so obvious. Janet would have seen it herself had she not been so close, distracted by her own conflicted feelings for Anthony and Neil and what to do if she got the new appointment. I towelled off and practically ran to my desk.

I booted up the computer and went online. Google fed me a whole bunch of archived links on Janet's speeches, and it was all there.

Maybe innocuous to you and me, but ringing an alarm for somebody.

Somebody with money. Somebody who had enough of it to hire operatives.

I rang Helena. "I need to see you and Janet."

There was a sigh from the other end of the phone. "That might prove a little difficult. She's lying low at her house in Notting Hill until the reporters lose interest in Anthony Boulet."

"She'll want to come out for this," I answered. "I think I've discovered what this is all about."

A surprised silence from the other end of the line. "Oh," she said gently.

"And Helena, I think I'd better move in with you for a little while."

"I pay you enough to make rent, darling."

"Very funny. It's the safe thing to do. Trust me."

A sigh of mock exasperation. "If you must. Well, don't expect a mint left on the pillow. But don't you think you ought to stick close to Janet? Wouldn't that make more sense?"

"No, I think she's safe for now. I'll explain more when I get there."

I rang off before she could ask any more questions. I didn't want to confirm her fears over the line, and it was bad enough that she suspected what I was thinking—that she could be targeted as the next murder victim.

♦

A quick ride on the District Line, and I was at the house. I was surprised when Janet showed up only twenty minutes later. I expected her to have more trouble ducking the journos camped outside, but she informed us their numbers were down. There was a good reason for that.

The good news was that the TV reporters were still calling Anthony a "trusted colleague" and "friend" of Janet Marshall and not picking up on the innuendoes in the tabloids or the occasional hint of speculation in the broadsheets. If it became a nightly story for BBC or Channel Four, she could kiss the ambassadorship goodbye.

Thankfully the coverage took a hard right turn that very day because of the Met investigation.

There was my old pal, Carl Norton, unflappable in the scrum of cameras and microphones, making a public statement.

"We now believe," he told the reporters, "that Mr. Boulet was murdered not over any personal grudges or involvements but because of an investigation into criminal activity he was conducting himself and was close to bringing to the attention of the authorities."

Bless you, Carl.

"What's the nature of this criminal activity?" asked one of the reporters.

"We cannot divulge that at this time." But in point of fact, I was pretty sure they simply didn't know. I did, but it had only come to me in a lightning flash of insight about an hour before the news conference.

In the jumpy, hand-held camera view, Carl kept marching towards the double doors of a police station. "I've read our statement, and I'm sorry, but we can't answer any further questions regarding the case—"

Of course, the reporters ignored this. "Is Ms. Marshall aware of what Mr. Boulet was working on?"

There was a millisecond pause before he decided to field that one. "No, Ms. Marshall has no knowledge whatsoever of what Mr. Boulet was looking into. We now believe he was trying to contact her that evening to divulge his findings, and that his late hour of the cab booking was due to his feeling of urgency."

"Then you've formally questioned Ms. Marshall?"

"I'm sorry, no more questions. You have our statement."

The flurry of fresh questions started up again, but the doors closed behind him, and the scrum was faced with three burly constables making sure they didn't follow him in. Helena muted the sound on the television.

I turned to Janet. "When did they question you again?"

"Very early this morning. That detective was quite a gentleman about it, I must say. He apologised and said it would be better if we met at about five. His men would create a distraction for the photographers downstairs. So five o' clock came, and from my window, I watched them all scrambling down the road because a couple of tow trucks came along for their cars. I have no idea what excuse the police used, but I can't say I felt very sorry for those men."

I smiled. Carl once told me he had thought of going into engineering instead of police work, and it was just like him to come up with a mechanical solution to humans being a pain in the ass.

"What did you tell Carl about Anthony?"

"The truth."

Both Helena and I were instantly sputtering in surprise. "The *truth*! Why would—"

"No, no," said Janet quickly. "I didn't talk about us, and they didn't ask. I meant the truth about his work—I haven't a clue what Anthony was working on. And I got the impression neither do they."

"Good," I said. "Did they say they'll need you for further inquiries? Do they want to bring you back?"

She shook her head.

"Okay, I think they will, but if you're smart, you won't volunteer what I'm about to tell you. I think I finally know what this is all about."

They waited.

I rolled my eyes, thinking how I had come full circle to fighting against the plunderers of Africa again.

"Coltan," I said. "It's about Coltan."

11

Janet didn't react for a moment. Too flabbergasted to speak.

"But ... But the threats! Lionel being tortured and killed, Anthony's murder! Are you telling me someone went to all this trouble, killed these men just for—"

"It's not a lot of trouble," I broke in. "Not from their point of view. You know yourself we're talking about billions."

Helena was lost. "Would one of you like to fill me in here? I haven't a bloody clue what's going on or what Coltan is or what either of you are talking about."

"It's got to be right here in this room," said Janet with a sad smile, "or the end product, more precisely." She was still trying to get her head around the idea that this was the cause.

I took Helena through it, explaining how it was a substance that looked like black mud, heavier than iron but only slightly lighter than gold, made up of columbium and tantalum, hence *Col-tan*. Refine the tantalum, and you get a great conductor of electricity. Fantastic heat resistance. Perfect for tiny circuit boards.

"It's in your laptop, Helena, your pocket organiser, and you couldn't have mobile phone networks without it. That's a billion-pound industry right there. They use it in aviation and atomic energy plants, too. The biggest mines for the stuff at the moment are in Australia, but . . ."

"But everyone thinks most of the world reserves are in central Africa," said Janet, picking up the thread. "Right in the Congo. *That's* what's behind all the continuing bloodshed, not all this rubbish in the media about tribal fighting." I heard the note of simmering outrage in her voice over the issue.

"I don't understand," said Helena innocently.

Janet leaned forward on the sofa. "About five . . .? No, six years ago, a bunch of Tutsi rebels with backing from Uganda and Rwanda tried to topple the Congolese president. They made out he was sheltering Hutu militias who slaughtered the Tutsis in Rwanda. So armies from Angola, Zimbabwe, Namibia and Chad all came in, supposedly to back the Congo. But it was really an excuse to make a grab for the Coltan. There's always this talk about fighting Africans, but Helena, that war was funded by a whole slew of European and *British* companies! There were UK firms that had export licenses to sell them arms, and there are still front companies getting the Coltan out, whether they've got a 'fragile peace' or not. Down there, you've got forced child labour for sifting riverbeds and mining in abandoned mines. There's mass murder, rape and torture going on all for the sake of mobile phones."

"I've never heard anything about this," remarked Helena, "and I like to think I'm reasonably well informed."

"The TV networks don't want to have to explain Africa,

they'd rather show pictures of all the dark people fighting," I said bitterly. "About three years ago, though, the UN came out with a report that implicated a whole list of companies in the Coltan trade at the time."

My hand fell on the mouse of her PC. Her ADSL was already on, and within a few seconds, I had called up the report. There they were: Amalgamated Metal Corp., Afrimex, Euromet, De Beers and on it went.

"These days, you find disclaimers on certain corporate websites all over the place, saying the firms buy their tantalum now from sources outside the Congo. Coltan's not as easy to trace back as, say, conflict diamonds. Problem is, only about two thirds of the stuff could possibly be coming from other places. That's why Anthony was killed. He had figured out the paper trail of manufactured capacitors to the tantalum, and the money changing hands all the way back to Kinshasa."

Janet was overwhelmed by a new tide of grief. "Oh, my God."

Helena and I both froze.

"I'm supposed to address a conference on African unity next month," Janet went on. "We ... we couldn't decide what the topic of my speech was. I said maybe I should give Coltan a rest—perhaps I should look at economic development instead. Anthony said wait a bit, maybe he could find something new for me, but no promises ..."

Helena gave her a comforting squeeze on the shoulder.

Janet was still in shock. "This is really over me speaking out on it?"

I nodded. "I'm afraid so. You know the stakes. You're a black female politician who could end up as Britain's voice in South Africa. You could have a great deal of influence on the region. And *they* know you won't be toeing the line

246 · LISA LAWRENCE

from Downing Street. You'll also have crucial input into Britain's decisions. They know you won't play ball with them."

"We've got to go back to the police," she said impulsively.

"We'll do no such fool thing!" snapped Helena. "Not unless you want to toss your bloody career down the drain and take me with you."

"But—"

"She's right," I said. "What are you going to tell them? I don't have a shred of tangible evidence to offer. Just because I've figured it out doesn't mean I've got proof."

Janet was pressing hard. "But you do know who's behind this?"

"It's not that simple," I answered. "We're dealing with deep pockets that I'm pretty sure are on the continent. This could be one company or several that have ganged up all for the 'common good' to stop you being a pain in the ass."

Helena tapped the screen of her computer with a pen. She may not have been up on the issue, but she was a smart lady, and she noticed the absence of one particular firm.

"I realise this list is three years old, but Buccaneer Cape Mining isn't here," she pointed out.

"No, it wouldn't be," I explained, "because Buccaneer Cape was a late bloomer when it came to the trade. I was just coming to that."

I crossed over to the folder of goodies I had next to my handbag on the sofa, and I pulled out the company's annual report.

"Before these conglomerates got embarrassed, they didn't mind writing about Coltan for shareholders. Here. Buccaneer Cape Mining saw it was too late to get in on the Coltan boom near the end of 2000, but it had access to copper reserves and germanium in the Katanga region. It has a presence in the country, but no one ever made a stink over it because Coltan was the hot issue, not copper."

Helena drew a blank. "So if they weren't there for Coltan, then why . . . ?"

"Why was Lionel killed? With the 'official' peace on, the media flap died down over Coltan, and Lionel discovered that another big player, Orpheocon, had thought of re-exploring an area north of Goma in the east of the country. It was being under-exploited. That was part of his job, to keep an eye on the competition. Here he was in London, noticing something that even executives and engineers in the field weren't picking up on. When he said the word, it would take only a few bribes to secure the mining licenses and export permits, and Buccaneer Cape would pull the rug out from under Orpheocon's feet."

"So we know at least that Orpheocon's involved," said Janet, shaking her head.

I nodded. "And there could be others. We can't be sure yet."

Helena was solemn. "They killed Lionel for a stupid analysis report."

"They've bankrolled rebels and done arms sales over Coltan," I replied. "They've slaughtered thousands for it already. How much more nerve does it take to arrange the murder of one mining executive here in London?"

"Bringing that war here," Janet noted in disgust. "And that traitorous Tom son-of-a-bitch brought it on himself."

"Yes, I suppose he did," I said quietly.

I could lay claim to all the feelings she was having now. We had both surrendered our bodies in turn to Lionel in a casual, almost perfunctory way. For myself, the betrayal I felt didn't hit me square in the eyes. Try a few inches lower.

I had that man inside me, I thought, and he was one who didn't care that with a few anonymous keystrokes on his computer, he could spell more misery for people who looked like me, like *him*.

I couldn't understand it, but then I didn't know why I thought I should be able to. I didn't understand the Rwandan guerrilla who took cash from a European bank in trade for his skill with a machine gun.

But if Lionel could have had a change of heart, if he could have been persuaded of the culpability of his firm and others, someone took away any chance he had for redemption.

Janet stood up and went to the bay window, muttering, "Bastard ..."

Lionel. Guilty in her mind as much as the one who tortured him to death.

"For a long time," I said, signalling that I wasn't done with my explanation, "our killer fooled me exactly the way he intended to fool the cops and everyone else. He didn't go after Lionel. He had to kill him to cover up his business— same reason he had to kill Anthony. Janet was always the original planned target."

I had Ms. Marshall's attention again. Turning, she asked, "What do you mean?"

"Not to be morbid," piped up Helena before I could respond, "but he did torture Lionel."

She looked a little embarrassed for saying it, as if she expected Janet or me to feel more deeply about the guy than a one-night stand. In truth, it was Helena who knew him the longest.

"I'm certain now," I explained, "that making him strip and jerk off, all the sexual humiliation, was his attempt to kill two birds with one stone. It made the police think the motive was personal if they didn't buy the suicide, which still threw them off the scent of Lionel's business dealings. And the killer knew the cops would look into his sex life, which conceivably could lead back to Janet and blow the lid off the poker games."

"Why send him the letter, then?" asked Helena. "All it did was tip Lionel off that he was in danger."

"But it didn't, really," I argued. "Pull out the note and consider its phrasing."

She did, retrieving the note from her desk. I looked over her shoulder as she checked the now familiar words:

POKING DRIED-UP OLD BITCHES HAS BEEN PROFITABLE, HASN'T IT? LUCKY AT CARDS, UNLUCKY AT LOVE. YOU'RE GOING TO WIND UP DEAD YOU KEEP SEEING HER

"If you keep seeing *her*," I said, tapping the page. "Lionel wasn't tipped off about the *real* danger he was in because the note supposedly warned him to stop seeing Janet, that's all. And that's why we were all confused, including him. He wasn't seeing Janet! As a matter of fact, he wasn't seeing any woman lately. So he went on with his business, sat in on the poker games, thinking if he didn't try to win Janet anymore, whoever was pissed off would clue in. But the note makes a reference to strip poker. 'Lucky at cards.' All of us reasonably assumed we were dealing with an insider, and yet any regular at the games *already knew* that Janet and Lionel weren't an item."

"So what are you saying, darling?" asked Helena, getting confused.

"I'm saying the purpose of the note all the time was misdirection. Had to be. If he simply blackmailed Janet, I think he was afraid he'd give the game away. Knowing how passionate she is on the Coltan issue, he couldn't be sure she wouldn't figure out it had something to do with her crusade. By threatening Lionel he made all of us think—for a while—it was just about sex."

"But that's what I mean," insisted Helena. "He threatened Lionel, and then he killed him."

"You're assuming that the letter and the murder were each part of an orchestrated plan, that one was sure to follow the other. I don't think it happened that way. When he discovered what Lionel was up to at work and decided to kill him, he must have known there was a possibility his note might surface. So he arranged the murder to fit conveniently with his blackmail scenario."

"But you said Lionel was gay or bi or whatever," Helena pointed out. "You said there was gay porn on the DVD, and ugh, too sordid!"

"It still works," I argued. "Gay jealous lover says stop seeing *her*. The police didn't even need to learn about the note. Carl Norton and I went in that wrong direction for a while."

"Then why didn't the killer send a note like that to Neil, too?" asked Janet. "He must know about Neil. Why not embarrass me with him? Or Anthony for that matter? That would have been easier."

"Not at all," I replied. "Think about it. All the evidence that Neil is an escort for you is with Helena, and while I'm sure the blackmailer considered burglarising her house and getting the records, our girlfriend here is very careful. Sure, our blackmailer knows about your poker playing. He has to know—he knew about Lionel through the games. He made reference to the agency in your note and to the poker circuit in Lionel's. But you told me Anthony never took part in the games. Never showed up for even one. It was Anthony's own phone call to the minicab company that suggested an affair between you two. *Not* our blackmailer."

"So he might not even know," said Helena.

"About Anthony, no," I said. "About Neil, I'm sure he does. But that's where he got clever."

"What do you mean?" asked Janet.

"Lionel was always the wild card. Neil would do what he could to rescue your political career and deny everything. That's the kind of guy he is. You two could simply claim you're 'romantically involved,' which in fact you are. But suppose it came out about you and Lionel? He couldn't be controlled or swayed by personal loyalty. He could go sell his story to *The Sun* if he wanted to. I think our villain was actually counting on *your* ethics."

Janet was riveted. "How?"

"Sometimes we're on our best behaviour towards the people we don't like," I said. "We feel we ought to be. Neil could get a note, and you'd say, 'I can't let you get hurt because of me,' and he'd say, 'Don't worry, baby, I'm not going to put up with this,' and off you go to the police hand-in-hand. You wouldn't feel the weight as much. But our black-mailer made you feel responsible for Lionel's safety. A man you may have slept with but hardly knew and couldn't trust. You felt responsible for protecting him. It was the right thing to do, the honourable thing."

Janet didn't comment, and from her silence, both Helena and I knew it was so.

"And here's the kicker," I added. "Technically, the black-mailer never put you on the hook for Lionel at all."

"Of course he did," she said automatically.

"Nope."

Before I even turned to her, Helena read my intention and fetched the note delivered to Janet's house.

"It's all there," I said. "Just like in Lionel's note."

TIME FOR YOU TO RETIRE UNLESS YOU WANT THE WORLD TO KNOW ABOUT YOUR SATURDAY NIGHTS. SAD OLD BAG, AREN'T YOU? HAVE TO PAY TO GET OFF. WHAT A JUICY STORY IT COULD BE

"Oh, shit!" muttered Helena, and she collapsed onto the couch.

"What?" asked Janet, confused. She turned from Helena to me. "What? I don't get it."

It was Helena who answered. "Don't you see? The bastard used me!"

"I don't understand," said Janet.

Helena was still groaning. It was up to me to spell it out.

"Like I said, if he delivered a note to Neil, Neil would merely come to you. No way to predict how you'd decide to handle it. Lionel may well have been selected because he *wasn't* deeply involved with you. Whether he was or not, who would he confide in? Who could he show the note to? The blackmailer had a better than fifty-fifty chance he would bring it right back to Helena. It's her escort agency. It's reasonable he should ask the boss for help. And when you got your note, you remember that none of us was sure whether the whole thing had simply to do with Lionel and you, or the guy was going through Helena's client list, picking them off. Same paper, same type font. Carefully hand-delivered as well. Obviously the same blackmailer. We all forgot your note mentioned only that 'you have to pay to get off.' Doesn't say *with whom*. So you cut back your schedule. You kept a low profile. Didn't go to the games for a while. Not for your own sake, because you're not about to let yourself be intimidated into the shadows. But if others are in trouble? You didn't cut back your schedule to protect Neil or Anthony, but for Helena's sake and Lionel's."

A glimmer of comprehension now in Janet's eyes.

"And that's how he knew you were shown Lionel's note," I went on. "Who else could have shown it to you but Helena? Who else had access? One note alone, he's not sure what you'll do. A second note to the right person, and he manipulates your good intentions. He's had you all pegged. He knew Lionel wouldn't confide in you, but *Helena* would trust you with it. In fact, he needed Helena to show it you, to make you keep a low profile for a while."

"He played us, darling," sighed Helena, looking up at Janet. "He played us all."

Janet Marshall shivered, nearing her breaking point. "This is insane. I mean . . . what kind of sick people are we dealing with? Why all the head games? Why didn't they just come out and expose me with Lionel or Neil when there was talk of my getting the appointment? Why not ruin me now and be done with it? God, I hate this!"

"It's timing," I said calmly, because one of us had to stay calm. "You haven't just been played, you've been herded. He wanted to make you behave yourself so no one else would stumble accidentally onto the story—and too early. He expected you to shut up and stop making speeches—but it can still come out after you get the gig . . . or not. You decided you weren't going to play his game—after all, you did that awards thing. And so he's forced to go to Plan B."

"Which is?"

"He waits. If you're thrown out of the running now, who knows which way the political wind will blow? But if you get Pretoria, your appointment will let some very dangerous corporate people know that the UK is coming out quite firmly against the Coltan trade. A sex scandal will embarrass London and hurt Britain's prestige and influence with the African states."

"Bastards!" she muttered again in frustration. "If they want me out of it so badly, why don't they use spy cameras or bugs or whatever and—and simply video me fucking Neil or Lionel? All of these sick games!"

"We're not dealing with a professional mercenary or

operative here," I said. "At least I don't think so. Anthony's rushed murder is a good indication of that. I think we've got a corporate executive who's a wannabe spy. He happened on the strip poker craze, and he persuaded his masters this would be the perfect ruse to take you down. After all, he's in. He's accepted. He knows everyone. He's been clever about the psychology, but he's still making it up as he goes along."

I pointed to Helena. "I don't want to scare you, but that's why I better stick around. I think our guy may start to worry that someone could put it together."

Helena smiled faintly. "Someone has."

"But I'm not a cop. Knock on wood, he doesn't even know I'm after him. But he may start to believe someone could figure out this isn't about sex. So he may try a 'gratuitous' murder to throw everyone off track. I think you're the best target. If something happens to you, the agency will fall under the magnifying glass. For all I know, maybe you are part of his plan."

"Maybe it's time you told us who *he* is," suggested Helena.

At that instant, my mobile rang. It was Carl Norton, sounding quite exasperated—with the murders, with the media, with me. This is not a good thing, I thought. But at least he had news for me.

◆

I motioned to Helena I had to take this and jogged up to the master bedroom.

"I don't know why I'm telling you," Carl said tightly, "but that pill residue you tipped us off about?"

"Yeah."

"It's GHB. And you're right, the blood is Anthony Boulet's—from his right palm. A slash across it."

"A knife?" I asked. "I thought he was strangled."

"He was. And it wasn't a knife. The pathologist says it came from a hypodermic needle. The tox screen couldn't find traces of the GHB in his system, but perhaps he was given an extremely low dose, and that's why he was less than manageable for his killer. Fought the bloke off as he tried to administer another kind of sedative—or something worse. As he lifted his hand, the needle raked across his palm."

"So the killer whips out his cord or whatever and strangles him."

"Right," said Carl. "Did you see any glasses on his desk? Like he was having a drink with someone?"

No. No, I hadn't.

"I wasn't there, remember?"

"Ah, yes," said Carl in an impatient snide voice. "You only had a *psychic vision* of what was in the room. Okay, for your information: when the forensics guys went through the office, they found the residue of Scotch in the loo sink. Like someone poured the contents down the drain, but didn't bother to flush it with the tap. Didn't need to, really. One glass left behind with only Anthony Boulet's saliva on it."

"Took his own glass away with him," I said. "Smart."

"Yep. A bottle was in the top drawer of the filing cabinet. Mr. Boulet liked his Glenfiddich."

"The killer dropped one of his magic pills and inadvertently stepped on it. And it got forgotten in the commotion and his hasty cleanup. By the way, I bet if your people do a test, they'll find drugs used on Lionel Young as well."

"Way ahead of you."

"So we're looking for a doctor type, a pharmacist or perhaps a veterinarian."

"*I'm* looking," said Carl. "*You* are supposed to stay out of trouble."

"Yes, Dad."

"No joke this time, Teresa. Please. I heard about how you gave the cops in Paris the slip during that whole au pair scandal thing."

"What? What did I do?"

"You know what you did. I don't know how you did it, but they must be really gullible or stupid or both."

"What?" I asked innocently.

"Teresa! You do *not* look a thing like Michelle Williams."

"Some people say I do," I lied. "I could be in Destiny's Child."

"Uh-huh. And they let you through de Gaulle Airport? They bought the whole 'assumed name' rubbish?"

"Yes."

"With what you were carrying?"

"Yes. In Milan, they bought that I was Macy Gray." I adopted a throaty voice and started to sing: *I try to walk away, and I choke* . . .

He hung up on me.

♦

I went back downstairs into the living room to find a still-anxious Janet and Helena. "That was our friend, Inspector Norton. The cops found GHB in Anthony's office."

Janet's face went blank. "GHB . . . ?"

"Gamma hydroxybutyric acid," I supplied.

"It's one of those date rape drugs, darling," Helena told her.

I briefed them quickly about the GHB, feeling a little

distracted because there was something bothering me about Anthony's murder. I had the nagging sensation that I had missed an important detail or maybe something about the whole psychological rationale.

Of our victim? Our killer? I wasn't sure. I would have to mull on it later.

Of course, the GHB told the cops—and me—that either Anthony Boulet knew his killer or that the guy approached him in such a way that it was natural for them to have a conversation over a friendly drink after office hours.

But why would Anthony Boulet sit down with a representative of the Coltan trade over Scotch?

After I finished with Janet and Helena, I knew I'd better take a look at everything again. The timelines of the phone call, the discovery of the body. The digital photos I took inside the office. The works.

"You were about to tell us who you think is behind it all," prompted Helena.

"Yes," I said, coming down from the clouds. "I have no proof, and I hope I'm wrong. But I think it's Simon Highsmith."

◆

"Why him?" asked Janet.

Why him indeed?

"For one thing, Simon Highsmith dropped out of medical school years ago but would still know how to administer narcotics and sedatives," I answered. "That may sound very circumstantial, and it is, but I've had dealings with him before. In Sudan."

"Wait a minute," said Helena. "Simon Highsmith. That's *your* Simon from Africa?"

"He's not particularly *my* Simon," I grumbled.

"But you've got history," prompted Janet.

"Yes. And for me, he's still the primary suspect."

"If I'm guilty of letting my involvement with Neil cloud my judgement, isn't it possible that you're not totally objective when it comes to him?" she asked.

Never easy with this woman!

And there was Helena, waiting expectantly for me to tell more. My friend who had just blurted out this personal detail that now undermined their confidence in me. I was irritable because only a moment ago, I had calmly, painstakingly guided them through my logic over what was behind all this, and now when they asked me to point a finger at the culprit they assumed emotions were affecting my judgement.

"Sure, it's possible," I conceded, "but the reason I think it's him is because I do know him from before. I know what he's capable of. I watched Simon Highsmith pick up a rifle and shoot a man right in front of me. Some of the aid workers I knew there were kind of like adrenaline junkies in a way, and Simon ... Simon went all the way, became a mercenary on the side of the SPLA in the south. I think he's done a Kurtz."

My invented expression puzzled Janet. "Done a Kurtz?"

"*Heart of Darkness,*" supplied Helena, getting it. "You know, Janet—the bloke who goes into the jungle, supposed to be the great missionary, goes nuts and becomes a warlord? Didn't you ever have a boyfriend who made you sit through *Apocalypse Now?*"

"No," answered Janet with an arch of her eyebrows. She seemed to count herself lucky for it. And she was still baffled. "But if Simon Highsmith fought with the rebels, I mean his sympathies would ..."

"Years ago, there was this American journo who went

down to the Philippines to write a feature about child prostitution," I offered. "He wrote this incredibly moving story about the kids, the corruption, the whole shebang, and then later he dropped out of sight. What happened to him? Another reporter goes looking, and lo and behold, the crusading journo is in Manila. Now *he's* one of the pimps running his own child prostitution ring."

"Good Lord," muttered Helena.

"Somewhere along the line," I said, "Simon may have gone from a white guy fighting for Africans because it's the right thing to do or for good karma or whatever to thinking what am I getting out of this? From his perspective, maybe Africa hasn't got better and never will. So he asks why not cash in? Big country, small world. Easy to walk across the street to the competition. It can't be coincidence that he turns up flush with cash, crashing the party when there are all these Coltan links and you're in the running for the High Commission. Can't be."

What had he said to me back in my apartment? *It's a different country this time.* And I had assumed he meant Britain. Uh-uh.

"So why didn't he blow your cover?" asked Helena.

"Truthfully? I can't be sure." I pointed to Janet. "He came over to my apartment and assumed I was working for you, trying to chase down a blackmailer. Told me you should book a holiday, and I should get out of London, too, that things were going to get uglier."

"That sounds like a threat," said Janet. So much for doubting me about Simon.

"No," I argued. "That wouldn't be his style. He knows I'd dig in my heels. If he outs me, I can out him back. Mutually assured destruction. My bet is he decided to try to be allies, to make me think he's up to something else."

"Which is?" asked Helena.

"I asked him who he was working for, and he wouldn't tell me," I said. "He won't tell me right away because that would be too easy. But at the right moment, he'll come back with some rubbish story to lead me in the wrong direction. I can almost guarantee it."

"You're still playing poker," observed Helena.

Yes, I thought. Yes, I am.

"If not a threat then a warning," suggested Janet, flip-flopping. "He told you things were going to get worse, right? He'd advised you—and me—to get out of town."

"Which may sound very nice and sincere, but gains you nothing," I countered. "It may even play into his hands if you're out of town. The story can break while you're off on this holiday, and you'll be none the wiser. No chance for damage control. Remember: our blackmailer wants to set off his little media bomb on his timing, not anybody else's."

"So how can you stop him?" asked Helena. "He's killing our friends, and it looks like he's going to ruin both of us . . ."

"I prove he killed Anthony," I said. "Or I prove he killed Lionel. Or both."

Janet, her nerves eating her away, fell back on sarcasm. "Oh, that's all! The police don't have a clue, but you'll have it sussed."

Helena tried to rein her in. "Janet . . ."

"But this is way past a joke!" she insisted. "Men we know—one man I deeply cared for—are getting murdered. And with all due respect to your talents, Teresa, you're not with the police. You're not a forensics expert. You're not even a trained investigator by your own admission. I think it's time we gave up and went to the authorities!"

"Do that, and this bastard wins," snapped Helena. "There's no guarantee that what we tell them will lead to this creep's arrest. But his employers over in Geneva or down in Jo'burg or wherever the hell these slimy types operate from will still get what they paid for! Please, darling, you have to be strong with me. Let Teresa do her job. She's good at it."

"Thanks," I whispered.

"I'm sorry," said Janet, regaining control. "But I do hope to God you know what you're doing."

So did I.

12

I missed him. I wanted him back. Took me a while to figure out how to do it, if only for a little while. The obvious. Wendy the receptionist gave me an odd look when I made my request, but something in my eyes suggested that she please not pass it on to Helena.

Hell, it would turn up on Helena's bill later anyway as expenses.

"I don't usually entertain clients at my apartment," said Neil when I turned up at his door.

He was knotting his tie as he answered it, a dash of bright purple against a dark purple shirt, subtle blue pinstripe pattern on his Armani jacket and trousers. God, his aftershave made him smell good.

I played innocent. I played it about as well as I can do a Yorkshire accent.

"I just thought this would be more convenient," I said.

"You look lovely."

I was wearing the same outfit I'd worn at the last poker

game: long skirt with a deep slit up the side, the elegant hal-ter top with the tie neck and sequins around the trim. Go with a winner.

"You don't look happy to see me."

"I thought you wanted me to call when I figured out what I want."

"You didn't call," I said.

"Teresa . . ." Groan of exasperation.

"She doesn't have much time for you again these days, does she?" I asked. "Doesn't want you by her side when she shows up crying at his funeral?"

We didn't have to pretend anymore that I didn't know who she was. If Janet had gone remorsefully back to his place after her mini-orgy, no doubt she'd dropped a refer-ence to me having been there. And what kind of behaviour I was up to.

"She's a politician," said Neil. "She's got an image to maintain."

"You minded it a lot more when she didn't show up out-side the police station," I argued.

He sighed and rubbed his forehead. "Nothing's simple. Look, I do love Janet. You told me to go and ditch all this baggage over the games and my gigs with you when maybe that's good advice I should used with her. Once and for all. You know . . . You didn't call either."

"I'm here tonight," I said, moving in to him.

"You're too late."

"No, I'm not. I'm right on time, and I've paid for it. The Time. The full service. And I don't want to spend tonight arguing."

"Just because you rent my ass, doesn't mean you *get* my ass, babe," he laughed, leading me by the hand to the door. "Escort means I take you out. A show. Dinner. Whatever your pleasure—out there. In here is my choice."

"Yes, it is," I said.

I planted my feet, back to the door, and stayed put. I began kissing him. At first, sweet little pecks, then more insistent. My fingers felt his ribs and muscles under his shirt.

"So what's it going to be?"

In answer, he sank to his knees in front of me and began to lift my skirt. I felt his large hands grip my buttocks, kneading them, sculpting them, and then I felt his breath hot and passionate on the inside of my thighs. I stumbled back against the door.

He had my panties tugged down in an instant, sucking my clit in his mouth and making me moan. I felt a concussive wave of heat flow from my groin through my entire body. My fingers in his hair, touching the fabric of his jacket. My skirt was cast aside, Neil gorging himself on my pussy, overwhelming me with pleasure. His tongue flicking and nudging inside my vagina. I tugged on his necktie to get him to rise, and we kissed again violently. My hands ripped down his fly and worked blindly at his shirt buttons, but I didn't want him completely naked. Oh, no.

Shoulder blades hammering the door with our exertions, his brown cock jutting out of his pants, he penetrated me right then and there. Half-clothed. Wild abandon. I bit his lip and keened as his hands ducked under my top and fondled my breasts, revelling in the heat from his thighs, his huge penis, the touch of fine silk and cotton of his clothes. Shoe clunking to the floor as he hoisted my right leg. I panted as he increased his rhythm, and then he savagely yanked on my hair and kissed me, pumping me, fucking me, making me scream for mercy so that anybody out in the hall heard the show all the way down to the lift. And just as I thought I couldn't take any more, I ripped his shirt open, buttons cascading on the tiles like spilled mints, and I let out a wail, sinking my teeth into his chest.

"Oh, fuck, baby!"

"Teresa!"

His cock boring into me with sweet and precious extra depth as it tensed and shot. He was so long. Hard like a rock inside me.

"Teresa . . ."

Of course, it didn't resolve anything. But it felt good, and that was enough for this evening.

◆

I left him three hours later, thinking it might be better not to sleep over this time. A cab took me into the West End, and it was still comparatively early. I figured I could always hail another ride to get me to Richmond. Helena should be all right tonight, having a couple of her friends over for a "night of normalcy," as she put it. A wholesome game of Scrabble. And Sex on the Beach cocktails.

I was walking along the embankment, doing my mull thing over pieces of the case, when I noticed my shadow. He had tagged along since the cab dropped me off, and I wasn't sure whether he didn't have the talent for this or he wanted me to know he was there. Either way I wasn't in the mood for games.

"Don't you have anywhere else to go?" I called out impatiently to the darkness. "A tipple down at the pub? Lead a few insurgents in Iraq or something?"

"I don't do that kind of thing anymore," said Simon, walking into the light from the streetlamp.

"I'm not sure what you do lately, except be a pain in my ass."

"I see you didn't take my advice," he replied. "I did say it would get worse. It's getting to the point where I might not be able to help you."

"Help me?" I laughed scornfully. "How are you going to help me, Simon? You won't tell me who you're working for! And what you're after."

"Because you won't believe me."

"I may surprise you."

He shook his head. "Doubtful. I don't believe it myself sometimes. It's too fantastic."

Right on schedule, I thought. I'd warned Helena and Janet he would leave me baited on a hook and then try reeling me in. Here goes.

He pointed off to the great complex looming in the distance over the bank of the river. He was right. It was too fantastic. He had to be kidding me.

Legoland. Babylon-on-Thames. Vauxhall Cross.

MI6 Headquarters.

"Oh, come on!" I laughed. "I stand corrected. No, Simon, I don't believe you."

I started walking again, and he fell in stride next to me.

"I was recruited in Khartoum two months after you and I said goodbye. They didn't have anyone in the region who could find his own arse. And they're a cheap outfit, cheaper than you'd think. They expect a bloody freelancer to have oversight on Uganda and Congo as well."

"Spy work's a bitch, huh?"

"You asked who I was working for. Teresa, think about it. The region's barely stable. The British government went through a shit storm over Coltan like everyone else, and now it's determined that the traders don't fuck up their interests *or* their representatives."

"Why not come to Janet then and tell her to behave? Your alleged employers have a lot of muscle."

"Kind of closing the barn door after the horse is out, don't you think? And given Janet Marshall's political leanings . . ."

268 · LISA LAWRENCE

"Oh, please," I said. "This is a Labour government that jumped on board George Dubya's Baghdad invasion! I'm sure they've learned not to see every leftie as a potential security threat."

"Yes, well ... Let me put it this way. They're not worried only about martyr red or conservative blue."

I stopped walking. Every black person on this cloud-covered island has a little invisible Geiger counter, and the needle on mine just ticked into the hot zone.

He watched me hit boiling point and put up his hands. "Hey, don't shoot the messenger. I made a case for briefing her."

"Well, isn't that fucking typical!" I snapped. "Our cloak-and-dagger brigade doesn't want to trust a woman who could be our next High Commissioner because she's black, even though she's the victim of an international conspiracy! Nice to know the Cold War's over but the Race War's still going strong. So they won't brief Janet? Which means they allegedly care about the Coltan trade but not how these bastards are willing to ruin a British politician over it?"

"In a word, yes. They're afraid if Janet is briefed and decides to go public in her outrage, it will, umm—" He cleared his throat dramatically. "It will embarrass old friends who haven't quite extricated themselves yet financially. They're *supposed* to be hurrying up with that."

"And you work for these pricks?"

"Now just a minute," said Simon. "I'm trying to hunt down an illegal mining network. That's what I'm in for. Your Ms. Marshall is a big girl, and no one put a gun to her head and made her pay to fuck Neil, and no one said go spread your legs for Cahill, Westlake and Giradeau the other night. Don't look so surprised. Yes, I heard about it. Cahill's got a big mouth sometimes."

"What she chooses to do in her private—"

"She's a politician, Teresa! In Britain! She has no private life."

I didn't have an answer to this because he was right. Janet herself admitted she'd been stupid from day one. And lately she had almost resigned herself to public humiliation like a walk to the gallows.

If I wasn't so sure it would go to her head, I would have told her the truth of how I gave her a lot of credit. Facing tabloid ruin had not made her change who she was. It hadn't intimidated her into diminishing her own sexuality.

"You all right, miss?"

A curry delivery guy on a scooter. Must have been zipping by when he saw us arguing. Helmet on, but the voice sounded about eighteen at most.

"She's fine," snapped Simon. "Piss off."

Delivery Guy ignored Simon, looked at me.

"Thanks, I'm okay," I said.

He looked doubtful, so on the spot, I did a roundhouse kick to Simon's shoulder, prompting an "oomph" and nearly knocking Mr. MI6 to the pavement.

"You sure you all right?" asked Delivery Guy.

"Jeez," I muttered, losing my patience.

"Not talking to you anymore, love. Was talking to your husband."

"Piss off," groaned Simon.

And Delivery Guy started up his bike again, cracking wise again about the happy couple before his scooter putputted away.

"Nice shot," growled Simon, rubbing his shoulder.

We resumed the stroll. I didn't say anything for a moment, and neither did he.

Then I pointed out, "They don't need you here. They've got home-grown spies to pick up the thread. You could have stayed down in Africa."

"They needed me exactly because I am known down there," he explained. "A new fellow popping out of the blue, dropping names and waving African credentials that can't be checked out? Looks awfully suspicious. So they called me home. And the trail led to the games."

"What trail?"

Simon shrugged. "A long and winding one, having to do with a mining concession north of Goma for Buccaneer Cape. Past that, I can't really get into it. Classified."

"That's convenient," I snapped. "So who's behind all this?"

"Our old friend Orpheocon. They were once head-quartered in Johannesburg, now they have offices in London. I can't prove it yet, but the jigsaw is slowly coming together. We've got a whole dossier of shell companies, go-betweens, a bank in Herzegovina—"

"Whoa, whoa, whoa!" I cut in. "Herzegovina? That makes no sense. Banks in a place like that can't do international money transfers at the speed London wants."

"Oh, these guys can wait!" Simon laughed mirthlessly. "Time is money, but what they really go for is the lack of 'transparency' in the process, as the bankers put it. The money gets funnelled to Brussels, and then—"

I hurried him along. "Simon, what I meant was, who is behind all this *here*? Who killed Lionel and Anthony?"

He didn't respond.

"Simon. If you know . . ."

"No. No way, Teresa. For Christ sake, I've already told you too bloody much and compromised myself. When the moment is right, they will take the bugger out."

"Who's *they*, Simon? You mean *you*, don't you?"

He didn't answer.

"Before or after Janet's career gets ruined by this creep?"

Again, no reply.

I spotted a cab with its light on and flagged it down. Simon could get his own.

♦

I didn't believe anything he'd told me, and I had learned next to nothing. In so far as Simon Highsmith could be a spy, well, sure, he could be a spy. He had been an Englishman down in Sudan, fighting the Khartoum regime, and he spoke fluent Arabic. He could also muddle through one or two of the southern dialects and knew the terrain and the players. Acquaintances had heard rumours about him popping up everywhere from Zimbabwe to Mozambique. If not a spy then at least a mercenary.

What I had problems with was that he was a spy for *them,* and that they would care at all about the destructive toll of the Coltan trade. I didn't think the powers that be in this country, whatever the political party, gave a damn what happened there, and the fact that it all grew worse in Darfur last year was my proof.

He had really insulted my intelligence. The big mining and oil conglomerates were not so embarrassed by what they did that they needed to launder their money through the back end of Europe. Once their front companies made their transfers to respectable branch offices of European banks in say, Cairo or Johannesburg, the money was "clean" as far as PR trouble went.

I had to sift through Simon's bullshit to decide what, if anything, was true. This whole thing was about Coltan. Lionel had analysed it. Janet had protested it. Anthony had followed it—the same trail Simon claimed to have uncovered.

Okay. If Simon subscribes to the old theory that a whopping fantastic lie works better than a small one, and knowing this Herzegovina bank business has got to be rubbish, let's assume he's trying to send me in the opposite direction. Look at the opposite of everything he's telling you.

He wouldn't name the killer, but he gave up the company. Why? He must know I'll try to find a link between Orpheocon and one of the suspects, unless he wants me to be spinning my wheels. Which brings us to his next assurance: "When the moment is right, they'll take the bugger out." Which really meant he would take the bugger out.

Translation: you shouldn't interfere. You should do nothing and wait. *Wait, because he didn't know who it was yet. Or perhaps he did, but he did have to wait for the right timing.*

A stall, a big stall. Had to be.

And then there was the most valuable bit of information he had given by trying to steer me off course. He implied that his employers didn't give a toss about Janet.

Only a couple of weeks earlier, he had suggested Janet and I go on holiday until the whole shit storm blew over. He had suggested things would get more ugly—the corollary of that was he would be powerless to stop them.

Okay. So for his MI6 cover story he had to come up with a plausible explanation for why his taskmasters didn't warn Janet. Simple. They didn't care about Janet. Well, he had always been a cynic, and he could reasonably assume I'd be cynical, too, about MI6.

Uh, uh, Simon. Not buying it. I'll believe you're a spook, just not their spook.

Opposites. He had wanted me to think his employers didn't care about Janet. Yet he had also wanted her out of the way, had suggested she go on holiday. Perhaps someone cared very much what happened to our Ms. Marshall.

If there were powerful corporate forces at work trying to

prevent Janet from getting Pretoria and speaking out on Coltan, was it possible that someone *else* wanted very much for her to get the appointment?

Not exactly a guardian angel or concerned for her personally, but who thought she would be the right appointee for their interests?

Which brought us back to the same question: if so, why hadn't *they* warned Janet what was really going on? There could be only one possible answer. They couldn't. To tip her off about their involvement meant a risk to Janet's chances of actually getting the job. Any kind of meeting could be construed as Janet being allied with their powerful organization or whatever it was, this someone else, and it would look like she wasn't impartial or ready to act solely in Britain's interests.

And I think I knew who that someone else was. I just wasn't sure how they had dreamed up sending Simon Highsmith.

♦

When I got back to Richmond, Helena asked me how it was going.

"Simon has told me he's working for MI6," I said blandly.

She was flippant as well. "Ah. Naughty girl for telling me. I'll tell Janet. Then we can all break the Official Secrets Act."

I plunked myself down in front of Helena's computer and surfed through archive pages of *The Star* newspaper in Johannesburg. I thought that if someone was eager to get Janet into the High Commission, the current situation in South Africa could use a little more scrutiny. They would want more of an ally in Janet Marshall than just another diplomat who spoke out against the Coltan trade.

One innocuous item a few months before caught my eye, and I hit the link. Last September, there were angry words exchanged in the country's National Assembly during a debate on black empowerment. Minerals and Energy Deputy Minister Lulu Xingwana let fly, complaining about "rich white cartels that are continuing even today to loot our diamonds, taking them to London; that are continuing today to monopolise the mining industry."

The heated row in the House happened only days after Tony Trahar, CEO of the Anglo American mining company, told *The Financial Times:* "I think the South African political risk issue is starting to diminish—although I am not saying it has gone." Oh, oh.

South Africa's President Thabo Mbeki had fired back a salvo in his Internet column, writing: "Both the ANC and the government would not know what political risk Mr. Trahar is talking about. What is this risk that has started to diminish, but has not gone? Is this the risk that persuaded Anglo American that it should list and re-domicile in London, while speaking to us only about the size of capital markets?"

He observed tartly that black South Africans had been paid a pittance while working for Anglo American and other companies in the years of minority rule yet they had "chosen reconciliation rather than revenge"—they hardly deserved to be "computed as a political risk."

The Star reported that Mbeki and Trahar apparently patched up their political differences over a phone call.

Fine, but it got me speculating. There had to be many like Lulu Xingwana who thought white cartels were still trying to suck their country dry after apartheid was gone. Just as you could bet there were other white corporate CEOs who thought democracy in South Africa was still somehow "at risk."

Goes to show that out of sight, out of mind. There's a nice sculpted head of Nelson Mandela outside the Royal Festival Hall, and most folks in London can tell you blacks rule in Johannesburg now, happy outcome long overdue, the end. But of course it wasn't as simple as that.

The country did have to worry about its neighbours. It did have to worry about how stable the region was. The newspaper websites had conflicting reports on whether South Africa had handed over intelligence that helped get those alleged mercenaries picked up at Harare Airport last year. You know the ones—accused, along with Margaret Thatcher's son, of trying to topple the government in Equatorial Guinea.

It seemed South Africa had grown very concerned about security in the region.

It was time, I thought, to ratchet up Helena's BT bill. I had a friend down in Johannesburg, Thembi Sindiswa, who worked as a documentary producer for one of the radio stations. They were only one hour ahead down there, so no worries about phoning, except it was late in the afternoon and getting into crucial drive time for journo types. She'd want to kill me.

"Hey!"

"Hey," I half-yelled back. Lousy line, she could barely hear me as I made my request.

"Listen, T, give me a day or so. I'll phone around. I got a source with the Scorpions. Maybe he knows something."

The Scorpions. South Africa's version of the FBI, the Directorate of Special Investigations. They looked into major, high-profile crimes, ones involving organized syndicates and millions in profit.

"No promises, though," she warned me.

"I understand. Thanks, Thembi."

◆

I should have learned my lesson after the very first time a boy tied me up.

I remember the boy, Jimmy Sanderson, and I recall we boldly did this outdoors. Of course, we were both seven, and Jimmy used my bright pink skipping rope. We were supposed to be playing cops and robbers, and I had the double part of being the hostage at the bank hold-up, but after he had me good and knotted, he ran off with my Action Man doll that I used for occasional rescues of Barbie. The big liar.

Men, huh?

This time, of course, was very different.

Daniel had called me, wanting to continue my "sexual tuition," as he put it, and though I was wary, I had my own agenda, wanting to check something out. I didn't know why he insisted on a special request, but I complied. "You got any clothes you're giving away? You know, to charity? Goodwill? Wear 'em."

So I didn't feel terribly sexy when I showed up at his door in a long faded, ratty Janet Jackson concert T-shirt, a hand-me-down from a boyfriend, and old red track pants. As soon as I stepped inside, he quipped that he wanted to show me "an old rope trick," and I had a good idea what he had in mind. I submitted.

Stupid, right? Because for all I knew, this guy could be *the* guy. Lionel was bound up before he was murdered. If Daniel was the one, if he was onto my role in this whole drama, he could kill me then and there in his flat. Really stupid. And I had gone there to take another look around and try to rule him out conclusively as a suspect. If I was wrong—

Taking all kinds of stupid risks on this case. With my health. My safety. My heart.

"I believe you said you weren't into this Halloween shit," I reminded him.

"And I believe," he replied smoothly, "I was referring to all the doggy collars and leather fashion victim stuff. I do believe in erotic restraint—"

Out of nowhere, he produced a paring knife, and before the acid in my stomach could churn with reflexive, instinctive panic, he poked its point into my shirt and began to tear upward, cutting my bra clasp in the blade's wake. Then he was slicing away at the track pants and my knickers, and within thirty seconds, I was not only bound, I was naked as well. My nipples were hard, and my thighs were drenched in my juices, getting off on him slicing away my clothes. I watched the mirror flash of the knife as his other hand roamed over my breasts and my belly, his mouth kissing me with urgent hunger.

He pushed me gently to the floor, and I heard myself gasp out, "Wait, wait," but he didn't, and I only put up a half-hearted fight. Too turned on, getting too slurping wet, breathing too hard. Feeling my bare breasts against the low-pile carpet, starting to feel the muscle ache in my arms behind my back. He had another long stretch of rope, and within a moment, he had my legs bent and then hog-tied to my wrists. And I moaned in anticipation. Delicious vulnerability.

His hand first. Fingers feeling me from behind, penetrating me, and then he rolled me onto my side and masturbated me as his mouth sucked on my nipples. My wrists squirmed, my legs began to tremble from this game of violation as much as the stored energy of being kept in place, needing to be set free. He brought me to a squirting shower all over again, coming violently until I thought my limbs shaking would loosen the bonds enough to pounce on him. But the ropes held. Perspiring badly now, my own scent thick in my nostrils, and still he kept me coming.

When he thrust his cock into me, I screamed but no sound came out. Such overwhelming waves of surrendering release, the pleasure of helplessness, as his hard cock filled me, and I fought only for show. Oh, fuck me, please fuck me hard, take me completely! A revelation of rope. I came again and again, and when at last he untied me, I was dying of thirst. I thought I had sweated five pounds away from struggling against my bonds. Incredible.

◆

Daniel was in the bathroom when I took a moment for my scheduled snoop around. Naturally I wandered over to his desk, but I wouldn't have time to boot up his computer. In fact, I didn't think I needed to, because I spotted something that piqued my interest right away. The fax machine.

Yet more and more pages lying on the out tray, each one almost blank except for the reassuring message:

Transmission:OK

Transmission:OK

Transmission:OK

Transmission:OK

Transmission:OK

I remembered I had considered an explanation for this—that Daniel was sending sketches of his work to his client for approval. But then I noticed the time intervals—they didn't add up. I don't care how good an artist or architect you are, it begged credibility that anyone can whip off an impressive drawing and then send it across the Channel to Paris all in the space of 47 seconds.

But it did give you enough time to type out a message and send it.

The time intervals, however, weren't the clincher. What sealed the deal for me was that the exact same sketches still sat on the drafting table right where they were the last time I was here. There was even a fine layer of dust on the edge of the T-square. Daniel would have to be pretty lousy at his job, for which he was brought all the way over from the States, to abandon his project like that. Or else he was working at a glacial pace. It occurred to me that maybe I wasn't looking at tools. These were props.

He wasn't an architect.

What if I was right about an intelligence presence involved in this whole scandal? I had thought corporate intelligence, but what if Simon was telling the truth about MI6 only he was telling it about someone else? He had simply appropriated Daniel's motivation to make himself look innocent.

That fax machine wasn't for sketches.

Maybe it was for checking in with higher-ups.

Okay, you're a spy, and you need to report. If you're faxing a typed message, why not simply use a Messenger programme or email? Yeah, they can be hacked into, but wouldn't it be the same with a fax?

◆

"Actually, no," explained Jiro Tanaka as he cinched up his belt in front of me about five hours later. Get your head out of the gutter—he was cinching up his black belt, and we were at the dojo where I train. Jiro was not only a buddy, a karate student with his third dan who liked to slingshot his reverse punches across the floor at amazing speed, he was one of the sharpest minds in IT in London. Kind of weird reconciling those Japanese features with the Liverpool accent, but hey, his dad was a merchant seaman originally out of Buenos Aires, so Jiro had quite a diverse background. He'd been my answer-man on computer stuff before, and now I was trying to wrap my head around his techno gobbledegook before we got down to practice.

"It's very difficult to tap a fax message, Teresa," Jiro was telling me now. "If this is your baddie, he's got a bloody brilliant scheme."

"I don't get it," I admitted. "It works on a phone line like email, but you've got hackers ripping off messages on those—"

Japanese people almost never interrupt, but Jiro was Japanese-British, and his wincing expression told me I was on the wrong track. I ought to shut up and listen.

"Fax technology gave IT wizards the notion for email," said Jiro. "It's kind of like the granddaddy of the web. But faxing also works like your television. All the data is converted into a serial stream, going left to right. Now just like telly, if the receiver loses sync, the result isn't viewable. When the receive end loses sync or senses an error it asks for a resend. Right, you want to eavesdrop. If you lose sync, who do you ask? And because of line noise, this can happen several times during a message. With me?"

I nodded, barely keeping up.

"I'll try to simplify this a bit for you," Jiro went on. "Unlike email, it's bloody difficult, if not close to impossible, to hack into a fax because faxes are sent in packets of data. And *that's* because all phone lines aren't created equal. You know that irritating *skree* and *squelch* noise you get when you accidentally call up a fax number? That's the fax machine trying to talk to another fax machine. First, there's a speed-up test to determine how fast the incoming stuff can go—a test message. That's the protocol for start-up, then you have what's called a check-sum, and—well, I don't know how much you need all this, but the point is you get varying speeds of transmission. The two fax machines kind of shake hands before they do business."

"Okay," I said. "Got it."

Jiro grinned. "No, love, you haven't, have you?"

"Nope," I confessed. "I don't. Faxes use modems, don't they? So why can't you just tap in and ..." I shrugged. I didn't know how to put it in geek-speak.

"Remember what I said? All phone lines aren't created equal. A fax transmission algorithm is a complicated animal, and they came up with this bird back when folks still had to make do with 1200-bit modems. As a result, it's completely different to the modem you got in your shiny new PC at home today, which by the way uses a different algorithm. Like I say, if your guy is thinking fax for foiling hacks, he's got imagination."

Or his bosses do, I thought.

"Okay, I'm with you," I said. "I am with you this time."

"Then," Jiro went on, "your baddie can go one better to make it impossible to eavesdrop. Now all this is based on somebody attaching a connection directly to the phone line, yeah? In theory, you *could,* I suppose, record all the tones and use a sophisticated programme to download the message—if you know what you're doing."

"And you have something like that?" I said coyly. Jiro shook his head. "I can get one, but it wouldn't help."

"Why not?"

"Nowadays, your intelligence agencies use equipment that scans large groups of lines looking for key words instead of whole messages. Okay, it takes several scans to reproduce a text line, and their gear looks for the predictable bits that make up text letters. But if he knows what he's doing and wants to keep his messages secret, he can do something very simple to spoil any salvage operation you've got in mind."

"What?"

"*Hand write* his message."

I stared at him blankly.

"Told you before," explained Jiro. "A fax is sent in a serial stream, left to right, like lines on a picture tube. Now that's all well and good if you want to intercept a *typed* message, but nobody's handwriting is uniform."

He took a pen hanging by a string on the dojo bulletin board and scribbled on a tournament notice. In neat block printing, he wrote: "Teresa is a girl." And he wrote it on a slant.

"My 'e's are different, even if this is subtle. My 'g' is different from my 'l,' and if I write it on an angle, you're buggered," he said. "So much for trying to replicate a left-to-right serial stream. The only way you're going to be able to tell what was written is if you're looking directly at the page itself. And this is assuming your monitor doesn't lose sync. You want to confound modern technology, you go back in time to old technology."

Yes, I thought, but the new can always come back with a second wind. If the only way I can tell what Daniel is writing is to view the pages themselves, then I would just have to get myself a good look.

Since I was getting my fair share of exposure to webcams lately, my next shopping trip would be for a nifty hidden eye. And then I would have to either charm my way back into Daniel's apartment or do some more "scrubbing."

♦

Five hours of doing the spider, watching and waiting outside Daniel's Canary Wharf apartment.

I decided it might look a little strange me doing an about-face and dropping my frosty bitch act with him, calling him up out of the blue for one of our liaisons. Especially when he seemed to get off so much on calling me when he felt like it. It was tempting to tail him for a while and check his movements, but he knew I drove a Beamer, and I still had my hopes pinned on that fax machine upstairs to reveal all.

I figured I should keep it for caution's sake to a tight five minutes to snoop around. Still nothing moved or disturbed on the drafting table. Nothing today on the output tray of the machine, not even confirmation pages. Good. Maybe I haven't missed anything.

Fifteen minutes to install my little pin camera and make sure it would give me the view I wanted. Amazing thing. Don't ask me how it worked, that would need another explanation from Jiro, but suffice to say, I could see what Daniel saw when the print-outs emerged, all the while back at the surveillance monitors in Helena's house in Richmond.

Of course, now I had to wait until he got something.

◆

It was mid-afternoon when my friend Thembi called me back from South Africa. I was in a robe at Helena's, having poured myself a glass of wine, watching a bit of television as I thought about the case. I was just about to finally crack a book on winning poker strategy when the phone rang.

Thembi's voice was all business, asking me—no, telling me: "Get out of where you are, go down the street and call me from another line. Not a cell."

"Yeah?"

"Yeah. Do it. I'll wait."

I quickly dressed, grabbed my purse and locked the house

up. I would have a long walk before I hit a BT call box, but I had to humour Thembi. For one of her documentaries, she had looked into surveillance networks like ECHELON. That's the international version of Big Brother (NSA, Britain's GCHQ, Australia's DSD and more alphabet soup) that allegedly spied on millions of people's cell phone calls and emails. France had its network. So, apparently, did China, Israel, India—it's enough to make anyone paranoid.

God, had I brought enough change? Who makes a long-distance call using a pay phone anymore? By the time I realised I had only £2.10 in coins, I was on the high street.

I went into a certain department store that shall go nameless but that I loathe because of its return policies, and I slung a pair of slacks over my shoulder. Shameless, I breezed up to the sales counter.

"Hi. That girl over there"—I pointed towards empty air—"she says it would be all right if I was to use your phone. My card got declined, and I know I've paid my bill, so I just wanted to check with Visa and see what the hell's going on."

Stone-faced clerk. "I don't think we can do that. Our phones are not supposed to be used for personal calls."

How I love the cooperative attitude in this nation of shopkeepers.

I replied sweetly, "Well, she went and checked it with your manager, so I guess it has to be all right, doesn't it?"

"Wait right here," the woman said. She actually said it like a command. "I'll go ask."

"You are getting a sale out of this," I argued gently.

"Just wait, please."

And she was off. Once her back was turned, I was dialling.

Thembi answered on the first ring. She picked up the

sounds of the Muzak and the PA staff announcements and laughed. "Oh, God, you're using them again! You're terrible."

"They should have exchanged that blouse, you know they should have," I said. "What's going on?"

"*What* are you mixed up in?" she demanded.

"What's the matter? What's up?"

"Your friend Simon Highsmith. You're right. All the 'private military firm' stuff is rubbish. The best information from my source says he's probably never been to Sierra Leone. But he can set off bells. Big ones."

Not the MI6 gig, not that, please.

"A few years ago when the Scorpions were formed, the first thing they started was a data bank on British nationals because of all the hell raised over the conflict diamonds. They have an old photocopy of the stamps in Simon Highsmith's passport. Ones showing entry in and out of Nigeria, Angola, Egypt, Sudan, Ethiopia ... So they plugged in the passport number to check recent entry here. Makes sense, doesn't it? British passports are still good for ten years, right?"

"Yeah."

It was one of those obvious facts that made you double-check your own common knowledge. Were they valid for ten years? Of course they were.

"The passport for Simon Highsmith in their database was issued in 1993. The passport he waved in front of a Customs officer here seven months ago has a completely different number and was issued in 1998. No stamps anymore for Sudan or Ethiopia. Passport Control in London and Pretoria both say the 1993 one was never reported as lost or stolen. Then my friend says phones began to ring, and he was told politely to stop asking questions about this guy."

"Why?"

"The information is on the level, believe me. I could get

into a lot of trouble for telling you this, but I pleaded with my source that you're good people."

"Tell me what?"

"Teresa, this Simon Highsmith—he's South African Secret Service."

13

That's great, I thought, back at the house and pacing Helena's living room. That's just great.

I had to figure out what to *do* with this information. Telling Helena or Janet would mean more anguished soul-searching on our Ms. Marshall's part, debating with herself whether her integrity had been undermined, compromised, blah, blah, blah. The way I saw it, if she didn't have a clue as to who else was out there and how they were watching her back, there was no conflict of interest. Simon and company might foil the plot to ruin her, but they had no pull in crowning her. Either she'd get the appointment or she wouldn't.

Apart from being able to rule Simon out as a suspect, I didn't know what this revelation did for me. I still felt I was right in one assumption: Simon had no more idea who killed Lionel and Anthony than I did. And though he had come to the games with more background than I had, I was catching up fast.

I could always go to him and tell him what I had learned.

Simon, however, wasn't a team player. Our time in the Nuba Mountains had taught me that.

I wanted to throw in my vote with Janet for believing I was in over my head. Blackmail, double murder, corporate greed and now political interference from foreign agents.

And let's not forget the orgies.

♦

I sat up as Helena and Janet practically rushed into the house, Helena doing a little run into the kitchen and calling over her shoulder, "I've got champagne!"

"God, champagne," laughed Janet. "I'm ready for vodka!"

"What's going on?" I asked, though I had a pretty good idea. Janet was bursting with it.

"I got the call," she said in a small voice, quietly beaming.

"Wow," I said. "That's great, that's ... Congratulations."

We had one of those awkward moments where one person puts out their hand to shake—me—while the other makes a move to hug you. I hugged her back clumsily, and Helena returned with the bottle and the glasses.

"Right, you've got packing to do," she warned.

"Hey, don't push me on the plane yet," said Janet. "There's probably going to be briefings and more briefings, and I'll have to get an estate agent to rent out the house. Then all the security stuff and media interviews—"

Helena clinked her glass to Janet's to cut this off.

"Drink up, darling. It'll be fine. Teresa, tell her it'll be fine."

"It will be fine." I tried to sound confident.

In truth, I wasn't so sure. If our blackmailer had been forced to kill Anthony to cover his tracks, maybe his whole timetable had been upset. With mumblings and innuendo over just what the man's relationship had been with Janet, maybe her friends in government had pushed hard for a quick decision to spare her any more anxiety. And to get the media to shut up. Editors would shrug and think: well, she's going, story's over.

Not as far as the blackmailer was concerned. In the euphoria over the good news, Helena and Janet forgot that I'd said it was all about timing.

My job had just got a whole lot harder. If I didn't find him soon, he could still pull it off.

"George Westlake wants to throw you a big party at The Lotus Eaters," Helena was telling Janet.

"And let me guess," giggled Janet. "There'll be a game."

"Of course there'll be a game," replied Helena. "You don't get to play, though. Too respectable now."

Janet pretended to pout. "That doesn't sound fair ..."

And I stood by, still thinking to myself: timing.

◆

Damn it, I had been sloppy. Since I knew Simon had dropped out of medical school and that he was somehow mixed up in this, I had broken off checking deeper into the backgrounds of my other suspects. We knew our killer used drugs on Lionel and had tried to use drugs on Anthony, sooooo ...

I love the web—a living, ever-growing encyclopaedia where you can find almost anything. The General Medical Council regulates and licenses doctors to practice in the UK, and you can easily check a doctor's registration on its website. Problem was, just because we were in the UK didn't mean I was looking for a British physician or a disgraced doc who had lost his licence *here*. It was like the UN at the strip poker games. Simon, I now knew, was an operative for South Africa, while Ayako was Japanese-American and Giradeau hailed from Boston.

The Federation of State Medical Boards in the US had its Federation Credentials Verification Service set up in 1996. According to its website, it allowed somebody "to establish a confidential, lifetime professional portfolio that can be forwarded at the individual's request to any interested party, including, but not limited to: state medical boards, hospitals, managed care plans and professional societies." Terrific. Assuming my guy had applied and was in there. And they probably didn't just hand out that kind of information to anyone.

Maybe I was going about this the wrong way. I could go to Simon and suggest we join forces. He had the broad strokes, but I had key details about the actual murders themselves that, paired with the right information networks, could nail our blackmailer. If the Scorpions in Johannesburg could pick up Simon on their radar, certainly he must have spook resources to find out whether one of our players had also been jetting back and forth to his neck of the woods. In fact, South Africa kept back channels of communication going with Zimbabwe, so the net could spread a little wider.

But he must have done this already. Damn, it would have been the first thing he'd do, Teresa. Think.

◆

It came back to me in a flash, the thing that bothered me about Anthony's murder, that nagged at me even while I was briefing Helena and Janet Marshall about the GHB found in the law chambers. Carl had said a Scotch bottle was in the top shelf of the filing cabinet. Anthony Boulet "liked his Glenfiddich."

When Anthony had a drink with his killer, it was Anthony who had likely suggested it. It was his bottle, and it's not like it was out in the open—it was in the filing cabinet after all. But Anthony booked a minicab to pick him up at his house in Islington. The police found he had used the service before, and the dispatcher recognised his voice.

Now if Anthony was going to stop in at his house first before going on to Janet's, what was he doing using up precious time on drinks with our anonymous killer? He knew he had to get going. No one books a minicab from one spot that'll pick him up from somewhere else, unless he's about to leave.

So why offer the killer a friendly glass of Scotch? It was late. If it were somehow a business-mixed-with-pleasure, sociable occasion, Anthony would have put off the call for the cab. He could have shot the breeze, no pressure to get home in time. No, Anthony was surprised by the guy's arrival. He had felt threatened. Let's talk it over. Here, have a drink.

But the more important question, the question I didn't ask because we all thought we knew the answer, was: Why did Anthony Boulet feel he had to rush over to Janet Marshall's home in the middle of the night?

At first people thought they were having an affair. They were, but Janet claims things had cooled down between them. Even though he had his own key, he probably would have phoned first. If she weren't home, he would merely wait. I had concluded he must have wanted to tell Janet about the Coltan, the whole reason for this nightmare she was being subjected to. That's why Anthony was killed, I had told Helena and Janet. He had figured out the paper trail of manufactured capacitors to the tantalum, and all the money changing hands right back to Kinshasa.

Only I was wrong.

It's not enough, and I should have known it. It didn't ring true. When I figured it out myself, I had waited a little before going over to brief Helena and Janet. I arrived with a reason, sure, but I only had suspicions about Simon. And Anthony could have told Janet the next morning as well. He had the paper trail. The information wasn't going to change overnight, so . . .

When do you rush to someone's home and wake her up in the middle of the night? When you know the woman you love and idolize is in imminent danger from a specific individual. When you can point an accusing finger and be sure it's at the culprit. Only that person confronted Anthony first in his office.

Anthony had to talk to her immediately because he knew it was one of her strip poker acquaintances. And yet both Helena and Janet said he had never taken in one of the games. That meant our killer's name had to have been dropped in conversation, probably more than once, and Anthony put two and two together.

It wouldn't be a name that popped out at him from the mining files on Orpheocon. If it were that simple, Simon would have known the murderer's identity ages ago and hunted him down first. Work locally, think globally, Teresa. Corporations are wheels within wheels. Orpheocon was a large conglomerate, and that's why I had wrestled with the question of Ayako's involvement, finally ignoring it as mere coincidence. Look for the wheels within wheels.

The killer had wiped out Anthony's web pages and the files linked to Coltan. But *only* those files. He assumed that if he covered up the reason for the murders, he covered up his own discovery.

Or maybe . . . He was ignorant of just what tipped the solicitor off so that it wouldn't occur to him to delete any other files.

Either way, the reference to the killer had come as a thunderbolt to Anthony, and it must have been through a case that at first looked totally unrelated. But like Simon Highsmith of Sudan appearing out of nowhere to get dealt into strip poker games, it couldn't be coincidence.

Our blackmailer would turn out to be someone who wasn't what he appeared to be. That's what I had told myself weeks ago, and I was pretty sure it would still be true.

♦

Afternoon became early evening as I stared at a computer screen and photocopies of notes, print-outs of archived files. More cups of coffee than were probably good for me.

Orpheocon, it seemed, had a pharmaceutical division. And why not? Especially when its forestry division in South America probably got its hands on the plants used for scores of patented drugs. And digging through web archives and my photocopies of scribbled notes from the law office, I learned that about ten years earlier Anthony Boulet, as a young investigator, had been poking around in the Orpheocon pharmaceutical company. He was working for a long-forgotten royal commission started during John Major's term in office. It was supposed to look into the over-prescription of anti-depressants, and Anthony was concerned chiefly with the over-medicating of black British males.

And one of his case histories was a teenage minor named Neil Kenan.

Jeez. It explained a lot. Here was Anthony, doing his best to be on the side of the angels, but part of his ambivalence towards Janet's lover could be explained by his own wrestling with the stigma of Neil's mental illness.

And it got better. In Anthony's correspondence was a letter from a law firm in Massachusetts requesting information on his old research. The lawyers in Boston had launched a class-action suit against Orpheocon Pharmaceuticals over one of its drugs. "Clinical trials and post marketing reports" showed it caused in "both pediatrics and adults, severe agitation-type adverse events coupled with self-harm or harm to others. The agitation-type events included: akathisia, agitation, disinhibition, emotional lability, hostility, aggression, depersonalisation. In some cases, the events occurred within several weeks of starting treatment."

I watch the news. I knew what this was about. There had been studies done recently that showed heightened suicidal behaviour in kids taking anti-depressants. Not that it was relevant to what I was doing, but the law firm in Boston planned to demonstrate Orpheocon knew about these trials and didn't adequately advise physicians about the danger. So. Their pill-makers and their mining and oil executives all worked from the same ethical songbook.

What concerned me was that Anthony got regular updates on the case, and he must have bolted upright in his chair when he saw who Orpheocon was calling as one of its star expert witnesses.

Doctor Daniel Giradeau.

A doctor attached to a respected clinic in Bruges. As in Belgium. As in Belgian Congo.

But Anthony wasn't the only one recognising old names. What do you want to bet that when the decade-old commission research made it to those Boston lawyers, Orpheocon made sure they got their copy? Or maybe it had to be passed along under disclosure rules? I'll bet they took great interest in Anthony Boulet's name.

And Neil Kenan? Sure, he was a minor at the time with a private medical history, but it wouldn't take much for that big corporate octopus to learn his name. Two black men near the top of the enemies list for the UK.

Oh, my God. Knowing Neil's clinical history, Giradeau could whip up quite a cocktail to mess him up and implicate him in anything that happened to Janet.

I ran—I didn't walk, but ran—to where Wendy the receptionist had reserved a monitor for me. It was to spy on Giradeau's fax machine, and it took me a moment to recall Jiro's instructions on how to download the thing.

After a moment, the image popped up—exactly as Jiro had theorized. Bloody brilliant. In neat bold printing on an angle was written: APPROVED USE OF GAMMA HYDROXYBUTYRIC ACID & KETAMINE HYDROCHLORIDE DO ASAP DUST HER & PERSONNEL AS YOU DEEM FIT.

14

I stared at the page and the names of the drugs. Took me all of thirty seconds on broadband to learn that one, gamma hydroxybutyric acid, was a colourless liquid. Ketamine hydrochloride was usually in pills. Oh. Shit.

Date-rape drugs. There could only be one reason he would use these, and it wasn't for rape.

I picked up the phone and dialled Helena's mobile. No, she wasn't in Richmond, but at The Lotus Eaters club in the West End.

"Where are you?" she asked. "Aren't you coming?" *Damn it.* The game, I had practically forgotten all about the game. George was playing host back at The Lotus Eaters, and he had insisted everyone come for Janet's sake. His party to celebrate her appointment. Of course, it would be better if she didn't play, not when the media jackals would be sniffing around at this critical time, but she could make an appearance.

"Helena, this is very important," I said as I ran out the door to the BMW. "Who's there tonight?"

298 · LISA LAWRENCE

"Gosh, darling, I don't know, everyone—Westlake, of course, Vivian, Neil, Simon, Ayako, me—"

"Is Janet there already?"

"Yes, but we don't need to worry. She's just staying for a couple of drinks and then going home with Neil to be a good girl. Bad enough someone thought they spotted a *Sun* photographer hanging around—"

I was stalled at a red in Brompton Road when the policeman spotted me with the mobile to my ear. He glowered at me and with a pantomime gesture, ordered me to ring off. *Shit.*

"Helena, keep her there," I ordered. "And keep Neil there, too. Don't let either one of them out of your sight until I get there. I don't care if they have to go for a wee, you make sure neither one is ever alone. Don't let them drink anything, not even water! Understand? And worst of all, don't leave Janet and Neil together alone!"

"Oh, my God! You're not telling me Neil's the killer?"

Now the cop was making a beeline for the car. And still that light was on red, no escape.

"No, Helena, he's not, it's—I can't explain it right now, but I'll get there as soon as I can!"

"Should I tell Simon?"

"No!"

Simon's regular answer to big problems was to start shooting, and while I had no doubt he had learned from his Secret Service trainers how to do it quietly, he might treat the others there besides Janet as collateral damage. No, thank you.

I could only give Helena so much information over the phone. If I told her it was Giradeau, she'd freak and any suspicious behaviour around him would probably make him bolt. Helena would have a weird vibe going with Janet and Neil, but better that than my friend taking on our blackmailer all by herself.

I had Giradeau's true background, but I was still running with a light load when it came to hard evidence tying him to the murders.

No answer at Carl's extension at work. Please pick up, please pick up, please pick up—

No response on his mobile either. As they say, you're on your own, kid. I bring regular cops into this, it could end up a shooting gallery or at the very least a tabloid scandal.

Unfortunately, the cop in front of me at the moment was getting really pissed off, yelling more orders that I could barely hear through the windshield and practically on top of me. I raised my hand in surrender and dropped my Nokia onto the passenger seat. Shit, shit, shit—

But just before the policeman reached the driver's side window, the light turned green, and I roared off. I heard him curse after me.

From the passenger seat, my phone bleeped, and I saw from the caller ID it was Helena ringing back. I took my eyes off the road for an instant to stab the green button with a finger, and I heard her start a protest. She would be even more upset when the cop's ticket caught up with her.

"Teresa, if Janet hangs around, she'll have to play!" bleated the tinny voice from the mobile on the chair. "She can't risk public embarrassment now. It's only days after her appointment!"

Raining again. I turned on the wipers as I passed Hyde Park Corner. "I don't care if she has to do tag-team humping, don't let her leave!"

Because the minute Janet was out of sight, Giradeau would kill her. Even better that Neil had accompanied her tonight. Daniel would make it look like a crime of passion, murder-suicide, and that was the reason for the GHB and the ketamine.

He would slip them into the couple's drinks, and while

Janet on the GHB might black out and be more docile or unconscious, vulnerable to attack, ketamine could induce not only date-rape drug symptoms like memory loss and blackouts, but aggressive or violent behaviour. When the cops arrived, if Neil was still awake at all, he would look drunk, and his judgement would be impaired. The set-up would be perfect.

Dust her, they had scrawled across the page. What is it with these operations that they always have to find euphemisms for killing?

Yes, Carl and his detectives knew drugs were used on Lionel and would have been used on Anthony. But it wouldn't matter. They didn't have a viable suspect to pin it on yet, and our Belgian doctor was going to give them one. Janet would be dead, and Giradeau would have enough time to fly out of the country.

A line came back to me from Neil's favourite play, a famous line that could fit a new context: *Yet she must die, else she'll betray more men.*

♦

I flashed my invite to the doorman at the club's main entrance, and bolted through the revolving door. I knew where the party was (up on the third floor, conference rooms), but I had no clue if the poker game was nearby or on another floor. I flew into the party room and saw about a hundred people, more than I would have expected. I guess this was George Westlake's idea of a "small" affair.

That meant the poker game would probably be held at a discreet distance away from the festivities. Bouncing on my heels with frantic energy, I scanned the crowd—no Helena, no Neil, no Simon, no Giradeau. No Janet. All at the game. Damn it.

I couldn't find one familiar face that would be in the know about the cards and frolics.

Okay. Do the chicken with its head cut off.

I walked briskly across the floor and began checking side corridors. In these big club/hotels, there's always more than one exit out of a conference. The first one, I found nothing but little alcove rooms with walnut desks and green-shaded lamps, old-fashioned paintings that depicted fox hunting.

Next corridor. Same furniture, same bad art. And a whump. What goes whump all by itself behind a door marked STAFF?

Helena. Her weight hitting the door as her body stirred. Her green silk dress didn't go with handcuffs. Or the electrician's tape over her mouth.

She was unconscious, completely out of it, so I took advantage of the moment to spare her the pain and rip the gag off. Breathing, thank God, but I bet she'd have a hell of a hangover in the morning. She didn't look like she'd been roughed up or molested. Just drugged.

But there could only be a couple of reasons Giradeau had deposited her here. She'd either tripped onto what he was about or he was factoring her in as another one of "Neil's victims." He'd be coming back for her.

The cuffs weren't police issue—they were the novelty kind you can buy in sex shops. A standard key works on them all, and I pulled out the one I keep on my ring next to my house keys and the key to my parents' house in Oxford. Yeah, sure, I could explain why I keep a handcuff key handy. Let's just say it's good to have one on you.

"Hel? Helena? Wake up, darling."

No good, don't know why I bothered.

But I couldn't leave her there. Giradeau would be coming back for her.

I had to think fast, so I put one of her arms around my neck and half-carried her, half-dragged her to one of the other alcove rooms with a closet that locked. I was gambling that she could sleep it off there, and if she happened to wake up, she could let herself out but Giradeau couldn't get in. Best thing to do was to reach him first.

Back to headless chicken mode. Only three corridors on this floor, and as I crossed back through the party and hit the third one I spotted Neil. He stood in the hall with a drink in his hand. And by himself. Not good. But he looked reasonably sober and in control.

"Where is she?" I demanded.

"Who?"

"What do you mean who?" I shot back in panic. "Janet! Where is Janet?"

The drink. The drink he was holding. Giradeau's drugs. I knocked the glass out of his hand, spilling it onto the carpet. He took it for a gesture of anger.

"Oh, shit, please, Teresa, don't make a scene. Not here. This is a big night for her—"

"No, you don't understa—"

"No, Teresa, you don't understand! I care about you, but I'm in love with Janet, and we—"

"*She's in danger!*" I shouted over him.

"What? What are you talking about?"

"Lionel's killer! And Anthony's! For God's sake, tell me where—"

"Lionel killed himself," he answered, and I forgot he wasn't in the loop. Talking to himself more than to me. "And some burglar killed Boulet—"

"Damn it, Neil! Is she at the game?"

Got to be on another floor. And if he wouldn't tell me, I'd have to hurry up and look for myself. I tried to push past him, but he held me back.

"Tell me where she is, Neil! Please!"

"You're out of your mind—"

I'd have to hurt him or throw him or something in a moment.

"We're running out of time! Look, babe, I don't work for a biotech firm, I'm working for Helena—"

"Working for *Helena*?"

"You have to trust me, Neil! I knew you were at the police station that day because Carl Norton and I go way back—"

Staring at me like a wax dummy.

"Did anyone pass you a drink tonight?" I asked.

"You passed mine to the floor—"

"Did you get them at the bar?"

"Y—yeah."

"What about Janet?"

"I don't know, maybe, I mean—oh, God, this is for real, isn't it?"

"Yes! Now take me to her!"

I tugged his arm, and then he was running with me down the hall. He led me upstairs, and we hurried to the game room.

Pushing the door open with a rude slam, and it was an absurd scene in front of me. Off in a corner, Vivian, naked, was all but ignored as she had the penis of a certain sportscaster in her mouth on the settee. And at the table: George Westlake clothed, Ayako topless, Cahill clothed, a white girl I didn't recognise completely nude, and Simon topless. A couple more new faces. By the bar, Janet wore a navy blue evening dress and a paper gold crown that read "Queen Godiva." Chatting with Daniel Giradeau in a tux with the bow tie undone around his open neck.

Everyone suddenly staring at me. And Neil coming up fast in tow.

"Simon, get your shirt back on," I snapped.

"Why?" he sang gaily.

"Because I might need you," I said, my voice grim.

Perfectly quiet. Waiting for me—me who stared at Giradeau. Stepping closer. Then another step, staring at him all the time.

No woman-scorned look, no expression of feeling betrayed on my face, because truthfully, I didn't feel that at all. I was in The Zone, I think. In case mode. I just stared at him, accusing him and accusing him, mongoose to cobra, wanting to get Janet safely away and really not sure what I would do with him after that.

And now everyone could tell who I had in my sights.

"Where's your little black bag, doctor?" I said at last.

"Doctor?" asked George. "He's an architect."

"No, he's not," I said.

Even I didn't notice Simon dressed now and inching his way close. Without warning, he dropped to the floor and didn't go for Giradeau—he tripped Janet and yanked her under her arms across the carpet. To safety. She was too bewildered to protest. Then Neil went over to her, nodding to Simon and understanding what he'd done. Neil didn't know how the guy was involved, but he was appreciative.

"What's going on?" asked George.

Cahill assumed it was a joke. "We get theatre with striptease now, Westlake?"

"I don't know what this is about, Gary—"

"Teresa?" asked Ayako.

Her mouth slightly open, covering her breasts and starting to get scared. So was the girl at the table. People began to back away from the confrontation.

Heads turned for answers to Janet and Neil, but the couple didn't have any for them. Simon was back by my side.

"You sure?" he asked softly.

"Very."

Giradeau offered a thin smile. Still speaking English like

a perfect American, and maybe he'd learned it that way when young.

"Him, I was suspicious of," he said, indicating Simon. "He drops in out of the blue. And all that soldier of fortune bullshit we kept hearing? But you, sweetheart ... I didn't hear you coming. Oh, wait a minute, yes, I did."

"I was playing a part," I replied. "Just like you."

"Teresa," said Simon calmly. "Your 'doctor' here needs surgery. Surgery like we saw in the Nuba Mountains."

No. No, no.

I shot him a look.

"Let me take care of it," he whispered.

I kept an eye on Giradeau as I whispered to Simon, "You said it yourself. This is a different country. Your bosses in Pretoria should know that."

"I'm not deciding what's best this time," he argued. "This white man's under orders."

"You think it's better because of that?" I scoffed.

"Excuse me, I have no idea what you two are squabbling about," Giradeau cut in, "but I'm walking out of here right now."

"I don't think so," I said. "I bet we dig through your pockets we'll find a hypodermic syringe and maybe a bottle of pills. Drugs you're not supposed to have. The police will be very interested in that."

"The police," groaned Simon, having no faith.

"I *am* leaving," said Giradeau.

"Will someone kindly tell us what's going on?" demanded Cahill in exasperation.

That was when Giradeau made a break for it. Simon was closest, got to him first. Being a spy, however, didn't make him an acrobat, that nifty manoeuvre to get Janet free notwithstanding. Did show he had imagination. But now the bull tried to wreck the china shop with a clumsy tackle.

Giradeau, more agile than I would have expected, side-stepped him and rammed an elbow into his back. Simon sputtered as he went headfirst to eat carpet.

There were shouts and yells all around and one genuine "Eek!" from that silly naked girl at the table, and Daniel ran down the hall to the fire exit stairs.

I paused all of two seconds to look at Janet, make sure she was all right. I had no idea if Giradeau had got his chance to drug her, but she was already saying, "I'm fine, I'm fine." Neil must have asked her about her drinks when he rushed to her side.

Neil. Trying to be chivalrous. Or plain enraged at the thought that Giradeau could have killed her. I saw his back getting smaller down the hall. Shouted his name as I broke into a sprint.

As I rammed the bar for the fire exit door, I heard the ping of the elevator arriving and glanced over my shoulder. Simon was back on his feet, getting in and trying to beat us to Giradeau. Shit.

Jumping the last four stairs on every flight. Of course, he still beat me out the door.

Who knows how much of a lead Giradeau had by now with Neil hot on his heels.

As it turned out, not much. I think Neil must have tried to tackle him at some point, Giradeau throwing him off, but Neil had got back up and given chase again. I could see them in the darkness ahead, running south, but I couldn't spot Simon. Maybe he was trying to cut Giradeau off.

I don't know how we all did it, but Giradeau was doing the Roger Bannister, leading everyone on a merry chase out of the rabbit warren of side streets behind Trafalgar Square, trying to lose Neil and maybe Simon in Charing Cross Station. No good. He thought better of it and ran down Villiers

Street, and I don't know, maybe he would try to lose us in Embankment Station. Cut off again? Simon? I couldn't see.

Lungs killing me. I was using all I had to keep up. I'm normally good for short sprints, not long hauls like this, although I can punch it if I have to. Neil obviously ran regularly. I don't know what Simon's gym regimen is, but if he got knocked on his ass again like he did in the club, his execution threat was nothing for me to worry about.

I wasn't fond of him these days, but I didn't want Giradeau to kill him either.

Or Neil.

Racing up the steps to Hungerford Bridge. Trains squealing and roaring behind it on the elevated tracks as they made their way from the West End to the South Bank. I couldn't see any tourists taking photos or casual pedestrians crossing the span, and thank God for that because the uphill climb finally took the wind out of Giradeau's sails.

Neil caught up as our Belgian doctor came in sight of the panoramic view of the Houses of Parliament lit up for the night. He lunged for him.

Giradeau grabbed his wrist in a blur worthy of Sky Sports slow-mo playback, spun him around and dumped him on his ass. Then panting, he stood his ground. Seeing me coming.

Oh, that's just great. That's terrific. He knows aikido. I *hate* guys who know aikido.

Here I am, a girl who likes to punch, and I have to tangle with a lover (make that *ex*-lover) who can throw me into a wall. Make one more mistake in my timing of a blow or a kick, and he'd swing me around in the air like a lasso.

At the moment, however, he didn't want to draw me in. He was keeping me well back, and with good reason.

He'd grabbed a syringe out of his inside coat pocket, and now he crouched down to push the needle firmly against the skin of Neil's neck. Neil was still trying to shake off his rough landing. Giradeau grinned at me.

"There's a lovely solution in this, just ready to kill your boyfriend here," he warned.

My imagination fled me. All I could think to say was, "The minute you do I'm going to push you off this bridge."

"I'm a very good swimmer."

Getting nowhere.

"I'm not leaving," I announced quietly. "The police will turn up eventually, and then it'll be a whole new game. You'll never make it home. By the way, flawless accent. You had everyone fooled. What I don't understand is why you simply didn't pass yourself off as a doctor."

"With no affiliation to the British medical community?" he shot back. "And no hospital privileges? What would I be doing here? Besides, too close to my regular persona."

And what ultimately tripped him up with Anthony Boulet. The name alone twigged Anthony to go investigate.

"Just for the record," said Giradeau. "It's nothing personal, Teresa. We're talking billions of pounds here. I'm sure you read a *racial* factor into it, but it's not like that. It's business, and as far as you and I—"

"Please, don't," I cut through him. "Just don't. Spare me any 'greed is good' speech. As far as you and I are concerned"—I sighed away some of the tension—"we never pretended to have feelings for each other before. I certainly don't see any reason to start now."

"To think I had you all nice and trussed up. I could have ..."

"But you didn't," I snapped. "Why do you think I let you do it to me, Daniel?"

"You wanted me to do it! To make you feel in danger. That's why, honey! You—"

"Uh-uh. I was never in any danger."

"Like you could get free—"

"Never needed to worry."

"I was one of the thrill rides of you

"You *know* you wanted—"

"What I know," I said, "is your thrill ride comes

own passenger airbag—that enormous ego of yours. All so

and mushy. That whole 'mysterious reserve' of yours? The

whole non-involvement thing? You can get that with a

dildo. It gives me orgasms, too, Daniel, and I don't need to

flatter it."

"Shut up. Just shut up."

I laughed cruelly. It was a dangerous game, but I needed

to buy time.

"You think you have an advantage by seeing my tits or

making me come? Was that part of the whole 'international

corporate spy' thing you talked yourself into? Have to be a

big stud as well? You got lucky, finding out about the poker

circuit. That's the only real initiative you showed, isn't it?

Dreaming up these little head games for the players. Oh,

yeah, besides going around and killing guys to make more

waves. Bet your employers *loved* the extra sniffing around

after that! You're an errand boy, Daniel."

"I'll be a rich errand boy. I won't even need to practice

again."

Again. A hint of a backstory there. I smelled professional

misconduct screwing up our good doctor's life along the

way, leading him into the employment of Orpheocon. I

didn't have time to consider that at the moment. The old

Hippocratic Oath line of "First, do no harm" had been thrown

out the window as he kept that syringe firmly planted against

Neil's neck.

"You're dreaming if you think you're going back across

the water to a quiet life," I said.

He arched his eyebrows at me and put on this wolfish

. "That's the great thing about working for a multi-
ational. They've got corporate apartments all over the
world. South America. Africa . . ."

The notion of this creep spending his fee money on the
very continent he helped rape made my blood come to a
fresh boil.

Neil had his senses back, fully alert, but confused. I tried
not to show him any fear that might increase his own. I
met his eyes and silently pleaded: *Don't do a thing. Trust me,
babe.*

He couldn't nod. I understood the yes in his eyes anyway.

Better think of something. Giradeau was a sociopath
who thought murder solved problems, and at the moment
his problem was how to abandon ship. And while he claimed
there was no "racial factor" involved, I thought he must enjoy humiliating successful black men—guys like Lionel and
Anthony. And Neil. The bastard liked his job. I had to re-
mind him he didn't have time to indulge himself anymore.

"Daniel," I said calmly. "I'll start walking across the bridge.
I won't be able to reach you. I'll turn my back. You'll have a
head start back into the West End."

Giggles now. "Oh, marvellous! Will you cover your eyes
and count to a hundred, too?"

"If that's what it takes."

"Okay."

I hesitated. Couldn't think for a moment.

"Do it!" he barked.

My eyes locked on Neil's, still asking him to trust me. Not
that this manoeuvre was guaranteed to work anyway. But
hey, from the moment Giradeau stuck the needle close to
his skin, I was buying Neil extra minutes of breathing without cardiac seizure. I passed him and began to walk backwards
towards the South Bank, taking little steps.

"One . . . two . . . three . . ."

"Very cute, Teresa. You're supposed to turn your back before you start counting."

"All right, all right!" I yelled, nerves gone.

I backed up about thirty feet, knowing I had to turn around soon when I spotted the tiny red dot on Daniel's arm.

I didn't know what to think. My eyes must have gone wide, the surprise reflected in Giradeau's expression, and then he suddenly winced and cursed as something went *fffft* into the hand holding the needle. He let Neil go, muttering, "Fuck!"

Whatever it was, it changed everything. Neil fell forward onto his hands and knees, the syringe flying to the ground but it didn't shatter. Giradeau was still cradling his wounded hand.

Me? I was running like hell back to them.

Lunge punches aren't my strong suit. I'm a defensive sparring partner, or so Jiro and other teachers tell me. I think Giradeau had time for coffee at Starbucks by the time my fist approached his chin.

He caught my arm with his good left hand and performed one of those twirly, somersault aikido thingies that if I didn't know how to roll would have left me winded. And still we're talking a touchdown on hard cement.

Ow. Big ow.

I heard his size 12 Church shoes clicking past me in a mad dash towards the other end of the bridge. You're going to lose him, Teresa.

Another set of footsteps past me.

Get up. Get up now. Dolce & Gabbana looks lousy on pavement. First things first. I scrambled over to Neil, grabbing his shoulder.

312 · LISA LAWRENCE

"Are you all right? Tell me you're all right!"

I inspected his neck as best I could in the dim light available. So far as I could see, the needle hadn't punctured his skin at all. He was fine. A little shaken up, but fine.

"I'm okay, I'm okay," he said.

He looked at me with such complete bewilderment. He'd heard me talk with Giradeau in the private language of culprit and pursuer, heard us refer to things he hadn't a clue about, and now he didn't know me. He looked at me like I had grown another head.

"Teresa . . . ?"

I pulled my sleeve over my hand and very gingerly picked up the hypodermic, depressing it so that the lethal contents squirted harmlessly into the Thames. I had to make a split decision about whether to dispose of it since it was evidence. I couldn't run after Giradeau with it, and I didn't want to throw it into the river where it could wash up somewhere and prick some kid. I put it down carefully near the curb.

"Don't touch that thing," I ordered. "Stick close to Janet. Did you see Simon? Had to be him. Neil?"

"N—no. No, I didn't."

The red dot. And whatever little projectile had struck Giradeau in the hand. Had to be Simon catching up to me. Whatever he had fired, he must have done it from the steps leading up to the bridge.

"*Shit,*" I muttered. Then I broke into a sprint. I had lost precious seconds, and knowing I would stop to check on Neil, Simon was free to go after Giradeau.

Thames Path? The London Eye looming over me. Or had he gone down Concert Hall Approach, trying to lose Simon and me in the small streets leading towards Waterloo station? Damn it. The guy could have a Eurostar ticket in his pocket right now. Course, I didn't know what the schedule was for Brussels, but that hardly mattered. He could bugger off to Paris. Or Penshurst. Who knows? Get himself a new passport from his masters to sneak out.

He had to be stopped here. But not Simon's way, not like that.

There. Yep. Making his way to Waterloo.

Running after him in the darkness, and he stopped all of a sudden, as if he expected to be ambushed by Simon cutting him off. Then he heard my quick heels behind him, and he turned.

I had to slow down my momentum to set up to hit him, but my fist caught him squarely in the sweet spot above his top lip, below his nose. No way you can roll with it.

A dojo's a lab. Everything's up for grabs in the street—no perfect technique there. All things being perfect, one hit should have sent him to la-la land. But I was rushed, both of us full of adrenaline, and one millimetre of hesitation in his head movement or my blow meant he staggered but didn't fall. I had to hit him quick and fast.

I came at him with everything, giving him a swift kick in the thigh—far better than the balls. Bigger target, still hurts like hell. He grunted with the pain and hobbled a bit, and then I threw a jab that fell short and tried a reverse punch into his belly to knock the wind out of him. Bulls-eye. Go on, give him another.

He pivoted away, our backs rolling against each other like gears, then I felt an open hand smack across the back of my head, and my vision exploded with pretty violet and blue lights. Next thing I knew, he had my wrist again, and gravity decided to go see what's happening at the Royal Festival Hall. Bye, Teresa. Up in the air, and not in a good way. Then landing hard on my side and tumbling instinctively, and still my head felt lawn.

"Ow," I complained flatly to no one in particular, because Giradeau was off again.

With an irritable huff, I picked myself up to follow. Stupid, Teresa. Very, very stupid. Should have hit him, jumped back. Hit him, jump back again. Keep your distance.

No worries. A rematch was imminent. I was panting hard as I sprinted forward, and I spotted him several yards ahead of me.

I opened my mouth to shout as I saw the return of the magic red dot, the beam of a laser sight, catch up to him. All at once it was as if two gigantic fingers yanked on his spine. The marionette began to rattle. Giradeau, his arms at his sides, shook in violent spasms. Oh, God, too late, far too late—

Too dark and too far away to see the invisible wires plugged into the Belgian's chest. The man who had just threatened Neil with a hypodermic was dying from needles of another kind. Two tiny barbs. Stun gun. Pull the trigger, and a compressed gas cartridge sends the electrodes shooting forward, and the ones for the newer models will work right through a bullet-proof vest. You can stand twenty feet from your target and still zap him.

Hurry up, Teresa. Insulated wires. Grab them and yank them out before—

Giradeau's legs and spine lost all will, and he crumpled to the ground. I could just make out the wires floating to the cement, his executioner using a Swiss army knife or something to quickly cut them loose so he could take off. I knew Giradeau was dead even before I caught the faint whiff of cooked flesh.

He was hit with way more than the 50,000 volts or whatever the safe amount was. Taser is the American company that manufactures most of the reputable sophisticated stun guns, but what was used a second ago was a ripped-off design, modified to be lethal.

"*Goddamn* you, Simon!" I shouted loud and long.

I'll bet he was still close enough to hear me.

Not that it mattered.

Yes, Giradeau was a sadistic killer. But bringing him to trial could have ripped the lid off the whole dirty business. Simon's masters weren't interested in moral victory. They wanted what was expedient. Remove the player. Leave the table with the smaller pot.

I suppose Giradeau's death ended any threat of the strip poker circuit being exposed. By the time the cops arrived, everyone would have their clothes on and look sober.

◆

As I trudged up to The Lotus Eaters, George Westlake was standing outside the front door, waiting for me, looking strangely apologetic.

"We've called the police," he said, sounding quite formal.

"Who's 'we'?"

He understood what I meant. Which ones were decent enough not to scamper off to save their reputations? Surprisingly, most of them. Vivian had a minor meltdown, insisting neurotically over and over that she had to go, and within five minutes, she grated on everyone's nerves so much that they told her it's okay, go already. But keep your mouth shut. If Vivian wanted to come back on the circuit, I knew she wouldn't get in. Cowardice does wonders for reducing one's sexual allure.

"Um, Teresa?" started George, and he sounded unsure whether to call me that. As if he thought maybe it was an alias or something.

"Whatever's going on, whatever you think of us, we care about Janet. We can count on the porter and catering staff.

They've always liked her, and I've ... Well, um, I've greased a few palms for extra goodwill. It's better that she was never here."

"I agree," I said. "That has to include Neil too. When Giradeau showed up, there was a party, that's all it was."

He nodded. In the games, George never won me, never fucked me. He had always treated me with respect. I stepped close and kissed him sweetly on the lips.

"I wasn't always acting," I told him.

He looked down at the ground shyly. He was all right.

I made sure that Janet had the good common sense to leave with Neil, and then I fetched Helena and waited outside the club for the police. Three Met cars pulled up, sirens on, lights flashing, and I had to run through my spiel again ten minutes later when Carl showed up in an unmarked vehicle. I showed him where Giradeau's body was.

I told him I didn't see who actually fired the stun gun at him. That much was true.

15

Helena was all right when I got her out of that storage closet. Taken to hospital but released the next morning. She could remember Giradeau hanging on her every word for a long time at the party, then things blurred, and he was "helping" her to sit down, only it seemed to take a long time to reach a settee. Next: blackout.

Yes, she told Carl, she knew Daniel Giradeau from society functions and such. No, she had no clue as to why he should want to attack her. Or Lionel. Or Anthony Boulet. The Coltan motive never made it into the papers.

It was three days later when Neil called me at home, and the call wasn't unexpected. He said he wanted to talk, and I invited him to come round to my place.

I buzzed him in and greeted him at my door, watched him remove his shoes and step forward cautiously to take in the surroundings. He checked out my CD stack and my bookshelf, examined the African carvings on the mantelpiece and the family photos of me, Dad, Mum, my brother.

Me outside one of the Oxford colleges with friends, a framed snap of Helena and me.

"So," he mused sombrely, still looking around, "this is you. This is who Teresa Knight really is."

"Yeah," I nodded. "This is me. Um, would you like a drink?"

"I can't stay that long."

"Oh."

He took a deep breath and announced, "Janet and I have talked. We hashed out a lot of issues that, well, I suppose have made us both a little crazy. And ... it's good, I think we've made a couple of breakthroughs. She wants me to go with her to South Africa."

Lionel's words back in his office were beginning to ring true. I had assumed they had only been meant to hurt, but he had called it right.

He won't even think he's playing you. He'll believe what he feels for a while then drop you.

"So you're going," I said softly.

"Yeah."

Oh, hell, Teresa, I thought. It's not like you two had anything to build from. You don't even know if he would like who you really are. And who you really are seems to change with the job. When this guy's done for the night, he puts away the script. Maybe if you had met him in a pub or something. Nah.

Poor Lionel knew. He'd called it. All Janet and Neil had required was a crisis to make them grow up and start being responsible towards each other.

"You take care of each other, okay?"

"Yeah," he promised.

He loomed over me, tilted my chin with a finger and kissed me goodbye. We melted into each other, tongues playing, but I knew he'd pull out of it in a second so I finished first. Had it lasted a little longer, I would have covered his hand with mine and lifted it to my breast, making a silent invitation. I really wanted one last time with him before I had to give him up.

But it probably wasn't a good idea.

"Get out of here," I said.

He smiled and went for the door, slipped on his shoes again. "You really are incredible, you know that, don't you?"

I laughed. "Thanks? I guess. You, too."

He closed the door after himself, and then I heard his shoes clicking down the hall. I stepped out of my apartment and leaned over the railing to watch the top of his head disappear down the stairs. In a second, he was gone.

I sincerely hoped it worked out for those two and that they had a happy ending. I think they deserved one.

♦

Simon on the phone. Sounding very far away.

"Please don't hang up," he said. "I know you're pissed."

I let out a long sigh. "I'm not pissed."

"You mean anymore."

"Anymore, yes," I said a little too irritably. "Janet's all right. So is Helena." And my cheque cleared.

"That's good," I heard Simon say. "You should feel good, Teresa. I didn't clue in on Giradeau, and neither did my office. Email told me nothing. We'll have to watch out if anyone tries that fax stunt in the future."

So. He knew. Don't know how he'd traced my steps on that one, but I guess he had his ways.

"You stopped the whole mess from breaking open."

"Don't patronise me, Simon. You finished him off so you

look pretty good to your bosses. That's why you're chipper. People should know what they tried to do. What they *are* doing."

"They will know. Janet Marshall is still breathing. She can talk about Coltan all she likes now."

"Oh, please! The murders, the blackmail, all the facts that back up her case can't be pinned on Orpheocon. You used your fancy spy gun and made Giradeau extra crispy! He was our link. The trail ends with him. He can't be turned. He can't point any fingers at who hired him. He's dead! Thanks a lot."

I heard the steady noise of the long-distance line as he considered this. When he finally replied, his voice was calm, gentle.

"And what would that accomplish, Teresa? A lengthy court and appeals process in London and Brussels? Probably Washington, too. Years dragging on and for what? While the fat cats at Orpheocon go merrily along raping these countries? And who would go to prison? No one. No single individual held accountable because it's everyone to blame and no one. Orpheocon would lose a PR war for maybe six months. I'm fighting the real war."

"They must feel pretty good about themselves, whoever they are," I said. "Your bosses. From Mandela to this in a decade. The country's really grown up. They kept the president and all the other officials out of the loop, didn't they?"

I took his abrupt silence as confirmation.

"Oh, that's great. That's marvellous, Simon. Now they know how to solve problems just like the CIA, the Mossad, and our local boys here."

"Teresa, we both love Africa. So do the people I work for. We saved a bit of it, all of us."

"No, Simon. We could have. You bought it a little time, that's all."

Another one of those trademark Simon Highsmith pauses.

"I hope we get to work together again, darling."

"Jeez, I don't," I said, and I rang off. These cordless phones are a drag because you can't give someone a really good slam in their ear anymore.

◆

That was my second goodbye of the week. The third took longer and was far more fun—especially since I instigated it. I screwed up my nerve and called Ayako.

"Hi."

"Hi," she said, all of her curiosity packed into one syllable. "I didn't expect to ..." She stopped herself before she said something rude. "It's good to hear from you."

"I'm glad you feel that way," I said, "because I was hoping we could get together."

"Oh? What's the occasion?"

I sighed. "End of the case. A couple of friends leaving town."

"I see," she answered. *"Him."*

"Well ... yes."

"He can get under a girl's skin."

"Yes, he can."

"So I get consolation prize?" she laughed, but she didn't make it as sarcastic as the cold words on the page.

"That's not exactly how I would, uh ..."

She was giggling hard. "Okay, I guess I've made you squirm long enough. Take a cab to my place."

"When?"

"Now, baby. Let the healing begin."

◆

So I did. Like I keep saying, I learned a lot about myself on this case.

She was waiting for me in an outfit that was meant for one of those twenty-year-old ingénues. With her youthful looks she could easily pull it off. Low-cut neck, bare left arm, full sleeve on right, bare midriff, no bra. Very short leather mini, so short I could see she was wearing no panties. She smelled good. She tasted good. She had me up against the door the minute I walked in, and like a man, her hands were all over me, stripping me in fifteen seconds flat.

"Lie down," she said, and I complied, listening absently to the smack and squelch of something being coated onto something else. Then I felt the slippery nudge of a dildo against my vaginal lips, the thick rubber dick slick with lubricant, and my pussy gates opened and accepted it greedily.

"Tell me how you want it," she whispered. "He could really take you hard, right?"

"Y—yes," I whimpered. "Fuck me hard with it."

And she began quick hard strokes with her toy, watching my fingers clench the pillow, and she listened to me moan and didn't switch on the little motor until I was nearing my peak. I came and lay there for a long moment, rolling over with the red rubber dick still inside me, and the spell was broken. She had unzipped her skirt and tossed it aside, her self-control unravelling. Her pussy slurped with her juices, and she looked amazingly sexy like that, no bottoms, just that single sleeve top and the hard points of her nipples poking through the cotton. Forget Neil and his magic dick. I wanted her now, and I sat up and gathered her in my arms, kissing her deeply and tracing my fingers down to her sweet little thighs.

I must have kissed her and stroked her for ages before my hand even strayed to her mound. She was powerfully erotic to me, half-dressed like that. Just to kiss her soft pillow lips, to look into her almond eyes and touch her straight black hair. I studied the gentle curve of her body as her top ended, and my eyes were rewarded with her lovely hips, the colour of porcelain.

My girl. I was going to make her wake the neighbours tonight.

♦

I stayed at her place for three days, and it was like the beginning of a passionate affair. You know how it is in the beginning, right? You can't keep your hands off each other. You don't bother to go out but you order in, and the bed becomes a square little mattress planet, deserted except for you and your lover. We did that.

We sat naked on her big king-size bed with a pizza box in front of our legs, a towelling roll for napkins, and we watched *The L Word* for laughs. I confessed I really could go for Jennifer Beals, even if the show must be some American network executive's excuse to put on soft-core lesbian action under the guise of drama. We watched DVDs. Ayako could make a kick-ass cappuccino in the morning.

We parted, I think, on pretty friendly terms. Despite the wildness of the poker games, she was one for routine. She liked sex on the side but companionship at home, easy access hand-holding when she took a break from reports on her laptop.

She said she never wanted to turn into a "Japanese wife," the term loaded with more references than I guess I'd know, but she didn't realise she'd wound up shopping for one for herself.

♦

When I got home to my flat, waiting in the email inbox were PDFs from the publisher of my kids' book. Sample sketches of the kind of illustrations that would accompany the text. Completely different style from Roxanne's, but they didn't suck. The stylised refugee camp backdrop looked like it was cut out of a newspaper photo, contrasted with the drawing of my plucky little girl detective heroine, who had big brown eyes and squiggles for hair—a kind of African Manga child, if you can imagine it. More cute than I would have liked, but I could live with it. It had been a week of compromises and graceful surrenders.

◆

Greece. Hot. Sandy. Sunny. Gorgeous. I was nude again, on display for everyone to see. This time in Crete, in Paleochora, on the western beach where naturists frolicked. Helena and me. The Mediterranean was a stunning blue, and I looked out at the water and ignored the "textiles" as they call them, the killjoy clothed and the clothed gawkers. Helena had said we could both use a vacation, and a grateful Janet announced it would be on her.

"This is nice," I declared, sitting up to open a bottle of water.

Helena gave me a mother hen's look. "How are you, darling?"

"Me?" I laughed. "I'm fine! Come on, look where we are." After a couple of seconds, I gave it up. Sighing, I added, "I'm okay. Really."

Helena wasn't convinced. Maybe I wasn't either. I meet a nice guy, someone who could maybe hold my interest for the whole stretch, and I don't top his list. And that whole moral debate again with Simon? Ugh. Then there was the business with girls. I liked them. More than I ever thought I could. I may have to do something about that, like act on it occasionally.

I think I could give up my taste for fucking in front of other people. And I probably didn't need to get tied up again. Fun, sure, yet I could take it or leave it. At least, I hoped I could leave it. But girls . . . I like to think I knew myself pretty well. If I met a nice girl, yeah, I'd try to chat her up. And if it led somewhere, well, that was going to make for some interesting family conversations when I visited home. But it would be all right.

Girl or guy, *I* would be all right.

I patted Helena's arm and said, "When we get home, I may take a few days out just to take stock, you know? Read. Cook. Take in a museum or something. A little 'me' time. It was getting crowded upstairs, all those people I had to worry about and what they were supposed to mean in my life. And now they're gone."

"And you're on a nice beach, away from it all," Helena emphasized. "Sounds good: a little 'you' time."

"Yeah."

"A celibacy break?" she teased.

"I wouldn't go that far."

I flashed her a smile and went to cool off in the sea. The shallower depths were warm at this hour, and I splashed my way in up to my hips. I was trying to screw up the courage to plunge in and handle the chillier currents when a big wave rolled in and just soaked me. That decided that.

As I trod water, thinking about sampling all that life threw at me like these rolling waves—the good we did in Sudan and the good we failed to do, the good we might have done for the Congo, affairs with Simon, Neil, Ayako— I spotted a guy on the beach. He strolled along and tried not to make too big a deal out of checking me out.

I had seen him before near the *taverna* the last couple of

days. Talked just enough with him to exchange hellos. American, I think. Mahogany skin, hair cut very short and *damn!* You see all kinds of less-than-ideal physiques on a beach that allowed public nudity, but this guy was cut. Washboard stomach, good muscle tone in his slim arms, and what dangled between his legs looked like it would do the job for me. My first good look at him.

He flashed me a polite, shy smile and was about to move on when I gave him a reason to pause. I swam for a couple of strokes and stood up, letting the water drip off my breasts and arms, rivulets of water trailing down my belly. I smiled back and waved to him to come join me. A quick glance to check on Helena. Reading her book, or pretending to.

The guy on the beach pointed to himself to ask: me?

I crooked my finger at him and made a face. Yeah, you. You know I mean you. Don't get cute. He smiled back and waded into the sparkling water, and then I watched him swimming towards me.

ABOUT THE AUTHOR

Lisa Lawrence lives and works in London as a freelance writer, contributing to newspapers and various women's magazines. She blames an early boyfriend for inspiring her to write fiction after he regularly dragged her into the West End's various bookshops for mysteries, science fiction and comics. She went looking for erotica all on her own. This is her first novel.

Don't miss the next sexy novel featuring
Teresa Knight! This time she's on top,
in control, and going beyond
every boundary she's ever known.

PLEASURE IS THE ULTIMATE POWER TRIP.

Beg Me

Lisa Lawrence

An erotic thriller by the author of *Strip Poker*

It's the ultimate erotic experience: a handpicked group where every man's craving can be satisfied. But for Teresa Knight, it's also a place where sensual adventures can spiral dangerously out of control. Hired to probe a suspicious death, the part-time investigator enters the sizzling New York fetish scene—a seductive, uncertain world that will test the limits of her own sexuality with every potential lover she meets. For gaining entry into this elite BDSM cult means that Teresa must let down her defenses—in more ways than one.

Her search for answers brings her into contact with an enigmatic businessman who takes her to the brink of her own untapped desires even as he enlists her help in solving a crime that dates back forty years and crosses continents. From exotic Bangkok to gleaming Manhattan, Teresa finds herself locked in a sensual power struggle with a shadowy man who has a deadly agenda. What she uncovers is a shocking conspiracy of murder that will imperil her life while giving a whole new meaning to going all the way.

Beg Me

Available from Delta Trade Paperbacks in June 2007